MY HIGH HORSE CZAR

BRIDGET E. BAKER

Copyright © 2023 by Bridget E. Baker

All rights reserved.

No part of this book may be reproduced in any form or by any electronic or mechanical means, including information storage and retrieval systems, without written permission from the author, except for the use of brief quotations in a book review.

✿ Created with Vellum

For Emerald, my shining star

Never doubt that you deserve the very best.
Demand it every single day.
You are so much more amazing than you think.

ABOUT THE BOOK

Adriana's stuck between a rock and a very hard, very dangerous place. It's not the first time she's ever been in trouble, but it is the worst.

When her twin sister calls and tells her she's going to be killed unless Adriana surrenders herself in half an hour, she figures she doesn't have much to lose.

But Adriana has no idea how much excitement her future holds, or whose protection she's about to awaken.

The scrappy fighter who has vowed never to date or marry is about to meet her match in the highest horse-shifter in existence—the displaced Czar of Russia himself, Alexei Romanov.

My High Horse Czar
by Bridget E. Baker

Fight or flight.

The experts say that humans experience one or the other under stressful circumstances. As a female who weighs less than 6 stone, I should really have learned to run. It's not like I'm equipped to take out mean men who are twice my size.

But my twin sister got all the flight response.

Mom always says I'm fifty pounds of dynamite in a five-pound bag, and I don't have a very long fuse, either. I just wish I was more like a thousand pounds of dynamite in a hundred-pound bag. Then maybe I'd have blown another way out.

My stepfather really caused everything. If he hadn't been so unbearably gross, I never would have felt compelled to move out of my mom's apartment. Leaving home meant that I needed to find another place to live, and being on your own is expensive. It's worse when you have no education or skillset, other than riding. It didn't leave me a lot of options.

My sister's best friend gave me two horses who weren't good at jumping, and I used them to run races, earning money more often than not. At first it was enough, but as bills began to pile up, I needed a bigger win.

To make enough, I needed more money than I had, so I borrowed it. But then. . .I didn't win. I lost. And then I was really in a bind. I kept paying things forward, staying a half step ahead of where I needed to be all the time.

Until I wasn't.

The first time I met Nojus, I thought he was cute. He had a little-boy air about him. I must have been delusional, because the second time we met, when I had to tell him I didn't have his money, he was busy gutting someone when I walked through the door. I nearly lost my breakfast, and I couldn't bring myself to tell him the truth. I lied and said it had been stolen. I think he knew, but he gave me an extension with outrageous interest, which would double the amount due. It felt better than being gutted, at least.

Only, now, almost a year later, after throwing a race to cover some of the compounding interest, he basically owns me.

All he has to do if I stop listening to him, aside from kill me, is hand in his evidence of my criminal activity to the policija. Which is how he's been able to use me to run his errands, threaten people in higher positions where the more obvious goons could never sneak through, and dig up information from people who would never talk to him.

Even so, I'm way past the grace period.

And I'm still broke.

"Adriana." Nojus's hand strokes the top of my head and my heart hammers.

I can't help looking around desperately for anything I might be able to use to defend myself. Why didn't I bring something? Oh, right. Because the second I pulled anything out, one of his men would just shoot me.

It's not like I even know how to use a gun.

"You still haven't repaid me."

"I've done you a lot of services."

"None of that discharged your debt." His hand slides down my jaw slowly and hooks beneath my chin. "I've told you what you *can* do." He lifts my face toward his. "I can't figure out why you keep refusing. It's making me self-conscious, to be honest. Do you not find me attractive?"

He makes me want to claw my own nails down my face until I'm so hideous no one would ever look at me. He reminds me so much of Mārtinš, my stepfather, that the thought of him touching me makes bile rise up in my throat.

"I vowed years ago never to date, never to fall in love, and never to marry. You've met my stepfather. You know why."

"What I know," Nojus says, "is that I'm right here, telling you that you can pay me back, or you can *die*. Isn't breaking a promise better than dying?"

My hand itches to slap him, but I doubt my jujitsu classes will do much for me in this situation. Seeing that he's got at least six men in the next room, I know that even if I beat him, I'll still lose. "My sister has a new boyfriend," I finally say, my voice trembling. "She just won a huge jumping contest. It's why I was already here in Riga when you called."

"And?" His hand slides across my shoulder.

I need to think about something else. Anything else. If I can't distract myself, I'll punch him. Or I'll puke. Either one will likely get me killed.

"If you let me go talk to her, I'll come back with your money."

"You think your crippled sister's boyfriend is just going to give you half a million euros?" His laughter grates on my ears. "What an optimistic slut you are." Without warning, he slaps me across my face, sending me sprawling across the floor. The rubber band holding my hair back snaps and it falls loose across my face.

I welcome the violence. It's much easier to handle than the misery-inducing caresses.

"You have one hour. If you're not back here by then, I'll send my men to either collect you or kill you, Adriana. You'll be given the choice, but I really hope they collect you." His hand drops to his crotch and he rubs, his eyes on mine.

I drop my eyes so he can't see how disgusting I find him. Few people in this world are worse than Mārtinš, but Nojus, the Lithuanian arms dealer who supplies the criminals on the eastern side of Latvia, might be one of them.

"One hour. Don't forget to keep this with you." He sets one of his burner phones in front of me. "I'd hate to have to add the cost of locating you to your already increasing debt. You might never repay it, even between the sheets."

Not showing him how repulsive I find him is hard, but Nojus is notoriously fickle. The last thing I need is to tick him off before I can even beg Grigoriy to save me. I've barely reached the street outside when an unknown number calls my regular cell phone. I'm pretty sure I know who it is. It must be either Mirdza or Kristiana, calling from the arena. After all, when Nojus called me, I basically threw Blanka's reins at Kris and ran.

Mirdza's probably furious.

She just made a huge comeback, the likes of which I never imagined she could, and not only did her boyfriend not go to see it, our mother skipped, too. Then her lousy sister ran away and left her instead of celebrating. I'd be super duper ticked.

Maybe she'll forgive me. My twin sister's nothing like me.

She's the one everyone loves. The one people want to be like. The one people want to help. She's also the reason Kristiana gave me the starter horses, and without them, I'd never even have been able to race. I should be grateful to have a sister like her. I know I should. I'm the worthless sack of crap, and I'm the one always taking, taking, taking, but for some reason that knowledge just makes me angrier.

Every time I think about Mirdza, I'm overcome with the same guilt. The guilt I've always carried around. She's crippled because of me. I should've stepped in to help her—I'm the fighter—or help my mother, or call the authorities, or. . .well, anything. I should've done *something*, but instead, I ran.

Her life was forever wrecked because of me.

Until Mr. Handsome Prince showed up, I guess. He seems willing to cut the world in pieces and run it through a blender for her if she just mentions she'd like an earth smoothie. When she moves around a room, his eyes track her every movement. It's like he's a magnet, but instead of tracking north, he tracks *Mirdza*.

I know Aleksandr's rich. I hear Grigoriy is, too. He's a prince, for heaven's sake, or he says he is. He must have money. Is there any chance she might be able to get. . .but *half a million euros?* How could I even ask her for that?

And there's *no one* who can come up with that much in an hour.

Just before the call's about to go to voicemail, I swipe to answer. "Hello?"

"Kristiana," she says. "It's me, Mirdza." It's definitely her, but why's she calling me Kristiana? She didn't stutter or stammer or correct herself. And she doesn't sound upset that I left, either.

What's going on?

"Thank goodness you're calling." I open my mouth to force the words out—to ask her for money. Maybe I can drill down to the final amount later, after she's agreed to talk to Grigoriy. I'm going to have to tell her the reason, and that makes me want to scream. I wonder how much he might be able to come up with before my deadline is here. What do banks let you withdraw, assuming he has it?

"The men you were worried about have taken me after all, just like Aleksandr thought they might," she says.

What? What men?

Before I can ask, she plows ahead. "But you're the one they want, Kris. Not me."

Whoa, she knows I'm not Kris. She wants me to get a message to Kris, clearly. But why didn't she just call Kris? Or why not just tell me what's going on?

Someone must be listening.

"Okay." My mind finally wraps itself around what she said. Those men Aleksandr was worried about. . .took her?

My brain rebels against the thought. I deserve to be taken, beaten, whatever. But not Mirdza. She's never done anything bad *ever.* How dare Aleksandr and Kristiana endanger her life?

"They want you to come to the following address in

the next half hour." She pauses, thankfully, and I flip the phone to speaker so I can enter the address she reads into the notes app. My heart was beating fast before, but now I'm probably close to the heart attack range.

I need to get to this place in the next half hour. . .or what?

"But you know me," Mirdza continues. "I hate the idea of someone trading themselves to save me as much as I hate Polish sausages. I've never wanted any, and I don't want you to show up in the next thirty minutes, either."

Polish what?

I remember it, then. The stupid code she made up after Mārtinš nearly killed her. Something about Polish sausages means I'm supposed to call the police.

But she said she hates them, and that she doesn't want any. Then she told me *not* to come. Does she mean to tell the cops, but not to go?

It hits me then, why she's calling me and not Kristiana. I really am a moron. I should've known from the start. If she called her best friend, Kris would rush to her side. The men would kill them both. Even if they released Mirdza, they'd definitely kill Kris. She said it herself.

My sister's a total martyr—she'd trade herself for someone else in a heartbeat. Actually, I'm probably the only person she could be one hundred percent sure would pick myself. Which means she's sending Kris and Aleks a message. . .through me. She won't want me to share it until the time has passed.

"If you don't come alone," a man's voice says, "we'll kill her."

A chill shoots up my spine. This man sounds worse than Nojus.

"If you're late, we'll kill her." The man hangs up.

With shaking hands, I look up the distance to the address and find out that, shockingly, it's not that far away. If I take a cab and run, I'll have a little time. I stop at the local post office, scrawl out a hasty note, and mail my own phone to our apartment at Liepašeta.

I was never going to get the money.

Part of me knew that already. There's also no way I was going to repay Nojus in the way he wanted. Since I was clearly doomed to die today, I may as well do it for a good cause.

I'm terrified as I march into the park where the men told me to go. My heart's racing. My palms and pits are sweaty. My head's throbbing from dehydration, too much panic, and the incessant darting of my eyes, looking for the horrible mastermind who wants Kris and didn't mind kidnapping and threatening my sister to draw her out.

What do they want with Kristiana?

I expect a dozen men in all black. I expect knives and guns and flinty eyes. I don't know what kind of people Kristiana pissed off—or maybe it was her husband who made them mad. They're probably Russians, right? The Russian mafia? Maybe Aleksandr borrowed money, too. That would be rich, if I get killed for the same thing I did, only by someone else's mob boss. Won't Nojus be shocked when he can't rape me? I hope he finds out that I'm dead—I want him to be deprived of the satisfaction of doing it himself.

Or maybe he'll spend several years and thousands of dollars searching for me. That would be even better.

As I glance at my watch, I realize that if I can just delay whoever it is that comes for Kris for twenty minutes or so, Nojus's lackeys should show up to collect me. That might be interesting.

And of course, as always, the second I see a glimmer of hope. . .I start to make a plan.

The people who wanted Kris here will be strong. Powerful. Probably scary looking. And I have no idea why they want Kris. Mirdza knew something, which means Kristiana would have an inkling of who they are. Other than dealing with her dad's gambling, her life was pretty blasé before she got engaged.

Plus, Mirdza said, 'like Aleksandr thought they might.' It has to be related to him. He's Russian, so the guys will likely be Russian. It's probably about money. Everything is, at its most basic.

I start watching people intently as they move around the park.

No one's wearing black. No one's carrying any weapons I can make out. No one even looks very ominous.

Actually, there aren't really any scary men.

There's a woman leading her two young children. A lady carries a bag of groceries as she briskly walks past. There's a teenage kid with a dog. And there's one man, talking on a cell phone. He's wearing a bright blue scarf, he has hair so dark that it's almost black, and when he looks up at me, his eyes exactly match his scarf. I mean, sure, he's wearing a dark suit, but it's like Dior or something.

No mobster would ever wear what he's wearing.

Plus, he's drop-dead gorgeous. Like a print ad model for Calvin Klein, or a movie star here on holiday. He smiles, and even though I never date and have no intention to ever change, I still swoon a little.

I can't help smiling back.

A moment later, he hangs up his call and stands. Then he strolls toward me. I mean, this happens some-times. I'll meet some stranger's eye, and he'll approach me. Then he always asks for my number. I may be a mess, but like Mirdza's bestie, I'm blonde, thin, and pretty.

It's just a really bad time to deal with this sort of thing.

I'd hate for the beautiful stranger to get caught in the crosshairs of my surrender. I glance at my watch and realize it's now only five minutes until Nojus's deadline, and the stranger's a few paces away and closing.

"What's your name?" he asks, and his accent is *Russian.*

It can't be the bad guy, right? There's no scar on his face. He doesn't *look* like the henchmen that people like Nojus order around. Nothing about him sends me *danger* vibes. Even so, when I answer, I say, "Kristiana Liepa."

Just in case.

When he stands there, half-smiling, I feel like I should warn him off.

"I'm dating someone," I say. "Sorry."

"I know," he says. "I wish I could give Aleksandr my regards. Maybe someday soon."

Turns out, I was wrong. My villain-radar sucks.

But how could this man be the one threatening my sister? He looks like he could be mugged by a Backstreet Boy with a pair of safety scissors. I'm suddenly much more worried about the men Nojus is sending, and annoyed by the fact that I *mailed* my cell phone to myself with a dramatic note.

"Is this some kind of prank?" I ask. "Because Mirdza—"

"I just told my men to release her." He tilts his head sideways, examining me. "You're taller than I thought from the press images after winning the

Grand National. And have you gained a bit of weight?"

This guy's *rude*, too. "Now, listen here."

"Oh, I'm delighted to listen to anything you care to say," he says. "You're really a marvel to me, you know. When the men told me their powers just dissolved when they touched you, I thought they were lying. They're creative in excusing their failures, you know, always have been. That's the problem with people who were raised wealthy. They're always full of excuses."

Raised rich? Kristiana grew up with money, too, but not like, Aleksandr levels of it.

"What did you want to tell me?"

I decide to tread lightly. Maybe he has men stationed where I can't see them, in the buildings all around the park or something. He looks like a trust baby that people might report to about things.

"Why did you want me when your problem's with Aleksandr?" There. That's a good question. Maybe he'll tell me something I can use.

"My problem isn't with Aleksandr. It's with someone named Baba Yaga, if I have a *problem* with anyone, but even she did us all a huge favor." He gestures at the bench.

I think he might be insane.

If the men following him are also crazy, that would explain their threats. No one was really in trouble, but when someone threatens you, it's hard to realize that. Especially Mirdza. She's been afraid of everything and everyone since the Mārtiņš incident. Once you start running, it's hard to stop.

"Baba Yaga? Are you serious?"

When he smiles, he looks even prettier than I realized he could. "You don't believe me?" He sighs. "It's a shame that the revolution I started created so many complete zealots, but when you light a match, it's hard to control the flames entirely. They burned so many things that we really should have kept."

Revolution? Fire? What's he saying?

"Here's the thing, Kristiana. I'm genuinely worried that you pose a threat to me. So while you arouse my curiosity, I think I'm probably safer just killing you."

The idea that this fop might kill me is laughable.

Then again, he thinks I'm Kristiana. She hasn't trained in martial arts. She hasn't thrown a high-stakes horse race, or cut off someone's finger when they were groping her. Luckily, that stunt made Nojus laugh—he was actually angrier at his man for doing it than he was at me for defending myself.

He always thought I'd come around to wanting him, and he wanted to keep me *pure*.

As if my thoughts summon them, his men show up right then—early. I'm actually impressed to see that he sent a dozen men. I've met all but three of them, and the ones I'd met are all reasonably competent. The others look like kids who probably tagged along to learn something.

"Who are they?" the print model asks. "I thought Aleks might be somewhere near—hoped he would be, if I'm being honest—but it didn't occur to me that he'd hire goons to come after me." He laughs and it's surprisingly melodic. "What's the point?"

"Who are you?" I ask. "Aleksandr doesn't know."

"I'm Leonid Ivanovich, the true heir to the Russian throne. My great, great, great, great-grandfather was locked up by the Romanovs when they stole my family's throne. Your darling boyfriend Aleksandr was Alexei's best friend, and Grigoriy was always following them around too. If they'd just sworn to me a hundred years ago, things wouldn't have gotten nearly as nasty."

Oh, no. He's a raving lunatic.

He may be gorgeous, but I've learned that sometimes lunatics are the scariest people of all.

"We have a chance here to set things aright, five hundred years late, but better late than never, right?"

"Five hundred years late?"

He stands. "I'd rather kill you than deal with another bloody battle. I mean, they both sound fun, but the battle's slower and the end result won't change."

"She's coming with us," Nojus's second-in-command says. He's tall, he's stupid, and his Latvian is terrible. He usually keeps things pretty short, which is his best quality.

"She's definitely not." Leonid glances back at me. "They're with you? Really?"

I shake my head. "I don't like them. They're here to kill me too, though, so maybe you have more in common than you think."

"You want to kill her?" Leonid's eyebrows rise. "Really?"

The men glare. About half of them don't speak Latvian. Lithuanian's similar, but I can only catch snatches of it here and there. I'm guessing it's the same for them.

"You're talking too fast, and your accent is too heavy. They don't understand you," I say.

"You're positive they want you dead?" Leonid asks.

I nod.

He sighs. "This is tedious, and I hate doing things out in the open like this." He glances around slowly, starting in the east. There's a popping sound and sparks fall from a camera mounted on the side of the brick building. Then he looks to the west, and the same thing happens to a traffic camera on a light post.

Again, and again, ten little rounds of pops and sparks, all of them disabling recording devices.

"What are you doing?" I ask.

"Do you really not know?" Leonid looks even more annoyed now.

"She comes with us," Nojus's cousin says. He's smaller, but he's covered in tattoos from head to toe. I've always thought he was one of the scarier lackeys. He's also really handy with a switchblade.

"Yes, you've said," Leonid says. "And now that I've made sure—" He cuts off with a grimace and there's a spark and a shout from a man standing on the closest corner. "Move along, loser!" Leonid waves, and the man actually scampers away.

"Okay, *now* that we're finally not being filmed, I can eliminate one more nuisance." He lifts his hands, and all twelve men are suddenly engulfed in flames.

I can barely believe what I'm seeing.

They're screaming and stumbling and the *smell*. I do retch, right over the side of the bench.

"Burning people alive is so messy and disgusting, but honestly, I did not expect this of Aleksandr." He sighs. "So what's his plan, then? He just sent you here like a sacrificial lamb to be roasted?"

"No," I say. "I'm not a lamb."

"Oh, no?" Leonid smiles.

There are a dozen men who are literally burning into piles of ash behind him, and he looks like he's forgotten all about them.

"Tell me, then. Why was he okay with sending you here alone like this, with just a few helpless, walking firewood sticks as company?"

"Those men weren't sent by Aleks," I say. "They were coming to kill me, because I owe a very bad man a lot of money."

"Wait." Leonid looks truly baffled. "If you owe someone money, why hasn't Aleks taken care of it?"

"For someone who seems to think he knows everything," I say, "you're not very smart."

When his eyes flash, it occurs to me that I should not be baiting him. What's wrong with me? Why do I always take swings at lions?

"I'm not even Kristiana, you idiot." Hopefully it's been long enough that Mirdza's safe. I think about telling them that I'm Mirdza's criminal sister, but then I realize that doing that would just lead them right back to Mirdza. The longer it takes them to figure out who I am, the better her chance of actually escaping. "I'm just a patsy she paid to show up today." I glance around. "And judging from what I'm seeing? She didn't pay me nearly enough."

Leonid does *not* look pleased, but he says, "Come with me."

And I do.

My options appear to be following him or becoming a pile of ashes. Not much in the way of robust choices.

❧ 2 ❧

When I was a kid, my mom used to try to make me and Mirdza eat our vegetables. For my sister, she'd threaten. If my twin didn't eat the turnips or beets or cabbage, Mom wouldn't give her anything else. Mirdza sometimes fought for a few minutes. Once she refused for an entire hour—she really hated beets as a small child. But eventually, she'd cave and shove the stuff down.

Eventually, Mom gave up on ever making me eat turnips.

She realized that, even at the age of three, if I didn't want to do something, nothing she did, nothing she threatened, and no wait, however long, would ever change my mind. I'd rather starve than eat those turnips.

One thing I never did, however, was throw a tantrum.

No, the child we knew who threw tantrums was Kristiana. She would initially argue with her mother or mine if something wasn't to her liking, but if they held the line, she wouldn't stubbornly insist like me. She rarely caved like Mirdza.

Kristiana Liepa threw epic, monumental, break-your-eardrums tantrums, the likes of which I had never seen, not before or since.

Until today.

Leonid thought I was Kristiana, and now that I've confessed that I'm not, well. He doesn't take it well. At first, only the trees in the park, the benches, and the parked cars nearby burst into flames. But as he stares at me, as his face darkens, more things begin to burn.

The building across the street. The one next to it.

People rush out of them into the main street and the alley beyond, and their screaming doesn't even seem to faze him. His nostrils flare, and more cars explode and burn. His hands clench at his side, and two more shops burst into flame.

I don't usually feel much guilt, but in this instance, I'm making an exception. When I came here in Kris's place, I figured I had nothing to lose. I was already as good as dead, and if I could spare Kris, who might actually help my sister when she's in trouble, I should do it.

But now?

How many others will die because I came in her place? How many others will lose their shops, their homes, or their health? I shake my head. "Knock it off, you big baby."

"Why did you answer the phone and come to this place? My men clearly told me that Mirdza was ordered to call Kristiana."

I sigh. "Well, she didn't. I've done some distasteful things for her in the past, so she called me instead, and now I see why." I glance sideways, unsure which direction we could even move to avoid the gusts of blazing heat now billowing outward from all sides. "I'm thinking I should have demanded more money." If I can get him to aim his anger at me, maybe he'll kill me already and stop destroying other stuff.

He scowls and another building explodes into flames. The electrical wire overhead pops and crackles and lightning bolts arc from it down to the ground.

It's very, very hard for me not to show how terrified I am.

"You're either very stupid, or you're lying." He crosses his arms. "And I mean to find out which."

An electric bolt from the power line arcs sideways and strikes me, and then everything goes dark.

When I wake up, I'm in a small, square room with a concrete floor. There's a drain in the center. There are two windows, but they're both near the ceiling, and they're very small. There's a single lightbulb dangling from the ceiling, with a chain hanging down beside it. Presumably that would allow me to turn it on and off if I could reach.

There's a solid wooden door with an iron handle, and there's nothing else in the room. I'm still wearing my clothing from earlier, including my jacket and long pants, but I'm now barefoot. Removing shoes is just prudent if you're keeping someone against their will, probably, but knowing I can't run bothers me. When I force myself to sit up, my head's pounding, my back aches, and there's a sharp pain in my shoulder. The fabric of my jacket is black there, so I'm guessing that's where I got zapped.

"Hello?" My voice is rough when I try to use it.

No one answers.

I clear my throat and try again with more force this time. "Hello!" I shove to my feet and circle the room, jostling the lock with no success. It's not one that would be easy to pick. There's a deadbolt above the knob, so even if I did manage to free the first mechanism, there's no likelihood I'll be able to open the door.

It's not my first time being locked up, and it probably won't be my last, but it's the first time I have no idea why I'm here or where I'm being held. I'm not claustrophobic, and I keep a level head in danger, so things could be worse. I wish I had something to throw. I'm guessing those windows lead to somewhere that someone's actually on watch, so I doubt it would help in any case.

"Hello!" I shout for another twenty minutes with no success, which is really a shame, because I have *got* to pee.

"Alright," I say. "I'm warning you. I've got to pee, and I can't wait. I tried and tried, but I'm about to use this drain."

Now's when we find out what kind of perverts we're dealing with. I unbutton my pants, slide them down, and crouch over the drain. I mean, this isn't exactly one of my finest moments, but it's also not a low point in my life.

Sadly.

I'm actually a little disappointed when no one interrupts me. I've been around a lot of losers, and perverts might be the easiest to understand. After I shake dry as much as I can, I pull my pants back up—wherever we are, it's chilly enough that I hurry—and sit in the corner, leaning against the rough, dirty wall.

"Why can't they ever hold hostages in clean rooms with en suite bathrooms?" I ask out loud, just in case they're monitoring me from somewhere. "It's not that I can't handle a little discomfort. Sleeping on concrete isn't going to break me, so would it really be so hard to toss a blanket and a pillow in here? A children's potty training toilet would also be fine. Sheesh. They're not even very expensive."

I go on like that, speaking nonsense, for another hour before I decide that no one's monitoring me.

It's a little hard for me, as I watch the sun set. I've peed three times, but less and less each time. No one has brought food. No one has brought water. My throat's dry—drier because of all the talking I stupidly did—and I've found not a single idea on which to formulate an escape. I don't have any tools I can use to attack or disarm anyone who does enter. And I still know nothing more about what Leonid wanted, or why I'm even here.

I've dozed off when the sound of the door rattling open wakes me. I shoot to my feet, blinking rapidly to clear my foggy brain.

When the door does open, it's not Leonid.

"Who are you?" I can't help glaring. "What do you want?"

The man sets a few items on the ground and kicks them toward me. Two bottles of water. A prepackaged meal—crackers and cheese that kids usually eat at school. That's it.

No utensils.

Nothing made of metal or even hard plastic.

Sadly, Leonid's hotheaded reaction before does not appear to have extended to his current treatment.

"Who are you?" the man asks in Russian.

Does that mean I'm in Russia now? I know Aleksandr's from there. Unfortunately, my Russian isn't especially good. Unlike Mirdza, I didn't suck up to Mom unbearably. I spent most of my visits to Russia sulking and pretending I didn't speak a word.

I do know my Russian swearwords pretty well, so when I tell the guy where he can go and what he can do, I'm reasonably certain he understands. Even so, he's half-smiling as he walks out the door.

Four days pass like this, with only two meals being provided each day—both boxes of prepackaged crackers and cheese—and two water bottles. Nothing's made available for my use other than the drain, and let me tell you. The room is not smelling its best.

That's actually what gives me the idea.

I'm not able to do much about freedom from here. I've located no ways to escape and had no ideas of how to incapacitate my food delivery service. I'm not getting enough food, so I'm slowly weakening, day by day. It doesn't bode well for my odds at escape, not unless I can change something major.

I've imagined lots of ways I might die, but slowly starving to death in a hovel that might or might not be in Russia has never been on the list. It's embarrassing, honestly. I mean, I don't suffer from any delusions that I'm important, but I figured if I died, it would at least be in a blaze of glory.

Seeing as someone has to come inside twice a day and give me food, and I'm assuming that at some point, someone is going to interrogate me, and since I'm already pretty gross. . .I decide to actively make it worse. What gives me the idea?

It's a little embarrassing to admit that the kids' cartoon *Finding Nemo* is my inspiration. Those fish fouled up that tank and it had to be cleaned. I'm not going to escape as things are, but if someone has to get me out to rinse me off, maybe I'll find some kind of way out. So I actively stop trying to rinse my poop down the drain. I pee in the corner. I smear my poop on the walls. All over myself.

Which makes me gag.

So I use the vomit too. It's almost ten hours before

I become so used to the smell that I stop suffering from it. I'm honestly having second thoughts about my plan when the man with the short-cut blond hair walks through the door. He doubles back immediately and drops the water and crackers, covering his nose and mouth with his hand. The swear words he uses in Russian are inventive, and I make a mental note of one combination in particular that I really might use next time I'm angry.

"What did you do?" He lifts his head and peers around the corner, his eyes widening in alarm. "What —why would you—"

"My stomach." I grab my belly and moan. "Sick. I sick." My Russian's not great, so I lean into my limitations. Plus, hopefully the more they think I can't communicate, the more understanding they'll be when I refuse to give them information.

The man kicks the packaged cheese and crackers through the doorway, and then he shoves the water bottles, too. He closes the door again so quickly that I wonder how tough he can possibly be. I mean, sure, it smells, but really, it's not *that* big of a deal. I've been in here all day.

But an hour later he's back, and he's carrying a blindfold, a pair of handcuffs, and a rope.

Jackpot.

He blindfolds me, cuffs me, and ties the rope in a noose around my neck. "Don't try anything weird."

"Leonid's letting me out for a walk?" I ask in Latvian. "How generous."

I can't see, but I can feel, and I don't have to walk very far before the concrete turns into hard-packed dirt. Blondie shoves me from behind, and I fall to my knees. I hear the squeaking of a water valve being turned on, and then I'm being sprayed.

It's not fun.

The spray hits my back. My front. My face. My arms. Moving around is pointless, because he uses the neck noose to shift me the way he wants me regardless. Eventually, he deems me clean enough, and that's when he turns me, rearranges my arms, undoes the handcuffs, positions me around a large metal pole, and redoes the handcuffs. Hugging a metal pole with a blindfold on isn't exactly fun, but it's also not *so bad*. I hear him head inside, his footfalls heading back the way we exited, the slithering sound of the hose dragging along behind him. Then I hear the same whooshing noises—he's clearly spraying out the inside of my terrible cave-room. I hope he leaves the unopened crackers and cheese in there. Maybe now that it's cleaner in there, I'll be able to choke them down.

My belly growls in approval.

When you're getting six or seven hundred calories a day, you really can't afford to miss any of them. Puking up this morning's breakfast didn't help much with my calorie deficit. While he's in there, I manage to shift my blindfold enough to look around. We're out in the country—I can't even see a neighbor. Pastures with small copses of pine and elm trees as far as I can turn—and the room I've been kept in is inside a very small, very run-down hut. It looks like a shepherd's cottage. There's a small chimney on top, and there's a run-down split rail fence circling part of the yard.

The fact that it has water feels a bit like a miracle, but other than the spigot with the attached hose, we could be standing in this same spot a hundred years ago, right down to the wash basin and washboard with the clothesline strung up next to it. The string's broken and dangling, but someone lived here at some point.

The state of this place is both good and bad. My

captors clearly aren't staying onsite. They may not even have Wi-Fi and monitoring set up, but there's also no one out here to hear me or see me and offer help.

When I hear footsteps shifting back in my direction, I use the pole to shove my blindfold back down, and I lean my head against it.

Super tired captive. Nothing to see here.

"You get back inside," he says in Russian.

I rattle my hands against the pole as loudly as I can, not willing to admit that I understand what he said, but answering his unasked demand.

He's rough undoing my handcuffs, like he's worried that if he's nice, I'll make a break for it. I'm not that stupid. I have no money, no shoes, and no idea where I am or where I might go. Running now, when he's holding a rope around my neck and standing right next to me? That's something a particularly stupid horse might do.

I'm not quite that dumb.

He's barely marched me back to the cell and removed my blindfold when I hear the sound of a vehicle outside, idling near the hut. It's probably parking. The tension in the lines of the face of the man who has been bringing me food tells me it's his boss.

Sure enough, when the newcomer finally clomps his way through the door, it's Leonid.

"Why's the room wet?" He's glaring, but not at me, and he's using Russian, presumably because he's not addressing me.

"She got sick or something," the blond man says in Russian. "The room smelled really bad."

Leonid arches one eyebrow. "You're sick?"

I shrug.

"I know your name, girl. We looked up the number

that your friend dialed, and it's owned by an Adriana Strelkova. You must be Mirdza's sister."

"So?"

"Why did she call you instead of Kristiana?"

I don't answer.

"I'm going to send a message to Mirdza, telling her that if she values your life, she'll—"

Now I'm laughing.

"What?" Leonid frowns.

"That's a huge waste of time. She called me because she doesn't value my life," I say. "I just look like Kris. Even though I'm her sister, trust me. She won't care what happens to me."

It's a bluff, but I need him to believe it. Because if Mirdza trades her life for mine now, then all this will have been a complete waste. My one good act will have been wasted.

Leonid studies my face as if he's evaluating my words.

"In a million years, Mirdza never thought I'd be selfless enough to show up. But she'd also never trade me for Kristiana. Trust me. I'm not the leverage you want."

Leonid paces, which can't be very satisfying in such a small room.

"Tell me why you want Kris, and I can help you figure out how to get what you really want." I only allow myself a half smile. I'm sitting in the corner of a concrete room, sopping wet—I don't have a lot of options in terms of pressuring this man, but a knowing smile sometimes helps. "You want her fiancé? Does he owe you money? Or do you have some kind of grudge against him?"

"This isn't about Aleksandr." Leonid scowls. "Tell

me how to separate Kristiana from her boyfriend so I can bring her here."

Oh, shoot. "You may as well give up. Now that you've kidnapped me and Mirdza, nothing on earth will convince Aleksandr to let Kris out of his sight. That guy's crazy."

"That's not good news for you." Leonid drops into a crouch, his head not much higher than mine. "Because if you have nothing to offer, we have no reason to keep you around."

"That's true," I say.

"You have one day to think of a way to be helpful to me," he says. "If you don't have any ideas for me tomorrow, *good* ideas, I'll dispose of you and spare Boris any more of his time."

With a threat like that, I have absolutely nothing to lose.

And that's when I do my finest work.

❋   3   ❋

At least I'm learning new things here.

For instance, today I've learned that there's a delicate balance, when you're eating under seven hundred calories a day, between how much poop to smear on yourself, and how much to spread around the room. If I spread too much around, I run the risk that Boris won't hose me down at all. If I spread too much on myself, he may not need to clean the room. For my half-baked plan to have even the slightest possibility of working, Boris absolutely has to take me outside and leave me.

As I'm working on my plan, I realize that my life has reached an all-time low. It's probably not surprising, though. I mean, I'm not a good person.

My twin's a good person. She goes to church every week. She prays for people. She steps in when there's danger, even when it means she's at risk herself. She stands up for the little guy, even though she's small herself. Even after she got injured, badly, she kept right on doing good things. She taught children to ride. She offered discounts to the people who couldn't pay. She stood up for my mother, and she's a stalwart and steadfast friend. If she were here, there would be loads of people who wanted to find her.

She's probably the only person looking for me.

If she were to get down on her knees and pray, that prayer would probably come easy to her. She'd know just what to say, and God would probably see her as an old friend.

Meanwhile, I'm like the bad kid at school who's getting ready to ask the principal for help. The whole idea of praying, for me, is cringey. I mean, I've never thought there was a God, because if there is, he's done nothing but ignore me at best. Cackle while I squirm at worse. First, my dad died. Then I got Mārtiņš. People all around me got great stuff, lucky breaks, and rich boyfriends.

And I get poop-smearing conundrums.

Even so, my plan's so flimsy that a light breeze would snap it, so I need any edge I can get. I crouch down on my feet, and I close my eyes, and for the first time in at least a decade, I pray.

"Dear God. I have no idea whether that's the right way to start a prayer, but that's how I was told to write a letter, so you know. I'm only talking to you today because I'm in a bit of a mess. I know I've never really done anything for you. I haven't been super grateful, and to be honest, I don't like you very much. I haven't had much luck, and I blame you for that. But I did try to help out my sister by coming in Kristiana's place, even though that's not what she wanted me to do."

I sigh.

"Anyway, now I'm stuck here."

My knees hurt. It's stupid, since all I'm doing is kneeling on rough concrete, but my knees are bony, and they're completely miserable right now. Maybe I'm supposed to be miserable. In the churches I've seen, their pews are always made of solid wood. They look really uncomfortable. It could be part of this. We suffer in payment for our request? Is that it? If so, I can highlight my suffering a little.

"Look, things are bad for me, okay? I'm starving, and I don't know where I am, and if I were to give them a way to trap Kris, I'd probably get out of here, but I'd undo the tiny good thing I did that got me stuck here in the first place. Plus, they might just shoot me either way." I groan. This prayer thing sucks. "So I guess here's what I'm asking for. Rome wasn't built overnight, and you already know that no matter how much I try, I'll never be as good as my sister Mirdza. But, if you help me escape today, I promise that I'll do three good things to make up for the help."

That seems like a pretty good offer. I'm not even asking for some kind of credit for the good thing I did to get in here.

"What I need is this. First, I need that Boris guy to wash me off again, before he does the room. If Leonid comes with him, or if he just ignores the mess because his boss is going to kill me, I'm done for." That's item number one. "And second, and this is probably the biggest thing, I need to be washed off in the same place, and I need there to be an old clothespin there. Not one of those crappy, split wooden ones. It needs to have the little piece of wire that holds the two pieces of wood together. I need that little piece of metal, alright? Or you know, another small piece of metal like that."

I sigh.

"And then, after that, if you could send someone—*anyone*—to drive past while Boris is cleaning down the room, that'd be great. I mean, I'm not sure how far I can get on foot, and I'm pretty sure Boris would just find me again, and then Leonid would probably incinerate me. So an escape truck or something would be ideal, but I'll leave that up to you."

I stop there, because I'm starting to feel like I have less of a plan, and more of a desperate hope. Do I really think every single thing needs to be done by God? Sheesh.

"Then again, I'm not asking for very much," I say. "I mean, you're God, right? And I've never asked for anything before. So, like, in the grand scheme of things, it's pretty small stuff. And in return, I promise that the next three chances I have to help someone out, I'll do it. No matter how hard it is for me, I'll do the right thing when I have to choose. Alright?"

It seems fair. God helps me out of here, and I help him three times.

"Okay, so that's my offer. If you help me with that stuff, I'll assume you accepted it. And if not, well, maybe you'll get to meet me sooner rather than later." I look up then, and I open my eyes. "And if you can't do those three little things for me, you should expect me to be pretty ticked off when we do meet. Brace yourself for that."

Maybe I shouldn't have signed off with a threat.

I bow my head. "Sorry. Amen." I was a little late, but I remembered the sign off. Maybe that will help.

And then it's time to smear poop. Again, the smell makes me sick, which just gives me more material to work with. I try to make sure that part lands near the drain at least, like I'm aiming to do the right thing. But honestly, this whole thing is just one of the nastiest experiences of my life. I should have, like, spent my time recruiting some kind of special forces team to protect me in cases like this.

Or, you know, figured out how to do magic.

I think about those fire balls and electricity zaps. Were they real? Did I imagine them? Leonid seemed nasty, but perfectly normal yesterday. Boris sucks, but he doesn't seem magical either. Could I have hallucinated the whole thing?

Maybe he just. . .but no matter how many times I try to think of a way to imagine that what happened didn't, I can't block out the image of those men being burned into piles of ash. My heart's already beating too fast when a car pulls up outside.

Please be Boris. Please just be Boris.

Either God loves me, or I got lucky, because it *is* Boris, with another box of crackers and cheese. He drops the water bottles and the box on the ground outside when he opens the door, and he swears up a storm again.

"You must be kidding me."

I shrug. "I told you those are making me sick," I say in Latvian. I toss my head at the discarded cracker box. "No toilet. No towels. No soap." I shrug. "What did you want me to do?"

Boris is fuming. He snatches the blindfold off the ground outside and storms into the room. I keep my head bowed, and I don't fight him when he knots it way too tightly around my head. Ironically, even though it's tighter than yesterday, I can see more out of the periphery, because the blindfold's also rolled into a tighter, smaller ring.

I trip and stumble when he drags me outside again, mostly so that he'll think I'm pathetic and uncoordinated, but also partially because I *am* shaky. It's been a week of virtually no calories and limited water. Even the twenty yards we travel feels like a long walk. He throws me to the ground this time, and I immediately start feeling around for anything that might be a clothespin.

He's spraying off my back when I find one.

But it's the bad kind. It's nothing but one piece of wood, split up the middle. I mutter a curse and keep looking.

"What are you doing?" Boris shifts the water off me.

I freeze.

"Are you trying to find a stick? Or maybe something harder?" He laughs. "I swept this area yesterday. You can't think I'm that stupid."

I exhale slowly, as if I'm now resigned to the idea that I won't be able to attack him.

"Besides." He walks closer. "A stick won't help you." His hand shifts—I can see it from the corner of my eye —and then he zaps my shoulder.

Once, when I was five, I backed up into Kristiana's mother's electric fence around the property line. That made me jump like a shocked cat and shriek like a baby.

This hurts far, far worse than that did.

"I can incapacitate you from anywhere." Boris doesn't sound like he's boasting. It sounds like a fact.

I shake my head, sticking to Latvian in spite of his Russian. "I'm not trying to attack you, I swear."

"Keep your hands still." He stands there for a moment, as if he's watching to make sure I understand.

I nod.

He clomps back to the water spigot and turns the hose on again. "No moving."

When the water hits my back, it's so cold that I fall forward involuntarily.

"Don't move!"

So much for God's help. No clothespin means no

way to pick the handcuff. And that means I'm stuck here.

As he recuffs my arms around the pole, tears are soaking the front of the blindfold. I never cry. I just don't. But right now, my life's as ridiculous as it ever has been. It feels so unbearably pointless.

And I feel like an idiot.

I didn't believe in God.

I've never believed that some benevolent being's watching over us. Even if he exists, I've never been one of the creatures he loved or cared about. So why am I so depressed that he didn't save me?

I don't even bother using the pole to slide the blindfold down. What's the point? It's not like I'll see anything helpful.

But then I hear a car.

A car, driving by on this Godforsaken stretch of road. I'm desperate to get the blindfold off, but by the time I do, the car's so far away there's no way it could possibly see me.

Rage floods my body, and I want to scream.

Instead, I kick the pole.

That hurts like a nail through my toe, which was just more idiocy on my part. But when I look down at my bare foot, I realize that right next to it, there's a clothespin.

How much time have I wasted?

My pulse beats in my ears. I shove the clothespin up with my toes, but I can't quite get it up to the top. It falls, and now it's farther away than it was before.

I bite off my swear words, and focus.

Please, God, let me get this clothespin up here.

Every second that ticks by feels like an hour. I drop the clothes pin again, but then I have an idea. If I lift my hands up and hang from them, I can bring my foot up much farther. . .

My abs scream. My shoulders cry. My heart races pell-mell.

But I make it.

I manage to get the clothespin right up to my fingers, and I nearly drop it a third time. But I don't. I almost crack a tooth freeing the metal part from the wood, but then it's out, and my hands are trembling as I work to pick the stupid lock in the handcuffs. I almost drop the pin twice, because trying to pick a lock with handcuffed hands is way, way harder. But I'm finally doing something I've practiced before.

A life of idiocy has prepared me for this.

Then I hear Boris's footsteps, coming back in my direction, the hose water splashing next to the steps as if nothing's wrong at all.

I'm still in cuffs.

He's some crazy electric shock person, and he'll fry me if he catches me trying to escape. I found the clothespin, but it's too late. I'm doomed anyway.

But then the mechanism in the lock catches, and I've freed one hand. I'll have to worry about the other one later. I need to *run* as fast as I can. Which direction?

I'm vacillating, first left, then right, when I hear it.

Boris's phone is ringing.

"Hang on," he says. "Lemme turn off this water." He's just around the corner.

I shove my blindfold down and throw my hands up, hoping he won't notice that I'm free.

My breaths are coming quick and shallow, and my hands and arms are trembling like mad, but Boris shuts off the water, tosses the hose to the ground, and marches back toward the hut. "Yeah, but this place is a dump, I'm telling you. Even in town, there's not a single decent place to eat."

And then he's gone again—back inside the hut.

He just left me here.

God is good. God loves me. I tear my blindfold off and start to run, heading to the right because it looks like there are more trees I might hide behind in that direction. Also, the car came from there. Maybe there's another house close. Maybe they'd take me to the police.

The handcuffs are dangling from my right hand still, swinging and whamming into my right leg, and I'm so weak that spots keep threatening my vision. My bare feet are already scraped and cut, and then I come down hard on a stick.

I bite off the involuntary whimper. I won't risk any noise at all, other than the sound of my feet against the dry ground.

You will not pass out, Adriana. You will keep running and never look back.

Only, I know what's back there. Any moment now, Boris will walk out of that hut, realize I'm missing, and take off after me. It spurs me to run faster.

But not fast enough.

I hear his shout when he discovers that I'm missing, and it's not nearly far enough away. "I should've asked for more, God," I whisper, my breaths coming quick and labored. "I should have asked—" Wait. I did. I asked for an escape car. I wipe sweat out of my eyes, and I smile.

"You brought just Boris, and he took me out to wash me off," I whisper. "And then you got me the clothespin. You gave me a freebie with that phone call. Now where's my escape car?"

But no car shows up. Boris is still shouting behind

me, closing in, when something bursts through the copse and into view.

It's a monstrously large white horse.

No bridle. No saddle. Not even a halter. He's not shod. But he's a grey, and not a young one. He's practically white, with a black mane and tail, a black nose, and black legs.

His nostrils flare when he sees me.

Is this it? I'm laughing in my head. *This is my escape vehicle?*

"I've never been one to look a gift horse in the mouth." I step toward him slowly, one hand extended, fingers spread. "Hey there, boy. I need a ride."

He shies back.

And then when he hears the shouting from not-nearly-far-enough behind us, instead of bolting, he whinnies.

Really, God? You couldn't have at least given him a saddle? I have no idea if this horse is even broke. I could wind up dying here instead of there.

But I groan. "Alright, listen. There's a maniac behind me, and he wants me dead. I made a bargain with God, and you're what he sent, so you're going to stand still and let me scramble up on your back."

Even with my speech, I'm a little floored when he stands and lets me approach him. When I reach up and grab the mane at the top of his withers, he snorts, but he doesn't move.

"Please don't be a maniac," I say. And then I say it over and over, like a chant or something. "I'm about to swing up."

He stamps.

I take that as consent.

Then I jump up, my years as a jockey making it fairly simple in spite of his impressive height, pulling on the ridge at the top of his withers as hard as I can, and swinging my right leg over his back. He stays remarkably steady through it all, as if he's been ridden before.

It makes sense. How many wild horses are really running around in this day and age?

"I can't believe that worked."

The shouting's close now, and I reach forward and grab a handful of his mane with each hand. I didn't consider the handcuffs, though, and they swing around and clock him on the side of his neck.

He jumps, and then he bolts.

The wrong direction.

"No," I'm shouting. "Not that way!"

As if he can understand me, he wheels around the other direction, and I crouch low on his neck as he picks up speed.

I've been a jockey for nearly ten years, and I've never felt afraid of speed, but that's on a controlled racetrack with steady footing. I'm not sure that I've ever gone as fast as I am right now, and chunks of sod and sticks and leaves are churning into the air and flying into my face as we race past.

I'm not sure how long we run like that, but it's more than two miles—I'm used to racing two miles, and my thighs are burning from where I'm gripping his flank. Sure, I don't have stirrups, but it's not like the crouch that jockeys use is easy. It's at least as hard, balancing on top, as it is to clench around this horse bareback.

We've long since left Boris behind, racing as we have been into the middle of nowhere, but I have no idea where we're going, or how long we can keep going this way before Boris will circle back and catch us in his car. I'm debating whether we should turn back and look for a road when that decision's sort of taken from me.

Because we stop sharply, right in front of a fence.

Clearly someone owns this land.

Do I turn right? Left? I'm debating what to do when two riders in full tack come running toward me on the other side of the fence. They wave wildly, and then they cheer.

Cheer?

I'm standing in front of the fence, totally unsure what to do, when the riders finally pull up in front of me.

"You brought him back." The rider in front is on a big, stocky sorrel, and he's wearing nice clothes—these people have money. His hair's short, as short as Boris's was. His eyes are alert and they look almost shocked. "How did you get on his back?" More Russian, of course, confirming my guess that we're in Russia.

I blink.

What do I say? I had no idea this horse was from here, and I certainly didn't race this way to bring him to someone.

"Do you speak Russian?" the other rider asks. He's riding a deep blood bay, and although he waited to speak, he has an air of authority the other rider doesn't have. He points. "That's our horse. You brought him back to us?"

I have no idea how to play this. On the one hand, I don't want to be branded as a horse thief and thrown in a Russian prison. On the other hand, I'm not keen on surrendering the one means of transportation I've found when I'm only a few miles away from Boris.

"I speak Latvian," I finally say.

The two men frown, and they start talking amongst

one another quickly. I can pick up some of it, but not all.

"—our horse."

"Not exactly. We found him."

"But he's worth a fortune." Something something. "She can ride him."

"—kicked us, and no one else will even try."

Finally, they turn toward me. The second man to speak, the one with the shiny black boots and the longish brown hair says, "I speak some Latvian. You found our horse. You are riding him, so you know horses."

I nod.

"You look. . ." His eyes scan my body, and I cringe at what I must look like. I've been wearing the same clothing for more than a week, and other than a few hose downs, which did nothing for my hair or skin, I've been sitting alone in a room. Covered with poop.

And I'm barefoot.

"I've been running," I say. "My ex is following me, even now." I glance back over my shoulder. "I found this horse, and he let me ride him to escape."

"Ah." The men nod, and they return to talking.

"—hide her, probably won't need. . .pay her much."

"Tuesday." Something something. "No one else."

My grey mount decides he's about done standing around, and he tosses his head and starts to move.

"Whoa," the first man says.

"Hang on," the other shouts.

"I'm not using a saddle or bridle here," I shout. "Not all of this is up to me."

"Okay," Shiny Boots says. "Then how about this." He's trotting along to keep up with my grey, who's dying to move.

"There's a gate up here," the second guy says in Russian.

The first guy takes over, back to Latvian. "If you can get the stallion to stop and follow us through, we'd be happy to hide you *and* pay you to break him for us."

"Break him for what?" I ask.

"To race," the man says.

"That's exactly what I do," I say.

But I have no idea whether I can get him to slow down and go through the gate. I haven't told the guys this yet, but so far, my ability to get on this horse and guide him mostly away from Boris has been entirely luck.

Or a little bit of leftover grace from my deal with God. There's no way I'm going to try and explain that. I already look like an absolute lunatic.

Ugh.

I lean down close to his neck, and I pat him. "Listen up, now, boy. These nice men have a deal for us. There's a very, very bad man behind me, and he wants me dead. I'm certain he'll kill me, unless I can find somewhere to hide." I pause. "And I need your help a little longer."

The grey snorts.

"I don't like being stuck in a cage either," I say. "I know why you broke free." I drop my voice to the barest of whispers. "So when I leave, I'll do my very best to take you with me."

He slows down a bit, and he tosses his head.

There's no way he understands what I'm saying, but I do. And I mean it. When I finally feel ready to run, I'll try and let him loose again, just like I found him.

"You'd have to hide me," I say loudly. "When my ex comes looking, you'll have to say you haven't seen me at all."

"If we do that," Shiny Boots asks, "do you think you can make the horse behave?"

I see the gate up ahead. "Let's find out." I turn him toward the fence and ask him to move closer.

He picks up speed, turns toward the fence, and before I can guide him toward the gate, he vaults over the center of the four-foot fence. I'm not a jumper like my sister, and I very nearly fall off, but thanks to a really good hold on his mane, I right myself.

"Looks like it's worth a try," Shiny Boots says. "I'm Viktor Baranov. I look forward to working with you."

4

I'm not sure how many times I turn around and look over my shoulder, but Boris doesn't show up. More importantly, neither does Leonid.

As we move away from the fence we just jumped and into the main paddock, it's quite clear that we've entered a different area entirely from where we were. Instead of wild underbrush, the grass is well tended, the paddocks are cross fenced with horses in them, and the water troughs are set at regular intervals.

There's a wide alleyway that's intersected by other small cross fenced paddocks, and luckily we leapt into the alley. It makes sense that the end of the long, narrow pasture would be the location of a gate off the property. Lots of horses rush their fences as we trot our way down the slim bisecting area, and I brace myself for nonsense. The grey I'm on doesn't react, other than swiveling his ears and pinning them a time or two. It's surprising to me, since he's apparently a stallion, but without a saddle or even a bridle, I'm delighted he's not too agitated about the other horses.

I can't help being nervous about where exactly

we're going or what their plan is. I'm on the run, I'm in a strange place, and admitting that I have no idea where I am seems like a bad idea. But mostly, I'm nervous because there's really only one thing I know about these men I'm following.

Somehow, they lost this horse earlier today.

I'm worried that they won't have a plan for getting me off his back safely and getting him into a pen or paddock that can hold him. One of the men immediately whips out his phone, texting someone I'm sure.

"What's the plan?" I ask. "What kind of operation is this?" I really hope Viktor speaks enough Latvian to understand what I'm asking.

"Don't worry," he says. "We're a full-scale racing barn with dozens of staff. Our trainer's one of the best in St. Petersburg, and we've let him know that we recovered Quicksilver."

"That's actually a pretty good name, boy." I pat his neck. "And you're definitely quick."

"What's she saying?" The man with short hair asks.

Viktor's talking so quickly in Russian that I can't entirely follow, but he appears to be sharing what I said, from the first question to my appreciation of the name.

"But he's dangerous too," the man with short hair says in Russian. "He's broken two grooms' arms and Olav's leg."

I can't react to that, since I'm not supposed to speak Russian. "What did he say?" I force a smile.

"He said you're right. He's really fast." Viktor nods.

So he's not being honest about the danger involved. That doesn't impress me. "Where are we going?" I haven't seen a single fence above about four and a half feet. "I'm assuming you have a taller fence somewhere?"

Two men pop out from around a barn in front of us, holding guns.

My heart stops dead, and I'm literally preparing to wheel Quicksilver back around and race back down the narrow alley when they fire. Two tranqs hit Quicksilver on his shoulder. The men both approach slowly, one of them walking with his hands raised like an idiot. They really ought to give the tranqs more time to work before they try to catch him and lead him to his stall or wherever he's going.

"You can slide off. We'll take him from here," Viktor says. "Pyotr here speaks Latvian, and he can take you to the grooms' quarters and get you some new boots."

The dummy with his hands up, like that might keep him safe from the fifteen hundred pound stallion, appears to be Pyotr. Goodie.

"She need clothes too," Pyotr says. "But where I find girl clothes? She really small." His Latvian's not amazing, but I can understand him at least.

"We have lots of jockey gear that's been left over the years," Viktor answers in Russian. "Let her take her pick. Even if it doesn't fit great, at least it won't smell, and it's all small."

Oh, good. They've noticed that I smell from several feet away on horseback. Excellent.

Quicksilver's starting to sway a bit, which means the tranqs are starting to kick in. I swing my leg over and slide off his back. My feet complain immediately, but at least the ground here isn't covered with sticks and rocks. "Where to?"

The second I move, Quicksilver lurches after me, whinnying loudly.

I pivot and place my hand on his soft nose. "Oh, boy, don't worry. I'll come and see you very soon." He whickers, and I rub my hand up and down on the wide, flat front of his face. "Very soon, okay? Once I have boots, I can even come see you later today."

Pyotr's more of a gentleman than I expect. He smiles and points up ahead. We start to walk, and I notice that he's keeping to the side of the path where the grass is thicker. He may not be very smart, but at least he's chivalrous.

For the next three hours, I jump at every new person who appears, convinced that Boris or Leonid is going to show up at any moment. I do finally know where I am, on the outskirts of St. Petersburg, Russia. Pyotr proudly told me that we're not too far from the Alexander Palace. For me, that's notable only because it's close to the Ropsha Racecourse. I've been there twice in the past, riding horses for one of my old employers. It's not the premiere track in Russia, but it's a pretty decent one.

The shower I take is nerve-wracking, because I hate feeling even more vulnerable in a strange place, but it's also heavenly. I wasn't sure my hair would ever recover, but even without costly conditioner, it looks worlds better without grime, oil, and sweat caked in it. Actually, I feel like the week plus of not showering might have worked like a deep conditioner for it. That's kind of gross to think about.

My kidnapping silver lining. . .

The biggest bonus was when Leonid killed off all the men who were coming to kill me, I suppose. But I have someone even worse on my tail now, so. . .

How hard will Leonid really search for me, though? It almost felt like he was planning to kill me just to make sure Kris and Mirdza wouldn't hear about his plans. Being honest, it doesn't sound like he has much of one. What could I really tell them that they don't already know? If he's Aleksandr's enemy, Kris's boyfriend will already know who he is, surely.

Leonid doesn't seem like someone who spends a lot of time on nuance, what with incinerating twelve people at once and zapping me and dragging me to St. Petersburg. He wasn't even the one caring for me. Boris was. Hopefully now that I'm gone, they'll let it go.

This horse farm wasn't exactly close, but it's not really far, either. A few miles away at most. And with this many people working here, I'm not convinced Viktor can really hide my presence. I'm also the only girl among the staff, as far as I can tell, but that gets me a special room away from the others and my own private bathroom. Once I'm clean, I change into one of the half dozen new outfits I cobbled together from their hand-me-down bag, and slide my feet into nearly brand-new boots that apparently the trainer's daughter grew out of.

There are some benefits to being stupidly small. Jockeying is only one of them.

Pyotr calls me. "Miss?" And then he knocks on the door of my small room. "I bring food."

Bless that tall, kindhearted Russian man.

I whip the door open, expecting a sandwich and maybe an apple. Instead, he's holding a tray with a stack of sandwiches, a bowl of pelmeni—the smell practically exploding against my tastebuds—and a plate full of lamb shashlik.

"I could kiss you," I say in Latvian, not caring whether he understands.

I think he does, though. Poor Pyotr blushes as he lifts the tray.

I take it gratefully and manage to eat nearly half of it. And finally, I'm ready to check on Quicksilver. I hope the Russian trainer's crew was able to get him safely to a decent stallion pen. Now that I've eaten, and I'm dressed, and I don't smell, I venture out of my room. . .

And there's no one else around.

I glance at the clock. It's nearly five, which means the horses may be getting a third feed, or perhaps they're being brought in from the paddocks. I walk out of the front door of the bunkhouse and follow the noise. . .to a large, open-air gathering area with picnic tables. The grooms and riders are all eating together, laughing and talking.

Viktor stands. "Ah, you look different." He beams. "You clean up quite well."

"Uh, thanks," I say. "Where's Quicksilver?"

"Sit." He sits himself and gestures.

I shake my head. "Pyotr brought me food, which was excellent, and I ate far more than I should have. I'd really like to check on the stallion."

Viktor nods. "He's on the far end." He points. "You can't really miss it. Head down the middle lane, and it's the last paddock on the right."

So he is in a paddock, in spite of escaping before. That's pretty generous of them.

"The devil himself couldn't get out of that paddock now." Viktor's dismissed me, and now he's laughing at something a very large, very red-faced man's saying.

It could be way worse. Most of my life, my main goal has been to avoid attention. Telling them I can't speak Russian seems to have been an excellent call. Way better than trying to parse through what everyone's saying with my broken Russian. This way, they mostly leave me alone.

He wasn't kidding when he said it was all the way down the lane. But finally, maybe a third or a half mile down the way, I see it. It's the Fort Knox of pastures, like they think all of America's gold stores are inside. There's a six-foot fence, with an electric wire floating above it all the way around. When Quicksilver sees me, he trots over, head held high.

He's an absolutely stunning animal.

I've never really liked greys much. They always seem to roll in poop. And if not poop, then mud. Their eyes are often not very pretty at all, but none of that's true with him. He's almost snowy everywhere but his muzzle, his legs, and his mane and tail. And those are a consistent dark grey that's breathtaking.

But his eyes are truly amazing.

They're intelligent, engaged, and a gorgeous shade of blue I've almost never seen on a horse. "Wow," I say. "You're a real looker."

He whinnies.

"But sheesh," I say. "Who do they think you are with this insane fence? Houdini?"

He's a horse, though, so he just stares at me.

Plus, he did break out, so. . . "Well, I think we both get the rest of today off, but starting tomorrow morn-ing, we'll have a full day. I know that normally, people wouldn't be in too much of a hurry to break a new horse, but you're clearly not a baby, and I can't stick around here for very long. So let's make some great progress, show them what we can do, and then I'll get paid. As soon as that's done, I can let you go in the middle of the night, and we'll both be on our merry way. Sound like a deal?"

He snorts.

I'm actually a little bit excited.

You know, when I'm not peering around every corner in paranoia. Viktor makes me walk Quicksilver to his stall, which is miraculously simple, and shortly after that, Viktor stops by my room.

"I wanted to make sure we're on the same page." He raises one eyebrow.

"I have some questions."

"I thought you might."

"How did Quicksilver get loose before?"

"He's a wild catch," Viktor says. "In Russia, any wild horses belong to whomever can catch them. About ten days ago, he simply showed up in that forest where we found you, blowing and winded. He was easy to catch. But the next day, instead of being calm, he became insane. He kept trying to get away. We had to sedate him."

That's not promising.

"So you have no idea how old he is?"

"His teeth look almost perfect. Our vet thinks five or six at most."

"Alright."

"And when we breezed him, the one time we got someone on his back, the time was almost record breaking."

"But?"

"He took the bit like he'd had one in before, and then he stood for the saddle. Once. But after that, any time we tried, he practically killed the people trying." Viktor frowns. "We've tranqed him nearly every single day that he's been here. We can't keep doing that, clearly."

"And that's where I come in."

"He seems to love you," Viktor says. "If you can get him to where he's manageable, we'll pay you a handsome fee. My boss and I talked—we know it's dangerous, and we know you're probably already itching to get out of here. We told the men that you're a distant cousin visiting from Romania. That way none of them will try to talk to you. They don't know Latvian, except for Pyotr, and he wants to keep you safe, so he's promised to stay quiet."

"Oh, that's nice."

"If you can break Quicksilver to race, we'll pay you two million rubles."

I manage to keep from whistling, barely. It's not a massive fortune by any means, but it's enough to buy a used car. And more importantly, it's enough to get me back to Latvia. Or even on a flight to America, if that seems wiser. Between Nojus and Leonid, getting far, far away from anyone who wants to kill me feels like it might be a smart call.

I'll focus on getting this horse broke for now, and then once that's done, I'll see what direction feels the best.

"Thank you," I say.

And I mean it.

5

The next morning, I'm cursing Viktor out in every language I know. From the second I stepped into Quicksilver's Fort Knox paddock, grooms started lining up along the edge.

I thought, since he seems to be an exceptionally smart horse, I might start with Liberty. It's a training method the Americans like to claim, but really it's been around since 400 BC when Xenophon the Athenian wrote *On Horsemanship*, which focused quite a bit on positive reinforcement with a horse instead of just moving off pressure.

The idea of Liberty is to get the horse to work with what it naturally likes, and to give it space to move away or say no if it wants to ignore you.

Unfortunately, Quicksilver seems to naturally dislike anything to do with a crop, which you usually hold to cue the horse, and from the second I walked in with one, he does nothing but run away.

The grooms find this pretty funny.

But after a few moments, Quicksilver notices they're laughing and *scowls*. It sounds insane, but I swear the stallion's glaring at the people watching. I've chucked my whip to the edge of the paddock at this point, and I'm standing near the gate, wondering whether to go for the halter and try a modified version of Liberty instead.

Quicksilver's still focused on the audience, but when I make a bid for his attention, he trots right up to me and places his face right against my hand. Then he whuffles.

"What—"

He snorts then, covering me with grass-flecked bits of snot.

"Thanks a lot for that."

I know horses can't laugh, but I'd almost say he laughed.

"Alright, boy, let's try this without a whip." I step a bit back, and I signal with my hands the direction I'd like him to go. "Times like this, I really wish horses could talk." I tilt my head. "Then you could tell me why you're here, what you already know, and what's freaked you out in the past." I shake my head. "But for now, we'll have to try and figure it out together, one tiny bit at a time."

He listens much better without the whip, and I find that the more I talk him through things, the better he does. If I were a starry-eyed girl, I'd have thought he could understand me. As a very jaded adult, I realize that he's almost certainly reading my tone. Even so, if it's working, it's working.

By the end of the day, after taking five breaks in between, I notice that even Viktor's in the audience gathered outside.

"That looked amazing," he says. "Will you try and get on him tomorrow?"

I frown. "Would *you* like to get on him tomorrow?"

Viktor's eyebrows rise. "You were on him yesterday. Doing ground work feels like a backtrack."

"I was on the run yesterday, barefoot, and I didn't have many choices," I say. "Today, with the assurance that you won't let my ex know I'm here." I shrug. "I'm going to start from the ground up and do this right."

"Suit yourself," Viktor says. "But you might want to know that your ex did come by today. He actually said he was your employer and that you owed him a lot of money." Viktor looks uneasy.

"He did?"

Viktor nods. "He said you're an expert jockey, but that you like to gamble, and that you owed him more than a year's pay."

I can't help cringing.

"I hate smooth talking Russian businessmen. I didn't buy his lie."

I exhale dramatically. "Oh, good."

He leans closer, his mouth right next to the fence. "He beat you, didn't he?"

I swallow.

"My sister's husband beat her, and if I thought I could get away with it, I'd rip his head off."

For only the second time in my life, I think that maybe there is a God, and maybe he is watching over me. When I finally walk Quicksilver to his stall that night, I lean against his head for a moment. "Thank you," I say. "For finding me that day, and for letting me get on your back. I know you don't want to be here, and I know that bringing you back was a pretty lousy way to reward you for saving me, but I am grateful, and I do remember my promise. Once we convince them that you're a solid citizen and I get paid, I'll release you."

Although.

Now that Viktor has proven to be such a solid ally, I'm feeling worse and worse about taking his money and leaving. After all, I made this promise to a *horse*, and it's not like letting him go is really the benevolent thing to do. Horses in the wild have dangerous, unsafe lives. Food isn't sure, footing isn't solid, and without a herd. . .

It's starting to feel like I'll be making the wrong decision either way.

I wish I knew where Quicksilver came from. We're nowhere near the Russian Steppe where wild horses often roam. Letting him go, no matter how smart he is, is starting to feel a little nuts.

The next few days are a slow and steady progression, and Quicksilver continues to listen to me and match me, step for step. I'm mapping out a three-week plan when Viktor comes by. "How's it looking?"

I point at my timeline. "I think that within a month, we'll have some solid progress to show your boss."

"A month?" He snorts. "That's not fast enough."

"You had several men break bones before I got here," I say. "All the guys gather round because they're expecting to watch me get hurt."

"Still, a month's way too long," Viktor says. "There's a big race in a week. Boss wants him in it."

I stand up. "Oh, well, by all means, bring the faster guy back and let him do it. Oh, wait. Your last guy broke limbs and can't ride for months."

"Your boyfriend came by again today," Viktor says.

A chill runs up my spine.

"A few of the guys overheard what he had to say. He had a photo this time, and they looked. . .interested. If I were you, I'd be more motivated to finish the job."

Is he threatening me?

Or is he just warning me? Either way, Leonid hasn't given up, and if he's got a photo, no one on earth can keep this many guys quiet. It's only a matter of time before he offers a reward. They'd all talk for that. I crumple up my timeline and draw a new one. "I could try to ride him this week, I suppose."

Viktor smiles.

But that means, it's time to saddle him.

Horses don't usually scare me. After all, what's the worst that can happen? I've been thrown plenty of times, and I've been bucked far more, but for some reason, this one scares me more than most, and I can't figure out exactly why. Maybe it's the bizarre awareness he seems to have that makes him feel more dangerous.

"You got a saddle on him before, you said, right?" I ask.

Viktor nods, but his eyes are round as saucers from his safe place on the other side of the paddock. It's not very reassuring.

"What happened to the guy who saddled him, exactly?"

Viktor swallows.

"Hey, I'm serious. He broke an arm or something, right?"

Viktor cringes.

I snap. "Just tell me."

He rubs his hands along his jaw, the stubble there making a scritching sound. "His ankle got stuck in the stirrup. He broke his leg and his arm."

I step back. "Why are you guys so desperate to break this horse? And why on such a short timeline?"

"I thought our timeline worked for you," Viktor says. "You owe us money now, for room and board, and you want to get paid and leave. No?"

I clench my fist. "But why are *you* in such a hurry? Wouldn't you rather I do this right?"

"Owner's tired of winning second and third place. There are three really big races—name-making races—in St. Petersburg each year, and one of them is in eight days. If he misses this one, he'll have to wait five months for the next. He'd like to start planning his breeding for next summer. He wants a new bloodline. He was looking at some pricey stallions, but then this guy just waltzed onto our property. He's convinced it's a sign from God."

My blood runs cold.

On that very same day, I was asking God for help. But could all of this be any more unclear? I told God I'd do three good things in a row, but which is the good one? Do I break this horse for them so they can finally win? Or am I supposed to free the horse *from* them, because he was free before they found him, and he broke free on his own before helping me?

That's what I hate about all this God stuff.

Churches want you to think everything in life's black and white. Good or evil. But I must be some kind of black-white colorblind, because I swear that everything always looks grey. I need someone to tell me what the right choice is, but who could I possibly ask? What would I even say? Even my sister Mirdza, who sort of landed me in this mess to begin with, wouldn't believe anything about my life since the day of her very own win in that showjumping competition.

I turn around, shove my uneasiness away, and lift the saddle pad into the air. It's just big enough for a small saddle—a racing saddle. Quicksilver's wearing a halter, but he's ground tied, because if I were to tie him to the fence, he might freak out and bolt, damaging the halter and his own pretty head.

Green horses are the worst.

I swore I wasn't ever breaking one again, but that was before I was brought to Russia with no shoes and electrocuted by my kidnappers. I suppose when I compare it to being melted by fireballs or zapped by electro-man, dealing with a nutty horse is a massive step up.

I'm still stuck talking to Quicksilver constantly, or he tenses up and acts like a fool. "This saddle isn't the one I usually use at home, and it's not the kind of saddle you'll use if you race. The one I race in is called a Clarino, and it weighs a single pound. Can you believe that? I had to pay a few hundred dollars for a saddle that weighs one pound. That's what I should be doing. Instead of risking my neck for chump change, I should've gone into saddle design." I lean closer to him, swinging the brown exercise saddle they use here over his back. "Do you know why I didn't? Because I hate math *and* science, and those saddle geeks spend more time measuring things and counting than they do on a horse. Maybe that's why I should've made one instead —surely I'd do a better job, since I actually ride. But my grades weren't good enough. I guess that means my head's not worth much. Even so, I'd rather not break it today. I'm fond of it."

I sigh.

"Please don't freak out."

Quicksilver's head whips around, and I brace for a bite.

But instead, he blows air on my arm and then licks me.

The insane stallion everyone's afraid of just *licked* my arm.

"This horse is whack," I say. "Like, I think he might legitimately be imbalanced. Has anyone tried medicating him? Maybe we could level him out somehow."

And *now* he bites me. It's as if he was just looking for a good spot before, and he finally found it. The saddle wasn't cinched on yet, so when I slap him and he bolts, it flies up in the air and the butt of it sails right into my nose. My stupid, brainless head's protected by a helmet, but my nose was totally exposed. The saddle may be lightweight—all the racing exercise saddles are—but it still stings like, well, like a blow to the nose, when it hits the cartilage on the bridge of my nose.

"Oww." My hand flies up to cover my nose. At least I remember to swear only in Latvian. I've been learning so many new Russian swear words that it's a real challenge.

"Let's give him the day and try again tomorrow." Viktor and the other guys who were watching are laughing, and it makes me want to bite *them*.

"She looks just like him," one of the men says in Russian.

I turn my head to look at Quicksilver, who is literally standing right by me, scowling at them too. For all the world, he looks like he knows they're mocking us. I mean, I've had smart horses before, but this guy is practically creeper-vibes with how much he seems to understand about human behavior and emotions.

"Try again tomorrow?" I'm fuming now. "I'm getting a saddle on this idiot today, and you jerks are going to feel really stupid when I do."

It's a dumb thing to say, really, since saddling a horse isn't that big of an accomplishment.

Luckily, only Viktor can even understand me, and I was muttering.

Hopefully he didn't hear.

I practically whip the saddle up off the ground and

stomp toward Quicksilver. Any other horse I've ever dealt with probably would've bolted with the ham-handed way I'm handling this, but for some reason, he shakes a little like flies are bugging him, and then he stays put. I toss the saddle pad over his back again, and then I drop the saddle in place. I don't waste any time chatting this go round, grabbing the cinch and securing it on one side and then on the other.

I wait for him to freak out, but he doesn't.

"Hand me the bridle," I say.

No one moves. Viktor doesn't even say anything. I whip my head around, and they're all just staring at me.

"What?"

"You speak Russian?" the man who was just laughing asks.

I cringe. I can't really say I just know a word or two, because I used a command properly and knew the word for bridle. "A little," I say. "Not much." I switch to Latvian. "We had a Russian rider for a while, and he always told me what to do in Russian. I know horse affiliated words the best."

Viktor nods slowly, opening the gate and passing the bridle through.

I snatch it out of his hand and walk back over to Quicksilver while he translates what I said. They're all talking amongst themselves now, trying to decide whether I've been lying this whole time, and how much of what they've said I've understood.

I'm mad at myself for slipping. I was too distracted by Quicksilver, I suppose. I'm not like Kristiana or Mirdza. I goof things up all the time. But in this moment, my attention shifts to the stunning grey in front of me. He's standing still, calm, and sensible.

"Okay, boy. It's been a *day* already, and it's only nine in the morning. I'm sorry we had that incident with the saddle, and I'm still mad at you for biting me, but let's call it even and move on. What do you say?"

He whinnies.

The hair on my arms rises. I swear, if I didn't know it was impossible, I'd say this horse understands everything I'm saying. Which is nuts, because he's as Russian as these guys.

Even in my head, I'm funny.

I can't help smiling at my lame joke—like the reason he can't understand me is that I'm speaking *Latvian*, and not that I'm a human and he's a horse.

"Alright. I'm going to lift this bridle up and slide this bit into your mouth, and it's going to fit in a place where you don't have teeth, so don't try to bite me again." Actually, I didn't think to check whether he has wolf teeth.

I swear under my breath.

"He didn't have wolf teeth," Viktor says.

In Russian.

"What?" I ask in Latvian.

"He doesn't have wolf teeth," he says in Latvian. "We checked the first time we sedated him."

I breathe a sigh of relief and start over. "Alright, sir, you've apparently been cleared for the bit, so let's see how you do." I pat his shoulder. "You handled the saddle well—the second time. That and the way you let me ride you the day we met make me think you've been broken before, but maybe by lousy jerks. So let's take this slowly."

I move the halter to his neck, and he stomps once, but otherwise stands. Then I touch his nose and ask him to move his head down.

He does.

Sliding the bit into his mouth is as easy as bridling a twenty-year-old veteran. He stands still and calm as I buckle the nose band and the chin strap, and then he turns his head toward me, slightly, as if to say, "Let's show them."

I would be a complete lunatic to try and climb on him, knowing what I know about what happened to the last guy who just hopped on.

Right?

But I *am* kind of a lunatic.

I always have been. And I am beginning to believe in my bones that he understands me. He bit me after I was saying he was crazy. He listens when I talk.

Is it possible?

Or have I cracked?

I look him in the eye and say, "Will you let me on for a ride? Or will you break my arm?"

He stares right back at me, and then he nods, slowly.

"Wait, are you nodding that I can ride?"

He snorts. And then he nods again.

I swear, not even sure whether it's Latvian or Russian. Can I really trust that a *horse* is communicating with me? I've probably lost my mind.

At least a dozen Russian men are staring at us, mouths gaping open, eyes wide as can be, as I pull the stirrups down, and then swing up and over his back. It's not like we can really do anything impressive, not in a paddock that's less than an acre in size, but at least I can distract them from my Russian slip-up and our saddle incident.

I hope I don't distract them with an even bigger spill.

But so far, Quicksilver seems to know how to react to cues from the bit. Unlike most racehorses, the slightest shift in my hand position doesn't have him bolting forward. It seems like maybe he was properly trained.

They'll want to beat that out of him.

When I ask him to walk, a lively walk, a working walk, he does it. His head's up, he's ahead of me, but not by too much. After a careful circle, I click to ask for a trot. He lunges right into a canter, but maybe that's not super surprising.

At least he's on the correct lead.

The men have their faces pressed against the fence, so this time, as we approach that side of the paddock, I lean closer to Quicksilver's neck and whisper. "Let's really race past them, shall we? Fast enough to cover them with dirt?"

Again, as if he can understand me, his head drops a bit, and he begins pulling against my hands. When we turn into that stretch, I don't even ask. I just release him.

He bolts.

We're moving so fast that if I wasn't wearing a helmet, my hair would be plastered against my head. I'm actually a little nervous, as we turn the corner, that we might careen into the side of the enclosure. I'm sitting up high enough that I'd get pretty well acquainted with the electric fence if we did, so I'm not keen.

Luckily, Quicksilver turns well.

I haul back on the reins, and he stops a little too fast. I don't go over his ears and into the dirt, but it's a near enough miss that it makes me nervous.

"Well," I say. "I'd call this good progress." I might be a little too pleased. I mean, this is my job, after all.

Viktor's smiling when I look his way.

But someone's trotting up the path, which usually means there's some kind of problem elsewhere.

"That guy's back," he says. "And he brought the police with him. They said they want to search the property for the Latvian girl."

And just like that, all the butterflies and rainbows in my heart drop dead. It's back to cobwebs and skeletons in there, like usual.

❧ 6 ❧

I love my mother.

I really do. And of course, because I laid it out like that, it's clear that there's a but coming.

My mother isn't a strong person.

I realized that for the first time when I was quite young—the day I met Kristiana's mother for the first time. When you're a kid, you don't realize you're poor. You don't know your mother's a bit of a mess. You don't know the food you're eating is bad.

It's all you've ever known.

It's not until you experience something *better* that you realize the first thing was wanting.

The day we moved to live at Liepašeta was that day for me. Having only ever lived in an apartment until that point, I was blown away by the magnitude of the place. It was *huge*, and it was *lovely,* and I couldn't wrap my brain around the fact that they owned a massive house, a gargantuan barn, and a smaller barn with living quarters attached.

On top of that, at the end of their large stables, there were apartments—bigger apartments than we'd ever lived in, and they simply used them for people who were working for them, as a perk.

We lived in one of those apartments for free, because my mother started cleaning for the Liepa family. I suppose I could have been filled with resentment toward Kristiana's mother. After all, I envied Kris for most of my life.

But Mrs. Liepa was spectacular.

She was strong. She was brave. She was talented. She was fiery. She knew more about horses and how to ride them than anyone I had ever met. She's the reason that Kristiana, Mirdza, and I all love horses. She's the reason I grew up to be strong myself instead of turning out like my mother. She's the reason I knew that women *could* grow up this way. She's the reason I got straight As in English, always. For a while there, I spoke it even better than Kristiana.

But at the end of the day, the easiest way out for me is still to tell Leonid and Boris how to capture Kristiana.

I could do it.

If I called her, she'd come for me. She'd do anything I asked, thanks to the guilt I'm sure she's feeling about how I took her place.

But her mother's also the reason I would never do that.

If there's a heaven, Mrs. Liepa's there. If there's a God, she's got to be one of his most beloved. And there's not a single solitary chance on this earth that I would ever repay her goodness, her charity, her love of Mirdza and my mom and me and all the broken things in the world, by handing her daughter over to those maniacs.

So as adrenaline courses through my veins, and as I start looking around for the closest exit, the thought never enters my mind to betray Kristiana to save myself.

Even I have limits.

Of course, the second Viktor bows out to go and talk to them, reassuring me it will be fine, but also signaling to all the men standing around that I definitely *am* the person they're looking for, I start devising a plan.

"Since the ride has gone so well," I say, "I think I ought to try breezing him on the track. Wouldn't it be nice to send a video clip or something to the owner? Show the progress?"

Of course, they can't understand me.

But I'm pointing, and one of the guys closest to the gate starts to open it.

His buddies are a bit smarter. They start arguing, gesturing, and shoving him. I open my mouth to argue, but before I can say a word, Quicksilver plunges forward, shoving his way through the partially opened gate.

"Whoa," I say, hauling on his face.

It's like he can't hear or feel me at all.

At least the guys can tell that I'm not in control. They're waving and shouting and eventually, running after us, but Quicksilver isn't stopping. He pounds down the alley-paddock that runs in segmented pieces from this far end of the property down to the line where we first entered.

Only, instead of tearing right down the main line, he hangs a quick right and heads straight for the main compound, which is right where Leonid or Boris or whoever is waiting. I'm practically positive.

I was trying to stop him before, but now I'm basically ripping his face off. I've never had a horse completely ignore me like this, and I ride racehorses.

I know how to release and yank and release and *yank*.

But this guy isn't stopping.

Just when I think we're going to sprint right into the main area, he pulls left, and that's when I realize what he's doing. He's heading for the one break in the perimeter fence, the four-foot run that circles around the side of the barn and out the back road.

I'm swearing under my breath, but I'm also patting the side of his neck. "You're freaking brilliant, you insane beast."

And when I stop fighting him, *we fly*.

As we exit the property, I can't help thinking that my situation just went from not-good to very, very bad. I mean, I'm a Latvian citizen without any identification, communication device, or money, and I've now stolen a horse. The stolen horse is literally my only means of transportation, and I have no way to feed or clothe myself, much less a mighty beast who could be rendered utterly useless by a tummy ache or a crack in his toenail at any time. And there's a magical villain who apparently has at least one cop in his pocket who's now on my tail. No matter how fast this insane grey stallion is, this is not the beginning of a fairy tale.

It's clearly the start of an epic tragedy.

While we're racing alongside a road—luckily a very rural road—I start to think. What's my plan here? If I just run around, I'm bound to generate some attention. Someone will call the cops. Then I'll be caught.

I need money.

I need identification.

I need a place to hide.

And eventually, I need a way out of Russia.

I could call Gustav. He doesn't really like me, but we were raised together until his mom died. He ran away and never looked back after that. The problem is that I don't know his phone number, but I could probably look up his family's business. I bet someone could get him a message. I would need a phone or reliable access to one to make that feasible.

It's a definite back burner idea.

But for now, there's really only one person I could call who might be able to help with all those things. Or rather, if I call Mirdza, she might enlist the aid of Kristiana and her Russian boyfriend. I know Mirdza's boyfriend is Russian too, and he allegedly has money as well, but they've been together for twelve and a half minutes, and in my experience, the fastest way to break a new couple up is for family to start making crazy demands.

At least if I wreck Kristiana's relationship, I won't feel as lousy for it.

And I have her number memorized.

If I can only get my hands on a phone. . .and make an international call. Why is everything so hard when you're penniless and in a strange country? "Phone. Phone. Where can I find a phone?" I spent so many days talking to Quicksilver all the time that I think I just do it now our of habit.

Quicksilver slows a hair and turns back to look at me, as if I was actually asking for his input. It makes me smile.

"You're doing great, boy. You just keep on going a little farther and. . ."

There's a sign for the Ropsha Racetrack up ahead.

It's a crazy thought, but it *almost* feels like God's intervening. I know exactly *one* person in Russia, and they work there. At that racetrack. Plus, a woman on a horse that's galloping full tilt down the road? The only place that won't cause people to call the cops is probably near a racetrack.

Of course, they may have to call a vet if he doesn't slow down pretty soon. He may drop dead. Ha. How far have we been running? Four miles? Five?

Looking up ahead, if I just leave this path and head up the ridge toward the road, I notice that there's a man sitting on the side of the road by his car. It probably has a flat tire. The fact that he doesn't have a working car is probably a good thing. He can't get in his car and follow me if he turns out to be a jerk. And since he's broken down, he might take pity on someone else who's also somewhat stranded.

In this day and age, everyone has a phone, right?

I take a gamble and ask Quicksilver to slow down, and then I guide him up, through the brambles, and toward the road. "I know this sounds a little crazy, but I need to get to that man up there. I'm hoping he'll have a phone, and that he'll let me borrow it."

Quicksilver stops.

No matter how hard I try to urge him forward, he won't budge.

Finally, I swing off, drop the reins, knot them so they won't get caught if he bolts, and walk away.

"Stupid horse," I mutter. "Thinks if he acts tough, he can decide where we go? What a lunatic."

As I get closer, I walk more carefully, hoping not to alarm this poor guy. That backfires a bit, because when I finally step out onto the road ahead of him, he shoots to his feet, swears loudly, and drops his phone.

"I'm so sorry," I say in the best Russian I can manage. "I didn't mean to startle you. I got stranded on my way to the racetrack, and there wasn't anyone around. Then I saw you, and I thought you might have a phone I can borrow."

I don't mention that it's to make an international call. What idiot would agree to that?

"Oh." He brushes his phone off. "Well, okay. A friend of mine's coming to pick me up. He could probably drop you off. That race track is close." He points and then holds his phone out.

I've stepped closer and I'm reaching for it when Quicksilver comes racing up behind me. We both turn just as he slams into me from behind, knocking me forward. I land in the dirt, which rips my already hand-me-down men's pants in the knee.

I'm swearing up a storm as I stand.

The guy ran all the way around his car, and now he's hiding on the road side of it, his head barely visible.

Freaking Quicksilver. Every time I think maybe he's a genius, he does something idiotic. "Look, moron. He was about to let me call my sister, Mirdza." I shake my head. "I'm so sorry. Racehorses are sometimes total lunatics."

"Maybe you should come over here," the guy says. "He looks dangerous."

"He's dangerously irritating," I say in Russian. "But he won't really hurt me."

"Still."

I walk toward the car, careful to stay on the forest side of it. "If I can borrow your phone to make that call, I'll take my idiot horse and get away from you, I swear."

He doesn't look too keen to pass me his phone this time.

"Please?" I use my best damsel-in-distress eye-batting, and he finally relents. He doesn't stand up all the way, and his hand shakes as he hands me his phone, but he does pass it across in front of the windshield.

Thank goodness.

I dial Mirdza without thinking, but she doesn't answer. I decide to leave her a voicemail. "Hey, M, it's me." I don't want to alarm the guy who's loaned me his phone, so I keep things pretty neutral, just in case he speaks Latvian. "I'm outside of St. Petersburg right now, near the Ropsha Racetrack. I'm kind of stranded, truth be told, and I could use some help. If you get this, maybe try to marshal a little help. I'll try and call again."

I hang up.

Nervous guy holds out his hand.

I cringe a little. "Can I try one other number? My sister didn't answer."

He frowns, but nods. "Okay, sure. Yeah. Go ahead."

It's funny that people who really want to say no usually wind up saying yes a dozen different ways when they finally do. It's like they have to say it over and over to reassure themselves it's their choice and not foisted upon them by the social pressure they feel.

I dial Kristiana. She picks up.

"Allo," she says.

She must have realized it's a Russian number. "Kris, it's me," I say in Latvian, pretty confident this guy doesn't speak it.

She inhales sharply. "Are you alright?"

"So far," I say. "I'm alive. But I'm outside St. Petersburg, and I have no way to get—"

"Are you safe?"

"No. I'm near the Ropsha Racetrack, and I'm broke."

"If you can find someplace to hide, anywhere, and tell me where you'll be, we can come to you."

"The thing is, other than this big idiotic horse that's kind of following me, I don't have—"

"Did you say a horse is following you?" Her tone's

urgent—like she's *more* concerned now than she was before.

"Yes, but—"

"A smart horse?"

"Sure," I say. "But also very, very stupid sometimes.

Behind me, Quicksilver snorts.

"What does he look like?"

"Hey, what language are you speaking?" The Russian man stands, his brow furrowing.

"He's a grey," I say. "But look, I need to go."

"Is that an international call?" He reaches across the windshield for me.

I back up.

But Quicksilver's there.

"He's a grey." Kris is talking to someone else, but I'm too distracted to try and listen. "Is he mostly white?" she asks. "With a dark mane and tail?"

"*Kris*," I say. "*This isn't my phone*. Can you focus?"

She can't, clearly. "But how did you find him?"

This woman's seriously obsessed with horses, like, in a sick way. I was *kidnapped*, and now I'm in Russia, and she's more interested in the horse I found than in my whereabouts. "Look, I have to go, okay? I'll try and call back."

"Adriana! Wait!"

But the guy's circling the car, so I hang up.

Quicksilver's racing toward him, actually placing himself between the rightfully irritated man and me. Like he's a guard horse, or something.

Horses are prey, so even for a stallion, this is pretty odd.

"I'm going to set your phone here." I hold it up, and show him that I terminated the call. "Thanks for letting me borrow it." I set it on the ground and back away slowly.

Quicksilver looks down at the phone, and then he looks up at the guy. He narrows his eyes at him, and then he snorts.

The guy backs up a step.

And Quicksilver stomps on the phone, shattered plastic bits scattering all over.

Oh, shoot.

I grab the side of his saddle and swing up and we're off before the guy's shouts can turn into more. It's surprising that the same guy who was hiding on the other side of his car is now practically attacking us, but people get crazy when their phones are involved.

"What was that for?" I lean closer to his neck. "*Bad* Quicksilver."

He tosses his head and keeps running.

Within less than five minutes, I see the town that's on the east side of the racetrack. If I stick close to the road, I can stay mostly hidden from people for almost the entire way to the east, and then swing around north, hopefully preventing people from placing any calls that will tell the authorities where I am.

As we fast-trot our way up and around, I can't help thinking about that phone call.

Why did Kristiana get so hung up on my horse?

Sure, she's given me lots of horses over the years. I mean, I know that on the balance sheet, I owe her. But is she really worried about me repaying her right now? I don't even own Quicksilver. I *stole* him. From someone who has quite a lot of money and power, too.

And Leonid's still following me, presumably still upset with Kris and her boyfriend for unknown reasons.

Which begs the question, can her boyfriend also shoot fireballs and zap people? Or does he know that Boris and Leonid can? What on earth is going on and who do they work for? What kind of strange government experiments gave them those powers, and why are they after Kris?

All of those would be good things to focus on, to grill me about, or to obsess over.

But no.

It's all about this stupid, idiotic brute who keeps biting me and smashing Good Samaritan's phones. "Ugh. Why did you crush that guy's phone? And why did you bite me earlier? When people try to help, you should be nice to them, not rude."

Quicksilver snorts, and I'm almost positive it was a reaction to my comment.

It had to be, right?

Compared to fireballs and electric zaps coming from people, is this really that strange? Could he be, like, some super duper smart horse? Like, maybe Kristiana and Aleksandr got involved with some kind of illegal horse trading or horse breeding scheme, and that's why. . .could that be why he was loose? Maybe he's Leonid's horse, and those other people stole him! Maybe they really want the *horse back*, but that jerk was telling me they were coming for me.

We're finally approaching the back side of the race track, and I realize that if Kristiana was asking all those questions about the horse, and if this horse *is* super smart. . . Maybe ditching him is my only way out.

"Alright." I haul on his reins, pat his neck, and swing off. "Well, I can't really see a way for us to help one another anymore at this point." I unbuckle his bridle and pull it off. Then I undo his cinch on one side, and then the other. I could just ditch the bridle and saddle, but they're literally the only things of value I have right now. Even if they only buy me dinner, I'm carrying them to the track.

"You've been a really great partner in crime, but I think it's time we go our separate ways." I pat his rump. "Hopefully there's a stream around here or something." I feel a little bad about ditching him. He's pretty sweaty and probably thirsty.

Then again, he's smart. He should be fine. Horses can eat wherever and surely there's water around.

But Quicksilver shakes his head.

The gosh-darn horse shakes his big old head at me, like he's emphatically turning down my proposition.

"The thing is, I have a friend here, sort of, and I'm going to see if he'll hide me for a little while." For a saddle and a bridle, he should give me at least two or three meals, right? I mean, they're used. But they have some value. "You should head south." I point. "There are a lot of low density little towns sprinkled all over for a day or two's travel, but then if you keep south and maybe a little east, you'll wind up in a no man's land called Khotnezha, and I heard there were some wild horses there."

If he's not a genetically modified kind of bizarre beast, that may be where he came from.

"Maybe they grow them smarter there." I pat his nose. "I really do appreciate your help, and I wish I had some treats to offer you, or really anything at all."

I remember something.

"Okay, there's a watering hole maybe two miles down that path." I point again. "I went on a trail ride with my friend Gavriil about two years ago, and if you follow that street right there, it'll open up and behind the big bushes, you'll see it. Maybe that'll be my parting gift, if you really do understand what I'm saying."

Quicksilver throws his ears back and paws at the ground.

"Alright, well." I brush my hands against themselves and pivot on one heel.

I'm about ten strides down the path toward the stables—really hoping that Gavriil is still in charge, and wishing that I'd kept in touch better—when I realize the stallion's following me.

Quicksilver's staying a few paces away, and he stops when I look over my shoulder, but he's *following me*. He's walking right behind me like he's a dog who just adopted me.

"You can't come." I turn around and fold my arms across my chest. "You need to go that way." I point.

He just looks at me.

No pawing. No snorting. No pinned ears. Just looking.

It makes me feel pretty guilty. He did save me, not once, but twice now. And his reaction to me was the reason Viktor was willing to keep me around at all. If not for him, I'd be back in that horrible cement cell smearing waste on myself, or worse, dead.

Plus, I promised God to try and help him. Sort of.

"How am I supposed to do anything with you? Huh?" I exhale and curse fate. "Look, you're like a neon sign pointing them at me. I'm small. I can hide. You're huge. You can't hide anywhere."

He tosses his head.

"I know, I know, you're fabulous. But the thing is, they *own* you—either the bad men I just left, or the bad men chasing me, and either way, I'm in the wrong, legally speaking. I've stolen you. The only thing worse than a Russian jail would be that horrible Leonid guy getting hold of me again. I swear, if that guy burns me to ash. . ." I shudder involuntarily. "Boris is almost as bad, with his electric zaps. Trust me. Neither of us wants to see them, and our best bet is splitting up."

Quicksilver freezes, his nostrils flaring, his eyes widening.

He looks like a horse that's just seen a plastic bag, blowing round and round like a ball, tossed by the wind —basically, he looks ready to bolt and pee himself at the same time.

"Whoa," I say. "What's going on with you?" I look around.

No plastic bags in sight. No big shadows, either.

"Look, if you do understand me, how about this? You stay here, and if I can find my friend Gavriil, and if he has a place to keep you, I'll bring him out here. Okay?"

He shakes his head.

The horse I'm talking to, as if he and I are having a conversation, shakes his head *no*. And I'm not even surprised. I'm bargaining with him.

Maybe they should commit me.

"This isn't a negotiation," I say. "You stay put. I'll try to come get you."

But when I start walking again, and then when I start jogging, he trots along even closer than before. When I stop, his huge head actually bumps into my back. I spin around again, angry this time. "I don't even have a halter for you. I can't very well go walking into a racing facility with a horse that's just loose—"

He bumps the saddle with his nose.

"For the love—Quicksilver."

He bumps it again, and this time he blows snot all over my arm.

I groan.

I can't believe a horse is forcing me to do things. A horse that I don't even own. But if I walk in there like this, with this big lummox of an idiot tagging along on my heels, they'll stop me for sure. It will draw *way more* attention than if I lead him in there, all sweaty and tacked up. At least he'll look like every other horse out there, more or less.

"Fine." I grit my teeth and throw the stupid saddle back on. "*Fine*, but you have to listen to *everything* else I say from here on out. Okay?"

He nods.

My stallion *nods*.

And I take that to mean that he's listening to me. Understanding what I say, and agreeing to behave. A stallion who was, until very recently, wild.

I've gone completely insane.

"Look." I clear my throat as I'm putting the bridle back on him. "If you actually understand what I'm saying, I want you to—"

"*Adriana?*"

When I snap my head around, Gavriil's standing behind me, just as handsome as ever. I've never broken my rule about not dating, but if I ever got close. . .it was with him.

"It *is* you. What are you doing here?"

My voice is small—embarrassingly small—and it cracks when I say, "I need help."

He doesn't pause. He doesn't hesitate for even a second. He strides toward me, his arms extended. "Anything you need."

And Quicksilver bites him, hard, right on the meaty part of his hand.

＊ 7 ＊

The first time I met Gavriil, he was mucking stalls at the nicest racetrack in Latvia. His very wealthy father had kicked him out, and he had left the country to really get away. He was taking any job he could get. After hearing his story, I lent him a hand, and he bought me a few beers at the local pub to repay me. With his dark hair and soulful, deep brown eyes, I knew I was walking a dangerous line.

For the first and only time in my life, I was actually tempted to date someone. It took all of my resolve and years and years' worth of accumulated trauma for me to turn him down. When I saw him in Russia later, managing this racetrack, I nearly changed my mind.

Twice now, I've held firm.

But this time around, I'm meeting him without a single friend or supporter. I'm lost, and I'm confused, and I'm scared, and Gavriil's face may be the most beautiful thing I've ever seen.

Even though he looks like he might shoot Quicksilver.

"I am so sorry," I say. "He's a very temperamental horse, but he's saved my life twice now, so. . ."

Gavriil's eyes widen. "Saved your—I had no idea you were even in Russia."

"It's a really, really long story," I say. "And." I glance around and then drop my voice. "There are some people looking for me."

He sighs. "Is this even your horse?"

I cringe. "Not exactly."

It's a little sad that he already knows me well enough to ask that. "Did you steal him?"

I'm not sure how to answer that. "Sort of?"

Gavriil closes his eyes.

I'm sure he's weighing his options and trying to decide what to do. The smart move would be handing me in. I know he and his dad kind of made up, but not really, which is why he's still working as a racetrack manager instead of running the family business. Even so, it's not like he's some powerless guy without options. Getting tagged for his affiliation with me won't break him like it might a normal guy.

I sound really selfish, even to myself.

"If I had anyone else I could go to. . ." I glance around again.

Quicksilver's pawing at the ground, but at least now that I've yanked him behind me, he's mostly staying put. "If you could just loan me a stall for him temporarily and hear me out, I'll do whatever you ask afterward."

He sighs.

But that's how I know I have him.

Unlike me, Gavriil thinks things through. He's methodical, he's prudent, and he always does the right thing. If he were going to kick me out without even hearing what I had to say, he would've done it already.

He finally tosses his head, and I realize he's taking me to the quarantine pen.

"We're going to find a place to rest for a bit," I whisper to Quicksilver as I pat his nose. "And maybe you'll even get some grain."

He bumps my side.

"Grain, yes."

He tosses his head. Then he bumps me again.

"Wait, do you mean me?"

"I have food," Gavriil says, his Latvian still excellent. "But I really doubt if that horse is worried about you eating. You may be crediting him with thoughts he's not capable of."

Quicksilver tries to bite him again.

"Maybe you're not giving him enough credit. He is smarter than any other horse I've met."

"He could do calculus, and I'd still hate him," Gavriil says.

I can't help laughing.

Quicksilver nuzzles my arm.

"I doubt he can do that," I say. "But I swear, Gav, I can't tell you how many times I've asked him something, and he's responded. It's uncanny."

We've reached his three separate quarantine stalls, which are luckily all unoccupied, and Gavriil slides the door to the largest stall open.

"Like, watch this." I pull the saddle off, and then I start to take off his bridle.

"Whoa," Gavriil says. "What are you doing?"

"Just trust me." I point at the stall. "Alright, Quicksilver. Show him what I'm talking about. Walk into the stall for me."

Quicksilver stares at me intently.

And does absolutely nothing else.

Well, that's embarrassing.

"I really thought that would work."

"He's a horse, Adriana. I know that sometimes it's hard—they *feel* so smart, but at the end of the day, they all have the mentality of a toddler."

Quicksilver's pawing at the ground, and I grab a halter. Maybe he'll be still and steady while I halter him, and then I can. . .

I stop dead.

His pawing wasn't random.

He spelled out a word.

It's not a very nice word.

It's a Russian word.

"Gav." I point. And I swallow. And I'm still struggling to believe what I'm seeing.

Clearly, in the dirt in front of me, my horse has just written the Russian word for. . .well, it's a rude name for illegitimate children. And he tosses his head at Gavriil.

He waltzes into the stall, stretches out, and pees on the shavings. Then he turns around, blows out a bunch of air in what sounds like a beleaguered sigh, and stares straight ahead, blankly.

Gavriil swears under his breath, closes the stall door, and kicks dirt over the large scrawled word. He points at the door to the small office by the tack room. "Let's talk."

The office only has one window, and it's on the door that opens to the outside. It doesn't let in a lot of light, but at least I can see Quicksilver out of the corner of my eye. He's turned away from us now, not agitated at all as far as I can tell.

I walk Gavriil through as much of what has happened as I can, glossing over the reasons for Nojus's men being after me and leaving out the fireballs and the electric shock magic. Even without those parts, his eyes get wider and wider, and when I tell him that Leonid allegedly showed up with a police officer, he takes my hand. "Adriana."

"I know. It's been. . .a weird few weeks."

"I'm—I can't believe you escaped."

"Well, I stole their horse to do it," I say.

"The horse none of them can ride and that they just *found* a week or so ago."

"Even so, in their mind—"

"They won't have papers for him," Gavriil says.

"Not real ones, anyway," I say.

"That's true." He frowns. "Listen, if I call my dad—"

"Are you guys fine, now?"

He stiffens, so that's a no.

"Then don't do it. Not for me. Not for this. I don't want to drag you into—"

"Like I'm going to let you. . .what? Run all alone again?"

"They can have the horse back," I say. "I mean, I feel bad for him. He hates them, and clearly he's not a normal horse. I don't think it's right for them to have him, or to race him against his will or whatever. But I'm not sure what else to do."

"I said, if I call my dad—"

"I don't want to force anything horrible for you. I just need a loan." I hate asking for money, but I don't see another way, and I don't have a single dime. "And if you know anyone who can find identification for people. . ."

"Then you're just running again," he says. "Stay with me instead, at least until these people can't hurt you."

It's tempting. In all my life, just like the last two times I was around him, I've never been more tempted to just surrender. I've never more strongly considered trusting a man to take care of me. But that always comes with strings, and I can't handle strings. I know I can't. I'm the kind of person whom strings will strangle in the end, always.

"Gav—"

He holds up his hands. "I'm not saying you have to date me. I'm not proposing marriage. I'm just saying that instead of running away, you could believe in me for a minute. You can hide, and I'll take care of this for you."

I think about what I know about Gavriil. He's honest. He's hard working, especially for a rich man's son, and he's kind. He's a beautiful, generous man. If there really are good men out there, he's one of them.

And no one like that deserves to be saddled with someone like me.

"I can't," I say.

"I'll get you cash," he says. "But it's a Sunday, and it's late afternoon. The soonest I can get it for you is the morning. Stay here tonight, and you can think about it. Alright?"

My heart starts to pound. "But what if they find me?"

"If you think I can't keep you safe for one night, here on my own track, you don't know me at all."

"They have the police on their side," I say. "If they show up with a warrant, what will you do?"

"They don't know where you went, or they'd already be here. They'll have a lot of ground to cover to locate you, and even when they do, they need a judge to give them a warrant. And if it comes to that, I *will* call—"

"I don't want you to have to call your dad for me."

He presses a finger to my mouth. "My uncle," he says. "I'll call my uncle. He's the Minister of Justice here in Russia—he's literally the boss of all the judges in the country."

Oh. Well. That's nice.

"Please calm down. It's going to be alright."

A single tear rolls down my face, and I wipe it away quickly, but Gavriil sees it, and he stands up. He pulls me to my feet, and his arms wrap around me, holding me tightly.

There's a horrible whinnying scream behind us, and then a whamming sound. We jump apart and look through the glass of the door. Quicksilver's throwing himself against the stall door and screaming. His eyes are wild, his nostrils flaring, and he starts striking the inside of the door with his hooves.

"That horse is possessed," Gavriil says. "We should call a priest to perform an exorcism or something."

But it's almost like he was watching us, and when Gavriil crossed a line. . . I move away from Gavriil and wave to Quicksilver. He stops banging on the door and hurling himself against the stall, but he's still watching intently.

"I think—"

"If you can loan me money in the morning," I say, "I'll take it. I'll release him into the woods, send him on his way, and then I'll get out of here."

Gavriil shakes his head. "I think it's a bad plan, but I've never had any luck telling you what to do."

I can't help smiling about that. "Don't worry. No one else has either."

He sighs, but he doesn't argue any more. At least, not right now.

"Oh," I say. "Can I borrow your phone?"

"Of course." He pulls it out of his pocket. But when I call them, neither Kristiana nor Mirdza answer. In fact, both the calls go to voicemail. It's a little deflating. I sort of thought they'd be waiting by the phone. I was hoping maybe one of them could wire me money, and I wouldn't have to impose on poor Gavriil. I leave them both messages, telling them I'm at the racetrack and that they can call me back at this number. Mirdza's met Gavriil, so she'll be able to guess that I've found some kind of help. Maybe that'll help her sleep easier.

Gavriil looks at his phone. "I've got to meet with a few grooms." He opens the office door. "I'll make sure they bring some feed for this one. Any idea what he's been eating?" He's glaring at Quicksilver, who's not looking very happy, either.

His ears are pinned to his head, and he's tossing his head at Gavriil.

I walk him through what we've been feeding him. "Don't take it personally," I say. "The attitude, I mean. He acts like this with literally everyone but me."

"Were all the grooms there male?"

I nod.

"Maybe he was abused by men," Gavriil says. "Or maybe his last owner was a woman who was abused *by* men."

I'd never even thought of that. "Almost every horse problem. . ."

"Is a human problem," Gavriil finishes.

At least he knows that. It's sadly very, very true.

"Before I get started on all that, I'll take you to my apartment. It's not far, and you're welcome to take a shower and change into some of my pajamas."

Quicksilver freaks out again, this time worse than the last.

"I might stay in here with him. It's a new place, and I'm leaving. I think it's freaking him out."

"Are you sure you'll be safe in there?"

"He bit me once," I say, "but other than that, he's

never hurt me. He's had plenty of chances."

Gavriil doesn't like it, I can tell, but he doesn't say. The only person I ever let win an argument is a horse, and even that's rare.

I open the stall door a crack and slide through. "You're lucky I love horses, mister, because otherwise, I'd have just walked away and let you break your leg kicking the wall."

He looks smug.

I've never seen a smug horse, but there's a first time for everything, I suppose. He bumps me with his nose, and I rub him under his chin. Then I slide my hand up, along his jaw, and scratch under his dark, thick mane.

"How do you keep so clean?" I ask. "I've never known a grey who wasn't covered in poop stains."

He snorts.

He does seem to only be going in the corner—I've heard that about stallions, that they're way neater than the usual horse.

"You really do seem to be listening to me." Actually, this is what we were talking about when I saw Gavriil earlier. I'd just tried to release him, and he'd refused to go. "One thing I was just telling my friend is that, after he loans me some money, I can finally honor my promise to you. I can set you free."

He freezes.

There's no doubt in my mind that this horse understands what I'm saying. Maybe not every word, but at least some of it. "On the day we met, when you saved me, I promised that after I was safe, I'd release you."

He's still not moving, not even a single twitch.

"But I tried earlier, and you didn't go. Then you walked right into this stall."

His head turns slowly, and he presses his nose against my hand.

"Listen, Quicksilver, no one loves horses more than I do, and the fast ones—I love them most of all." I rub his nose. "But we're in a country called Russia right now, and I live in a place called Latvia. There's not a good way, without a *lot* of paperwork for you, that I can take you back with me. Even then, there's a quarantine."

Horses are a little hard to transport in the best of cases, and the last thing I want to do right now, with Leonid on my tail, is start filling out paperwork declaring a horse.

"You were free when I found you, and I intend to make sure you're free when I leave. Instead of just shooing you away, Gavriil can help me. He'll take you in a trailer out close to the steppe and release you there. Okay?"

Quicksilver spins around quickly, and now I'm staring at his butt.

"Are you asking me to scratch this?" Most horses love getting butt scratches. They can't reach it easily, and if my butt was that big and beautiful and hairy, I'd probably long for a butt scratch, too. I do what any good horse girl does, and I reach out and scratch his butt with both hands, my fingernails digging in, especially right around the base of his tail.

At first, he jumps, like he was not expecting it, but then he does what horses always do and shifts a bit, then freezes, his neck stretching, his head lifting, lifting, lifting, and finally, his eyes closing.

"No horse can resist a good butt scratch." I can't help my laugh.

It startles him, though, and he spins back around.

"If you can just handle the stall in here for one night, I promise that before I leave on the train tomorrow, I'll make sure you're free and safe."

Quicksilver starts to whinny, and then he whuffles, and then he makes one of the strangest horse sounds I've heard, a kind of grunting snort whinny.

I shake my head. "You are one odd animal. Surely you know that."

He sighs, dramatically, like the whole world's against him.

I pat his neck. "It's going to be fine. I swear it is."

When his dinner arrives, he tears into it. But when Gavriil returns to collect me, Quicksilver freaks out *again*.

"I hate that horse," Gav says.

"Can you just bring my food in here?" I ask. "And maybe bring a sleeping bag? I think I'm going to have to sleep in here."

"Did you sleep with him while you were breaking him?"

I shake my head. "But we're both a little strung out right now, being on the run from not one, but two different groups. And, we can't really afford to draw more attention to him."

Gavriil doesn't like it, but eventually he gives up again. When he brings me a sandwich, Quicksilver tries to eat it.

I swat him. "Stop. You have yours." I shove him toward the hay. "Leave mine alone."

He pins his ears, but he goes back to his dinner.

And after we're done eating and I've had a quick bathroom break, I unroll my sleeping bag in the corner and lie down. Thirty seconds later, Quicksilver lies down too, right next to me. He sets his giant head close to mine and closes his eyes.

"I think that horse is insane," Gavriil says. "I'm sleeping in the office, so if you need something, just shout."

Quicksilver lifts his head and blows air right at him, as if to say, *go away*.

I'm tired enough that, even with the anxiety that we'll be found, I go right to sleep. When I wake up, I'm curled up against Quicksilver's side, my head resting on his shoulder. I sit up with a jolt, and realize that he's watching me.

There's just a little bit of light streaming through the side of the stall, so it must be close to dawn. I yawn and try to brush my hand through my hair. It's such a disaster that I give up on that right away.

Even with the shavings, the night's sleep did me a *lot* of good. I feel way better.

Until a man runs, shouting, into the barn. "Mr. Belov!"

Gavriil shoots out of the office. "What's wrong?" he asks in Russian.

I hear him close the office door, but I'm not sure whether we should stay somewhat hidden or hop up and get ready to run.

"There are men outside. They're claiming you're harboring a stolen horse, and they say they've called the police."

Gavriil swears under his breath. "It's fine. I'll call my uncle."

"Don't bother." That's a voice I know.

I leap to my feet, and I look over the edge of the stall. Quicksilver stands up behind me, too.

Sure enough, Kristiana and her fiancé Aleksandr, as well as Mirdza and her boyfriend Grigoriy, have followed the panicked man.

"Trust me," Aleks says. "If you give us a moment alone with Adriana, we can make it so that this all just goes away."

                              ❄   8   ❄

What on earth are they talking about?

I know Aleksandr's wealthy, and I know he's connected. But if anyone's connections are going to help us here, it's Gavriil's. His uncle's the Minister of Justice, for heaven's sake.

"I'm going to call my uncle," Gavriil says. "I think—"

Quicksilver screams, the loudest whinny I have ever heard, and instead of stepping back in alarm, Aleksandr and Grigoriy both smile.

And then they *salute,* which is really, *really* strange.

"Before you call in any favors, please give us five minutes," Aleks says. "In fact, you can go tell the people who are causing the problem that they have the wrong place. You do *not* have a large grey horse here, not anywhere. Tell them that, and invite them to search."

The man who came running over, shouting, looks totally incredulous. "But there *is* a large—"

"You want me to lie?" Gavriil asks.

"Trust me," Aleksandr says.

"But I don't." Gavriil folds his arms. "I don't even know you."

Aleksandr glares at him, and it's actually pretty scary. "Give me five minutes, or I'll be forced to do something I don't want to do."

A chill runs up my spine—I've never thought Kristiana's fiancé was particularly threatening. . .until now.

Gavriil must agree, because he stops arguing, and he and his groom duck out the side, presumably going to buy us a few minutes.

"What's the plan?" I ask. "Do you have a trailer or something? Because I bet at this hour, there's no traffic at all, and I know there's a dirt road that—"

"Adriana," Kristiana says.

I lift my eyebrows. "Yeah?"

"Hush."

Aleksandr opens the stall door and walks inside, completely unafraid that the enormous, insane stallion in the stall will attack him. I jump between them, throwing up both arms, my back to Quicksilver. "I should warn you. This horse isn't at all broke, and he gets pretty aggressive."

Aleks ignores me, ducking around my arms, and Quicksilver doesn't bite or kick or even pin his ears. He *leans in*, and Aleksandr *hugs* his neck.

"What's going on?" I ask. "Do you know this horse somehow?"

"Do me a favor," Aleks says. "Press your hand against his neck."

"But—"

"Just do it," Mirdza says softly. "Please."

I open my mouth to argue, but they're all looking at me so expectantly, like they know some secret that will just blow my mind. If they would listen long enough, I could tell them that he knows Russian letters and wrote a swearword in the dirt. Or I could tell them that he listens to what I say and responds. But since they know everything already, *whatever*.

"Fine." I press my hand against Quicksilver's neck. "Now what?"

"Repeat after me," Aleksandr says.

"Okay."

"I wish," he says.

"I wish," I say.

"That you were a human instead of a horse."

I drop my hand. "Of all the stupid—"

"Just say it." Aleks grabs my wrist and shoves it back up until my hand's touching Quicksilver's back. "But touch him while you do."

I roll my eyes, but I just repeat the weird phrase. "I wish you were a human instead of a horse." I'm dropping my hand as I say, "But who would want that? Everyone knows that a horse is way better—"

Only, something weird happens, like a clap of thunder, but not loud. It's like a clap of thunder might feel. . .and suddenly, Quicksilver *is* a man. A man with burnished golden hair, eyes the color of the sky, and a body that. . . I choke.

He's entirely and completely naked, and his body is *glorious*.

"Finally," the naked man who used to be a horse named Quicksilver says.

As if he's been waiting for the chance to talk for more than a week. As if this is totally expected. As if everyone already knew that he was actually a man.

Which is *insane*.

But, a little voice in my head asks, is it really any crazier than fireballs, lightning bolts, and a horse who understands everything I say? A horse who gets *jealous* when another man touches me?

If I'm being honest, this may be the thing that makes the *most sense* of anything that's happened to me in a while.

Grigoriy steps forward and thrusts a bag toward the naked man. The man takes it gratefully and begins dressing. I probably should avert my eyes. Kristiana would avert her eyes. My sister Mirdza would *definitely* avert her eyes, but that's not who I am.

I'm the kind of girl who stares at anything amazing as long as I can.

"Adriana," Mirdza says. "Come over here while he's dressing."

But the man knows who I am. He's been around me long enough that he's not even surprised to see that I haven't moved. "Adriana."

The way he says my voice—it's deep. It's slow.

It's *sensual*.

My heart races, my breath catches in my throat, and I nearly drown in the cliché feelings that burn in my chest, but I could stand here all day, waiting for him to say my name one more time.

I thought he was gorgeous the first time I looked at his human face. His facial features look nearly aristocratic, and his eyes and hair would be striking no matter how he sounded, but his voice. Oh, his voice is *glorious*.

It makes things inside of me vibrate.

No, that's not the right word. It makes them *quiver*.

"What's going on?" Gavriil is back, and he's looking around frantically. "Where'd you put the horse?"

"What horse?" the man asks.

Gavriil frowns, and then he tilts his head, eyeing the now-dressed man strangely. "Wait, who are you?"

The man's pulling boots on now, brushing the shavings off the bottom of his socks before sticking each foot into them in turn. This is not someone who has always been a horse and is suddenly a man. He knows how to do all the human things.

Was he somehow stuck as a horse?

I'm lucky he liked me well enough to save me both those times. Really lucky. But it's making more sense that he understood me. And that he bit me when I said he was nuts.

Oh my word. I scratched his *butt*.

Heat climbs up my cheeks until I'm sure they're both flaming red. *Get it under control, Adriana. You're embarrassing yourself* more *by freaking out.*

Now that his boots are both on, the man straightens. "This might sound strange to you." His smug look is disturbingly similar in his human form to his horse one. "But my name's actually Alexei Romanov."

Gavriil laughs. "Sure. And I'm Joseph Stalin."

"I'm not kidding," Alexei says. "I've spent the past hundred years frozen by some kind of curse, but now that I'm awake, I plan to retake my throne."

Oh, no. My beautiful horse-man is insane.

Or worse, I'm afraid that I might be, because I want to believe him.

$$ \text{❦} \quad 9 \quad \text{❦} $$

Gavriil insists on coming with us when Aleksandr and Grigoriy start ushering us all toward their Land Rover Discovery.

"There's no room for him," Alexei says.

"The car has seven seats," Gavriil says.

Grigoriy's frowning.

Aleksandr's scowling.

I climb into the car and scoot past the middle row to sit in the back. Gavriil moves to follow me, but Alexei stops in front of the door and slams his hand up against the doorframe. "I'll sit by her."

"Why can't anyone tell me where the horse went?" Gav looks pretty agitated, understandably. If I'd experienced a few less fireballs, lightning bolts, and sentient horses in the past week, I'd probably be right where he is now.

"I freed him," I say. "Like I told you I wanted to. After being in that stall all night, the second I opened the door, he bolted."

Gavriil looks like he's going to argue, but he doesn't. "And now you're all just rushing away?"

"Did you hear the part where there's not one, but two different groups of men after her?" Alexei asks.

"I did," Gavriil says, "but when did *you* hear that? I swear there were only four of them earlier."

I can't blame him for being confused. He had mounted his figurative white horse, was ready to throw down his visor and charge to my rescue, and then this insane man shows up—my insane horse disappears—and suddenly he's being shunted to the side.

"Gavriil," I say, half-shouting from the back seat of the car. "You have no idea how grateful I am for all your help. I'll call you later, okay?"

He opens his mouth to talk, but then he closes it again.

"She'll call you." Alexei's smiling as he hops in the car, pulling the door shut behind him. Grigoriy and Mirdza are already climbing in on the other side, and Kris and Aleks are sitting in the driver and passenger seats.

When the car starts to move, Alexei slings an arm up and around my shoulder.

"Whoa, there." I shove his arm off. "You stay on your side, and I'll stay on mine, *Czar* Alexei."

"You think he's crazy." Mirdza's turned around and is looking at me with what looks a lot like pity.

"What?" I can't help my gusty laugh. "Crazy? The horse who just turned into a man right in front of me and claims he's the emperor's son who was killed by the Bolsheviks?"

"The whole thing's pretty hard to process," Mirdza says.

She's saying she already knew. "It is." I swallow. "Although, it's easier when your brain has been tender- ized by watching a supervillain incinerate a dozen men, lock you in a cell for a week with no food, and then send his lackey to electrocute you."

Mirdza closes her eyes, and I hate how pained she looks.

"It's fine," I say. "I wasn't trying to make you cry or whatever. It's just that *those* things I saw with my own eyes, but I struggle to believe that he's Alexei Romanov, the murdered child of Russia's last Czar."

"Why is it harder to believe that than it is to believe that I'm a horse-shifting mage?" Alexei's right eyebrow's raised, but he's keeping his hands and arms to himself, so that's progress.

"Who took you after the show?" Aleksandr asks from the front seat. "I'm less worried about whether you believe us, and more concerned about the reason—"

"Wait." I say. "Do you all believe that he's a displaced czar who should be ruling Russia?"

Kristiana turns to face straight ahead.

Mirdza won't meet my eye.

"You really all believe him?"

Only Alexei will look at me. He's still staring calmly, his gorgeous, intelligent blue eyes steady, and his enormous, well-muscled yet lean frame casually upright next to me. He isn't desperate or angry or frantic. He looks. . .assured.

"They believe me because it's true."

"Even if it is true, why does none of this surprise them?" Especially Mirdza and Kris.

"They were stuck in their horse form, frozen in time, just like me, and they're from the same time period."

"You're saying both of them—" I point at Grigoriy and Aleks. "Are also super old dudes who should have died. . ." I trail off then, because something very strange occurs to me. "Wait." I stare at the back of Grigoriy's head. "*Charlemagne?*"

Mirdza turns back to face me, her nose scrunched. "I wondered when you'd put that together. I wasn't afraid to ride him, because he knew to be careful with my leg."

"The horse you rode—you knew all along that he was really a person pretending to be a horse?"

"He wasn't pretending. They really do become horses." She shrugs. "There's also always a risk of injury, but yes. Grigoriy's Charlemagne."

Grigoriy looks supremely annoyed. "I am *not* Charlemagne. I'm the same person whether I'm a horse or a man. You made up that name, and you persist in calling me—"

Mirdza pats his arm. "Yes, yes, I know. But still."

I whip my head sideways. "Are you going to insist that you're not Quicksilver?"

Alexei shrugs. "You didn't even make up the name, but if you want to use it while I'm in my horse form." His lips twist and his eyes sparkle. "If it helps you accept it, I'm not opposed."

For some reason, his mischievous, flirty words remind me—again— that last night, I was scratching him. All over. "I can't believe that last night, I scratched. . ."

Mirdza's suppressing her laughter, but Grigoriy, Aleks, and Kris don't even bother.

"I kept trying to tell you I wasn't a horse, but you persisted in believing it," Alexei says. "It's not my fault. And, it felt really nice. I was a horse at the time."

I'm going to kill him.

Aleksandr pulls onto the M-11 and I realize we're all going the wrong way. "Hey, shouldn't we be headed for the E-95?"

Aleks eyes me in the rearview mirror. "You don't have identification, right?"

I blink.

"It's going to take me a little time to pull all of that together, and it'll be way easier to do it from home."

Home? I forgot he was Russian. Or, to be more precise, I knew he was Russian, but I didn't really think about the fact that he had a home in Russia. "Where are we going, exactly?" It feels like everyone already knows everything, other than me.

"Novgorod," Aleksandr says.

"Still?" Alexei smiles. "That's good to hear. Plus, it's not too far away."

My insane horse is speaking flawless Latvian and knows all about Russian geography.

"Hey, if you're really a hundred-year-old czar, why do you speak Latvian, huh?"

"Actually, we're not sure about that either," Mirdza says. "But it seems like they can all speak whatever languages the woman who helps shift them can speak."

"The woman who. . .*what?*" This makes less than no sense.

"From the moment I saw you, racing away from that idiot Boris in the woods, I could understand everything you said," Alexei says. "But I do speak six other languages fluently as well." He shrugs. "Future czars are always highly educated from birth."

"I want to go back to the 'woman who helps shift them' thing," I say. "How did I shift him? By saying I wished he was a man?" But talking about shifting him, especially in the context of breaking a curse, reminds me of my promise to do three good things. That weighs on me. I've never owed God any favors, and I've repaid exactly none of them.

"About that," Mirdza says. "We have a lot to talk

about, and some of it might be weird, and some of it might be. . .painful."

"We can talk when we get settled," Kris says. "There's no huge rush."

"Well, sort of, there is," I say. "You should probably know who's after us."

"We do need to hear all about that," Aleks says. "We know Boris and Mikhail are awake, but we're not sure who's the force behind them. Mirdza said they were answering to someone else."

Leonid. Even thinking his name makes me shiver. "He's crazy, and he has some kind of magical powers."

"We figured that much," Aleksandr says. "But once we get to my home, they won't be able to just waltz in after us. I have wards."

Wards? As in magical barriers that exist only in strange fantasy books about witches and stuff? Things just keep getting stranger.

"I still don't get why you did it," Mirdza says. "Why on earth did you go yourself that day?" Her kind eyes well with tears. "Why?"

Grigoriy takes her hand, their fingers intertwining.

"I owe a Lithuanian a lot of money." Two weeks ago, I wouldn't have been able to say that. I'd have been too ashamed—so ashamed I'd almost rather die than confess the truth. Pride is a terribly funny thing.

"Why?" Mirdza asks.

I shake my head. "Why what?"

"Why did you owe him money? Did you have a surgery?"

My sweet, sweet sister. She's always been happy to live on a shoestring in a tiny cupboard under the stairs. She'd never impose on others, not even for a surgery she needs. She can't even comprehend someone like me, someone who *yearns* for things she can't have. Someone who keeps thinking that with a little luck, she can get ahead. She can change her future.

Someone who keeps gambling and losing.

"Because I'm a selfish, greedy person," I say.

"Stop," Mirdza says. "None of us believe the crap you think about yourself."

Her quiet words strike like a slap.

"Maybe we should talk about it once we're home," Kristiana says.

Hearing her call Aleksandr's place *home* is strange. The entire time I've known her, she's loved only Liepašeta. I can't even imagine I'd be able to love someplace else, if that was my home. She does look comfortable with Aleks, though. She's at ease in a way I've never seen.

It's silent for a moment. A long moment. The road flies past, the noise from outside the car muted by the high-end engineering.

"What year is it, exactly?" Alexei asks softly.

For some reason, that question makes me laugh uproariously.

"Is that a funny question?" He narrows his eyes at me. "Why?"

I can't seem to stop laughing.

Maybe it's because he's a horse man. Maybe it's because he says he's a long-lost czar. Maybe it's because the other people in this car believe him. Or it could be that I was held by a lunatic who shoots fire from his fingers. Who would ever have thought my life would be anything like this?

But I think it's the *normal* way he asked, as if it's perfectly reasonable that he might not be sure what year it is.

"You have a lot to learn," Grigoriy says, telling him

the year. "Smartphones. Airplanes. The internet. But best of all, automobiles have really come a long way."

"I can't believe it's been more than a hundred years," he says. "That means that the humans are unlikely to believe I'm really Alexei Romanov."

"That's the first rational thing you've said," I say. "The *humans* aren't going to buy it, true or not."

"Even Adriana's having trouble," Alexei says, "and she's seen me shift."

"Bingo," I say. "I'm having trouble, and I saw it with my own eyeballs. But with the special effects out there now, with CGI, no one's going to believe any of this."

"I'm not sure," Mirdza says. "With live streams, with fantasy shows, and with the way people have started to embrace weird things, I think they might be more likely to believe it today than ever before."

I snort.

"Still, the adjustment's going to be steep," Grigoriy says.

"At least you have some good friends to help you," I say.

"And you," Alexei says.

That makes me laugh again. "Oh, trust me. I'm the least adjusted adult in this car. Or didn't you notice that I'm the one on the run from not one, not even two, but three different people?"

"All bad men," Alexei says. "But you won't need to worry about that anymore."

"Why?" I frown. "Why won't I need to worry about them?"

Alexei looks at me like I'd look at, well, a horse that I'm particularly proud of. "Because now you have me."

"I—I *have* you?"

He nods.

Staring at him like this, so close up, it's hard not to

be distracted by his strong jaw, covered with golden stubble, his dramatic blue eyes, his shining hair, and his sheer presence. He was a massively tall horse, but his human form's almost more powerful. It makes sense, if what he's saying is true. Someone who was trained to be the new czar of Russia would have been taught to stare people down from an early age.

But none of that excuses him acting like he *owns* me. "I don't *have* you," I say. "In fact, I have exactly one person—myself. That's how it'll always be, so maybe quit saying things that are crazier than the czar thing, or I'll have to do something that neither of us will enjoy."

"Your constant threats are endearing," he says.

"She's going to kill him," Mirdza whispers.

Alexei's head snaps her direction. "Why would she do that?"

"I thought I had it hard," Grigoriy says with a knowing smile.

"I'm basically a cream puff compared to Adriana," Mirdza says. "If he isn't careful, she'll gut him like a carp."

"What are you guys talking about?" I glare at Mirdza. As my sister, she should be making this easier, not harder.

Mirdza glances at Kristiana in the front, but I can't see her face, so I have no idea what their meaningful glance is about. Then Mirdza turns around slowly. "So, we think that Aleksandr woke up because Kristiana was in trouble—her dad's gambling was pretty bad and some terrible men were after her. The farm was in jeopardy, too."

"Woke up?"

"We were all cursed by Boris and Mikhail," Grigoriy says.

"And Grigoriy woke when I was attacked," Mirdza says. "The first thing he remembers is feeling a *pull* toward me."

"I saved her when she was tossed off that train," Grigoriy says.

"That makes sense. That's why I was able to find you in the woods," Alexei says.

"Umm, think again," I say. "I had been caught a week or more before, electrocuted, and then tied up for days. Where were you then?"

"That's when I woke up," Alexei says. "I felt a terrible pain, and then I rose from the darkness that had consumed me."

"You're saying that my being caught by Leonid is what woke you?"

"Leonid?" Aleksandr asks.

"Leonid Ivanovich?" Alexei asks. "Is that who caught you?" He's sitting up straighter.

I look around the car slowly. Mirdza and Kris look confused, like I feel. The men all look alert and cautious. I nod slowly. "That's what he said his name was."

"He takes great care with his appearance," Aleksandr says.

"Is that your way of saying he's gorgeous?" I ask.

Alexei scowls.

It's actually kind of funny to say he's beautiful in this group. I'm not sure I've ever seen this many handsome men in one place. Even good-looking men usually have one feature that's too prominent. A jaw that's weak. A nose that's too large. Acne. A wide mouth. Close-set eyes. But as I look around this car, I'm struck by their bizarrely impressive and perfect looks.

Aleksandr looks like the mysterious lord who broods while living on a massive and dark manor. He's all stark lines and sharp cuts. His black hair still brushes his perfectly defined brow, even from the rearview mirror.

Grigoriy's an interesting contrast. He's not as carefully refined, but there's a magnetism to his brutal strength. His brown hair's rich, his eyes bright, and he looks like the horse that's about to explode out of the chute, ready to hammer the other competitors. Shiny, intense, and explosive. His face is almost square—his eyes bold and his frame blocky—and yet somehow still perfectly proportioned.

Then there's Alexei, the painfully beautiful one. As pretty as Leonid, but without the sadism that radiated from that lunatic like strobe lights from a disco ball. With his light and bright coloring, he looks like a young Travis Fimmel—the man who played the king in *Vikings*.

Whereas Leonid looks like an evil Paul Walker.

They're like two sides of the same coin. I wonder whether they'd be upset if I said that. I decide to keep quiet about my comparisons for now. "Who is he?"

Aleksandr turns down a long drive and clicks a button. The massive iron gate in front of us opens, and we're headed for one of the largest homes I've ever seen. I'm not sure why the technology surprised me. Maybe because he said wards.

Even so, I'm a little relieved to see some familiar, twenty-first century inventions.

"We're home," Aleks says. "I think we should go inside, get you a shower, eat, and then we can really talk."

It's been more than two weeks since I've worn clothes that fit. I'm not sure I've ever appreciated Kristiana being my size more than I do today.

And I got a lot of amazing hand-me-downs over the years.

After a much-needed shower and hair detangling, I'm clean and I don't smell, and it's time to find something to wear. Kristiana to the rescue.

"That looks better on you than it does on me." Kris is frowning.

I roll my eyes.

"That's because now that you're happy, you're eating more." Mirdza coughs, hiding behind her hand.

Kris kicks her boot, but not very hard. "Rude."

"I recognize it, because. . ." Mirdza trails off.

Watching them has always hurt a little. They act like they're twins. I'm always the third wheel with my own sister.

"You don't look like you've gained weight," I say. "Either of you. You could probably do to gain a bit more, honestly."

"Look who's talking." Mirdza arches an eyebrow.

She's not wrong. I've always been quite small, and being a jockey has only made it worse. But I've lost so much weight since being caught that Kristiana's jeans would slide right off without a cinched belt holding them up. I've never had the curves I envy on other women. I look more like a stick figure.

But the way I look now is ridiculous.

"Maybe you'll get fat and happy soon." Kristiana's smirk is irritating.

"Why would I?"

"No reason," she says.

"If you're talking about Alexei, stop. You know I don't date, and if I were going to break my rule it would *not* be with a horse-man who claims he's the rightful czar of Russia."

Mirdza shrugs. "I wasn't looking either."

"I'm not just 'not looking,'" I say. "I will not date, and you know why I never have, so stop."

Mirdza sighs. "Alright."

"Speak for yourself," Kris says.

"You've met Mārtiņš," I say. "You know better than most my reasoning."

"Not every man's like him," Kris says. "It took me a while to trust, too, but—"

"Enough of them are." I walk toward the door. "And I'm not you. Okay?"

Kris nods. "Alright."

"Let's have the talk already," I say.

"There should be food prepared," Kris says. "At least we should go eat some of it."

"Amen," Mirdza says.

I follow Kristiana down a massive hallway, and then through heavy wooden doors into a cavernous room with tall, stained glass windows. There's a long table along the wall that's absolutely weighed down with platters of food. Blini with three or four different rich toppings, syrniki with sour cream and berries, plump, savory pelmeni piled up on top of one another, stroganoff and borscht in tureens, bright, chilled okroshka with loaves and loaves of fresh rye next to it, and platters of shashlik—lamb, beef, and chicken. Piles of fresh fruit and veggies are mounded up on either end.

My mouth's watering like crazy.

When Kris starts piling up her plate, I jump in to do the same. Even after several days of consistent food at that stable, I'm still ravenous. Skipping breakfast this morning didn't help. By the time we've all loaded up our plates, the men have also joined us. Grigoriy pulls out the chair next to Mirdza before heading over to grab food for himself.

Aleksandr sits next to Kris and tosses his head at one of the men standing by the doors. Apparently His Royal Highness doesn't fill his own plate.

Alexei takes the seat next to me and does the same thing as Aleks, catching the eye of one of the footmen standing by the door. I suppose if he really was in line to be the next czar, he's accustomed to having people serve him.

What a strange thought.

"Alright, what do you want to know first?" I ask.

What happened, essentially. That's what everyone wants to know. I'm light on the details about Nojus, not sharing his name for instance, but I do go over how Leonid met me at the park, how he burned twelve men, how he destroyed the cameras first, and how I wound up locked up in a hut in Russia.

Even though I try to skip over the more miserable parts, like the electrocution and the lack of proper food or accommodations, Kristiana looks like she might throw up.

"But who's the man who was after you in Latvia?" Alexei asks. "You never did say."

"If you can just get me papers that will get me through to Latvia, I can take care of that myself." I have no idea how, but the last thing I'm about to do is sit here and tell them all my horrible problems so we can rehash my idiocy. It's especially not going to happen with all these shiny, rich people staring at me.

"Adriana," Kris says. "You took my place. You endured misery that was meant for me. The least we can do is repay whatever debt made you feel compelled to do such a rash thing."

"I chose to take your place," I say. "As far as I'm concerned, now that you've saved me, we're even."

Kris frowns. "But—"

"Before we get into all that," Mirdza says, "just tell us who was after you. We need to know who we might encounter on our way back to Latvia."

That's reasonable. "Well, you know the Leonid man, apparently, and he's got connections with the police. So there's that guy and Boris, his little henchman."

"And?" Aleksandr wipes his mouth, which is too bad. I liked him with a magenta mustache. Borscht can be messy. "Just give us a name, Adriana."

"The owner of that stable I was staying at was Sasha Sorokin," I say.

"I'm not too worried about them. They won't have papers or any evidence of theft," Aleks says.

"And you won't have the horse," Alexei says. "They won't have a case to present even if they do find you."

"Still," Aleks says. "Maybe we reach out and let them know she isn't friendless. Sending them some money might resolve any ongoing risk they could pose. She's part of the racing world, and it's a small one."

"I suppose." Alexei doesn't look pleased with the idea of paying for his own release.

"That's enough distraction." Mirdza pins me with a glare. "That Lithuanian followed you into Latvia. Tell us who he is so we can deal with it."

"He didn't follow me into Latvia. That's where I met him in the first place. He won't follow me here, either."

"How can you be sure?" My sister may be kind and soft-spoken, but sometimes she's a little like a bulldog. She won't ever let go, even when she should. "You don't understand how men like that work. He's probably making plans right now. He could already be here, actually."

"Trust me. I've known Nojus for a long time. Leonid incinerated his twelve best men. That'll leave him reeling for a while. Plus, he'd have no way of knowing where I even went."

"Nojus?" Aleksandr's smile is infuriating.

I can't believe Mirdza needled me into saying his first name. Still, there are probably lots of Lithuanians with that name in Latvia. I doubt he's put any property into his name. Maybe they won't be able to find him. "Please, just leave it alone."

"Someone who would send a dozen men to threaten a woman doesn't let things go," Alexei says. "When those men were killed, he probably doubled down. You won't be safe while he's alive."

"Alright," Mirdza says. "I know that you guys always want to kill everyone."

"Not everyone," Grigoriy says. "Just evil men."

"Can we talk about the stranger, more threatening thing now?" I ask.

"What?" Grigoriy asks.

"Who's Leonid, and why's he magical?"

Grigoriy and Aleks both turn toward Alexei.

"Is Alexei your boss or something? Why do you both keep looking at him? Didn't he just wake up? He didn't even know what year it was."

"Old habits," Grigoriy says.

Alexei sets his fork down and finishes chewing his shashlik. "When I knew him, he wasn't magical at all. But to explain Leonid, I'll need to explain a little Russian history." He looks around. "Everyone okay with that?"

I shrug.

"Russia was actually founded by the Vikings," he says. "The Varangians were Norse raiders, and the one who matters the most for our story was a chieftain named Riurik. He had two younger brothers who helped him, all great kings of the Rus, but they both died without having children."

"That's sad," I say.

Alexei shrugs. "We now believe that Riurik had at least two children, though most history books record only one. When he died, his wife ruled in his stead, along with a trusted advisor and a warrior named Oleg. They kept the kingdom in check for his young son, Ivor. His line ruled Russia until the beginning of the 1600s when Vasili the Fourth died."

"After that, the rule of Russia was thrown into chaos," Aleksandr says. "They called it the Time of Troubles, and it only ended in 1613, when Michael Romanov was elected the new Czar."

"He was my 'great times eight' grandfather," Alexei says. "Mom always called him that."

"I always heard you were weak and sickly," I say.

"And I thought you were like ten or something when the revolution happened."

"History's written by the victors." Alexei's lip is curled in disgust. "Sickly, pah." He inhales slowly, his nostrils flaring.

It occurs to me that for him, his family's deaths would still be raw and new if he's been asleep this whole time. I'm still struggling to believe all of it, but I can at least understand that it's sad and pretty horrifying if it's true.

"Leonid showed up when I was in college," Alexei says. "His father claimed they were descended from the lost Riurik line, from a daughter who was not widely known, and as far as I know, they didn't have any powers at all. At least, they never mentioned them, and we never brought it up either."

"The Riurikid line, on the other hand, was always popping up," Aleksandr says. "Or at least, claims of it."

"But in this instance," Alexei says, "when we investigated their claim, it looked like it might have been true. They had a decent amount of evidence that they were descended from Riurik." He sighs. "My father made the decision that he would destroy all the evidence of it, and that he would bury the claim."

Aleksandr doesn't look surprised.

Neither does Grigoriy.

"Sometimes, for the peace of the people, it's better if the truth isn't broadcast," he says. "But I thought at the time that my dad made a grave error. I think that error cost him his life."

Aleks blinks.

Grigoriy's head whips sideways.

"I think it got my entire family killed." Alexei looks so tragically beautiful in that moment that my heart twists.

"But how?"

"After my father ignored them, buried their story, and set them aside, Leonid and his father went on to found the Bolshevik party, and that, combined with the famine. . ." Alexei shakes his head. "It was the perfect storm, but still, our family could have easily prevented the famine."

"How?" I ask. "Did you hoard food or something?"

"Remember how you saw fireballs and lightning bolts?" Kristiana says.

I nod.

"There were five families, noble families, that were given powers back when the Romanovs ended the Time of Troubles," Kristiana says. "Mikhail and Boris, whom you've met, are the children of two of them. They could shift into a horse form, which was extremely advantageous in a time when transportation was difficult and unreliable. They also were each bestowed power over a certain element."

"Fire and lightning," Mirdza says.

"And the other three families were the ones repre-sented here. Aleksandr's," Kristiana says, "was given the power over earth."

"Grigoriy's family controls wind," Mirdza says.

"And my family controls water." Alexei picks up his hand and holds it steady.

Nothing happens.

He frowns.

Then he swears under his breath.

"Actually, we didn't have time to explain that part of the curse yet," Aleks says, "but you won't be able to use your powers unless. . ."

"Unless what?" Alexei frowns.

"The woman whose need awakened you has to be touching you," Kristiana says.

You have got to be kidding me. "No way."

Mirdza drops her hand on Grigoriy's arm. "It doesn't have to be a big deal. See?"

Grigoriy looks up, and suddenly, wind starts to swirl around our heads. The chandelier above us shakes and clinks. Tiny bits of paper fly around the room in bizarre patterns.

And then it just stops.

"So you're saying that Alexei has some kind of magical powers he's only able to use with *my* help?" If I sound like I don't believe them, well.

I don't.

"That doesn't make sense," I say. "I don't know him. I don't need to know him. And I don't plan to stick around." I sound kind of mean, but if I have to spend a lot more time with the two lovesick couples, I might kill someone. "No offense."

"I did save your life," Alexei says. "And I'm sure we'll find a solution to this eventually."

"I knew, when you said we'd talk about things later, that there was going to be some catch." I stand up. My plate's mostly clean, and I have learned that Leonid's some kind of. . .wait. What have I learned about him exactly? "But who's Leonid and why does he have powers now? I'm not sure we really got there."

"Before we received our powers," Alexei says, "Baba Yaga gave the same powers to another ruler, one whose descendants governed in Russia for almost a thousand years."

"You mean Riurik, right?" I ask.

Alexei nods.

"So if Leonid can throw fire and shoot electricity, then he must be descended from Riurik, like he said."

"Perhaps," Alexei says. "But a hundred years ago, he

didn't have any powers. He also didn't have any money, and he didn't really have any supporters."

"At the time, there was a lot of unrest amongst the other nobles and among the people in Russia," Aleks says.

"We were discussing how best to mitigate the effects of the famine," Alexei says, "when we were attacked."

"Back up," I say. "I want to hear about that, but I also want to know how you know there's a second Riurik-born heir. It feels like you skipped that part."

"I agree," Kris says. "Why do you think there are two children when history records just the one?"

"We had access, after becoming the new rulers, to the old Riurikin records. Although they weren't super clear, they seemed to indicate a second line," Alexei says. "My father also had the journals left by my ancestor, Michael. Dad made me read them before he started to train me to use my magic. One of the things Michael recorded was that Baba Yaga gave the full strength of the magic to Riurik because she felt that he needed it. She realized later that she should have given them to several people instead of all to one. So when she granted the same thing to end the Time of Troubles, after she believed his line had ended, she split it into five relatively even powers."

"So if Leonid's descended from Riurik, he might be able to use all five powers?" Aleksandr asks.

Alexei shrugs. "At least two, for sure."

"If he can use all the powers, why didn't he just kill us back then?" Aleks asks.

"Could it be that, now that Baba Yaga gave out all five powers, Leonid can't use his?" I ask.

Alexei's smile makes me want to preen. Which is embarrassing. "Boris and Mikhail serve him, and he can use their powers." He nods. "I wonder whether it's connected. Maybe when Boris and Mikhail came to us, asking us to work with them, it was for Leonid."

"He'll make it harder for you to regain the throne," Grigoriy says.

"But there isn't a Russian throne," I say. "Not anymore."

Alexei frowns.

"The Russian people now have a government that's run mostly by the people," Aleks says. "More or less, anyway."

"For more than thirty years, they've had elections and let the people choose their leaders to some degree," Grigoriy says.

"That might make things easier," Alexei says. "My father was moving toward a government that listened to the people and allowed them to make many of the critical decisions."

This conversation is very, very strange.

"But I still don't understand what Leonid wanted with Kristiana," I say. I've been thinking about it, and I can't figure it out, even with all this new information. "After he realized I wasn't her, he became obsessed with figuring out how to get her. He'd given me one day to come up with a way to get her away from you, or he was going to kill me. My time was up when I ran."

"We aren't sure why he wants me," Kris says, "but their powers don't work when they're used against me. We think maybe it's because of that."

"So if he had kidnapped you," I say, "he couldn't have burned you or zapped you?" Maybe I shouldn't have taken her place after all.

"Which would have made her more vulnerable than you," Aleks says. "We think he wants her dead. Somehow, she poses a threat to him."

"Why would the magic not work on you? Are you, like, Baba Yaga's granddaughter or something?" I joke.

Alexei and Aleksandr frown.

"Could she be?" Grigoriy asks.

"I was kidding," I say.

Alexei shoves his plate away, finally done. "Leonid claims to be descended from Oleg," Alexei says. "But the records that discuss a second heir mention one that was hidden in the histories."

"Why did they hide one?" I ask.

"Because that child was born out of wedlock," Alexei says. "Riurik never recognized her, but she would have had the same magic, maybe. If Kristiana's somehow connected to this other line. . ." He shakes his head. "If Kristiana's like him, a true Riurikid, her very existence weakens his claim. Leonid won't give up in his pursuit. Maybe not ever."

"Looks like you guys need to do a little genealogy," I say.

Once, my mom came to school for a career day.

I was happy she was coming. Mom didn't come to many school things, and I thought it would be nice to have her there. She and Mārtinš had just gotten married, and she was wearing a ring.

The mother of one of my classmates, who had known us for a while, commented on it. She asked when my mom had remarried, and how she had the bravery to try again after losing our dad.

Mom launched into a story then, a story I'd never heard.

"It was all fate," Mom said with a twinkle in her eye. "My husband hadn't been close with his older brother. His brother had inherited all their father's fortune, and had left my first husband with nothing. His older brother was better looking, smarter, and had lots of women chasing him." Mom had blushed.

"I don't understand," the woman said.

"Well, my first husband's older brother had to come through town for business," she says. "We'd never met before, because of the bad blood. But when he came through, he decided to stop in and pay his respects. The second our eyes met. . ." Mom sighed. She shivered, like she was sharing some kind of fairy tale.

"Wait," the woman said. "Did you marry your *brother-in-law*?"

Mom nodded, oblivious to the fact that the woman was horrified. "He really is handsome, and so attentive. He never leaves me alone for a second. From the very moment we met, he's been by my side. And now all the work that broke my back, all the troubles that wore on me, they're all gone." Mom beamed. "It was destiny."

I watched Prince Charming beat her that night for burning the bread.

That's when I decided that destiny could rot for all I cared. I was never going to let some good-looking man convince me to surrender my independence. I would *never* hand over my life to fate or chance.

And that's why, the better looking the man is, the less I trust him.

"How long will it take to get my identification?" I ask.

"Two days, maybe?" Aleks shrugs. "I asked them to expedite it."

"And after that, I'll be free to go?"

"Go where?" Alexei asks. "Back to Latvia?"

I nod. "It's home."

"But you heard all that," Mirdza says. "Alexei won't be able to use his magic without you, and there's a villain who wants to kill Kristiana."

"I figure that'll keep him pretty busy here, which means I'll be safe to head back." I shrug. "You should come with me."

"You won't stay and help Alexei?" Kristiana asks.

I stand up. "Here's the thing. You two are both very

kind. You're generous. You're big-hearted. I love that about you, and I'm sure Aleksandr and Grigoriy do as well." I shrug. "I'm not any of those things, and while I appreciate that you're in a bit of a bind, it's not really my problem."

"Would it kill you to do the right thing for once?" Mirdza asks.

The right thing.

An image comes to mind of when I was on my knees, begging God for help. I promised I would do the right thing, three times. I vowed that when someone needed help, if he helped me, I would pay it back. This feels like a kick in the teeth, though.

I don't even believe in God. It's never been my thing.

Until I thought I was about to die, and then I got down on my knees and begged for help. And Boris did wash me off just as he had before. I found that clothespin just when I needed it. Then a magical horse showed up to save me.

I groan. "What exactly do you want me to do?"

If it's being at Alexei's beck and call, then this counts as all three nice things. Having to cater to some guy who has delusions of grandeur and needs me to hold his hand so he can perform magic?

It's definitely *all three*.

"Because there's no way I'm going to—"

"Calm down," Mirdza says. "He just needs a little help getting acclimated to life in this century."

"What does that mean?" I can't help my frown. I didn't promise to be happy about doing the right thing.

"Go with him to the dentist," Kristiana says.

"Take him shopping and help him pick some clothes."

"So we're not talking about, like, helping him fight

Leonid and try to reclaim the Russian throne, or whatever?"

All of them shake their heads.

"As if I'd let you risk yourself that way," Alexei says.

I lean over the edge of the table so my face is right in front of his. "Let's get one thing straight, though, mkay?"

He frowns, his gorgeous brows drawing together over those stunning eyes.

"You don't get to *let me* do a single thing. The only person who gets to decide what risks I take is *me*." I stare.

He blinks, confusion setting in.

"I'm not a dog, or a servant, or one of your little subjects. The next time you say you won't *let* me do something, I'm gonna take a crop to your happy-to-be-scratched backside."

Alexei swallows.

I turn around and march out the door, because that's what you do when you make a big declaration like that. Only, now I'm alone in the hall, and there's some kind of servant staring at me.

"Um. Where's my room?" I force a smile.

"You've been given the blue room." He points.

I nod, and then I march in the direction he points. It's pretty clear which room he's talking about, since everything in here is blue. Blue pillows on top of a blue duvet on the massive bed. Blue curtains, blue lampshades, light blue striped wallpaper. Blue carpet. "Talk about overkill," I mutter.

But now that I'm here, I have no idea what I'm supposed to do. I mean, I'm in Russia. I have no phone, no clothing, no car, no purse. . .nothing. And I've stormed off to hide in my room like a toddler who didn't get the flavor of cake she wanted.

I should have learned to think stuff through by this age, but here we are.

Someone taps on my door and I spin around expecting my sister. It's not my sister.

No one's further from my sister than Alexei Romanov.

"Hi." He leans against the doorframe. "You seem upset."

My scowl's practically a reflex.

"I usually get the most upset when I feel powerless."

I hate him.

"I came to make sure it's not that."

"Excuse me?"

"Aleksandr's family owed me some money when we were all cursed." He smirks. "They owed us quite a lot of money, in fact. They'd borrowed it to pay—it doesn't matter." He holds out his hand.

He's offering me some kind of bank register.

"What's that?" I arch an eyebrow.

"He has generously repaid my debt, with interest. I find that having resources at my disposal puts me in a much better mood. While I appreciate what your sister and her friend were trying to do—forcing you to help me—I'm not interested in coercing anyone. Your reminder there was timely."

"My reminder?"

"You said that I can't let you do anything." He shrugs. "You were right. If my mother had been here, she would have beaten me for implying something like that."

"Your mother?"

"Alexandra, born Alix of Hesse, a princess from her first breath."

"She was a feminist, it seems?"

Alexei smiles. "She insisted that her only son be named after her. She taught me to ride horses herself. She spent weeks furious with my father when he made one comment about a woman's place. I'd say that she was quite a women's rights activist, yes."

"I think I would have liked her."

His expression's suddenly weary, and I remember that for him, it's like she just passed away.

"I'm truly sorry for your family's death."

He shrugs. "Grigoriy tells me the records are fraught with incorrect information, describing me as weak, hemophilic, and quite young."

"Are you really wanting to try and reclaim the throne?" It seems like a mad idea. "Aleksandr lives quite a nice life here, and I'm sure that if you really can control water, you could do the same."

"I'm not power mad," he says. "If my people are safe and healthy and the government's caring for them well, I have no reason to try and change anything."

I think about the government in Russia. It's not always caring for its people, and I'm not at all convinced it's keeping them safe, but it makes me feel better that he's not gunning for some kind of insane restoration right away.

He's still holding out his hand, so I finally reach out and take what he's offering. It's a bank ledger, and it also has a debit card on top of it. "This says Alexei Romanov," I say.

"We can transfer the name, according to Aleksandr."

"Do you even have identification?"

"Aleks, as the first to wake, has already taken steps to prepare for my awakening."

"He's a pretty good friend." I flip open the book

and glance at it. In big black letters, it has an amount printed—balance. *Sixty-three million rubles.*

I drop the book.

"You agreed to help me acclimate," Alexei says, as if he didn't just hand me an absolute fortune.

"I can't take that," I say. "Aleksandr gave that to you, and you'll need money. Surely the world hasn't changed that much—it's as important today as it was back then."

Alexei frowns. "That's the smallest of the accounts Aleksandr gave me to repay the loan."

"The smallest—accounts? Plural?" I can barely believe what I'm hearing.

"With that, hopefully you can feel more able to leave, if you're insistent on doing that."

It's enough to repay Nojus with a little left over. It's enough to change my entire life. "I can't take it," I say.

"I did save you twice," Alexei says, "but you saved me, too. I was stuck in my horse form, and I need your help to even access my own powers."

His powers.

This entire thing is so surreal that I'm still struggling a little bit. "I did promise to help you acclimate."

He smiles, and that makes his eyes light up. His beautiful, strong lips curve, and he shifts a bit, the muscles in his shoulders, his arms, and in his lean frame shifting—no, rippling. "You did."

I reach over and grab the bank book—one token protest would have been enough, and I tried giving it twice. Now it's mine. "What did you have in mind?"

"Grigoriy tells me that they have entire shops that have lots of readymade clothing you can simply choose from. No tailors needed."

"Yes, that's true."

"I'd like to see one of those shops. Also, he says we need something called a phone."

"Grigoriy knows a lot."

"Don't worry," he says. "I'll catch on even faster than he did." He leans closer.

The hair on my arms stands up as a bizarre kind of thrill shoots through my entire body.

"Grigoriy's a bit of an idiot compared to me."

"Hey." Grigoriy's passing by the doorway, and he looks ready to punch Alexei.

"And he's very, very fun to tease." Alexei's grin widens, and I notice for the first time that he has dimples. Not one. *Two* absolutely lovely dimples, one on either side of his mouth.

I am in a lot of trouble. I may have sworn off fate, but it looks like it's not going to be so easy to shake. "Alright, so we're going shopping, then?"

"I think you should practice using his magic first," Mirdza says. "No way of knowing what might happen when we go out."

"That's true," Alexei says. "Do you mind letting me practice it a bit?"

"If you're rusty at all, it could get messy," Grigoriy says. "Go outside. Aleks and Kris just finished renovating."

"This room could stand to be redone next," Alexei says.

That makes me laugh. "It's like the color blue got the flu and threw up everywhere."

Alexei's eyes are dancing. "And I love blue—hello, water powers."

"Kris already did that room." Mirdza's frowning.

"Oh." I snort. "Well, it's *lovely*."

Alexei laughs, too. "Maybe we could call it the ocean room."

"Can your powers speed redecorating?" I'm kidding, but I'm also genuinely curious how they work.

"Follow me outside, and I'll show you."

"Can you even get outside of this place?" I whisper. "Because I got lost trying to go from the dining room back to here."

"Compared to the winter palace, this place is a hovel," he says.

"A *hovel?* Really?" I roll my eyes. "Lesson one in your assimilation. Don't use the word hovel."

"Really?"

"I'm pretty sure only authors trying to show off use words like that these days," I say.

"That's a shame. A broad vocabulary is a hallmark of the educated mind."

"Educated?" I snort. "Or snobby?"

"Educated," Alexei insists, hanging a right at the end of the hall, and by golly—he found a door that dumps us outside.

"Wow, you weren't kidding. You already know your way around."

"To be fair, Aleks merely renovated his now-very-old family home, so I've known my way around this place for quite some time."

"I haven't renovated my family home yet," I say. "But when I do, boy. You'll be impressed."

"I'm sure that I will." Alexei looks entirely serious.

"No." I follow him outside, and then I stop. "It's a joke, man. I don't have a family home. Normal people don't have family homes."

"Everyone has a family home," he says. "It's where your family lived when you were growing up. It's where they live now."

I shake my head. "Sorry to disappoint, but we lived in a sequence of apartments, none of which were owned by us. And now my mom's sponging off Kristiana's dad, living in one of the apartments they built for the grooms who help with the horse stalls, but doing no work to earn it."

"Oh." Alexei frowns.

"It's fine, though. I'm teasing you. It was meant to be ironic."

"Ah, yes. Irony—the use of language that usually means the opposite of what you intend," he says.

This acclimation's going to take a little longer than I originally thought. "You're a real hoot."

"Ah, more irony. Yes, I saw it right away this time."

"Actually, that's sarcasm, because I'm mocking you as well."

"Of course," he says. "Well done."

"Now, about the magic thing," I say.

He nods. "If you would be so kind." He holds out his hand.

I swallow. "I want to be clear on something." My eyes slide up from his outstretched hand to his face. "I don't date."

"You don't. . ." He frowns.

"I have never had a boyfriend. I don't want one. I'm not romantically interested in anyone, and I never will be. That's not a challenge, either." Some men get a little crazy when I say that, like Nojus. "Got it?"

Alexei's brow furrows. "You've never been involved with a man. That's what you're saying."

I nod.

"I'm just asking you to touch me, and holding my hand seemed the most expedient way."

Heat rises in my cheeks. "Right. I know. It's just that earlier, you said you'd never allow me to—"

"I apologized for that," he says.

"You did." I nod. "I just wanted to make sure. Aleksandr and Kristiana, and Mirdza and Grigoriy. . .I didn't want there to be any confusion."

"You're going to help me get settled, and then as soon as possible, you're going back to Latvia. Without me."

"Exactly. You understand."

"I do."

"Perfect."

He's still holding out his hand, and he wiggles his fingers.

I draw in a deep breath—reminding myself that this is no big deal. So I've never held a man's hand before. So what? It's not like this is significant. I'm just helping the rightful Czar of Russia to use his magical powers.

My life is so weird.

What's a little skin-to-skin?

I tighten my hand into a fist, and then I stretch it out and wiggle my fingers. "Okay." I lift my hand, but for some reason it's moving really, really slowly. My eyes shoot upward, meeting his.

He's staring at me with curiosity. Like, the kind I might have while I evaluate a new horse. One I really, really want to ride.

No. That's crazy. He's just waiting for me, because I'm the one being weird. I shove my hand forward, knocking my fingers against his. His hand's strong, warm, and very big. He shifts as my fingers crash over his, and slides his hand against mine, entwining our fingers.

Then he squeezes my hand tightly, gently tugging me closer. "There."

Nothing explains the shiver that starts in my stomach and rolls outward, like something really, really exciting just happened to me.

Like I took first in a stakes race. Or I won my bet at twenty to one odds. Or I dipped my toe in a hot tub on a freezing cold night. While someone who looked like Alexei watched me with intense eyes. Something is definitely wrong with me.

He tugs me again, and I take a step, moving even closer to him, my shoulder far below his, my head barely reaching his shoulder, my eyes staring right at his very solid, very well-sculpted chest muscles.

Alexandr's t-shirt looks way too good on Alexei.

"So, what exactly are we doing?" I lick my lips and look up.

His lip's twisted a bit, and his head's cocked sideways. "You've never been involved with a man. Right?"

I shake my head.

"Good."

Before I can protest his bizarrely possessive statement, he lifts his free hand, and tiny particles of water start to come together from all over the place. Within seconds, there's a floating orb of water in front of us.

"Ah." He closes his eyes. "That feels good." He shifts his head from side to side and stretches his shoulders. "Like flexing a muscle I haven't used in far too long."

"What can you do with it?"

"What can't I do with it?" He smiles. A million more tiny water molecules coalesce all around us. And then they begin to dance.

"What purpose does that serve?" I arch one eyebrow.

He laughs. "None at all." He brings it all together by bringing his hands together, my hand dragged along with them.

There's an enormous ball of water floating in front of us now, the size of a refrigerator.

"My father used to make me do that to improve my reach and my control."

"But what do you really use water for?" I can't think of much you could do with it, to be honest. "Mirdza says Grigoriy can fly with air."

Alexei's lips purse together. "He can."

"And?"

"Grigoriy spent countless hours practicing with a sword, you know." He shakes his head. "He was always considered to be the deadliest among us, even more terrifying than those who controlled flame, as he could put out the worst fires. But water can also douse flame. And." Alexei waves his hand and the huge ball of water disperses, spreading evenly to splash onto the bright green lawn. "Everything in the world that lives needs water." He points. "The flowers. The leaves. The trees. They're all sustained by the power of water. Our most important function was to move water from places that had it to places that need it. I'm able to take salt water and distill it and then move it to where it needs to go."

That's helpful, but still kind of boring, not that I'd tell him that. "Cool."

"It made the Romanovs the wealthiest family in Russia for generations," he says. "But there are military applications as well."

"Really?" I ask. "Drown a lot of people?"

He shakes his head. "It's slow and inefficient. I have much faster ways to kill than that." He points. "Which of those flowers do you not like?"

"I like them all." I frown. "Why wouldn't I like any of them?" I glance around. On the far end are huge, blooming azalea bushes. Next to them there are bright pink peonies with striking yellow centers. The brilliant lilac crocuses are stunning, too. But the most beautiful bloom is the hot pink Russian lotus. "That's my favorite, I think." I point.

"Alright, well, this isn't what I had in mind, but I can also control water that's being used by a plant right now. See?" His fingers gently shift, and the buds on the lotus unfurl, blooming in front of my eyes.

"That's—that's amazing."

"I can preserve them so they last three times longer than they normally would. I can also. . ." He throws his hand back and the azalea bush on the end withers.

"Oh, no."

"And restore things." He circles his hand slowly, and the azalea revives. "None of that is very exciting, but it can be vital."

Interesting.

"But if someone were to attack me, I wouldn't need a sword or an army," he says quietly.

"What do you mean?"

He frowns. "Those are weeds." He points at the thistle. "You'd agree that destroying them wouldn't work a hardship."

I shrug.

He stretches his hand and I watch intently, but nothing happens. Maybe the thistle swells a little? And then he closes his hand into a tight fist.

And it explodes into a million tiny pieces.

"What just happened?"

"Anything that's made up of water, I can destroy," he says softly.

It hits me then. All animals, and all humans. . .they're all made up of water. "You're saying. . ." I'm hyperventilating.

"There's a reason my father insisted on a very strict training regime for me."

"That's." I pull my hand free. "No one should have that power."

He shrugs. "And yet."

I can't look at him the same, not anymore. "How many people could you. . ."

"I'm not sure right now. I haven't practiced in a very long time," he says. "But before, thousands."

He could destroy an entire army all by himself. "What's your reach?"

"Miles, at least."

Forget electric shocks or burning a dozen men. Those feel like party tricks. His power over water is horrifying.

"That's just the beginning," he says. "Water rights have always been hotly contested, but it's simple for me to reroute streams, rivers, and even shift the tides to a certain extent."

"No one should have that much power," I say again, dumbly.

He shrugs. "If it helps, we've always used it to help people, like mitigating the effects of droughts and staving off widespread famine."

"Have you ever exploded a person?" I ask.

Alexei's eyes study mine, his beautiful face distracting, but I hold his gaze. I need to know the answer.

"Hey, guys. It's time to go." Kristiana's waving at us, and Aleksandr's car's idling in the drive.

"Go where?"

"Shopping," she says. "Duh."

❦ 12 ❦

The first thing we buy is a phone, which is really helpful, because I need an internet tool to calculate exactly how much of the money I just got will be needed to repay Nojus. Figuring a percentage for the exchange rate and transfer fees. . .I should have almost eighty thousand euros left over, even after repaying him.

"What are you doing over there?" Mirdza asks. "Texting Gavriil?"

Alexei's head whips sideways, staring as hard as he can at my lap while the sights outside the car whiz by.

"No." I slide my phone into my pocket. "I'm not. Not that it's any of your business."

I don't even know his number, though an internet search would tell me the number of the racetrack, and I should let him know that I'm safe. And thank him profusely.

"What's *texting?*" Alexei frowns.

"It's sending a message to someone," Mirdza says.

"How do you do it?" He holds out his phone. "I want to text someone."

"Who?" Mirdza asks. "You don't even know anyone."

"I want to text Adriana," he says.

Kris laughs.

I roll my eyes. "You don't need to text me. I'm right here."

Alexei frowns. "But I want to know how to do it."

"Are you sure he wasn't fourteen when he was cursed?" I whisper. "He's awfully interested in texting." I pull out my phone, realizing I haven't entered Kris's or Mirdza's phone numbers yet.

"What messages has he sent you?" Alexei's craning his neck, trying to see my screen.

I drop it, facedown, in my lap. "Alexei Romanov."

"It's Alexei Nikolaevich." Aleksandr's practically shaking, he's trying so hard to suppress his laughter.

I ignore Kristiana's fiancé and focus on the idiot who knows no modern etiquette. "You can't look at other people's phones. It's considered very rude."

"It's even worse than peeping at them naked," Grigoriy says.

"What?" Mirdza slaps his shoulder. "What are you saying?"

"I mean, that's how it seemed to me. You spent plenty of time casting sideways glances at me when I shifted, but you never let me take a peek at your phone."

Mirdza's spluttering, but she doesn't really look angry. It takes me a moment to realize that he's kidding. I didn't think Grigoriy had much of a sense of humor, but I guess I was wrong.

Aleks is pulling into a parking lot, finally, and he looks just as amused as he did before. "We're here."

"This should be interesting," Mirdza mutters. "It's nice not to be the one under a microscope this time."

"A microscope?" Alexei glances at me. "Are you a scientist?"

Now I do laugh.

"Ah, you mean that you're being examined." Alexei nods.

After we all pour out of the car and head for the first store, I hear Grigoriy whispering to Alexei. I sneak up a little closer, a little too keen to hear what they're saying.

"Whatever you do, if you suggest she buy something, make sure it's an extra small. That's denoted with the letters x and s on the tag on the garment."

"She is small," Alexei says. "So that makes sense. But surely Mirdza isn't the same size as Adriana."

"You don't get it," Grigoriy hisses. "No matter what woman you're with, hand her an extra small."

"Aleksandr told me the clothes come in different sizes that vary, and that each person can find one that's just right."

Grigoriy sighs. "That's patently untrue. Plenty of things, no matter the size, just won't work for some people's body shapes. But if you hand her a size large or extra large, you're going to offend her."

"Why?" Alexei frowns. "Large women are also beautiful."

"I know," Grigoriy says. "But for some reason, they don't think that anymore."

Alexei blinks.

I hate to interrupt this stellar sharing of misinformation by Grigoriy, but we've reached the shop. "Sounds like you have this shopping thing figured out," I say. "So you can go over there with Grigoriy." I point. "And I'll stay on this side in the women's clothing section, where plenty of lovely women wear size *large*." I glare.

"You don't want to stay and give him some input on what he buys?" Aleksandr asks. "Kristiana always wants to do that."

"Because you're romantically involved," I say. "Whereas Alexei and I are not. So, even if he decides to wear green basketball shorts, a polo shirt with a tiger on it, and yellow galoshes. . ." I fling my hands in the air. "It's all the same to me." I point. "Over there. You guys can help him."

The look on Alexei's face as he walks away from me *almost* makes me feel bad. I did offer to help them. But it's not like God cares which loafers he buys, for heaven's sake.

I only buy a handful of things—enough to tide me over for a few days—and I'm waiting when they finally finish. When they approach the register, I'm shocked.

Aleksandr wears a lot of black, grey, and dark blue. Grigoriy wears warm, earthy tones. They both look like the things they wear could work in the office, but would be a decent fit for meeting clients in the field. Business casual, their style could be called, or maybe rugged outdoorsman occasionally.

But the clothing Alexei's carrying. . . "What on earth are you thinking?"

Alexei freezes. "What?"

"Is he wanting to look like the rightful ruler of the country or a pimp?" The brightest, loudest prints I've ever seen are piled up on top of ripped, acid-washed jeans that a teenage drug dealer would have trouble pulling off. "No." I shake my head. "No way. Put all that down."

"Where did they even find that in the store?" Kris asks.

"I have no idea."

"I thought you said he could wear galoshes," Aleks

says. "Alexei is a much more vibrant person than either of us. He likes bright colors and—"

I intentionally bump into Aleksandr's shoulder as I walk past. "So it's your fault."

"He picked those," Grigoriy says.

"I do like bright colors," Alexei says.

I sigh, and point at the dressing room. "I think you're probably a men's large." I stare at his shoulders. "Right?" I turn toward Kris and Mirdza.

They both shrug.

"You two are even worse than the men."

They're talking amongst themselves while I stalk to the back of the men's section. "They're closing out summer styles," I say. "And the front of the store is full of things you can't even wear right now."

"Okay," Alexei says.

"But we can get a good deal on some of the clearance stuff."

Alexei blinks. "That's where I found those things."

I scrunch my nose. "The thing about buying clearance is that you need to be discerning."

"Why?"

"The reason it's on clearance, if there are a lot of them especially, is usually that it wasn't something people really wanted. There's always a reason for that."

His brow furrows.

"Sometimes you get lucky, and something that looks great on you is still on sale. Occasionally, someone returns something in just your size, and it winds up here."

"Returns?"

"You know what?" I ask. "We're getting a little advanced."

His eyes widen. "Are you saying that other humans came here, put these clothes on, wore them, and then they brought them back for other, unsuspecting people, to purchase?" The look of horror on his face would be hard for anyone not to laugh at.

"Yes," I say. "That's exactly what I'm saying."

He shudders.

His Royal Highness can explode flowers, or people, into small bits, but the idea of wearing clothing that has touched another human being first reduces him to quivering. It makes me grin. "Alright, well, if you feel up to it." I pluck a blue polo shirt and a couple of bold colored plain t-shirts off the rack. "Let's try these on to get a baseline idea of what works on you and what doesn't."

He follows me back to the dressing room. I duck inside to hang his clothes on the rack, but before I can leave, he shuts the door.

"Whoa," I say.

"What?" He frowns.

"You can't close the door until after I've left."

"But you've already seen me naked," he says.

When he shifted from a horse into a human this morning, I didn't shy away from taking a peek. But now, the image rises up in my mind like I'm being punished. His long, lean legs. His well-muscled torso and defined chest muscles.

And everything else.

My face must be bright red. "No way. I have to get out."

"You need to see the clothing, though. What's the problem with—"

I press my hand against his chest, and then I realize my mistake. Even through his t-shirt, he's warm and hard and. . .

My mouth goes dry.

I drop my hand and back up, but there's exactly

three feet of space in this ridiculous little cube, and he's taking up two and a half feet of it. He's staring at me, watching my reaction carefully. "Why are you blushing?"

"I'm not. It's just hot in here." I pinch two fingers together and fan the front of my shirt. "That's all. Now, let me out."

"Surely you can't object to me trying just the shirts." He whips his shirt up and over his head, and suddenly it's all right there in front of me. Shoulders, rounded, rippling, gleaming.

Oh, no.

My eyes do not listen to my brain's commands, traveling slowly down his frame toward his lovely, well-rounded chest muscles, where they just stop listening to any part of me and gawk openly, my mouth even dangling open a bit.

"Is there something wrong?" He tilts his head. I'm aware of the movement, but I ignore it.

Because now my eyes have dropped to his abs, and holy abdominal bliss. I've heard of people having a six pack. I have. I didn't really think they existed, outside of airbrushed print ads.

I must have spent too much time with thugs and jockeys, because there isn't an ounce of beer belly, and there isn't an inch of squidge on his midsection. He's also far more densely muscled than any jockey in the history of *ever*, and I find myself counting the rows of abs, and I just stop at four rows, because looking below that line would just be. . . Well. I stop.

It's not a six pack.

He has an *eight* pack.

And I'm dying to touch it. My hand starts to move, and then I realize what I'm doing. I'm standing in a dressing room, staring at Alexei's naked torso. I reach behind myself, snatch a shirt off the hanger, and shove it at him. "Here."

Then I push past him and shove him aside with my hip. Before I can whip the door open, someone bangs on it.

"Excuse me," the woman says in Russian. "But we don't allow men and women to—"

"I'm so sorry," I say. "I was just leaving."

"Why?" Alexei asks.

I open the door, but he puts his hand on the edge of it, preventing me from walking through the gap.

"Why won't you allow my friend to help me choose which shirt looks best?" He looks genuinely curious. "I'm not very fashionable. I need help."

"It's not decent for her to be in here." But then the woman notices Alexei, her eyes widening as she stares at his face. And widening further as they drop to his shoulders, chest, and abs. She gulps. "Although." She shrugs. "I mean, I suppose I understand that you might want a woman's. . .help."

"No," I say. "It's nothing like that." I step out. "Just put that shirt on and come back out, alright?"

While I walk to the front of the dressing room area, the woman follows, trotting after me with a conspiratorial smile. "Wow," she says. "I mean, his face was. . ." She whistles. "But that body. He was kind of hiding that under there before."

"Uh huh." I say.

"Sorry for kicking you out," she says. "My manager's really strict on that rule."

"It's fine." I don't tell her that she was helping me. "You were right."

She shakes her head. "If you want to go back in there, I won't tell."

I can't help my laugh.

"Seriously." She chuckles. "I'd claw someone's face off to get back in there if he was asking for me."

Alright, this woman is funny. "Do you have anything you'd recommend for him?"

"Clothes, you mean?" She grins. "Girl, please. Who cares what he wears? I'd be thinking about things to do once you've taken them off."

Oh my word. "Clothes," I say. "Definitely clothes."

"Sure," she says. "But it sure seems like a shame."

I nod slowly. "Like covering up the Mona Lisa with a car cover."

She giggles. "Exactly like that."

But someone like Alexei's utterly wasted on me, because no matter how delicious he is, I'll never take a bite. "Listen," I say. "He needs some help picking out clothing, and I'm definitely not the right one to provide it. How about you do me a favor and pick out a wardrobe you'd want him to wear?"

And just like that, I walk away from the temptation and wait in the car with Mirdza.

Kris jogs out to join us a few moments after I escape, and the girls almost immediately pounce.

"Do you seriously never plan to date anyone?" Kris asks.

"Yep. I really don't."

"But why?" she looks genuinely confused.

"One word, that I've already said." I pause. "Mārtiņš."

"But Mirdza had the same stepfather, and she dated Danils too, and now she has Grigoriy."

"Listen, I know you're both really happy with your horse men, and I even see the draw." Oh, boy do I see the attraction. "Hot, powerful, rich Russians, who have magical powers and can shift into amazing stallions?" I shake my head. "Believe me. I get it."

"But?" Kris is not letting this go.

"Do you remember when you had that birthday party—your twelfth birthday?"

Kris nods.

"Your mom served shrimp."

"You'd never had it, and you ate, like, the whole platter." Kris is smiling.

"Correction," I say. "Neither Mirdza nor I had ever had it, and together we ate the entire platter."

"Mom was so embarrassed," Mirdza says.

"And that night, we both got really sick, puking our guts up."

"I forgot about that," Mirdza says. "That flu was awful. It lasted for days."

"You missed a lot of school," Kristiana says. "I remember too."

"Well, after that, Mirdza still loved shrimp," I say. "Whereas I've never eaten it since. Even the idea of it repulses me."

Kris leans her head against the back of her seat and expels all her air. "But what does shrimp have to do—"

"People can go through the exact same thing and react differently," I say. "Just like that incident with the shrimp, a lifetime with Mārtinš has soured me on ever dating. Now let it go. Please."

Because no matter how much they push, and no matter how happy they are eating shrimp, they'll never make me into a seafood girl.

No one has a perfect mom. I mean, Kristiana kind of did, but I'm sure even she had her flaws. I know that. I've always known that people aren't perfect, and I never expected perfection from my mother.

I did expect honesty.

That was pretty stupid in retrospect. I mean, how many times do parents lie to their children? It starts nearly as soon as kids can talk.

"We're almost there," they say, with hours yet to go in the road trip.

Or how about, "Children in China are starving, so you better eat these lima beans." That one may be true, but it has very little bearing on the nasty food on my plate. It's a manipulation at the very least.

One of my favorites has always been, "If you make that weird face too long, your mouth will get stuck that way." In twenty-six years of life, I've yet to see anyone walking around with a face that was stuck with their tongue out or anything similar.

But at least in those cases, your parent's trying to

help you.

My mom started lying to me about a lot of things after Mārtinš came into our lives. She'd say she had fallen. She'd tell me that she *wanted* to spend their money on beer instead of food. She'd tell me she was happy when she clearly was not. Most of those lies were still calculated to spare me from pain and fear. But the very first time she told me that she was going to leave him. . .and then she didn't? The first time she told me she really thought he'd change?

Those lies were really hard for me to take.

She didn't tell them to help me.

She didn't say those things for my benefit at all. She did them to cover for her own cowardice and fear. They made me very, very leery of anyone who lies. Ever. The reason that I have virtually no friends is that as soon as someone lies to me, my trust is just gone, and it can't be repaired.

There are really only two people in the world that I trust—Kris and Mirdza.

As we drive back, I get a little emotional thinking about how they dropped everything when I called and flew to Russia. I mean, sure, the guys might have come because they heard about the grey horse that saved me.

But Kris and Mirdza came for me.

Dinner's ready when we arrive—I could get used to this—and it's even nicer than our meal earlier. Being rich is just as good as I always thought it would be. "Do you always eat like this?" I ask. "Because I would gain so much weight that I'd have to find a new job."

Actually, forget a job. If I could afford to eat like this, I wouldn't *need* a job, right?

"Worth it," Mirdza says, spearing a pierogi.

I've loaded my plate up with way too much food. I have no hope of actually finishing it. Alexei appears to be making pretty good progress. Maybe he'll want to eat whatever I don't.

But that thought makes me wonder.

"Hey, do you guys ever colic?"

Aleks freezes. "Do you mean, do we get a stomach ache and die from it when the weather changes or we eat something odd?" His lip twitches.

"Well, it sounds dumb when you say it like that."

Kristiana laughs. "Horses only colic because they can't vomit. These guys can change forms and puke out anything at all. It did take Aleks a while before he was ready to embrace junk food, though."

"Preservatives taste funny," Aleksandr says.

"But they also help delicious things last way longer," Mirdza says. "I'm not sure we'd have survived without preservatives when we were growing up."

Kristiana slides a large platter toward me, and I can't help grimacing.

It's shrimp.

Stupid jerk.

"No thanks," I say. "I never eat shrimp."

"I heard you haven't even *tried* it in years," Kristiana says. "Maybe you'll like it now." She pushes it closer, still.

"Shrimp was only available in certain seasons before," Alexei says. "I assume that's changed." He pulls the platter even closer, totally oblivious to the message as he snags a few more. "I really love it."

"I just bet you do," I say.

"Come on, Adriana. Just try one." Mirdza's getting in on it now, too.

"Maybe I should." I bump the plate with my elbow, and it slides off the table, shrimp scattering all over the place. "Oh, darn. Looks like no shrimp for me this time."

Alexei's brow furrows and he slides the ones he just took onto the edge of my plate. "It's fine. You can have mine."

"I hate shrimp," I say. "I knocked the platter over on purpose, because Mirdza and Kristiana think I don't know my own mind."

But now the wait staff's rushing over to clean it up, and I feel pretty bad. I push my chair out and drop to my knees, desperate to clean up the mess myself.

"It's okay," the woman says in Russian. "This is my job."

"Cleaning up food isn't your job," I say. "I caused this mess."

But she insists, and finally, I'm forced back to my feet. "Well, I'm full," I say. "And it's been a long day. I think I'm going back to my blue room where everything I see is blue to. . . be blue ah ba dee ah bah dye."

Mirdza snorts.

Grigoriy and Aleks look very confused.

"It's an old song," I clarify. "I really shouldn't sing any more of the lyrics. I mean, if this was in a book, for instance, the author might get sued for using actual song lyrics. But also, you don't know the song anyway. So, never mind."

"Can you stay for just a moment?" Kristiana asks. "I promise I won't tease you anymore. I actually had something to ask you. All of you."

That's weird. "Wait." I look at Mirdza. "Is this about the wedding? Because I know it's next month, and I do *not* want to be a bridesmaid. If you think that throwing me the bouquet—"

"It is about the wedding, but it's not what you think." Kris points.

I sit. "What, then?"

"I've been thinking about this all day, and any way

we turn, we can't get our answers without catching Leonid."

"He's pretty smart," I say. "I doubt he'll be easy to catch. Plus, he's dangerous. Did I mention he incinerated a dozen men? Because he did. Like it was nothing."

"I'll be around," Grigoriy says. "I can prevent stuff like that from happening."

So can Alexei, with a big ball of water or something, but only if I help. "You want me to stick around to power Alexei up."

Kristiana sighs. "I have a pretty big favor to ask. We've been planning a small wedding, but if we change that, if we open it to more guests, I think we could use the wedding as a lure to flush Leonid out. Maybe then we can catch him and finally get some answers."

"Absolutely not," Aleksandr says.

"I think it could work," Alexei says.

"It's far too dangerous," Aleks says. "No way."

"But I'll be there," Alexei says.

"Which is meaningless without Adriana," Aleks says. "You won't be able to do a thing."

"But it could draw them out," Grigoriy says. "And sitting around, waiting for them to attack, is even worse."

"I can keep Kris safe," Aleks says.

"What about when you have children?" Mirdza's voice is small, nervous. "Will you keep them all inside all the time? Never let them leave your warded estate?"

I stand up again. "I can't really speak to whether it's a good plan or not," I say. "But this isn't my war. I'm not trying to be a jerk, but I've already been a captive once. I don't want anything to do with it from here on out." It's above my paygrade, for sure.

I square my shoulders and walk out the door,

around the corner, and down the hall to my room. I refuse to change my mind or let guilt creep in. What I said is true. I've already been caught, starved, tortured, and threatened. I've had to run for my life twice, and this isn't something that really impacts me.

It doesn't even impact Mirdza. No one wants to capture or kill her.

At least, not now that they failed in forcing her to lure Kris out.

I care about Kris, of course I do, but as Aleks said, he can keep her safe. Whether they choose to risk her now isn't my problem. I didn't create Leonid. I didn't ask for them to be cursed. It has nothing to do with me, and unlike my mother, I do know how to walk away from things that threaten my life.

Only, as I'm changing into pajamas I borrowed from Kris—I didn't even think of buying any today—something keeps bugging me. That clothespin. The magical horse. The terrible plan I concocted that actually worked. It shouldn't have worked.

I should have died.

And I promised God to do three good things. So far, I haven't really done anything. I even failed at advising Alexei on polos. At the very least I should help friends who are specifically asking me. I don't really have a risky role. Sure, Leonid knows who I am, but he never wanted me.

Kris is offering herself up as bait—on her wedding day.

All I have to do is hold Alexei's hand. Is that really so bad?

That's when the truth stares me in the face. I'm afraid to do that, because I'm worried my resolve will crumble. The dressing room today. The time he showed me his powers.

Thinking of his hand on mine still makes me tremble, hours later.

I believe that those three lunatics in there, those magical stallion shifters, can protect us. I believe that they're the light to Leonid's darkness. I'm just not sure whether, if I keep seeing Alexei Romanov every single day, touching him, sitting next to him while he gives me anything he thinks I want. . .

I'm not sure I can continue to resist him.

And I know I need to.

After Mārtiņš, after my dad's death, and after watching what Danils did to Mirdza, I know better than anyone that most guys are not Aleksandrs. Most guys aren't Grigoriys, either.

Most guys are trash, and I don't want that. I can't risk it.

Maybe the scariest thing of all is that, even if Alexei *is* one of the good ones, there's no way I'm a good match for that. The kind of person I am, the kind of life I've led, I'd be lucky to score a Danils. There's no way a truly good guy—the only one I'd want—would like me for very long. Once he truly got to know me, he'd split, and I wouldn't even blame him.

So Alexei is *right out*.

But for once in my life, I need to do the selfless thing. I need to be brave in a way I never am. I need to support the only two people in this world I really trust. I pulled an Adriana in there, and it's time to eat a little crow and try to make it right.

I snatch the robe Kris left hanging off the back of my chair and wrap it around her ridiculous silk pajamas and knot the tie around my waist, and then I head back to the dining room.

Only, no one's there.

I pad in little circles all around the house, and I

don't see any of them anywhere. The stranger thing is that there aren't any support staff out and about either. Did they all go home? How did we go from the five of them all eating and chatting to no sound or people anywhere?

Then it hits me.

The house is so massive that I thought I didn't hear them, but maybe they went outside. I think back to how we found that side door, and then I retrace my steps, and sure enough, there it is. I'm pretty proud of myself when I burst through it.

And I'm even prouder when I hear them, just on the other side of the large azalea bushes Alexei wilted and then revived. I open my mouth to call Mirdza when I hear my name.

"—Adriana really won't do it?"

"She doesn't like to be forced," Mirdza says. "She's always been like that. She may change her mind, but only if *she* gets to make that decision."

That's true enough. It's a little embarrassing to hear my sister telling them how bullheaded I am, but I know she means well.

"Let's assume she doesn't come around," Kristiana says. "How would we do things?"

"It's one less person to defend," Alexei says.

Alexei's there? One less person to *defend?* He won't be able to use his powers if I don't agree to help. Why isn't he more keen than everyone else on convincing me?

He should be pushing, but I realize that he hasn't. Not once.

"I think the plan's the same either way," Grigoriy says. "We can plan out a few times that it'll look like Kristiana's off on her own, like if there's a problem with the catering, or if one of the flower girls gets lost or something. Then we can make sure that Alexei or I are close, ready to put out any fires that may spring up."

"Air's everywhere, but we need water close enough for you to use it," Mirdza says. "Right?"

"Water's everywhere too." Alexei lifts his hands, and water molecules from the air coalesce, just like they did earlier today. He brings his hands together and they form into a ball. "But even if it wasn't, guests will be holding drinks, and sweating, and the food will have water in it I can steal if necessary." He shrugs. "It'll be fine. Believe me."

It feels like someone just slapped me in the face.

I'm not standing anywhere near them, and I'm certainly not touching him, and Alexei just used his magic, and no one's the least bit surprised. I think about just storming off. I mean, that's what I ought to do. There's no point in confronting them.

Except that's who I am.

I'm the kind of person who's categorically unable to pretend that I don't know something.

"Why did you lie to me?" I ask softly.

Even in the moonlight, every single head turns toward my voice.

"Adriana?" Mirdza asks.

"What's the point of telling me that he needs my help?" I shake my head. "Is this all some kind of bizarre ongoing setup? Because that's sick."

"It's not like we weren't going to tell you," Kris says. "We just—"

I hold up my hand. "Never mind. It's not like I can believe anything you say." I turn around and race back to my room.

Only this time, I really do feel blue when I get there.

❦ 14 ❦

My identification arrives by courier early the next morning—it's on the entry table in the basket marked 'mail.' I should have an adult conversation with my sister and her bestie. I should hash things out, but. . .

I just don't want to.

They lied.

I pick a fight with my Yandex Taxi driver on the way to the airport. I practically come to blows with a passenger who tries to tell me that I'm boarding too early. And then, when the person next to me spills orange juice on my new shirt, I'm so angry that I shake.

Clearly I need to get myself under control.

By the time I get home, I'm doing much better. I'm not fuming for no reason. When my mom gushes and gushes that I'm back, and complains that I should never leave for so long without word again, I don't get annoyed or snappy.

I've let it go.

In my life, I've had plenty of experiences to prepare

me for Mirdza, Kristiana, and their two boyfriends lying. It's not like I really even know the guys. At the end of the day, people will always lie when they feel like it will help them get what they want. It's just what humans do.

No biggie.

After I get things settled, I decide not to put off finding Nojus. I have the money, so I have nothing to worry about. I mean, twelve of his men died. I'm a little nervous, but *I* didn't kill them, and he'll surely know that. I'm many things, but a killer isn't one of them, and I wouldn't even know where to begin with burning a person to cinders.

It takes me forever at the bank—it's complicated when you've done two transfers in two days—but finally I have the cash, and I brace myself to face what will surely be a very angry Lithuanian. I stand outside the door to his place for several minutes.

The paint's peeling. There's a line of ants tracking from the corner of the door to the spigot for the hose on the porch. There are loose boards on the porch, and there's a cracked windowpane I don't recall seeing before. Spending time at Aleksandr's mansion didn't improve my opinion of Nojus's house.

For someone who makes a bloody fortune, pun intended, exploiting others, why does he live in such a run-down pile? I suppose when you don't put any effort into maintaining what you have, it doesn't take long before it looks like this. I almost turn around and head back home. I haven't heard anything from the inside of the house, so maybe this is a bad time. It's not stupidly early, but still, he might be asleep. I could come back later today or tomorrow.

But this will just keep hanging over my head, and

that'll be horrible in its own way. I rap on the door, and then I force my hand to grab the loose handle and turn. "Nojus?"

Only, no one's here.

I'm not surprised it's unlocked. Anyone who might steal from an unlocked home would know not to steal from here. But also, in all the time I've known him, I've never seen the main room in the center of his house empty. There's always someone playing poker at the card table, drinking something at the bar, or arguing over what to watch on the television.

He had at least two dozen henchmen, and he found more regularly.

Sure, losing twelve of them was probably a significant blow, but it shouldn't have cleared everyone out. Where did they all go? I try again, calling out a little louder this time. "Nojus?"

Walking into his house is one thing—it's always had a bit of a revolving door. But I've never barged my way into his bedroom or really any of the rooms down the hall. That feels. . .different. "Nojus? It's Adriana. I have your money."

Still, nothing.

I'll have to come back later. I pivot on my heel and turn toward the door just as it opens. Nojus barges through, slamming the door so hard that it hits the wall and bounces back. He nearly plows into me.

"Oh," I say. "Sorry. I came with money." I hold up the bag.

"You did."

I nod.

That's when I notice that Nojus isn't alone. The two men with him walk in slower, eyeing me strangely. One's shorter than Nojus, which is hard to do, really, and the other's much, much taller. They both look about his age, and they're both glaring at me.

"I told you I'd get it, and I did. It's all here."

"A half million?" He arches one eyebrow.

I nod and hold the bag out.

He takes it, his nostrils flaring. "Where are my men?"

"I had nothing to do with that," I say. "That man kidnapped me, and I've been stuck in Russia. It took me forever to escape."

"What man? What happened?" Nojus looks desperate.

I really thought he'd already know. I mean, their ashes were right there. "His name's Leonid Ivanovich. They threatened me, and he—he burned them." Even saying it makes me feel sick, because I can't forget the image, the smell, and my horror.

Nojus's face twists. "No one could have—"

"He did it in a park," I say. "He's sadistic, but I didn't have anything to do with that."

"The man who took you killed them," he says. "In my book, that makes it your fault."

"Interesting," the man behind Nojus says, the man even shorter than he is. "So you think that, because the men you sent to kill her were killed by the person who *took* her, that's her fault, not yours?"

Nojus freezes.

My eyes slide sideways to the man who terrifies the Lithuanian arms dealer. He's not big. He doesn't look very scary. It's almost impossible to look scary when you're wearing a simple button-down shirt and jeans, but the short man also has no tattoos, no special markings, and he's not very muscular. "You think it's not your fault that your enforcers were all killed—you're blaming her for their deaths?"

As Nojus swallows, his Adam's apple bobs.

"I've been here for days, and all I've heard are excuses. None of them help me clean up the mess you've made." The short man looks sideways at the tall man next to him. "Is this the woman who owed him money for more than a year?"

The tall man nods tightly. "He kept offering to let her repay him in the bedroom."

Apparently they've talked about me.

Nojus isn't moving—when a tiger holds very, very still, that means there's something even scarier in the room. I'm just not sure why this man's it. Is he from the tax office or something?

"I've heard enough." The short man pulls out a gun and shoots Nojus in the back of the head.

Blood spatters all over me as his entire face explodes. I can't breathe, and I drop to my knees.

I've seen men killed before.

Heck, I saw twelve men burn to death at once, but they weren't eighteen inches from me, holding money in a bag that was still warm from my hand. The unassuming man who just shot him sticks his gun into a holster on his back and rucks his shirt up over it. He steps over Nojus and walks past me, too. "Clean that up."

Does he mean me? My brain rejects that order.

But my hands begin to twitch. If I don't start cleaning, will he shoot me next? He looked so casual, so unaffected by it.

Before I can decide what to do, the tall man sets to work, wrapping a blanket from the sofa around Nojus's head and dragging him out the front door in broad daylight.

The short man collapses onto one side of the small sofa between the kitchen and the family room. "Your name." He isn't asking. He isn't even turned to face me. He's just telling me that he wants my name, and expecting with absolute faith that I'll give it.

"A-a-adriana," I stammer.

"Adriana what?"

"Strelkova."

"You killed a dozen of our best men?"

Our? Who *is* this? "I didn't, sir. The man who captured me did, because they kept telling him to release me and threatening to attack him."

He shakes his head. "What a waste of resources." He turns to face me. "You know, most people think that there are predators and there are prey, but it's much more complicated than that. In fact, if you study patterns in nature, predators are often eaten by other, larger predators. There are even instances of predator-prey reversal where the larvae of beetles have been known to eat the very amphibians who pursed them. As the species evolved, they would even draw those amphibians to them specifically so they could consume them. A one-time defense mechanism changed a creature's essential makeup."

What's he talking about?

He shifts to the edge of the sofa and points at the chair opposite it. "Let's chat. I'd like to know a little more about you and your predilections."

I never heard Nojus use a single word as large as that one. Not ever.

Seeing as I don't have a choice, I sit, but I also say, "That bag has all the money I owe Nojus."

"It may contain what you owed him two weeks ago," he says. "But you didn't *pay* him two weeks ago."

Nojus was a known quantity. He would've taken the money—I'm sure of it. I would've been square, finally.

He knew the sum he demanded was already far, far above what I had borrowed. But as he just said, that was two weeks ago, and that was Nojus.

Who's now dead.

"My brother was always the one people watched," the man says. "He fought better than me. He intimidated and impressed other men much more effectively than I ever did. I was the nerdy, nose-in-a-book little brother. But my brother wasn't ever very smart, God rest his soul."

Is he *Nojus's brother*? Because. . .he just shot him like it was nothing.

He steeples his fingers in front of him, pressing his index fingers against his lower lip. "Most people would've seen him as predator and me as prey, but one little tool takes that edge away. One bullet, and I'm the predator." He inhales slowly and smiles. "Unlike my brother, I'm not rendered idiotic by a pretty face, even when it's spectacular."

That gives me even more heebie-jeebies than I got when Nojus tried to compliment me.

"He's left our family business in a shambles, and I'm stuck cleaning up his mess. I suppose you could say that, seeing you here, this little tiny girl, and realizing that he trained his men so badly that they didn't flee from an alpha predator and lost their lives. . ." He tsks. "It helped me finally see that only his death could turn our image around."

He murdered his own brother, and he doesn't even seem upset.

"The real question is, do you also have to die?" He drops a hand and taps his lip with just one finger. "I can't honestly think of another use for you. I'll be able to tell people that both the cause of the problems and the incompetent leader during the disaster were dealt with."

He reaches behind his back, and I realize he's going for the gun again.

"Wait," I say. "I'm a jockey. Your biggest rival is—um—" Why am I blanking on that Belarusian mobster's name. "It starts with an R. Radzivan!"

"What about him?" He's frowning, but he stops going for his gun.

"He's got that Akhal-Teke Thoroughbred cross he's been bragging about for months."

He frowns. "So?"

"I can pay my two weeks' interest by winning a race against him. Nojus has a new thoroughbred filly that's been clocking better than that cross—he had a guy who was sending him times from Radzivan's operation."

"Thanks, but I can pay for a jockey." He stands.

I stand, too. "Why pay for a mediocre one when I'm the best?" I hate the quiver in my voice. "If you kill me, you'll be out whatever you'd pay a trainer and a jockey leading up to the race." I pause. "And you'll lose."

He's thinking about it. He sighs. "When's the next race?"

"It's—" I'm not sure. I've been gone too long.

"Three weeks from tomorrow," the tall man says. "Jurgis said that yesterday. Nojus already paid the entry fee on a horse."

"And you're positive this filly of my brother's will win?" He lifts one eyebrow.

Who's ever positive a horse will win, really? No one, unless they've fixed the race. "Of course," I lie. My other alternative is a bullet through my brain—I'm not dumb enough to say I'm not sure.

"I'll give you a three-week reprieve. If you win, we'll be square. But if you lose, I'll kill you *and* someone you love." He turns toward the tall man. "Does she have a boyfriend?"

The tall man shakes his head.

"Mother?"

He nods.

"Great. You and your mother."

I would not have agreed to that. "Whoa—"

"You clearly need to put something more at risk. Your life's already forfeit." He tilts his head as he reaches for his gun again. "If you don't want a deal, I can just wrap things up now."

My heart races. I want to be the kind of person who wouldn't ever risk her mother's life. I want to be as brave as my sister. But at the end of the day, I'm not Mirdza.

Surely if I tell Mirdza what's going on, she and Grigoriy can keep Mom safe, right?

No.

However much I may fear this man and his trigger-happy finger, I can't do it. I can't kick the soccer ball down the field and hope I don't kill my own mother.

"Just shoot me," I say.

The man steps toward me. "The Americans have taught us the importance of motivation in this life. When you dangle a prize in front of people, or wave a gun behind them, they run faster. That's what capitalism is all about."

I'm not sure that's quite true. "I don't accept your offer. I'd rather die now." I close my eyes.

"But surely you must understand that there must be a deepening of stakes. Otherwise I do have to shoot you."

He should have done it already—that means he's

vested now. He wants to win. But he needs a way out. That means I have to offer him something nearly as awful as killing my mother.

There's a special seat next to the devil for this man.

"What's your counter offer, Adriana?"

"I can get you another eighty thousand—"

He scrunches his nose. "Don't offer me money. The damage you did when those men died, it wasn't monetary. I have a reputation to uphold. Weak predators become prey, remember?" He tilts his head, examining my face.

"I have a few horses," I say.

He shakes his head again, and then he circles me, his eyes studying me. "My brother was obsessed with her?" He looks at the tall man.

The tall man clears his throat. "He was. For years."

"But she always denied him." He grunts. "How about this? You put what my brother wanted on the menu for me, willingly, if you lose. Instead of killing your mother if you lose, I'll just kill you when I'm done."

If I had a knife or a gun, I'd murder him right now. "Sure." I grit my teeth, the words coming out clipped and flat. "It's a deal."

"We'll need witnesses in the event that you lose, of course." He smiles. "What fun would it be without people to watch?"

"I'll need daily access to the filly, to work her, to control her feed, and to make sure her vet care's up to par."

"Done." His smile broadens. "I think it's going to be a pleasure to have you working for me."

I hate him. Like, I really, really hate him. Maybe even worse than Leonid, who at least never demanded anything filthy. I force a smile. "Absolutely."

I'm shaking when I walk out the door. I'm halfway home when I realize that I didn't even ask his name.

That afternoon, when I show up at the track to run his filly, Nojus's trainer Lukas meets me in the parking lot. He walks me through the basics of how they've been preparing for the race, including feeding schedule and workouts.

"I heard you just got back into town," Lukas says. "I'm surprised you came today."

"Your new boss motivated me," I say.

"He's. . ."

"Right behind you," I whisper.

And indeed, the murderer's nearly reached us, still wearing the same button-down as earlier. I'm pretty sure the stain on the collar is blood. "Mister Rimkus runs a tight ship," Lukas says. "He does seem to inspire people's energetic efforts."

"I didn't realize you'd be here," I say.

"You're upset I came," Mr. Rimkus says. "That's okay. I don't expect employees to love me."

How magnanimous. "Let's see what she can do."

"Minnie," Lukas says. "Her name's Minnie Meteor."

"That's cute," I say. "I like it."

"But is she fast?" Mr. Rimkus arches an eyebrow.

"Let's see." I walk to where one of the grooms is holding her—she's dancing, which could be from excess nerves. Some of the best mounts I've had have been stressed-out disasters before the bell rang. After warming her up, I breeze her for a few laps, and then I stop her. She moves alright, a little jumpy perhaps, but her muscle condition's alright.

"She's usually a front runner the whole race," Lukas says. "Pulls a little when someone's ahead, but she's more of a hand ride. Doesn't like the crop. Her ears go back and she slows up if you use it."

That's good to know. "How's she look up against that Akhal-Teke?"

Lukas frowns. "No way to know since they haven't gone up against each other."

"Take her for a lap at her top speed," Mr. Rimkus says.

It's not really going to help him, not without any other horses to compare, but I tend to listen when lunatics talk. At least, when they're threatening to injure me, I do.

Lukas is right—she moves way better when I scrub my hand on her neck than when I pull or when I crop her. I'm optimistic when I put her away, until I look down and notice something very, very concerning. Mr. Rimkus has already left, but Lukas is talking to the groom.

"Hey," I say. "Come here."

Lukas frowns, but he listens. "What's that?" I point at her back left hoof, where there's a clear quarter crack.

"We're managing it."

I crouch down. "Managing it?" I shake my head. "This horse will be lame within a week if you don't take her off all the strenuous activity."

"You can't tell that from glancing at it. You haven't seen it for the past few weeks."

I glare. "You're telling me that it has been improving with her under saddle every day?"

Lukas sighs. "The race's three weeks away. It's a balancing act, for sure. Rest her enough that she can recover. Keep her in condition for the race."

She should be off for six months to regrow that hoof. But what's he going to say? He's probably in as deep as I am.

Both our futures now rest on the performance of one lame filly.

We're so screwed.

15

When I get home, I ask Kristiana's trainer if there are any horses who need a nice long hack. I really need to get away and clear my head. Luckily, Kris has so many horses that there's usually one who has been a bit of a basketcase and needs some time outside on the trails. Their biggest vice is usually racing too fast. It terrifies most riders, but it's not a problem for me.

I saddle up the leggy red roan and head out.

We've been out for almost an hour when he finally calms down fully. I ease up on his reins a bit, breathing a sigh of relief, and we walk for a good five minutes. Of course, once my guard is down, that's when it happens. He jumps at his own shadow, nearly tossing me over his head into the bushes.

I pat his neck. "Really? There's nothing out here, goofball."

He doesn't believe me, pawing at the ground and tossing his head relentlessly. I let him trot and puff for a little ways until we finally reach the stream. "You could use a drink, huh? Me, too." I can't help smiling at my corny joke.

I never do this, but I left his halter on underneath his bridle just in case we got to the stream and wanted a minute. I pull his bridle off and clip his lead line on, and then I sit down on the edge of the stream, letting him walk forward and rest.

In this spot, in the middle of nowhere, with no one around, I can finally think about the situation I've found myself in. Weeks ago, I thought that was the end. I was sure I'd played my last hand, and I'd gone bust. But then Leonid granted me a reprieve.

And I went from the frying pan right into the fire.

I was held captive, interrogated, and then finally freed, sort of. My savior turned out to be another pile of mess, but I escaped that disaster with a get out of jail free card. Only, when I played it today, I got smacked *again*. Sheesh.

I wiggled my way free yet again—because though I can't do anything else very well, I really am one of the best jockeys in Latvia. If you give me a horse that has an ounce of go in them, I can squeeze it right out in a race. One thing I have *never* done is put a horse in a situation where racing actively damages them.

People are usually in messes they've made. Horses don't get that kind of choice, but if I don't keep my mouth shut and watch Lukas medicate this poor filly so she can run in three weeks, Nojus's sadistic brother will rape and kill me.

Fabulous.

I mean, people matter more than animals, right? I'm not sure I believe that. That's probably why I devolve into a puddle of tears on the bank of the stream. I'm sobbing enough that even my sketch ride bumps the side of my arm with his nose.

"What?"

He does it again.

"I'll stop crying in a minute, okay? If your life was as bad as mine, you'd figure out how to cry, too." I laugh. "Or maybe you'd just get your leg stuck in a barbed wire fence, go sideways, deglove the skin off your leg, and cost me nine million dollars in vet fees. Is that why horses do that dumb stuff? Is that your solution to the fact that you can't cry and you don't have control over your own life?"

I inhale slowly, and then I finally manage to stop the bawling.

"What's wrong?" a voice asks from a few trees away.

I jump to my feet, and my idiot horse pulls so hard he escapes, trotting at least two dozen yards away, his nostrils puffing.

"Who's there?" I look around, but I don't see anyone.

"It's me," the man's voice says again.

"Two words aren't helpful," I say. "Not unless they're your name."

"Grab your horse first," he says.

I swear under my breath, but he's right. My red roan's moving farther and farther away. I walk toward him, hands back behind me, a calm and friendly expression plastered on my face in case he's an idiot who bolts.

He jolts and shifts a half dozen times, but eventually he lets me grab him. I'm not gentle as I walk him back. I have little patience for flighty idiots. "Alright. Just come out, then."

"Are you sure?" he asks. "The thing is—"

"Just come out," I say. "For the love of Pete, what's with the hiding?"

When Alexei steps out, I see why he was hiding. He's buck naked.

I clap my hand over my eyes. "Hide again, hide! Geez."

He's chuckling when he ducks back behind the tree.

"What on earth are you doing out here *naked?*"

"I was out for a run," he says, "in my horse form, but then I heard something. When I followed the sound, you were crying."

He's what made the red roan go crazy near the end. That makes a lot more sense. "So you're a stalker, now."

"Not at all. Just a concerned citizen. What do they call those—a Good Samaritan."

"Did the Good Samaritan lie to Jesus before or after he gave him a ride and new clothes? I feel like they didn't tell me that part in Sunday school."

I can practically hear Alexei roll his eyes when he says, "Very funny. But listen, what's so upsetting? Maybe I can help."

"Oh, I was just crying about how my twin sister and her best friend lied to me so that they could manipulate me into doing what they wanted, since they don't trust me to make good life choices myself."

As I say that, it occurs to me that both of them are engaged, wealthy, and happy, whilst I'm crying by a stream because some new thug is threatening to rape me before killing me.

They might not be *completely* wrong to want to guide me.

But still.

"I lied to you, too." Alexei's head pops out around the side of the tree, and I can't help ogling his upper body a little. "I'm sorry for that. Your twin sister, whom I assumed knew you better than anyone else, said you'd only stick around if you were needed."

"What a weird lie," I say. "It doesn't even make sense. Why tell me that I have to *touch* you for your powers to work?" It's like they knew that every time I touched him, my brain stopped working. I might have hated that lack of control more than anything else.

"It was the truth," he says. "At least, for them it was. When Aleks first shifted, he could only shift back and forth when Kristiana touched him and commanded it. And then he could only use his magic when she was touching him. But they discovered that it has something to do with Kristiana—probably something to do with why Leonid wants her—when she told me that I was forgiven, I didn't need to have you touching me anymore to shift or use my magic."

"But they knew the solution, and they lied about it."

"They wanted to help you," he says, but he's wincing a bit.

"Yeah, help me, by forcing me to try and date."

"It was wrong." He shrugs, even though he's bent sideways around a tree. Human movements are really ingrained. Watching his shoulder muscles and his pecs expand and contract is really distracting. "At least their intentions were in the right place."

"And what about yours?"

He's standing so far from the tree now that I can *almost* see indecent things. "I hadn't really seen a woman in a hundred years, and you're breathtakingly beautiful. Can you blame me for wanting to keep you around or for trusting that your sister knew best how to interact with you? She lied first. I just didn't correct it."

They all conspired behind my back. That really ticks me off.

"Are you going to be angry at her forever?"

"Maybe." I put the bridle back on the red roan and force myself to turn away. "But listen, I don't need help. Everything's fine," I lie.

"Really?" Judging by the rustling sounds, he's stepped out from behind the tree.

"Whoa, there, champ." I have my hand over my eyes when I turn back toward him. If my fingers aren't very tightly clamped together, well. Looking isn't touching.

"Sorry," he says. "It wasn't a big deal when I was growing up—we found ourselves having to shift a lot." He ducks back behind the tree.

A big deal, it most certainly *is*.

"The whole reason I shifted was to offer to help. If there's anything I can do, tell me what."

"I appreciate the offer, but the only one who might be able to help me is Kristiana, and I'm still way too mad at her—"

"Why could she help?" He's frowning now, and it's stupidly cute. "But I can't?"

"She's a vet," I say. "A horse doctor. And the horse I have to ride in a race in a few weeks has a quarter crack that's not being properly treated." I sigh. "I really, really need to win the race, but I'm worried I'll be harming the horse."

"Do you have to ride that specific horse?" He looks entirely serious.

"Pretty much," I say. "She's my best bet to win. See, this other guy has an Akhal-Teke, which don't usually win mile-and-a-half races, but this one's built different, I hear. It's a cross, actually, but the point is that I have to beat it."

"You could ride me." He's smiling, and he's only half standing behind the tree, and I can't help thinking of *other* things.

My entire face heats.

"In the race, I mean." But now his smile is very smug.

"You don't even have proper papers," I say, "and—"

"I'm assuming the people you're working with aren't the most ethical," he says. "Have them *find* me papers."

"But—"

"Make sure you're my owner, though. I'll be a stickler about that."

He wants to make sure that *I'm* his owner. I'm not sure what it is about that phrase that sends a thrill through me. "Alexei."

"I know you don't want to date me, and I know you can feel the chemistry between us." He steps forward a half step, stops, backs up, and sighs dramatically. "But Adriana, I'm not some teenage boy who's going to be following you around. Before the curse knocked us out, before my entire family was killed. . ." He pauses, clearly collecting himself.

That got serious really quick.

"My mother had very particular requirements for any woman I might consider marrying. I don't know what the future holds for me, but I have a feeling that the current Russian government's not going to maintain the status quo for long. The more I learn about their actions, the more displeased I am. I'm not sure what role I might play in the future, but marrying a Latvian jockey won't make my duty easier. Am I being clear?"

"Crystal." He regrets lying to me. He's been awake a little longer, seen other pretty girls, and now he's not interested in me. I should be relieved, but it hurts a little bit, too.

"Any concerns you had about the propriety of any actions between us, I hope you can let go of those. I will be an absolute gentleman in all our interactions going forward, I promise you."

"Okay."

I didn't want to date him. I didn't.

So why does it sting that he just rejected me? Why do I have an overwhelming urge to sit down on the bank of the stream and cry even harder than before?

He slams his fist against the side of the tree, clearly frustrated to be stuck behind it. "Saving me from that race barn, and imposing on your friend to help us, and being held in a hut for a week in Aleksandr's fiancée's place—none of those things were your fault. A paltry amount of money doesn't begin to make up for what you've been through. If there's something else I can do for you, please allow me to do it. Let me make up for some of the misery you've endured as a result of your affiliation with me—with all of us."

Now that he's been human a little longer, he sure is well spoken.

"Adriana, ride me in that race instead of the filly. You can save your conscience, and I'm positive that I'll win for you."

"What makes you so sure?" As I say the words, I hear the idiocy in them. Even back in Russia, it was clear that he was very, very fast.

"Please."

"Do you promise there won't be any weird hand holding or flirting?" I arch one eyebrow, almost hoping he'll disagree, or say that he makes no promises.

Instead, he nods slowly. "On my honor as the rightful czar of Russia, I swear it."

Well, that's a bit disappointing. But it's what I asked him to say.

What am I thinking?

It's what I want.

This feels kind of like the Christmas I turned eight. All I wanted was a bike, but then when I woke up on Christmas morning and found a shiny, red bicycle, I realized it was a lot of work to make it move and the horses I rode daily were way cooler.

So, I do what I did that Christmas. I paste a smile on my face. "Alright," I say. "I'll ride you."

Alexei leans his face against the trunk of the tree, and there's a boyish twinkle in his eye. "There's one little catch."

There always is. I arch my eyebrow.

"If I do this, if we train for this race, and if we win for whoever this is, you have to do something for me in return."

Why does that speed up my heart rate? And why am I suddenly just a bit happier? "What?"

"You have to forgive me for lying. No more hard feelings at all."

Since my anger over it's already mostly gone, I think I can do that. "Fine," I say. "After we win the race, all is forgiven."

Alexei beams, and I realize I may be in a whole new kind of trouble.

16

There was this kid when I was in fourth grade who always stole my lunch money.

It was silly, really. I hardly ever had any money to begin with.

About two days a week, give or take, I'd have scavenged a few bucks from Mārtinš's wallet while he was asleep. Or I'd find money on the counter. Either way, it amounted to less than five bucks a week.

Mirdza never even dreamed of pilfering money, but I've always been a bit more of an opportunist than she is.

The days I had money to buy a lunch were amazing. The school lunch tasted way better than the stuff Mom made at home, which was mostly boiled veggies with a tiny scrap of meat for flavor. The things I looked forward to the most were crisps. My friends like cheddar or sour cream and onion, but I loved vinegar and salt. Either way, the days of crisps and hot lunches disappeared when Markuss started stealing my money.

Until I had an idea.

He was bigger than me. He was stronger than me.

He never beat me up, really. He'd just knock me over, take my money, and then wander off like he'd done nothing wrong. At first, I felt like I couldn't do much to stop him or to complain, since he was bigger, and he hadn't really hurt me.

But he was stealing from me, and it made me feel unsafe, too.

One morning, weeks after Markuss started stealing from me, I found a crisp twenty-euro bill in Mārtiņš's pants pocket that was in the laundry basket. I could almost taste the tang of the vinegar and salt crisps in my mouth. I thought about trying to hide the money in my shoe.

After all, more than half the time, I didn't have any money to be taken. Markuss had been conditioned to that fact. But if he did find it, he'd become harder and harder to shake on the days I had nothing. It was a huge risk. I thought about stashing the money under my mattress and going for crisps later at night at the gas station half a mile down the road. But Mom was good at ferreting out extra cash too, so that was also risky.

In the end, my desperate desire for the crisps was too much. I slid the money into my shoe, and as I walked to school, I had an idea. A terrible idea. Yes, Markuss was bigger. . .but he also used nothing but his fists. What if I changed one side of the equation?

I started looking for rocks that might work: small enough to fit in my pocket, but large enough to do some damage. About a hundred yards from my house, I saw a white hunk of quartz. I crouched down and dug it out of the soft dirt. I wiped it on my pants—Mom was going to kill me—until I could see what I had. It was smooth on one side, but the bottom was pointed and sharp. It was about the size and shape of an egg, other than the jagged chunk.

"What are you doing?" Mirdza asked.

"Nothing," I said.

"Be careful." Mirdza was always worried back then. Actually, she's been worried most of her life.

When Markuss showed up a few blocks from the school, I let him shove me down. But when he started rummaging around in my pockets, I pulled out the egg rock. I dragged my hand back as far as I could, and I flung it forward, striking him on the temple. The blow made him bleed like a stuck pig, and it got all over my white shirt. He also started shouting. Which is why I hit him again. And again and again.

His friends started running away, but Markuss stayed almost totally still, like a huge baby, crying and bleeding.

"You're a thief, and I hate you, and you deserve it." I kicked him, and then I finally ran.

Mirdza was crying as much as he was as she trailed after me. "He's going to tell the teachers," she finally sobbed.

By the time I cleaned most of the blood off my shirt, using the garden hose on the side of the school that we usually drank out of on our way home, we were both late to class.

But that twenty was still safely in my shoe.

I thought Mirdza was right, too.

All day long, I expected someone to come and get me. No one ever did. That's when I learned a second important life lesson—when you've done something wrong yourself, you can't exactly turn anyone else in for their wrongdoing, which is why there's no honor among thieves.

There's really just brute force.

It's stupid, but as I trailer Alexei and slide into the seat of Kristiana's truck that I'm borrowing without asking, I feel a little better than I did yesterday. The bully in the schoolyard's far scarier now that I'm an adult. His threats are devastatingly real, but I'm more confident in Alexei's ability to win than I was in that poor Minnie, and frankly, riding Alexei feels a little like having a rock in my pocket.

He may not be able to attack someone in horse form, but he can make plants and humans *explode* in any shape I assume, so. . .

I called Lukas and let him know that I'd found a suitable substitute, and that I had a proposal for Mr. Rimkus. I sort of thought I'd get the chance to show him to Lukas first, but when I put the truck in park, I notice another car. A familiar car. And when I lead Alexei toward the track, the devil's already there watching.

"You said that my brother's mare was a shoo-in," he says. "Why am I looking at a different animal?" Rimkus is frowning, but I have no idea what he could be upset about. Quicksilver—Alexei—is stunning. He's probably the prettiest horse I've ever seen. Maybe that's his worry. Some of the best racehorses look like the equiv-alent of a run-down travel-trailer: janky, tired, and kinda gutted.

Very few of them look like high-end show ponies.

Alexei does, though.

"This horse is wicked fast," I say. "And given the terms of our agreement, I'd like to ride the horse most likely to win."

"But the agreement was based on me owning the horse," he says. "I won't even get paid the prize money if you ride *your* horse."

"Minnie's lame," I say. "Or if she's not, she's close to

it. I didn't know that when I suggested running her, and now that I do, I'm giving you a suitable alternative. Most of the money on races is made from winning bets, as you well know, and I promise you that, as an unknown, this horse will decimate Radzivan's, and—"

"But it won't be *my* horse that does it." Mr. Rimkus scowls. "This is as much to repair our image as it is for any other purpose."

I hate this guy. I already gave him half a million euros, and he's loaded as sin, clearly. Quicksilver's nostrils are flaring, and he looks ready to kick the jerk. I really don't need that happening.

"Give him to me, and I'll agree to it."

Oh, no. He's definitely going to bite him now. "That's not possible," I say. "I'll ride in your colors. No one has to know he's not yours, but that's the closest I'll come."

"Anyone who sees the paperwork will know."

I shrug. "I can ride that nag, and you can hold me to the terms of the bargain, but it won't repair your image, and it won't earn you a single euro."

He sighs dramatically. "Fine. I'll buy him from you."

"He's not for sale," I say. "I'll ride Minnie, or I'll ride Quicksilver, and either way I'll wear your colors. You can bet on him and make a fortune, or you can run her and lose. Those are your two options."

His smile's disgusting. Far worse than Nojus's ever was. "But if you lose, I still win."

"I remember," I say. "But I don't think you value that kind of win the same way that your brother did." Though, with the way he's changed the terms, maybe he does. I suppress my shudder. That last thing I need to do is arouse Alexei's suspicion further.

He huffs. "Show me what he can do. Then I'll decide."

I warm Quicksilver up, and once he's warm, I ask him to move out a little. It's really the first time I've ridden him on a track, and I don't think he's been ridden by many other people. What I initially mistook as some experience under saddle was more likely to be experience *in* the saddle that roughly translated because of his human intelligence. Even so, as soon as I ask for speed, he *shoots* forward. The ground's literally blurry underneath our feet, and when I fly past Lukas, his jaw's dangling.

It's satisfying.

After our third time around, Mr. Rimkus shouts. "Enough, enough."

I slow Quicksilver halfway around and trot him near the edge until we reach them.

He doesn't look pleased, in spite of our performance. "I'll buy him."

"Sometimes," I say, "we can't get what we want. This is one of those times. But I'll ride him in that race, and you can tell people whatever you want. I won't argue with your story."

He spins around and walks away, no big movements, no loud outbreaks, just headed out. He's nearly to the parking lot when he stops. "Fine."

I barely hear the word.

He's the kind of man who never, ever shouts. He expects others to simply hear and obey. It makes me hate him even more.

"Well, that's one problem solved," I say.

"What does that mean?" Lukas asks.

"I do own him, but I have zero papers."

Lukas swears.

"I couldn't admit that to him, because he'd get fake papers saying he owned him and steal him from me."

"He would, yes," Lukas says.

"And now you're thinking of doing that." I frown.

Lukas laughs. "It's not a terrible thought. I mean, I've never seen a horse move like that. He *flies*, Adriana."

"He does," I say. "But look, if you knew what I went through to get him." I slide off his back. "He's not really in condition for a race. How aggressive should we get with just three weeks to go?"

"Are you training him here or at home?"

I arch one eyebrow. "What do you think?"

"That if you're as smart as I think you are, you probably didn't even turn your truck engine off."

I do like Lukas.

That's rare for one of Nojus's men. They're mostly as bad as he was, but there's something about true horse people. I don't mean the ones out there hawking a horse for a quick buck. I mean the people who really love them—they're usually decent people deep down inside.

And Lukas loves them.

"Are you worried he'll try to steal him in the end?"

"Not really, no." I pull the bridle off Quicksilver's face without replacing it with a halter.

"Adriana! What are you doing?"

"I'll show you." I point at Quicksilver. "Now you, be a good boy, and walk in a circle around me."

Quicksilver snorts so that I know he's annoyed with me ordering him around, but he listens, moving in a clean circle around me.

"What just happened?" Lukas asks.

"This horse is amazing on the track, but when I tell you that we have a bond, and that I not only broke him, but that I've trained him extremely well, I mean it. If someone tries to take him from me. . ." I shrug. "I feel sorry for anyone who tries."

"But would he really hurt someone?" He lifts one eyebrow.

"Try and touch him," I say.

Lukas gives me a significant amount of side-eye, but he reaches toward Quicksilver slowly.

And nearly loses a finger.

"Trust me, he does anything I ask, but he won't listen to anyone else. Training him at Kris's farm is the best idea for everyone involved."

We talk about a plan to practice racing basics and also improve his condition without stressing him, and Quicksilver stands by my side the whole time, attentive. I, of course, know that he's listening.

Lukas is just *floored* by how he's standing there, still and respectful.

Finally, though, we have a plan, and I can head back. "I'll send you videos," I say. "And you can come by, if you want."

"How did you make him fall in love with you like that?" he asks.

I freeze. It's a strange choice of words—fall in love. "A lot of training, and more carrots than you've even imagined."

"That's why he's a little fat for a track horse," Lukas says.

I can't help my laugh. "Sure. He's fat." I can't keep myself from thinking of the image of Alexei naked. "Or maybe he's just more muscular than you're used to seeing."

"Maybe," Lukas says.

By the time I drive us back and start to open the door, Alexei has already shifted back to human. I nearly get another eyeful. "Come on," I say. "A little warning would be good."

"You trained me with *carrots?* And he thinks I'm

fat?" He huffs. "That guy's eaten too many carrots himself."

I'm still averting my eyes, but this is getting ridiculous. "And how are you planning to get from here to Kristiana's house, exactly? Or were you planning to shift again now that you've told me how annoyed you are? Because if someone happens to notice that—" I look pointedly at the groom who's walking a horse right past us. I drop to a hiss. "A naked man in a horse trailer might seem a bit odd to them."

He blinks. "I hadn't really thought about it."

I step back and gesture toward the house. "Be my guest. At least most of the people who work here are men. You might not give them a heart attack."

Or cause a riot.

"I doubt Aleks and Grigoriy will thank you if their girls see you, either."

"Don't you have a jacket or something in the truck?"

"I don't, but I might have a saddle pad."

A dirty one.

I can't help my smirk as I offer it to him.

He frowns, but he takes it. And I have a lovely time watching him walk away, even if the view is somewhat obscured by a smelly little blanket.

17

I had no idea, when I went back to my apartment, that I was heading into an ambush.

"You borrowed my truck," Kristiana says the moment I walk inside.

"Well, hello," I say. "Yes, I did."

Mirdza pounces next. "That's a favor, so now you have to repay us."

"How, exactly?" I pull my boots off and drop them by the front door. "Did you want money?"

"We want you to sit there." Kris points at the fussy, over-embroidered chair by the lamp. "And you have to listen to us until we're done."

It's not like I thought I could avoid them forever, but I may as well let them think they're getting one over on me. "I'm busy."

"Adriana, you have to," Kris says. "Or you can't use my truck ever again."

I glare at her for a moment, and then I say, "Fine." I drop onto the corner of the sofa where Mirdza likes to sit. I should've just taken the chair they told me to take, but I can't help being a contrarian. Even when I was always planning to give in, orders don't sit well with me.

"I know you're mad." Mirdza perches on the arm of the chair across from me, and I'm legitimately worried she's going to tip it over. Its arms aren't very well made. "But you have to forgive us."

"You lied to me," I say. "Like I was a little kid who needed her mommy to tell her that if she didn't eat carrots, she'd go blind."

"I think it's more that your eyesight won't be as good and you might need glasses," Kristiana says.

I glare.

"Not the point," Mirdza says. "The point is that we never should have done that, but we know you never date, and you were the one who woke up Alexei. . ."

"Guys." I shake my head. "I know that you found your happily ever after. Or at least you found your happy-for-now." I can't quite bring myself to say they'll be happy forever. "I'm glad you did. I really am, but I've talked to your horse czar guy, and guess what? He doesn't even want to date me. So." I shrug. "The only people here who are trying to shove us together?" I lift my eyebrows.

They stare at me.

I point at them both. "It's you guys. That's who. I'm glad that big grey horse saved me when I needed him. I'm genuinely happy—for him and for me. If my need woke him up from that curse, then bravo."

"It doesn't work like that," Kris says.

"What doesn't?"

Mirdza sighs. "The only reason Grigoriy woke up to save me is that we were meant to be together."

I arch an eyebrow. "And you know that from your sample size of. . .what? Two?" I frown. "And didn't you say that Aleks was, like, being raced by your dad's enemy when you found and bought him? It doesn't sound like he did much to save you."

"I was in trouble," Kris says, "when he woke up. I just kind of found a solution myself before meeting him. But even so, without him, I'd have lost that first race, and then I couldn't have bought him." She looks flustered. "But that's like you guys. Alexei needed your help, and you needed him to save you as well."

"Well." I stand up. "This was a good talk. I'm happy you guys were able to awaken your men and go on to plan your respective weddings together."

"I'm not engaged," Mirdza says.

"Only a matter of time, I'm sure. But the next time a naked horse shifter shows up when I'm in trouble?"

Mirdza's face falls.

"Find him another damsel to save. This one can save herself."

"Speaking of," my twin says, "Grigoriy says he's helping you win a race?"

I sigh. "Technically, that's true."

"What's technical about it?"

"Fine. It's just true," I say. "I guess I added the word 'technically' to feel a little better. I wouldn't need him, except the horse stupid Nojus bought is lame."

"And so you're racing Alexei?" Kristiana arches one eyebrow and meets Mirdza's eye.

"I know. You raced Aleksandr, and Mirdza competed on Grigoriy, and now you're positive that if we just prepare for this race together, we'll realize that we're meant to be. But guys, I'm telling you, he just told me he deserves to marry a princess, okay? I'm many things, but a princess I am not."

"You're better than a princess," Mirdza says. "You're fiery and independent."

I can't help laughing. "Yes, that's what I hear all guys want. A girl who's *fiery* and *independent*."

"These guys aren't like most guys," Kristiana says. "They do like that."

"How lovely," I say. "I'll be sure to keep my eyes open for other fiery women who might want to date a displaced Russian czar who can turn into a horse and move lakes around." I start walking to my room.

"But Adriana," Kris says.

I turn around, beginning to get a little annoyed. "What now?"

"I love you like a sister. That's why we lied. We just think you'd be happier if you let people in."

"*People*?" I snort. "How many guys were you thinking I'd need? Two? Or are we talking more like five or six?"

Before they can tell me to shut up, the door opens and way too much masculine energy walks through our front door. Aleksandr alone is more than enough, with his brooding looks and his commanding presence, but when Grigoriy shoulders his way through the door as well, I worry about our furniture. He has an even stockier build than Aleks, and he looks ready to pummel something.

"What's going on?" I ask.

And then Alexei walks through and closes the door.

"Alexei says you're racing him in three weeks," Alexander says, looking at me.

"News travels fast around here."

"I think we should make our plan around that," Aleks says, "instead of the wedding."

"Is this about the invites?" Kristiana says. "I told you, it's going to be better to have five hundred people. Keeping it under seventy-five was too hard anyway."

"The last two times Leonid has shown up, it's been

at a race," Aleks says, "when at least one of us was in our horse form. It's a more solid option than a wedding, and we don't run the risk of ruining your wedding."

"*My* wedding?" Kris's tone is a little shrill. "Last I checked, it was yours too."

"You're the one who has all those things you wanted us to have and do," Aleks says. "Of course I'm excited. I'm just saying that the planning for the wedding hasn't been helped by trying to lure Leonid and Boris and Mikhail."

Mirdza's nodding at me furiously, until Kris looks her way. Then she stops and smiles.

"The race is certainly sooner," I say. "If your plan works, you can spend less time stressing, and hey, if it fails, you can save the money on the wedding thing."

"Huh?" Kris asks.

"No bride, no wedding."

Now they're all scowling at me. "Look, I'm assuming you all showed up to convince me that we need to enact your plan at this race, and I don't care when you do it. The race is fine." If I get lucky, Leonid will incinerate Nojus's brother in the melee. "Knock yourselves out."

"But you won't help us." Mirdza frowns.

"What did you want me to do, exactly?" I'm genuinely curious. "I can't shift my form. I can't control earth, air, or water, and I didn't exactly endear myself to Boris or Leonid."

"You're a fighter," Mirdza says. "You always have been, since the time you smacked that bully in the head with a rock."

"Sure," I say. "I'll be at the race, and if there's something I can do—"

"We'd like your help making the plans," Kris says. "That's what we're saying."

I can't help glancing at Alexei. He's the one helping me out, and he and I will be training each day. Does he want me to help them plan to deal with the people who are chasing them? He's looking at me, but his face is totally impassive. I have no idea what he's thinking.

"Sure," I say. "If you need my input on something, just let me know."

It's slight—so slight that if I hadn't been watching for it, I'd never have noticed that Alexei's lip turns up just a bit. He's pleased I'm going to be involved. That's really all I needed to know. Now I won't have to make up excuses to get away when they start talking about all this.

"Does that mean you forgive us?" Kris asks.

They're all looking at me. It's not really a great way to ask whether someone forgives you. An apology should be a healing thing, not a pressure-filled one. But to them, this room's a safe space. To her, there probably isn't a lot of pressure in this moment.

"It's fine," I lie. "I know you were trying to help." I just can't trust that they know how to help me, and that's kind of sad.

"We should all get food," Kris says. "Aleks will pay." She bites her lip and beams at him. "Right?"

"Have you seen how much these guys eat?" He's feigning irritation, but he's smiling.

"I should—"

Mirdza hobbles the few steps between us and grabs my arm. "You should let your family who has missed you and was worried about you take you out to dinner so we can all give you tips on how to win a race on a magical horse."

"Yes." I nod. "I think that's a good topic to discuss at a restaurant."

When Mom emerges from her room, her eyes widening, I realize something.

I'm part of a very exclusive group.

Mom has no idea who Aleks really is. What Grigoriy can really do. What's going on. No one else knows. Kris told me that her dad doesn't know. Her brother has no idea. No one, other than the six of us, understands what the stakes are, or who these men really are.

It does make me feel a *little* special.

"These guys sent me to Russia to deal with some business stuff," I say. "And they had me working the whole time." Lying to Mom has always been easy for me. "Now I'm making them take me out to dinner to repay me."

Mom smiles. "That's a good idea, but don't let them off with just a dinner."

That's my mom. She won't fight for anything, but she'll push and push to see how much she can get out of a situation.

"Oh, I won't," I say. "My mom taught me better."

Mirdza looks embarrassed as we walk out, but she often does. I've gone the other way with things. If people don't like my mom, or our family, then I don't need them. It's like my litmus test for friendship.

"Where are we going?" I ask.

"Insist on somewhere nice," Mom yells from the family room.

Once the door closes, I smile. "Let's go to my favorite place."

Mirdza cringes.

"What?" I can't help staring right at Alexei when I say, "Mr. Burger's the best. You can get a burger and fries for five euros. And they make all their own buns."

"That sounds great," Aleks says.

"It is," I say. "Did I mention it's my favorite?" I shrug. "I like things that are cheap and quick." I skip over to my janky, broke-down car that might not even turn over. Usually it doesn't. "I'll drive."

"We can't all fit in that." Kris eyes my twenty-year-old Toyota Corolla with the same disgust as always.

"Great. Then I'll meet you there." I wave as I open the door with a stiff yank. It creaks loudly and then makes a clicking sound. My car has its own soundtrack, basically.

Mirdza's struggling toward me, probably as a show of family solidarity, instead of heading for the shiny, new car her boyfriend bought her. If I knew she'd insist on following me all the way over, I wouldn't have been so irritating.

"What happened to her leg?" Alexei took advantage of how distracted I was watching Mirdza and snuck over by me. He's now standing by the passenger side door.

"Mirdza's leg?"

He nods.

"My stepfather, that's what." I can't help gripping the doorframe tightly and scowling.

"He hurt her?"

"Sure did, and then you know, subsequent injuries haven't helped."

"Would she want it repaired properly?" He's asking so matter-of-factly that I almost can't believe what he's saying.

"What?"

"I never want to presume that I know what people want in their lives. She's a very strong woman, and she may—"

"She wants it fixed." I lean closer, bracing my elbows on the top of the car. "Can you do that?"

He shrugs. "I mean, I can't be one hundred percent certain, but probably."

"You heal people? Really?"

"Each of us has that ability to a certain extent, but when combined with my water powers, yes, I can heal most things."

"That's—Mirdza!" I should wait and talk to him on the way. I should approach things in a measured way so that I don't get her hopes up unreasonably, but I'm not that kind of person. I'm a storm-the-castle-and-deal-with-the-fallout-later kind of person.

She's almost reached us now, but she was clearly talking to Grigoriy about something and not listening. She turns. "Yeah?" She looks at the car window. "Is your car too messy for me to fit?" Is that hope in her tone? Rude.

"No. It's just that—"

"Oh, no." She sighs. "It won't start again?"

"No," I say. "It's not that either." Though to be honest, I'm not sure. Sitting for a few weeks while I was gone—Mom almost never uses it—probably did it no favors. "Listen."

"Why didn't you ask me to heal her?" Alexei's looking at Grigoriy now.

"Heal who?" Mirdza asks.

"It's only been a few days," Grigoriy says. "They've been chaotic."

"I'm not sure what your boyfriend has told you," Alexei says, looking at my sister now with a gentle kindness I didn't expect. "I know he can heal injuries that are recent, but I can heal most anything. Even old injuries."

Mirdza freezes.

"Would you like me to try healing your leg?"

"Is it painful?" she asks, as if that would deter her. My sister's the toughest person I know.

"It can be," Alexei says. "But it's short-lived."

A whole range of emotions pass over Mirdza's sweet face. Fear. Hope. Excitement. Nervousness. And fear again. I hate that our lives have taught her never to believe in something good. Never to chase rainbows. Never to expect that things might go *right*.

"When?" she asks.

"Right now, if you want." Alexei steps away from my car. He looks at the big house. "We'd need to go somewhere quiet and calm."

Mirdza blinks. Then she nods. "Yes."

Hope surges in my chest. For ten years, I've lived with the misery of knowing I could've saved my sister. My cowardice wrecked her life. My fear cost her everything. But now. . .can he really help her?

I know exactly how she's feeling right now.

I'm not sure I've ever hoped for something this much in my entire life, and he just mentioned it casually, like it was nothing. While we were all figuring out how best to carpool over to a burger place.

Grigoriy takes Mirdza's hand, which is trembling, and they start walking toward the big house.

"What are we—" Kris stops. "Did Alexei offer. . ."

"You knew he could do it?" I ask.

She shrugs. "The guys thought he might be able to, but they weren't sure, and they didn't want to press when he'd only been back for a few days."

I jog to catch up to where Alexei's casually sauntering toward the house. "Are you sure?"

He stops moving and turns to face me. "Sure?"

"That you can do it."

"Of course not," he says. "I'm never sure about

healing something. But of the dozens of times I've tried, it's always worked."

"Have you ever healed someone whose leg has been broken, twisted, glued and screwed together, and then broken again, and then surgically repaired with more bolts and screws and a bone graft?"

He frowns.

I bet they didn't have procedures like that in his time. "It has metal and wire in there, holding the pieces of the bone together."

His brow furrows. "I'll do the very best I can."

It's not enough, though. He has to fix it. "Please do."

He steps toward me, his hand raised a little, and his fingers brush against the edge of my jaw. "If there is any way I can repair your sister's leg, I'll do it, Adriana. No matter what it takes. I promise."

I can't seem to say a word, but I nod.

Like sinners on our way to church, we all walk inside quietly, slowly, seriously. Heads bowed.

"Is everything alright?" Kristiana's dad hops up off the sofa and follows us to the base of the stairs.

"Just doing some wedding stuff, Dad," Kris says. "It's fine."

"You look. . .did someone die?" His eyebrows are drawn together.

I don't blame him for being nervous. The mood is *somber*.

"No one died," I say. "It's actually good news."

"Oh." His eyebrows rise and he rubs his hands together. "Did that caterer say they can do crab?"

Kristiana rolls her eyes. "Dad, it's not in season. We can have it, but it would be frozen. I already told you that."

I can't help laughing a little. His idea of what might have inspired our mood is the availability of shellfish?

"Alright, well, I guess I'll just wait to hear what the other news is until you feel like telling me." He shoves his hands in his pocket and shuffles back into the living room. I actually feel a little bad. He must feel left out a lot, what with all the planning sessions he can't join—given they were trying to expand the wedding to lure Leonid. Maybe now that they're using the race, he won't feel so left out.

Watching Mirdza struggle her way up the stairs breaks my heart.

My hope that this will work grows exponentially. Like, it's probably really unhealthy how hard I'm hoping. If I hadn't just asked God on my knees to save me a week ago, without doing much at all to repay him yet, I'd be praying again right now.

Ah, screw it.

Please, God. You listened before. Please, please, please save her leg.

Twice in one week. That's got to be a record for someone like me.

I don't bother offering something in return this time. Clearly God knows I'm not a good investment. I'm like that bratty little kid that just keeps showing up, asking for another cookie, even though I made a mess with the first one and didn't eat my dinner like I said I would.

Maybe he loves me anyway, for some inexplicable reason. Isn't that kind of his thing? Gosh, I hope I didn't just piss him off, right as we're about to see if he can heal my sister.

"Alright," Alexei says from the top of the stairs. "One of these is her bedroom, right?"

Grigoriy points, and we all follow Alexei inside.

"Do you need a glass of water or something?" I ask.

Alexei looks like he might laugh.

"Hey, there are no stupid questions," Kris says. "Only stupid—"

"There are lots of stupid questions," I say. "And I just asked one, but that's fine. I'm okay with it."

"Can you sit on the bed and swing your leg up?" Alexei asks.

Mirdza has to brace both arms on the bed to swing her legs up. I've gotten so used to watching her that I didn't really pay close attention to it. Life has been really unfair for her.

Alexei drags a chair up next to the bed and sits, closes his eyes, and holds his hands over her knee. He inhales sharply, drops his hands, and opens his eyes again.

"Is that it?" I ask. "Did it work?"

Alexei frowns and shakes his head. "Not yet. I'm just feeling it out." He turns back to Mirdza. "Your sister tells me there's metal inside your leg. I can feel. . .something foreign."

Mirdza nods.

"I didn't realize that when I offered. In order to try to repair this. . ." He sighs. "I'll have to remove the metal first, and any bone that's not yours, and only then can I try to regrow the bone the way it should've always been."

"Try?" Mirdza stiffens. "And what if it doesn't work?"

His brow furrows. "If I can't regrow the bone." He grimaces. "I think you'd be unable to use the leg until you had another surgery to replace the metal I removed."

That's one heck of a risk.

18

I really only remember one thing about my dad. He worked a lot, and he wasn't home very often, but when he came home, he would often bring us surprises. And then he'd say, "Guess what?"

He'd be smiling so big that it almost split his face in two. We'd jump up and down and clap. Then he'd give us something. It might be a thin plastic fortune-telling fish that curled into different poses—and each one meant something else. It might be a peppermint. It might be a slice of cake.

It was never the same.

But most of the time, after offering us this treat, he'd say, "Alright. You've gotten something fun from Papa. Now. Do you want to go double or nothing?"

If we said yes, sometimes we got a kiss in return. He'd take our surprise and then laugh about it. We'd cry and whine, but he told us that a kiss from him was the most amazing thing we could get. Once he was gone, I realized that was true, but at the time, it made me sad.

The other half of the time, we'd get something even

better. Once, I got a carved wooden bowl. Another time, I got a butterfly made of beautiful blue stone. Once, I got an entire cake.

Mom made me share it, which ticked me off royally.

But even after Mirdza and Mom and Dad each had a piece, I got to gorge myself on as much cake as I could eat in one go. Needless to say, I always chose to go double or nothing. I hadn't done anything to get the treat in the first place, so I always wanted to turn it into something more.

My sister never did it, not once. Mirdza's not a gambler.

It's just not who she is.

So when Alexei tells her the truth, that he's not sure whether it'll work, that he'd have to remove the metal—which sounds absolutely awful—I already know what she's going to say. I know Mirdza will do the safe thing. She'll just keep hobbling around, in pain and miserable, because she might wind up worse off than she is if she risks it.

The status quo is the safe play.

It's what she knows.

She's opening her mouth to say she'll just live with her leg the way it is when I leap in front of her and grab her hand.

"Just this once," I plead. "For one time in your life, please, please, please, take a risk."

I know I'm being selfish. I know I'm asking her because of my guilt, but I can't help it. I need her to get better. I need to see a miracle for her, so that *I* can sleep better at night. It's greedy of me.

I was already saved once this week.

I shouldn't demand more, and especially not from

someone who never, ever takes risks like this. But I am who I am.

And she is who she is.

Which is why I know what she'll say before she says it.

"A, I can't." Her eyes well with tears.

I squeeze her hand, unwilling to take the loss just yet. "You can. I'm right here. You can do it, just like when you went back that day when you stood up for Mom. Don't do it for yourself, because you don't take risks for yourself. Instead, do it for me." I'm crying now, like a big idiot.

She shakes her head.

"I was there." The words feel ripped out of me.

"What?" She blinks.

"I was there," I confess. It's like something inside me is breaking. "I heard him beating Mom. I heard you go inside. I should've followed you. Maybe with both of us there—" My voice cracks.

Mirdza leans forward and pulls me against her chest, hugging me. "I'm glad you didn't come in. If I could go back in time, I'd tell you to do just what you did."

Because she's bravery and sacrifice to my cowardice and regret.

"Please try," I beg. "I still have nightmares."

"Who did this to them?" Alexei's voice sounds like midnight. Like an eclipse. Like the end of things.

"Their stepdad," Grigoriy says.

"I'm going to kill him." Alexei stands up.

Grigoriy grunts. "They don't want you to hurt him. They're very insistent on it."

"They?" I ask. "That's just my sister." I toss my head at the door. "Kill him—the sooner the better."

Alexei smiles.

"But first, heal her." I release Mirdza. I wipe my face with both hands. "Please, please let him try it."

"There's not much bone left," Mirdza whispers. "If he tries and it doesn't work." She shakes her head.

She may never walk again.

I hate this.

I hate it so much.

"Killing him won't fix me," she says. "Two wrongs—"

"Stop," I say. "Don't try cliches on me. This might fix you, and it's the best chance we've ever had." Another tear rolls down my cheek. "It might finally erase what happened."

"Fine," Mirdza says. "If you promise to leave Mārtinš alone, I'll try it. He's not with Mom anymore. There's no reason to drag darkness back into our lives."

Alexei frowns.

Grigoriy grunts.

Mirdza is who she is. And I want my miracle.

"What do you have to do to get the metal out?" I ask.

"Aleksandr," Alexei asks. "Can you. . .?"

Aleks is slouching against the wall near the door. "Can I. . . Oh. Can I remove the metal?"

"It's part of the earth, isn't it?" Alexei looks nervous.

Aleksandr walks toward the bed, his eyes intent.

I back out of the way.

This time, he sits on the chair and holds up his hands. And then after a moment, he nods. "It's going to be really, really terrible, though." He cringes. "The only way to get it out. . ." He stands and backs up.

"I think I know," Mirdza says. "You're going to have to pull it out. Through my body." She swallows.

"I can't." Kris shakes her head. "I love you, but I

can't stand here and watch that." She looks pale as a sheet.

"You don't have to." Mirdza's as pale as Kristiana. "And you don't, either." She's looking at Grigoriy.

And me.

"I'm staying," I say.

"Me too," Grigoriy says.

"Wait, so I'm the only one who wants to leave?" Kristiana's lips compress and her hands ball into fists.

"It's fine," I say. "You should go. It won't help her to have everyone here watching." But it's my penance for making my sister do this.

"What will you need?" Grigoriy asks. "I can step in and heal the exit wounds from the screws and the wire."

Alexei nods. "That's a good idea."

"And I'll take them out slowly, backing the screws out so that it doesn't damage the bone."

"Can we put her to sleep or something?" I ask.

"I'm afraid not," Alexei says. "I need to be able to monitor her vitals and how they're responding, or I can't deal with any issues."

"I doubt a hospital would loan us an anesthesiolo-gist anyway," Mirdza jokes.

"Can't any of you mind control someone into letting us?" I hate this. I'm the one who pushed for it, and I still hate it.

"I have a feeling this is going to be loud," Kristiana says. "I'm going to get my dad out of the house by. . .I don't know. I'll think of something."

"Good idea," Aleks says.

The eight minutes it takes for Kristiana to race downstairs and convince her father to leave—and get his shoes and his wallet and his keys—are some of the longest moments of my entire life.

But then, when the front door closes, I almost feel worse.

"Alright." Alexei nods. "I'm ready."

Aleksandr pushes past him and sits down on the chair again.

"Wait." I leap over Mirdza on the bed and lie next to her, holding her hand in mine. "Okay. Now you can do it."

Everyone's staring at me.

"What?" I huff. "She needs someone to hold her hand, okay?"

But then, Aleks starts. Mirdza's entire body goes stiff, and then she bows backward, her shoulders arcing down and her belly flying up. She's brave, and she's strong, but she's screaming louder than anyone I've ever heard scream, and it's the worst ninety seconds of my life. I can't look away as the top of her leg splits open, chunks of metal and grafted bone sliding out in a spray of crimson.

Only when Aleksandr stops and Grigoriy steps in do I realize that I'm screaming right along with her. But faster than her leg ripped open, it magically, invisibly closes, the skin simply regrowing over the gaping, jagged holes.

There's blood everywhere. It's all over Aleksandr. It's all over the floor. It's on the bed, and it's on me. Poor Mirdza's white as a ghost. But the first step, hopefully the *worst* step, is done.

Which is why I feel absolutely and utterly ill. Because that's the part we knew they could do. Now comes the unknown.

Grigoriy presses a kiss to her forehead and backs up.

My heart's hammering.

My hands, clutching Mirdza's, are clammy and

trembling.

My breathing's shallow and labored.

Mirdza, on the other hand, looks utterly calm.

"Are you alright?" I whisper.

She nods.

"How can you possibly be alright?"

Her smile's the saddest thing I've ever seen. "That actually wasn't so bad. Being stabbed and thrown off that train was way worse."

And now I'm crying again. My sister's life has been so horrific that having metal screws torn from her leg and blasted into the world—that risking her ability to walk for yet another time—isn't *that bad*. "Oh, Mirdza."

She shakes her head. "Stop. It's fine. I mean it." Because even beyond all the misery and the suffering, the hope on her face shines like a star. In my desperation about her pain, for a moment I forgot why we're doing this. It all comes down to this moment, really.

Can Alexei heal the shattered bones?

The bones that have been through so much. The original trauma. Regrowth. Breaking again. Scraping and pinning and screwing and grafts. Remodeling over and over. The cartilage and the tendons and the ligaments that have tried to hold this train wreck together must be pretty sore and tired as well.

That's the thing about our bodies.

They're amazing.

They're miraculous.

But when one small piece breaks, the rest of our body has to compensate, and it causes unimaginable wear and tear and collateral damage. I can't even imagine what it's been like for my sister, compensating for a paper-mâché leg. And now I may have made it all worse by making her gamble on this repair.

As guilty as I felt before, how will I feel if she's in a wheelchair from today forward?

"I'm ready." Mirdza's smiling.

If there was any doubt in my mind that my sister was a saint, it's gone. She has so much hope, so much light, and so much peace in the face of all this horror.

Please, please God, help this to fix her.

Is it crazy that someone selfish like me is praying? Yes. Is it bonkers that I'm asking for God's help with a magical healing? Also, yes.

But here we are.

Alexei's hands extend over my sister's leg, and I watch for something, anything, that will show me what he's doing. Light. Sparks. An electric feeling. Anything.

But nothing happens.

Until Mirdza gasps.

Her body bows and her hands tighten on mine, and she stays that way— rigid, taut, miserable—for one heartbeat. Then another. For a dozen more. And then she finally collapses against the blood-stained comforter and groans.

"What?" I look frantically from Mirdza to Alexei and back again. "What happened?"

Alexei swallows.

Mirdza inhales and then struggles into a seated position.

"I think it worked," Alexei says. "The bone regrew."

Mirdza smiles. "It doesn't hurt anymore." She doesn't even seem to notice the blood—her blood—that's smeared all over everything. She pivots on the bed until her legs swing over the side of the bed, and then. . .

She stands.

The smile that spreads across her face is the most beautiful thing I've ever seen.

❧ 19 ❧

I suggested Mr. Burger because I thought it would shock Alexei. I thought it would show everyone how fundamentally different we are. There is no way on earth that he's going to like the burger joint.

His meals were made by a team of servants, for heaven's sake. He's accustomed to sitting in dining halls with linen tablecloths and fine China. His family had multiple courses and dinners attended by the elite of society.

He's not going to like a messy, smooshed-up burger. I'm actually excited to see it happen, but I can't focus. I'm too distracted.

By Mirdza.

She's literally *frolicking* everywhere she goes. She also can't stop beaming. It's about the cutest thing I've ever seen.

I mean, ninety percent of her giddy joy is directed at Grigoriy, and about five percent is directed at Aleksandr and Alexei, who did just work together to save her. But *I'm the one* who bludgeoned her into trying it.

Where's all the bubbly, effervescent happiness that should be directed my way?

One hug. That's what I got.

Which is fine.

Mostly I'm just happy for her. But I did let her grind the bones in my hand together during the whole ordeal, and I was willing to take all the regret and all the misery if it failed, because I was the one pulling for her to try it. A little "Oooh, Adriana, you're the best," or "You were *right*, Adriana," might be nice.

Still, even without any credit, it's nice to see her dancing around while they discuss the menu like we're at a five-star restaurant.

"Which one has pomegranate seeds?" Aleksandr asks. "I don't think those should be on a burger."

"If you don't want those, you'll hate the Hawaiian one too, because it has grilled pineapple." Grigoriy squints. "But what's a wrap?"

"What exactly is a *burger?*" Alexei asks.

It hadn't even occurred to me he wouldn't know what it was. "It's bread with a slab of beef in between. They also put toppings on the meat." Luckily, an order comes up just then. I point. "The toppings and the bread types are the big decisions. What I love about this place is how many buns they have. Charcoal infused, pretzel, sesame, whole wheat, and plain."

Alexei still looks confused.

"Are these burgers really only three euros each?" Aleksandr asks.

I nod. "My kinda place." Artisan burger and fries for five euros? Yep.

"But which one should I get?" Alexei asks.

He's not someone who's accustomed to choosing his own meals, I imagine, plus this is something entirely new. "Start by trying the bacon burger," I say.

"Everyone likes bacon, plus it's pretty basic. Maybe just get the plain bun."

Then it's sauces and toppings that stump them.

We wind up letting three parties order ahead of us, but finally we get them all chosen, and Aleks gives the cashier fifty euros—they all got milkshakes—and we wait. It's a little awkward when we look for seats. There's a four-top table, which Aleks, Grigoriy, Kris, and Mirdza take immediately.

Then the guys startle, stand up, and look at Alexei.

"What?" I point at the table next to them. "We can sit here." It has a bit of a triple date vibe, but that would be true with literally anyone I came here with. I don't blame Alexei. I'm not that crazy.

"Would you prefer to sit here?" Aleksandr asks.

"Or here?" Grigoriy asks.

"What's going on?" I glance at Kris and Mirdza.

Kris laughs. "They've been like that ever since he got back. I think they're so used to him being their Czar that they can't quite wrap their heads around not deferring to him."

"We still defer to him." Grigoriy's eyes are intense. "He's still our czar."

The people who just walked past are giving us strange looks.

"Maybe we should speak something other than Latvian when we say super crazy things," I whisper in my horrible Russian.

"You should never speak in our language," Alexei's smiling. "You were better off pretending you couldn't."

I think about kicking him, but that might get us more of the wrong kind of attention. "Just sit." I slide into a plastic seat.

Luckily the burgers don't take too long, and the

other two guys settle down a little. Once the food arrives, Alexei looks at it like it might bite him.

"Burgers are really good," I say. "I did pick this place to taunt you a little, but they're not disgusting."

"I'm not accustomed to mashing things together." His lip's curled.

"Oh, please. What's soup, then? Or dumplings? They're all just food, mashed together."

"This also looks quite messy."

He picks up the burger, carefully peeling back the paper that has fallen down across the front. "If you say so."

He watches everyone else eat a bite or two first, but eventually he brings his to his mouth. When the ketchup squishes out the side and drips onto the front of his shirt, I can't help laughing.

He drops his burger to the tray immediately.

"Oh, come on," I say. "It's funny. You're all prim and proper, but the rest of us can eat burgers without making a mess. You're like a toddler."

His scowl looks utterly real—no feigning there.

"You aren't a czar anymore, Alexei," I say. "You're going to have to learn how to wallow around in the mud with the rest of us pigs."

"I'm still a lord," Aleksandr says.

"As am I," Grigoriy says.

Kristiana shoves a handful of fries in Aleksandr's mouth, and Mirdza's rolling her eyes when she bumps Grigoriy's shoulder.

He may still be scowling, but I notice that Alexei finishes his bacon burger and wipes his mouth thoroughly.

"The burger's good, though, right?" I can't help my self-satisfied grin.

"It was edible."

"Oh, that's too bad." I turn to Mirdza. "He didn't like it. So next time, we'll go without them."

"It was decent," Alexei says.

"Decent?" I stand up and toss my trash on the tray. "I'm sure Aleks and Kris can find a personal chef for you while you're stuck here, and after you return to your rightful position, you'll be able to hire your own."

He sighs. "The burger was pretty good, but I don't like being bad at things."

Mirdza and I exchange a glance and start laughing.

"What's funny about that?" Aleksandr asks.

"I mean, that's nice," I say. "But if you'd lived our lives, you wouldn't have had much choice. Without private tutors and special magical powers, we were bad at everything. Until we worked hard enough to become better."

We've lived very different lives.

I reach to grab his tray so I can take mine and his at the same time, but he stops me. "I can clear the table."

He takes both trays, piling his trash on mine and stacking them, and I decide he must have been watching other customers to figure that out. There's no way they had trays and communal trash cans back in 1917. At least, not that he would have ever used.

I'm a little bit proud of him, which is stupid.

The others are already heading back out to the car—mine wouldn't start, which is hardly surprising. We all rode with Kris and Aleksandr. We're nearly to Aleksandr's Land Rover when I almost step on a stick—that isn't a stick, because it's all striped.

Danger noodle. Ugh. I can't help my shriek. I hate snakes.

"Whoa, there. It's dead," Kristiana says. "Look."

Something already rolled over its head. What a

terrible tragedy. My hand's still pressed against my chest as my heart tries to recover.

"Not a fan of snakes?" Alexei asks.

"Is anyone?" I shudder.

He shrugs. "I don't love them, but I don't hate them either. They eat rats, and I like rats less than snakes."

"Gross." I slide into the car and scooch over. Alexei hops up after me.

"You're just biased because of Lucy." Kris closes the door behind her with a loud thunk.

"Who's Lucy?" Alexei and Aleksandr ask at the same time.

"She was one of Adriana's favorite mares when we were kids."

"That snake killed her," I say.

"A snake killed a horse?" Aleks looks unconvinced.

"I mean, not exactly."

"What happened?" Alexei asks.

"So, one night, we were putting the horses away. It was getting colder, and we were moving to the winter routine." I still get upset thinking about this.

"And?" Aleks asks.

"Well," Mirdza says. "Adriana was, what? Ten?"

"Yep."

"And she put Lucy in her stall with no problems." Kristiana tightens her hand on the armrest until her knuckles are white. "But then we heard screaming. That mare was always so calm, but she flipped."

"The snake bit her leg," I say. "It had been hiding in the shavings, ready to sleep."

"Leg wounds are never great for horses," Kristiana says. "But that one was nasty."

"Even so, she got over that," I say. "Proudflesh

removal, and bandages, and all kinds of misery later, she eventually recovered."

"But she wouldn't go back in the stall after that, so we let her stay in that small pasture behind the barn instead." Kris shakes her head. "Mom thought that after a few weeks, when it really got cold, she'd calm down."

"She never did," I say. "She was convinced that going into that stall would kill her." It actually makes me chuckle a little, thinking about how irrational she got.

"A year and change later, her leg was fine, but we had that horrible cold spell." Kris looks as sad as I feel.

"We decided she *had* to go inside. We thought she'd fling herself around a little and then get over it."

"She didn't," Kris says. "She flipped out and flipped out, whamming against the stall, flinging herself against it, until she hit the waterer wrong and. . ." Kris closes her eyes.

"We had to put her down," I say. "It was really, really sad. We should've just let her stay out in that pasture with double blankets."

"Or maybe you should've worked with her on going into the stall more," Alexei says. "Sometimes horses, people, whatever, they think something that's good is bad. You have to be patient and take small steps until they realize it's not what they think."

"My mom had died by then," Kris says. "I think we were all unsure what to do. Plus, we were all scared of our own stuff, just like her with the stall. We were all trying to just get over it, too."

"It's hard to help others when you're hurting your-self," Alexei says. "You shouldn't feel guilty. I didn't mean that at all."

I can't help thinking about Lucy the rest of the way

home. Obviously I'm not a horse. I'm not keen on snakes, but I don't freak out about walking into a stall because I saw one there once.

I'm much smarter than that.

But I *am* afraid of dating. I got into a fight with my sister and her best friend who were trying to help me. They wanted me to spend more time with someone who seems like a pretty great guy. Were they putting me in a stall? Were they trying to get me past my irrational fears?

Or am I right? Am I better off just avoiding stalls and double blanketing for cold snaps?

I glance at Alexei out of the corner of my eye on the way home. He's staring out the window, watching as the city roads transition to country ones. The world has changed in a blink for him, but he's taking it well. He's magical. He seems noble of mind, but he's literally noble of blood.

In spite of that, he's a pretty decent guy.

Not that any of it matters. He told me himself that he should find someone much better than me. It's a relief that's what he wants. Clearly we're a very bad mismatch. But when I look down at his hand, his large, strong, warm hand, mine moves toward it slightly, my fingers stretching apart.

"What are you doing?"

My head snaps up, my eyes meeting his curious ones. "Nothing."

"Did you drop something?" His eyes search the seat between us and the floorboard. "Is it small?"

Heat rises in my cheeks. "No, I didn't."

He stops. "Is everything alright?"

I spin back toward the window and press my face against it. "Fine."

But every time I glance his way the rest of the ride, he's looking at me. I hate it.

And I love it.

I hate that I love it.

When we park, I practically sprint away from the car and toward my apartment. I'm opening the door when I hear Alexei say my name.

Irritatingly, it lifts my spirits.

Mom's watching the television inside so intently that she hasn't even noticed I'm home, so I turn around.

It's not only Alexei. Kristiana's next to him. "You forgot your purse."

Alexei holds it out toward me.

I'm reaching for it when something from the television catches my attention.

"When the State Duma indicted the President, no one thought that the Federation Council would vote to impeach him, but now it's happened. The Prime Minister was dismissed just two weeks before and hasn't yet been replaced. The Russian government's currently facing a state of crisis like none we have seen in recent history."

Alexei's face is frozen, his eyes concerned.

And I can't help thinking about what he told me before. As long as the people of Russia are free and well cared for, there's no reason to take measures to regain his position.

But what about now?

❧ 20 ❧

I knew that there had been a President who was impeached in the United States. We learned about it in school. But then I remembered that Russia has also had it happen three times.

So it's big news, but it's hardly *shocking* news.

Alexei and Aleksandr and Grigoriy leave rather quickly, presumably to keep talking about the history of Russia—from 1917 when they all went to sleep until now—until they can't talk anymore. That's fine with me. I haven't really seen my mother in more than two weeks.

Not that I'm expecting my time with her to be relaxing.

Mom's a fritter. So even when you're trying to do something fun, she wrecks that pretty much any way she can. She picks at my hair. She suggests that I need to polish my nails. She comments on the clothing I'm wearing and my lack of a boyfriend. Once that feels heavy-handed, she gushes about Mirdza's new boyfriend. Today, I was prepared for the inevitable questions about Grigoriy's friend Alexei.

I knew it would be tiring.

But today, when it feels like too much, I suggest something I almost *never* do, in the name of research. You'd think that someone like my mother would loathe romantic comedies. By all counts, my father was far from perfect, but whatever good qualities he had were eclipsed by the mess he left our family in when he died.

Then along came someone worse than the devil himself. Mārtinš.

After surviving all that, there's still no one on earth who loves love stories as much as my mother. So when I suggest we watch a romance, she squeals so loudly that I'm convinced it terrifies the poor horses outside.

I'm determined to figure out whether I'm right to reject every man I meet, or whether I'm insisting on double blankets in snowmageddon like Lucy. Am I harming myself because of an irrational fear? I'm hoping to discover some helpful insight or knowledge from studying the ideas of romance themselves. Mom picks one she's been wanting to watch for a while that was just dubbed in Latvian.

The men in this one—there are two of them—are best friends. They're partners in law enforcement, and they're both unbelievably good looking, just like the Russians who are currently hanging around. They're both excellent at fighting, which makes sense, because they're special ops. And. . .

They both like the same little blond girl.

I make a mental note that it's nice that none of our Russian stallion shifters appear to like the same woman. That's a major relief. How awkward would it be if Grigoriy and Aleksandr both pursued Kris? But as these two guys are doing ridiculous things—car chases, bugging the girl's room, and attacking one another—I keep thinking the same thing.

Alexei's better looking than either of them. He's also funnier, smarter, and more powerful.

This movie's not helping with my research at all. It's just making me sad that he wants someone better than me. Which is stupid. I don't even want him. I wouldn't want him even if he *did* want me. It's good that he doesn't want me. I started this research not because of Alexei, but because I wondered whether my basic premise might be flawed.

Right before it ends, I stand up and leave. My mom's distressed that I left, of course, but she's hardly surprised. This has been my MO for a decade at least. I shower, and then I toss and turn half the night, dreaming repeatedly of stupid Alexei leaving me in different ways. I hate that this has become my new nightmare.

When I roll over and see 4:30 a.m. blinking on my alarm clock, I groan and stumble out of bed. I have four horses to work before I'm supposed to meet with Alexei, so I'm surprised when I reach the barn around five a.m. that he's already there.

"Oh."

His eyes widen.

"Why are you here?" I blink. "Didn't we say eight-thirty every morning?"

He nods.

"Do you need help with something? Because I have a few horses I need to work, and—"

"I couldn't sleep."

Oh. "Me either."

He comes with me, and surprisingly, with no one else around, he's kind of helpful. He knows how to groom and tack horses. He's even a decent rider. I guess it makes sense. He was raised royal, and in the early nineteen hundreds, that meant skill with a horse.

He cuts my work in half, and we're tacking down the last two horses I needed to work today by seven thirty.

"I knew how to ride by the time I was three," he says. "Mounted cavalry was pretty important back then."

I googled him when I got back home. The first picture that popped up was one of him as a tiny kid on top of a huge horse. But that makes me think of other stuff. "Can I ask you something?" I frown. "This might sound weird, but—"

"You looked me up."

My face heats immediately. "I mean, it's not that—"

"I'd have done the same thing."

"It said you suffered from severe hemophilia."

His smile's wry. "Apparently *someone* didn't like me."

"Do you know this Leonid?" It's not really any of my business, but I can't help asking. "It feels like maybe you did."

He grabs both saddles and starts carrying them to the tack room. "We met when I was younger."

I realize I'm trotting after him. I want to stop, because that feels sycophantic, especially when he's trying to do something nice like carrying a saddle I don't need him to carry for me, but I also want to hear what he's saying. "What did you think of him?"

"His dad was crazy, I think." Alexei drops the saddles on their racks like they weigh nothing. "Certifiably, I mean. Mentally ill. I think that's what Aleksandr said people say now."

"It is."

"He wasn't well, that's for sure. They were starving. I don't know all the details, but Boris's little sister, Katerina, found him first. She said he was starving, and she took him in. At first she really liked him, and they spent several years studying and spending a lot of time together—he was educated and fed by her family. Later they had some kind of fight."

"And?"

"That's when he started pushing for things. Demanding things. Most of it happened with her family, but after they had a permanent falling out, he came to my father. He made some petitions, aggressive petitions, and when Dad refused them. . ."

"You're not sure what happened next?"

Alexei shakes his head. "Not entirely, no. It was a turbulent time, and Dad was trying to keep up with the social tornado that was sweeping through Russia. I think part of the force behind that wind might have been Leonid."

"But what does that have to do with—"

Alexei grimaces. "Boris's sister, Katerina, really liked me. I think Leonid liked her, and since he was around after we were all cursed, I imagine he made a few changes to the history book's records."

"You think he made it look like you were sickly?"

Alexei shrugs. "I've seen dumber things happen."

So have I.

It's the historical equivalent of drawing a mustache on the face of a movie star on a poster. "I think that may tell us more about Leonid than it does about anything else."

"Interestingly, people are very confused about Rasputin. I couldn't believe they thought he was a magician. I saw some reports that he was an evil mastermind." He chuckles. "That guy was a real weirdo."

"I did hear that he was magician. I thought it might be true, especially once I realized you guys are magic."

"Hardly," Alexei says. "He was quite talented with healing, especially for rare, difficult cases. Dad's cousin actually had a bleeding condition, and he's the one we brought Rasputin to court to treat. Once, my mom stormed into his room to yell at him about something and he was wearing a woman's ball gown and posing in front of the mirror."

Catching him up on current medical stuff and politics is going to be a whole thing, apparently. "He might have just been a little misunderstood."

Alexei shrugs. "Maybe, but the gown was Mother's, and she was not the slightest bit pleased to find that he had taken it."

I suppose she wouldn't be.

"Are you ready to start our training?" Alexei asks.

I nod. "Thanks for helping me today."

"I love riding," Alexei says.

"It's too bad I can't turn into a horse then," I say.

He laughs. "It really is."

"You're both here." Kristiana breezes into the stables like she owns the place—which I suppose she does. Alexei must've seen her coming, because he's already ducked into a stall, and he tosses his clothes over the side of the wall. I can't help swallowing and turning away—but the image of him naked still flashes through my mind. I shake my head to clear it. The last thing I need to be thinking about is Alexei without clothes.

The very, very last.

When he bumps the door with his big, dark grey nose, pushing it open and walking out, one of the grooms at the end of the walkway startles. I grab a halter and swing it over his head.

Quicksilver snorts.

I do not expect Grigoriy, Mirdza, and Kristiana to all be loitering along the side of the track while we're warming up. Once Quicksilver's really puffing, I pull him up short along the fence line. "What's with the audience? You planning to do this every day for the next three weeks?"

"Maybe," Mirdza says. "Kris helped me when I was getting ready, and it saved me."

"I don't have a broken leg, and none of you know a thing about flat racing."

Quicksilver tosses his head like he's agreeing with me, but when a car pulls into the lot across the training yard, I'm suddenly glad they're all here. Nojus's brother is the last person I want to see.

"Are they coming every day?" Kris asks. "Because that's annoying."

Annoying isn't the word I'd use.

"Why are they even here?" Mirdza asks.

"It's a long story," I say. "Let's just say that I owed them a debt, and this race should eliminate it, finally."

"Wouldn't it be easier to just kill him?" Grigoriy's scowling. "I can tell from here—that's a bad man."

Mirdza's hands tighten on the fence, but she doesn't argue.

For a brief second, I consider telling them to do it. What if I told Mirdza and her boyfriend the kind of man Mr. Rimkus is? Would they eliminate him for me? But who will take his place? I've been around long enough to know that the Nojuses of the world are always followed by someone at least as bad as they are.

Hopefully I can win this race, and then it'll all be in the past, finally.

"Are we late?" Mr. Rimkus glares at Mirdza, Grigoriy, and Kristiana like they're lying to him.

"Not at all," I say. "We just finished our warm-up, but surely Lukas told you we won't be doing timed runs every day."

His eyes cut sideways to Lukas and then narrow.

"Of course I did," Lukas says. "But he'd like to see one more today, just to make sure he's made the right decision not to run Minnie."

"That's fine," I say.

"When are you coming back to the track he'll actually be running on?" Mr. Rimkus asks.

"A few days before the race itself should be fine," I say.

Lukas nods. He starts asking Kris about the details of her track, and then he pulls out his timer.

"Four furlongs?" I ask.

Lukas frowns. "He wants eight."

A full mile, timed. It's a little early for such a long distance.

Quicksilver tosses his head though, dancing forward, and I can't argue with everyone. "Fine, but then we get a week off from timed runs."

Mr. Rimkus arches an eyebrow. "If it's a satisfactory time."

"What's a good time for eight furlongs?" Mirdza asks.

"A minute fifty would be good for a green horse," Lukas says. "But it would be nice if he was under a minute forty."

"The record's around a minute thirty," Kris says. "Right?"

"Each lap is how long?" Mr. Rimkus asks.

"Four furlongs," Kris says.

Twice around the track at top speed. We can do that, even if it's a bit optimistic for an early time.

Quicksilver's chomping on the bit as I wheel him around. I assume he's doing that to seem more like a regular race horse, who would likely be prancing around like a lunatic. Most trainers don't bother teaching very good ground manners to racehorses. It takes too long to turn one of them into a solid citizen when you're not sure whether they'll have what it takes. Plus, some people think the nervous energy makes them run faster.

"Why aren't you using a chute?" Mr. Rimkus asks.

"Next week," I say. "We're conditioning now, and he does fine in the chute."

It's kind of nice having a horse I can explain things to—a horse who never spooks because he notices his own shadow. My heart accelerates as we circle to the starting line. My hands tremble just a bit where they're gripping the reins. Quicksilver leans forward, flexing, and on the bit just like I want.

Lukas puts his whistle to his lips and blows.

We explode forward, clumps of dirt flying outward in all directions.

"Easy," I say. "Let's save a little bit."

But he's not having that—he's acting like he's angry at Mr. Rimkus for doubting us. I hunch down over his shoulders, not urging him ahead, but not hauling back. I've never had a horse who understood how far we were going and what our goals were until now. I feel more like a passenger than I ever have before.

I'm frankly surprised by the end of the first loop when he's still running fast enough to churn up chunks of earth, but shortly after we start the second lap, I feel it. He went too hard at the start, and he's tired. Lactic acid's a real misery. I let him ease a bit, but as we round the mid-point, I prepare to ask for more.

I'm not sure whether he has any left to give.

When I jostle the reins, his head whips up, and he plows forward, his ears pressed back. In the home-stretch, he really pushes, his powerful limbs moving even faster than they did at the start.

He's such a beautiful monster.

As we lumber past Lukas, his mouth's dangling open, his eyes impressively wide. That's not good. What time did we just run? I let Quicksilver cool down, but when I swing back around, Mr. Rimkus is arguing with Kristiana.

"—no way it's four furlongs. You must've measured wrong."

"At the end of the day, it's a practice track," she says. "You can't bring men in here to remeasure."

"I have a right to know exactly how fast he is," Mr. Rimkus says.

"What right is it that you have exactly?" Kris arches one eyebrow. "As Adriana's closest friend, I feel entitled to ask."

"It's a business arrangement between Ms. Strelkova and I, and it's confidential." But he looks ticked.

"What was our time?" I ask.

"A minute twenty-nine," Lukas says.

No wonder he's losing his mind. We just broke the world record by three seconds.

21

In the end, Kristiana's stuck agreeing that her track was probably shorter than she thought. It chafes for her, but it's better than them thinking that my horse is some kind of international champion in the making.

He is, clearly.

But the last thing I need is to have that thug breathing down my neck even harder, demanding I give him my amazing horse, or questioning where I bought him.

"Your fake papers won't hold up to international scrutiny," Kristiana says, once we're safely inside her house and Rimkus and Lukas have left. "You better make sure you pace off the other horses at the real race."

What a bizarre and strange turn of events. I've finally found a horse who could go *all the way*, but doing that would invite too many questions that we can't answer. Not to mention the pressure we'd have to breed him if he won. That thought makes me laugh.

"What?" Alexei asks, now human and dressed smartly again for our strategy session.

"Nothing," I say.

"We're planning to catch the villain of the century who wants me dead or alive it seems, and we're dealing with a thug whom I don't at all like," Kris says. "I think we could all use a little humor."

"I was just thinking that if Quicksilver goes out there and breaks a lot of world records, I could make an absolute killing selling his frozen semen."

It's worth a little irreverence to hear Alexei's strangled cough.

"You don't think the world needs a few more little Quicksilvers running around?"

Alexei turns toward me, and then he kicks his legs up on the coffee table right beside mine. "Actually, I think that's a great idea. Were you volunteering?"

My stomach does a cartwheel, and suddenly everyone's laughing—at my expense.

"All I'm saying," Kris says, "is that we need to keep things under a tighter leash on the day of the race."

"Agreed." I may be blushing, and they may have flipped my joke around on me, but Kristiana's point is a valid one. These are strange circumstances, so we need to be on our guard.

We all agree on a training schedule and begin planning the logistics and the times we think Leonid might show up. We've also crafted the press release saying that a horse jointly owned by Kristiana and me is racing. If that doesn't lure him, nothing will.

"How are the wedding plans coming?" I ask.

"Fine," Kristiana says.

"Liar. She's stopped doing anything," Mirdza says. "She's been too focused on this."

I'm sure it's hard to get excited about bridesmaids

and wedding registries when you know someone wants to snatch you and do who knows what to you.

Her phone rings, then. It's a client—their horse is tangled in barbed wire. I can't believe people still use that to pen animals in paddocks. Horses are always getting spooked and startled and running into it. The results are always catastrophic.

"I'll go with and help," Mirdza says.

"Me too," Grigoriy offers.

Aleks is meeting with someone about some kind of business thing—I suppose someone has to manage all their ridiculous piles of money. But when Alexei bangs on my front door, freaking out, there's no one else around to help.

"There's water going everywhere." It's moments like this that remind me that he missed a hundred years. "It seems to be coming from massive pipes at the front of the property. I throttled the flow, but now the entire property isn't getting water, and doesn't it need to go places, like water troughs?"

I follow him as calmly as I can manage, and after telling him to release the water pressure, I discover that it's coming from a busted water main. The men who were working on the power lines last week probably bumped one and with enough pressure, a leak can eventually become a burst. It takes me nearly ten minutes to figure out where the shut-off valve is, but then I can finally cut water to the entire barn without making Alexei stand there and do it himself.

But for a horse barn, no water is an emergency. Horses need water or they can colic and die.

"I'll fill the water troughs," Alexei says. "That's not a big deal."

"In case you haven't noticed," I hiss, "there are a dozen people on this property who have no idea what you can do. Or did you think it would be a good plan to just wander around, materializing water out of thin air?"

He frowns.

Kristiana doesn't pick up when I call, which means she's in the middle of saving a horse. I sigh as I start calling plumbers, but none of them are answering. Daugavpils isn't exactly a booming metropolis, so once I've worked my way through the first twenty, I'm down to just two left. I've officially reached the bottom of the barrel.

The second to last number's out of service. I dial the very last one without a lot of hope.

A woman answers.

"Hey there," I say. "I've got a busted water main, and I have over a hundred horses on property that need water. I'm hoping you can send your plumber out today to look at it."

"Of course," the young woman says. "I'll be there in less than an hour."

"Wait, you're the plumber?"

"I am," she says. "Is that a problem?"

"Of course not," I say. "You just don't meet too many female plumbers."

She hangs up. I hope I didn't tick her off.

When she arrives, I'm even more surprised. She parks and climbs out of a massive, lifted pink truck. She's young, she's perky, and she's wearing designer clothing. Her work bag's pink, and it's *Prada*. She looks like Monster Truck Barbie.

She drops the Prada bag on the ground like it's just any old canvas duffel. "Where's the busted main?"

I show her.

Surprisingly, she's competent.

Even while wielding a pink shovel.

"Did you need a hand or anything?" I ask.

"Maybe from that handsome one." She points at Alexei and smiles.

He looks decidedly uncomfortable.

"Actually, he has to help our trainer, John." I toss my head. "Remember, honey? You've got some work to do?"

Alexei's eyes light up. "Right. I almost forgot." He beams at me. "I'll be in the arena if you need me, angel."

Angel.

I hate how hearing him call me that makes me smile—like an idiot. I know it's fake. Under the guise of protecting him from a flirting plumber, I pretended we were together, and he went along with it. No biggie.

But for some reason, I'm standing here like an idiot, wishing it was real.

"You alright?" the pink plumber asks, her eyes sparkling in a knowing way.

"Of course." I hold out my hand. "Need me to dig?"

She shoves the end into the ground and leans on it. "Not really. I was just testing to see whether he was single."

"Oh."

"Looks like he's not."

I shrug.

"How long have you been together?"

This is getting awkward fast. "Not very long," I say.

"You look nice together," she says.

"I'm not much for boyfriends," I say. "The whole thing feels weird to me."

The woman smiles. "It should feel weird, but in a good way." Her eyebrows bounce. "If it doesn't, you're doing it wrong."

I can't help my snort.

"I've fixed it."

"Wait." I look at the main. "All you did was dig around it and. . ." I wrack my brain. Did she cut or replace any pipe?

She waves her hand and the dirt shifts, filling the hole.

My breath catches.

"Relax, Adriana." In front of my eyes, the pink, polished princess flickers. She's suddenly a hundred-year-old crone.

And then she's back. A polished princess again.

"My name's Baba Yaga, and I thought I should come by for a chat. I apologize for any stress over the plumbing."

My mouth's drier than arena footing in midsummer. "I—you're *Baba Yaga*? The Russian witch who lived in a house with chicken legs that moved around? Did you really make stew with small children?"

She's still smiling, so maybe none of that is true.

But what if she's smiling because *it all is*?

"Your sister and I met at her recent show. Did she tell you?"

I shake my head.

"I wasn't sure whether she'd recognize me."

"I—should I call Alexei back?"

She shakes her head. "I came to talk to you, Adriana."

"You did?"

"Men are pushy, always demanding more."

I'm not sure what to say about that.

"Plumbing's interesting, you know, following the rules of water." She circles the main, staring at it intently. "Water's even more fascinating than the plumbing itself. Without water, everything on earth would die. But with too much water, things either rot or drown." She glances at me, her perfectly puckered pink lips quite bizarre now that I've seen her old lady form.

"I guess so."

"Your young man has the best power of the five, I think. He's able to ensure that the balance of life is just right. Not too much water, but not a lack either. Perfect balance has always been the ideal."

"Where did they come from? The powers, I mean?"

Her laughter's like the warble of a nightingale. Like the rushing of a river. Like the susurration of a hummingbird's wing, at once small and also all-encompassing. "Mother nature. I think that's what you humans call the force that created me these days. It sounds benevolent with that name, but it's not really like that. The earth herself does have a consciousness, and it's vaster than you can possibly imagine. I'm but one of many handmaidens who serve her. I've always served this continent, and that means I'm a caretaker for her people as well."

"You—oh."

"It's hard for you to comprehend, I understand. But if I'm right, I think you may understand me better than any of the others. You, too, are brash. You, too, have made mistakes."

"You made mistakes?"

"Really just the one." She tilts her head, and the eyes staring at me are ancient.

And very, very sad.

"My one mistake led me to an experience a handmaiden never should have had." She sighs.

"What?" I blink.

"I've never told another soul, but I've watched you, and I've decided to share this with you." She steps closer, and I don't retreat. "I fell for someone.

Someone not unlike your man." She tosses her head toward the barn. "Tall. Handsome. Intelligent. *Off-limits*."

"A man?"

This time, her laughter's bright and happy with just one note of sorrow. "Our time together was glorious, Adriana. Glorious."

Who's she talking about? "Anyone I've heard of?"

She shrugs. "His name was Rurik—sometimes called Riurik. He was a Viking king."

Holy ergot.

"When he asked me for a boon, to keep our daughter safe, I couldn't bear to deny him."

Her *daughter*? A chill runs down my spine. The second child of Riurik that the secret records mention was the forbidden love child of the Earth's handmaiden and the conquering King of Russia?

"The boon he asked for—I was blinded by our love. It made me stupid." She's revisiting memories now, her eyes almost wistful. "All of Russia's children are mine—not just Riurik's. I forgot that for a time."

"So, you. . ."

"My power as a caretaker works much the same way that water does, you know. It flows, it ebbs, and it consumes. But once the valve has been flipped, it can't be closed." Her eyes swing back to mine, and they're *vast*. The emotions I see swirling in them can't all be identified.

"You gifted them with earth, wind, fire, water, and electricity," I say.

"I gave all five of those powers to the children of my beloved, but then my fickle Riurik, he and I fought. His vision for Russia and mine weren't the same." She sighs. "During a time when we were arguing, he fell for another woman, someone like him, someone simpler.

With her, he had another child." She swallows slowly. "He turned from me once he had what he really wanted in the first place."

Oh, no.

"A son."

"Were you angry?" I ask.

"I was broken." Her eyes are haunted.

"But at least you still had a daughter."

"They often ignored females then." Her voice is bitter. "Her life wasn't easy."

"Are you angry? Did you hate the son he had with the other woman?"

When she faces me again, she's fully in the present. "I'm not a woman. I'm *all* women. Those other children, they are also mine. I forgot that truth for a time. But I remembered—his other child, he was also mine. All of Russia's children are mine."

This is so weird.

"There's a reason fraternization with humans is forbidden to those like me," she says. "When Riurik's line failed, when no one was left to lead the Russian people, and then when good people came and begged for my help so that they, like the Riurkin, could effectively rule, I tried to set things right."

"What does that mean?"

"Have you heard of the Time of Troubles?"

"That's the decade before the Romanovs took over," I say.

She smiles. "I helped to end that. I flipped more valves, this time splitting my power into the five more-or-less discrete pieces you mentioned the noble families having so that no one person could control it all."

"But?" I arch one eyebrow.

"It all comes from the same place," she says. "I thought Riurik's line was gone. I couldn't sense any of them. That's why I did it." She snaps, and the water main bursts again. "But I was wrong. They had simply moved too far out of my sphere for me to sense their existence. They hadn't tried to access the water main in so long, I thought the valve had frozen shut."

I step back, but I'm too late. I'm already drenched.

Although she hasn't moved, although the water rains down all over her, Baba Yaga remains utterly dry. She's not a crone, and she's not a maiden. Now she probably looks forty years old, but her eyes are ancient —dark and intent. She clearly thinks that what she's saying next is the most important piece of information she'll be sharing.

"The water all comes from the same place, Adriana, from the same main." Her words are barely audible over the roar of the water. "Do you understand me? Only the highest valve up each line controls it."

I shake my head. "What does that mean?"

She snaps again.

The water stops.

But this time, she and her ghastly truck are both gone.

22

The pink truck.

The Prada duffle.

Monster Truck Barbie and all her matching accessories, gone with a snap of her fingers.

"You're saying she was here, on my family farm?" Kristiana looks like her head might explode.

"She did the same thing to me," Mirdza says. "She was here, talking, and then she was just gone."

Kris is pacing. "I hate her. Why can't she tell us enough? What's with this cryptic garbage? Is she on our side or not?"

"I think she's on humanity's side," I say. "It was like she was trying to explain something basic to me with the water analogy."

"What did she say *exactly*?" Alexei asks.

"She asked me if I had heard of the Time of Troubles." I start pacing, too, like a horse kept too long in her stall. If we're not careful, we may wear Kristiana's kitchen tile down to the wooden framework underneath. "I said I had. And then she said that she helped the Romanovs take over. She said she flipped more valves, splitting the power from the main one into five pieces so that no one person could control it all."

"No *one* person can control it all," Kris says. "But Leonid can use fire and electricity."

"She did say something else at the end. She said it all comes from the same place." I think about the last thing she said. "Right before she disappeared, she said, 'I thought Riurik's line was gone. That's why I did it.' It was almost like she was saying his line *wasn't* gone. Leonid says he's the real heir, right?"

"Maybe he is," Alexei says. "Does that mean—" He stands up. "But you said you saw Boris using electricity, right?"

I nod slowly.

"It comes from the same place." Alexei's pacing now too, and I'm worried he'll slam into Kristiana or me.

"The very last thing she said was something about the water coming from the same main." I shake my head. "But if that's true, then why can Boris and Leonid both use it?"

"You can split it off with valves, but if you split it, the flow strength can go down," Mirdza says. "Maybe it's something like that."

"I hate this," Kris says. "Why can't she just be clear?" She hops over the back of the living room couch and flops backward, staring up at the ceiling.

"It felt like she was warning us," I say. "Like she wants to help us, but she's not sure how."

"But if Leonid is Riurik's line, isn't he her child?" Kristiana sits up, her eyes wide.

I shake my head. "Maybe, but maybe not. She was pretty upset when she said Riurik moved on from her. I think his son was not hers—but she'd already made him the promise that his kids would have those powers or something."

Kris's mouth forms into a big, round O. "That sucks."

"Right?" I snort. "That's why you can't ever really trust a guy."

"By that logic, you can't trust anyone," Grigoriy says. "Male or female."

"I guess." I cross my arms. "None of us ever really know what'll happen next in our lives."

Alexei stops pacing and turns toward me. "But the surprises are not as bad when you have someone you love standing beside you."

Grigoriy wraps an arm around Mirdza and presses a kiss to her temple.

"You two are irritating," Kris says.

"You're just saying that because Aleks isn't back yet." Mirdza leans her head against Grigoriy's chest.

Even after Aleks comes back, we can't decipher much more from Baba Yaga's visit, sadly. We go round and round, not figuring out much more, hammering out our plan for the race, prepping Quicksilver, and pacing his runs to make sure they're not outrageously fast.

And then it's finally time.

Alexei isn't too keen on going to stay at the race-track for several days.

"I told you," I say. "I'm going to be staying at a hotel next to it, and I'll spend all day with you. You won't be stuck in a box all day."

"That's some dedication," Kris says as she helps me hook up the trailer. "You know, when I was riding Aleksandr, I often slept in the stall with him. I said it was to keep an eye on him, but it was really because I wanted to be with him all the time."

Alexei's smiling now. Probably thinks it's some big joke.

"Stop," I say. "He's doing me a favor, so the least I can do is stay close to keep an eye on things."

"Sure," Kris says. "That, too." But she's smirking when Alexei shifts, and she's smiling a self-satisfied smile that really irritates me as she watches us drive away.

When we pull up at the race track, I expect Lukas to be waiting for us. I do *not* expect my Russian friend Gavriil to be standing beside him.

"How on earth did you get that beast out of Russia?" He looks utterly shocked. "I could have sworn he just disappeared."

"Russia, huh?" Lukas whistles. "I had no idea there were such epic horses there. I may need to book a trip."

"Not like this one," I say. "He's a rarity in Russia, too."

"Is he calmer now?" Gavriil eyes the stallion through the window of the trailer.

I wish I could say he was, but I have a feeling Quicksilver's going to be just as naughty. "He's good for me."

"He always was." Gavriil frowns.

"What are you doing here, anyway?" I ask.

"If you're alright," Lukas says, "I'll circle back for the workout tomorrow."

I wave him off, half wishing that Gavriil would leave with him. I'm not sure what to expect from Quicksilver when I unload, but there's no way to put it off. I finally unclip him through the window, whispering, "Please behave. I'll get rid of him as fast as I can, alright?"

Quicksilver stomps.

I hope that means yes.

I drop the back gate, undo the butt bar, and make a clicking sound to get him to back out. He's calm and slow, and he stops right in front of me, thankfully.

"Wow, he is better," Gavriil says. "But let's talk about why I'm here over lunch. You can drop him off and—"

Quicksilver tosses his head, snapping at Gavriil.

"I usually stay with him for a while after I move him somewhere new. He's a little. . .temperamental."

"I can see that." Gavriil sighs. "I've got plenty of time. I'll wait with you."

And he does, sticking to me like white on rice. At least Quicksilver doesn't actually bite him again. Pinned ears, snapping motions, but no teeth in flesh. Part of that is because Gavriil's so fast about moving away.

"He really seems to hate me." His usually kind eyes are wary. "Horses usually like me. I can't figure it out." He shakes his finger. "I saved you, you idiot."

Quicksilver doesn't seem to care, but he does let me lead him into his stall. "I'll just hang out here." I drag a step stool over and sit down.

Gavriil moves a little farther away, but he also brings a stool and sits. "Well, this isn't exactly the atmosphere I was hoping for, but I guess it'll have to do."

Atmosphere?

"You already know that my dad and I have fought for years," Gavriil says. "He wants me to get married and take over the family business."

"I get that," I say. "If I had a family business, I'd want that too, probably."

"But the woman I fell for likes horses," he says.

"The only time I ever saw her was at races." His eyes are utterly serious.

I'm worried he's talking about me. "I told you, Gav. I don't date."

He sighs. "I know, and I know why, too. But you've known me for years. I'm not like other guys. I'm kind and caring. I'm smart, and I'm a good person. Thanks to my dad, I'm also rich. Which means I can support you in any horse stuff you want to do."

Quicksilver lunges at the side of the stall, hitting it so hard that the entire wall shakes.

Gavriil jumps to his feet, upending his stool, and swears loudly. "What's wrong with him?"

"He's tem—"

"Temperamental, yes, I've heard." He flips Quicksilver off with both hands. "I hate you, you stupid jerk of a horse. I'm glad you're stuck in that stall, and I hope you choke on your grain and die."

I can't help laughing.

"I know you're about to race him," he says. "But even that makes me nervous. He's not safe—there's something wrong with him."

"I think I'll be alright." I shove my hand through the slats, and Quicksilver presses his face against my fingers.

"Why doesn't he ever bite you?" he asks.

"I think he loves me." I expect the massive grey to snort or shake his head or do that half-laugh thing he does.

But he just rubs his head against my hand and whickers.

"I think he does love you," Gavriil says slowly, like realization is dawning. "It's like he's jealous that I'm even here, which I know is nuts, but that horse acts like a man." He frowns. He blinks. And then he turns toward me slowly, his eyes narrowed. "Adriana." Just as I think he's going to figure it out, he shakes his head and laughs. "Never mind."

Gavriil is really, really smart. He was right about that. Even after several days with Quicksilver, I didn't come close to suspecting the truth. But I'm also smart. Smart enough to know by now that Alexei isn't really in love with me. He hasn't done a single flirty thing or made any kind of move since our talk—since he told me his mom wanted a princess for him. Anything he might have felt at the start, when he'd been isolated for so long, was short-lived.

Other than our shared love for horses, we aren't a good match.

"Gav, I know you're a good person. I can't believe you came all this way, though. You and I aren't—"

He takes my free hand in both of his. "Don't just reject me without thinking about it, because we're perfect. You're tempestuous and exciting. My dad and mom set me up with women all the time, but you're the only person I ever think about. You're brilliant and fast and furious. I love that about you. I always have. And I have the resources to give you a million horses like this one, but they'll be well trained and not at all temperamental."

Quicksilver freezes, his nostrils flaring, his face poked through the stall slats.

"Marry me, Adriana. Move with me to Russia. Let me take care of you, and I promise I'll always let you run as wild and free as you like."

"How touching," Mr. Rimkus says.

I yank both my hands away, ball them into tight fists, and shove them down at my sides. "I thought you were coming tomorrow."

"I wanted to touch base today," Mr. Rimkus says.

"And I'm glad I did." He arches one eyebrow at Gavriil. "Who is this dashing prince charming?"

"He's no one," I say.

"I'm her boyfriend," Gavriil says. "Who are *you?*"

"What is it about this woman?" Mr. Rimkus asks. "Why are all the men around you perpetually in heat?" His smile twists. "I don't normally fancy small, thin twigs like you, but I find myself almost hoping you lose the race next week. Far be it from me to join the ranks of your pathetic suitors, but I feel the need to research the object of such obsession."

"What's he talking about?" Gavriil's scowling.

"Just ignore him," I whisper. "It's nothing."

But Gavriil's shoulders square and he steps forward. "I don't like the way you're talking to her. Apologize."

Mr. Rimkus was already smiling, but it broadens. "I'm not sure we've had the pleasure of making our introductions yet, but I always enjoy making new friends."

"Unnecessary." I grab Gavriil's hand. "After next week, when Quicksilver and I win, I won't be acquainted with Mr. Rimkus anymore."

But Gav's not letting it go. "I'm not sure you should be acquainted with him now."

An image of Gavriil, a bullet hole blooming in the center of his forehead, flashes through my mind, and I quiver. "No," I whisper. "Please just let it go."

"She seems to really like you." Mr. Rimkus tilts his head like a bird watching something from a branch far above. "Curious. I thought she never really fancied anyone. I thought she fancied women, honestly."

"Shut your mouth," Gavriil says.

I tighten my fingers around his. "Just ignore him," I beg. "Please."

The water hose on the end of the row starts spraying, water spewing hard and fast.

All over Mr. Rimkus.

He splutters, spinning around, his eyes wide and angry. "Who did that?"

But no one's anywhere near the hose.

I know what happened, of course, but no one else has any idea.

Mr. Rimkus heads toward the hose, intending to turn it off, perhaps, but he just gets more and more soaked.

Gavriil's laughing.

I shake my head tightly. "Don't laugh."

When Mr. Rimkus gives up on shutting it off and turns back toward us, he looks like a drowned rat. He never really looks angry, at least not that I've seen, but he's clearly fuming now. "I'll be back tomorrow, and I won't come alone."

The hose magically shuts off the second he's gone.

"What on earth was that?" Gavriil asks.

"How about this?" I ask. "I'm starving, but I need to talk to someone about the water, and I need to make sure Quicksilver has calmed down."

"I'll go get you food," Gavriil says, "but I'm looking into that man, too. I don't like him, and I hate that he's anywhere near you."

"Same," I whisper. "But he's a very connected, very dangerous Lithuanian arms dealer. I need you to listen to me, Gavriil. I have this under control. Please let it go."

He stares at me for a long time, but finally, he nods and leaves.

I'm guessing he's the easy one to convince—the hose sprayer is probably way angrier. When I circle toward the stall, Quicksilver looks *ticked.* I duck into the stall, and he snorts. "I know. You didn't like him from the start."

He paws the shavings until the mats underneath are exposed.

"You want to change so we can talk."

He nods.

"You can't do that," I whisper. "There are too many people around here."

He bumps my wrist with his nose.

My watch? Maybe he's saying he'll do it later if I tell him no right now. I glance up and down the aisle to see whether anyone is there. Then I notice the CCTV at the end of the row. I point. "That's a recorded image."

He huffs.

No matter what I tell him, I can't actually stop him.

He bumps my watch again. Then he opens his mouth and mimics chewing even though there's nothing in it.

"You're worried about Gavriil because he went to get food and he'll be back soon?"

He nods again.

For the love. "You're supposed to rest in your stall for the day," I say. "I can't take you anywhere."

He starts pawing the floor and slamming the edge of the stall with his shoulder.

"You're going to hurt yourself," I say. "Stop that."

He snorts.

I keep forgetting that he can heal—the guys said he's the only one among them who can heal himself thanks to his water power. How fabulous. "Great. Then you can throw as many tantrums as you want. I don't care."

He rolls his eye. Another thing I've never seen from a horse. Gavriil has already noticed he's not normal. If he keeps acting like this with him around. . .

I finally throw the halter on Quicksilver and grab the bag I brought that's loaded with clothes for him in case of emergency. "Fine. Let's go for a walk."

The looks from the grooms are not great. And Lukas acts like he's going to punch me, but finally I get past them all. It takes nearly thirty minutes of walking to get to a place that's not full of people, and I'm sweating by the time we reach the edge of the property. We circle around the back of the storage building, and we're finally alone, assuming there's no one in any of the cars parked around the corner.

I chuck his bag on the ground. "There. Change, you diva."

He doesn't wait for me to take off the halter or look away—he's too impatient after all that. I can't help laughing at him choking as he unbuckles the halter. But then I really look, and I regret not looking away right off.

Because now I can't stop staring.

Holy sloughing ergots, he's absolutely gorgeous. The David would be jade green if he were here, staring at the beauty that is Alexei Romanov, but he'd also get an earful.

Because my Grecian god is really, really angry.

"What were you thinking, not telling us more about that man? He's an *arms dealer?*" He's shoving his legs into his pants so fast that I worry something important will get caught. "I should've let Grigoriy kill him."

"In one week, when we win that race, I'll never see him again."

"Think again," Alexei says. "Men like that never let go of something they desire."

I laugh. "He doesn't even like me."

He shakes his head. "He's sick, Adriana, and now he

does want you. He's always wanted everything that other men wanted, and now that's become you."

"Hardly," I say. "We have a deal—"

"Deals mean nothing to men without honor." He shoves his hands into the sleeves of the shirt, but he doesn't bother doing the buttons. He starts toward me, his face stormy. "I didn't want to press, but you should've told me about your deal before."

When he comes after me like that, I can't help it. I back up.

His eyes flash. "How am I supposed to keep you safe when I don't know what danger you're in?"

My back hits the metal wall of the warehouse, but it doesn't matter. I'm done retreating. "You're not supposed to keep me safe." I fold my arms and glare.

Alexei's aristocratic nose rises, and he slams one hand against the wall, busting his knuckles open. He doesn't even seem to notice the blood dripping down them and dropping on the ground. "Yes, I am."

I chuckle. "I'm sorry, but I think you've forgotten. Or maybe you're a little more like Mr. Rimkus than you think. You want a *princess*, and I'm a gutter rat."

Alexei leans down slowly. "You're a glorious goddess, Adriana Strelkova, and the only one who doesn't see that is you." His lips are right in front of me, and I can't see anything else. "I lied to you—told you what you wanted to hear so you'd stop hissing and arching your back every time I came close. From the moment I woke up, you've been the only woman I've even seen."

The world narrows to one single point in space and time. "You—you lied?"

"I'm done lying now," he says. "I'm done waiting for you to come to me. I'm done letting you drive me around like I'm actually a horse. I'm not a horse. I'm a man—your man. And I'm going to kill that disgusting pile of filth who keeps looking at you like he wants to degrade you."

My hands reach up and grab both sides of his face and drag his mouth down to meet mine. The explosion when our mouths meet is unlike anything I ever imagined. He doesn't kiss me—he claims me. He brands me. He *consumes* me.

And I don't even want to stop him.

My hands slide upward, my fingers lacing through his hair. His hands grip my hips and lift, bringing me up hard against the back of the storage room wall, and then his body closes the space between us, pressing against me until there's no space left.

He's so hard and unyielding, so possessive and demanding, that I ought to hate it. But instead, like a cat arching against the exact right pressure, I *purr*. "Yes," I murmur. "More."

Thankfully, Alexei seems to know just what I want —what I need. I wrap my legs around him, my hands drifting down as his mouth explores the side of my neck. I'm moaning, when I hear it.

"You have got to be kidding me."

"At least it's not the inside of that crappy old barn," Kristiana says. "Though, the side of a warehouse might be worse."

My eyes fly open. Mirdza, Kristiana, Grigoriy, and Aleksandr are all staring at us. Aleksandr's laughing. Grigoriy's beaming.

Kristiana looks irritated.

At least Mirdza's properly horrified that I'm straddling Alexei in a fairly public place.

"How did you—why are you even here?" I drop to my feet, bracing my hand against Alexei's firm chest.

"Your *boyfriend* Gavriil called," Mirdza says. "He was

frantic. He got back with food, and you were gone. He was convinced 'that filthy Lithuanian' had kidnapped you."

"He's making a police report now," Kristiana says. "But a groom mentioned he'd seen you walking this way."

"Also." Aleksandr lifts both eyebrows, nods, and smirks.

"Nice work, man," Grigoriy says. "It's about time."

❧ 23 ❧

"That's when I got with Kris," Aleks says. "Before a race." He's smirking, and I hate it.

"We aren't together," I say.

"That makes sense," Mirdza says. "I usually try to eat men's faces off when we aren't dating."

"Shut up," I say.

"I'm confused," Kristiana says. "What on earth is Gavriil doing here? And why does he think you're his girlfriend?"

"He's terminally stupid," Alexei says. "That's why. She turned him down."

"I did tell him no," I say. "But when Rimkus showed up, I might have acted like he was my boyfriend. It seemed simpler than trying to explain—"

"That you were dating your horse?" Alexei's lip's twitching, and something deep inside my stomach flutters.

What's wrong with me?

"You all have horrible timing," Alexei says. "Have I mentioned that?"

"Sorry about that." Aleksandr looks a little embar-

248

rassed. "If I'd known, I would've delayed at least a half an hour."

"Half an hour?" Mirdza asks. "Five minutes would have been more than enough. In half an hour, I'd have wound up with a niece or nephew on the way."

I'm going to sink into the ground beneath our feet. "What you saw was just a lapse in judgment." But my tone isn't nearly as commanding as it usually is. Being embarrassed sucks.

Alexei takes my hand, sliding his fingers between mine. "No, it wasn't."

Mirdza's eyebrows rise.

I ought to rip him a new one. I should shout and yank my hand away, but I can't quite bring myself to do it.

"So this Lithuanian," Grigoriy asks. "He's dying, no?"

"What is with you men, always jumping straight to that?" Mirdza asks.

"It's the women who suffer when you stomp around killing people," Kristiana says.

"We do it *for* the women," Grigoriy says.

"Once he dies, then another guy just like him pops up to take his place." Mirdza's voice is small. "Elimination like that isn't a solution."

"That's true—this guy is the last guy's brother," I say.

"What would be better?" Alexei asks.

I shrug. "I just want to get through the race."

"That's a little ostrich of you," Kris says. "And then what? When he still won't let you go, what will you do?"

I puff out my chest. "I could marry Gavriil and run away to Russia."

Alexei drags me closer and releases my hand. . .so

he can wrap his arm around my shoulders. "I thought you didn't want me to kill anyone."

That makes me laugh.

"You're mine." He stares at me, daring me to challenge him.

"I don't belong to anyone," I say firmly, meeting his eyes to make sure he's getting it. "But I will admit that I have *considered* dating you."

The goofy grin that spreads across his face is nothing to the shouts and hoots from the other four idiots.

"Stop," Alexei says. "Or you dummies will change her mind."

Mirdza's grinning bigger than any of the others. "I'm proud of you."

I roll my eyes, expecting another joke. "At what?"

"When you weren't dating, that meant Mārtinš was winning. Now you're finally beating him."

That floors me. "Why?"

"If you don't do things you want to do because of him, that's letting him control your life. Now that you're finally doing what *you* want, without regard for him, you've beaten him."

I hate when she's so clearly right. Being the dumb one really sucks.

Alexei's brushing the hair back off my face when Gavriil comes jogging around the corner. He stops dead, his eyes wide.

Then his shoulders droop.

"Gav." I step away from Alexei. I expect him to try and stop me, but he lets me go.

"Gavriil," I say, louder this time.

My old friend swallows. "So all the stuff about never dating, that wasn't true. You just didn't want to date me." He's utterly still.

"It was true," I say. "I never dated anyone." I pause.

"So that guy is. . ." Gavriil's staring at me, intently. I can tell we're at the edge of something here. If I tell him Alexei is nothing, it'll hurt Alexei, and Gav will double down. I can't have that. So it's time to rip the band-aid off.

"He is my boyfriend." I shake my head. "It's brand new, though. Like, it *just* started."

I expect him to argue or try and convince me, but he doesn't. Gavriil nods woodenly, turns around, and starts to walk away. He's almost back to the corner of the building when he pauses and turns slowly. "I'm glad you're alright." His eyes shift past me. "Take good care of her. If you screw up, you won't get a second chance."

That's the thing about the good guys. They don't stick around when they know they aren't wanted. It makes my heart hurt a little bit, though. If Mārtiņš hadn't broken me, I might have started dating him a long time ago.

Although, then I wouldn't have met Alexei. . . Gavriil's a good guy.

He's just not the *right* guy.

"That was awkward," Grigoriy says.

"I thought it was fun," Aleksandr says. "I've been missing out on everything like this lately. I guess that's my punishment for being the responsible one who woke up first."

"We all appreciate it," Alexei says.

"What has been so important?" I ask.

"We're having some of Alexei's property reinstated," he says. "Yesterday, we got confirmation on the DNA—they've officially recognized that he's the Romanov heir, after literally thousands of fake ones. It'll hit the news outlets soon. Maybe tomorrow."

That's going to be fun.

"I've also been working with him to set up some ways to monetize the water magic." Aleksandr's good at that stuff. Mirdza says he helped Grigoriy turn his air power into money, too.

"It'll be good for him to spend a little time as a horse," Aleks says.

"I'm not so sure," Alexei mutters.

I can't help laughing.

Alexei's eyes light up again. "If we just kill that pervert, we don't need to race at all, right?"

"Think again, lover boy," Mirdza says. "That race is our trap."

He sighs. "Right."

"Speaking of," Kristiana says. "Time to go furry again."

"Maybe don't say that," I say. "That's actually a word they use for—"

All five of them are staring at me, brows furrowed.

"Never mind." I can't believe they're all so naive. "Alright." I point at the bag. "Time to shift back."

"You two, turn around," Aleksandr says.

"Why?" Mirdza asks. "You never seem to care who's around."

Grigoriy covers her eyes himself. "Naughty."

Mirdza's laughing.

Alexei doesn't shift though. He steps closer, wrapping one arm around my waist and dragging me right up next to him. "Did you mean it?"

"Mean what?" I look up at his face.

"What you said—that you were softening toward the idea of us."

Us.

The word vibrates through me, leaving me trembling. "I did."

His head lowers slowly then, his lips brushing

lightly against mine. "Mine." That one word is rough—practically weighed down with emotion. "I want you for mine, forever."

I go up on tiptoe and kiss him back, but forcefully this time.

His arms tighten, and his mouth opens, like he means to show me that we'll be mixed up together until the end of time. What's stranger is that it doesn't scare me.

At all.

"Come on. Let's go, man," Grigoriy says.

"Gavriil already showed up," Aleks says. "The police are next, and if you're not a horse by then, we'll have a lot to explain."

The inventive way Alexei uses swear words endears me to him just a little more, but I hate that he's changing into his horse form now—and that he'll be stuck in it for the next few days. It's terrible timing.

This time, Mirdza and Kristiana turn around without complaint, but I don't. Alexei's smiling as he strips, and I'm the one feeling pretty miserable when he shifts into a massive grey horse.

I mean, I love horses. I really do. But for once, I was really sad to see this beauty show up.

"I might like Adriana-in-love," Mirdza says.

"Hey." I shake my head. "Don't use that word."

Mirdza's smirking at Kris, and I don't like it.

Apparently Quicksilver doesn't either, because he bumps past them a little forcefully, splitting the two of them up as he trots ahead.

"Wait," I say. "You're not haltered."

And of course, that's when the police appear around the corner.

"Stop," I shout. "We've been chasing him around

back here forever. Be quiet and be still, and I think I can catch him."

A little quick thinking, and we've got our cover story.

Gavriil wouldn't believe it, but he's not there. When I ask around later, it turns out he was already heading back home. It makes me a little sad—I don't exactly have loads of friends—but I don't regret my decision. Even when I follow Quicksilver back, and I'm stuck sitting outside his stall while a dozen different people come to take my statement, I don't regret anything.

In fact, I catch myself smiling like an idiot over and over all day long.

From the moment I woke up, you've been the only woman I've even seen.

Aaaaand, I'm doing it again. Grinning like a complete moron.

"What's making you smile so much?" Mirdza asks.

I stand up, my face going blank. "Nothing."

She leans against the stall. "Liar." She's smiling now, too. "You look like I felt the day Alexei healed my leg."

I roll my eyes.

"Admit it," she says. "Something has healed in you since you met him. You're *happy*."

I shake my head. "I'm normal."

"In the twenty-six years we've been alive, I'm not sure I recall ever seeing you happy, you know? That's really, really sad."

Now that I think about it, she's right. "We never had much to be happy about," I say. "That's not our fault."

"I'm not sure that's true," Mirdza says. "But no one ever taught us to focus on the good things, that's for sure."

"Why are you here?"

"The guys are kind of obsessed," she says. "They're working on something—but while they're busy, they're sending me and Kris to check on you and look some stuff up."

"But Kris can't leave the property without one of them."

Mirdza nods. "They're right to require that. There's a reason Leonid wants her, and it's not a good one."

I can't argue with that.

"I'm fine, though," I say. "I'm with Alexei, remember?" Saying that out loud sends a tiny shiver through me.

"Are you worried?"

"Nah. I'm not the one who has to traipse around on my own after the race," I say. "Is Kristiana nervous?"

Mirdza looks a little worried herself. "She's not, and that feels wrong to me."

By general consensus, I'm not allowed to leave Alexei's side without one of the other guys around to escort me. At least Mirdza brought me a sleeping bag and bedroll, but let me tell you. Sleeping in a stall with a horse isn't exactly romantic.

Giant poops.

Enormous pee.

It's definitely a little different when you know the horse is a human who's *aware*. Stallions are always neat, but this... He won't dirty his stall until I step out, and I'm stuck cleaning it up when I come back in, and. . .it's weird.

There are good things too, though. When I'm crouched over his neck, and we're flying around the track, entirely in sync, I can whisper thoughts and he follows them. . .I've never experienced anything like that connection with a regular horse. And when I wake up in the middle of the night, and I'm sleeping against his huge, warm body, my head cradled next to his massive, soft shoulder, I've never felt more safe.

It's weird.

All of it is really strange, but it's also beautiful in a way I never expected to find. To be honest, I didn't think something like this would ever exist, not with a man or a beast.

Because I trust him.

When we're on the track and when we're not. I believe he'll keep me safe. I believe he wants to take care of me, and he listens, too.

Between training and last-minute details, even with our friends on guard, the next four days fly by. Surprisingly, Mr. Rimkus doesn't come by again. Maybe he's afraid of demonic hoses. Maybe he's just not as excited to come threaten me, now that my last memory of him was of him stumbling away, water dripping from every part of his body. Even thinking about it makes me laugh.

Either way, I take the win.

But the day of the race, he shows up, just like I knew he would. I'm dressed and ready, about to take Quicksilver out for a little warm up when I hear him.

"Miss Strelkova. I heard your Russian friend went home. I'm delighted to find you here. Alone again." His smile's filthy.

"I wish I could say the same," I say. "But I'm ready for the race. So is Quicksilver." I slide the stall door open a hair, not that Alexei would need to physically block him. His hose trick shows that he can find other ways.

"I just wanted to make sure you remember the terms of our bargain."

"Of course I do," I whisper. "You leave my mother alone, and when I win, you leave me alone too."

"Yes, but if you don't win." He smiles. "Then I *own* you."

Quicksilver's already at the edge of the stall, but his nose shoves against the door and he's snorting and huffing, his nostrils flared.

"I remember."

"If you lose, I lose money—quite a lot of money. Nothing makes me quite as angry as losing money." His head tilts, and he looks me over, from foot to head. "But I'll have a chance to do something I've been dreaming about for a while now." He's so unassuming, this small brother of Nojus. He's so mid—so utterly average. I'm still surprised that someone so regular can be so disgusting. When he lifts his hand and presses one finger against my cheek, dragging it down the side of my face, I'm filled with utter and complete dread.

Quicksilver shoves the door open and bursts through, exploding past me and knocking Mr. Rimkus backward. He lifts one huge hoof and slams it against his chest, barely easing up before shattering Mr. Rimkus's chest like a melon.

Rimkus coughs and blood splatters all over Quicksilver's leg. "What the—?"

"Racehorses are known for having bad ground manners." I should regret what happened—the last thing I need to do is make him angrier.

"Is that Ramūnas Rimkus?" There are half a dozen armed policeman, guns raised. They're gesturing at Nojus's brother, lying prone under Quicksilver's hoof.

I nod.

"We have an arrest warrant for him," the one in front says. "Can you get the horse off him?" The cop looks pretty nervous about Quicksilver, and I don't blame him.

My stallion looks absolutely insane—mane blowing, nostrils flaring, massive muscles taut.

"I can halter him," I say.

Quicksilver lets me slide a halter over his face easily, then backs up when I ask, like he's a lost puppy dog. "What's he being arrested for?"

"A longer list than you could ever imagine," the officer says. "We have a confidential informant who just handed a whole pile of evidence over on dozens of men, all of them connected with this guy." He shrugs. "It's the most impressive takedown our department has ever had."

Holding my horse still and steady is simple as they cuff Mr. Rimkus and walk him away. But I notice something on the ground as I'm circling Quicksilver around, and I reach down and grab it.

It's a claim ticket.

His bet was placed with a cash wire.

Ten million euros with an independent company out of Las Vegas that's not subject to the same limits.

The odds on Quicksilver, as he's an unknown, are ridiculous.

I ought to hand this over to the cops, probably, but there's not a chance I'm doing that.

I can't help smiling as I work Quicksilver. I should be nervous, but I'm not. There's not a single horse that can beat us today, and now, it doesn't matter, even if there is. A weight I didn't realize I was feeling has been lifted.

I know it was the guys, working to help me and Alexei. I should be annoyed that they stepped in to fix my problem. Old Adriana would have been. Instead, I feel nothing but relief.

Is this what having a family feels like?

The normal pre-race stuff flies by, with both Mirdza and Kris nearby wishing me well. The guys are in place, our plan laid. Grigoriy's working the perimeter, with Aleksandr sticking near the girls. Kristiana won't head out on her own until after it's over and we're *sure* that Leonid and his men haven't shown up.

Yeah, right.

"There's a chance they won't bite," Mirdza says. "They've shown up at two different public events, and each time they didn't catch us. They may skip this one."

"Then we could move things back to the wedding," I say.

Mirdza shakes her head. "Kris was so relieved when we nixed that and went back to a small ceremony. I don't think Aleks would have the heart to go back to it again."

Quicksilver's dancing around a little more than usual. I can't tell whether he wants my attention or he's just a bit nervous.

"Whoa," Mirdza says. "Look at that."

A jockey I've never seen in colors I don't know prances up on a striking golden pony. A *palomino*, which isn't that notable, except there are almost no palomino thoroughbreds in the world. The ones that exist are usually sold so fast that they never make it to a little track like this one.

I've certainly never raced against one.

Actually, I've never even *seen* one before today.

"That's a palomino mare," Mirdza says. "Wow. She's stunning."

Quicksilver's head twists around so fast that I find myself gritting my teeth. Does he really care what another horse looks like? "She is beautiful," I begrudgingly say.

Why am I feeling jealous about a palomino mare? I should be jealous of her owner. But why's Quicksilver still looking at her?

He whinnies then, loud and long, which he *never* does. Not unless he's trying to get my attention, anyway. Unlike other horses, he's never herd sour, or barn sour, or calling out to other horses.

But the palomino mare's head whips toward him immediately, and her head and ears both perk up.

She screams right back.

"Do you *know* her?" Mirdza asks, her voice dropping to a whisper. "Is she. . .one of you?"

Quicksilver paws the ground.

And then he nods.

24

I'd been counting on winning.

I mean, what horse can beat a magical freak of nature? All the guys in their horse forms are unbelievably talented. It must be part of the magic, but they run faster, jump higher, and they can *think*.

It's a deadly combination.

But it never occurred to me that there might be another one running against us in this race. "I'm suddenly wishing we'd trained a little harder." I feel sick.

"It doesn't matter whether you win, though," Mirdza says.

They're calling for us.

"Remember that." Her smile's forced.

She's wrong.

I may not need to win for Mr. Rimkus any more, but I could really use that prize money. Also, I'd rather be dragged by a rope from the back of a car all the way home than lose to some gorgeous blonde mare whom Alexei calls over and over. She probably shifts into an even more gorgeous woman, and now I feel sicker.

I lean low against Quicksilver's withers and whisper. "We're going to win today, do you hear me? Forget all that pacing and crap. You aren't going to lose to that. . .that mare. Got it?"

He snorts.

I pat his shoulder. "I'm serious."

He tosses his head.

"Good. We're on the same page."

But he's smirking, I can tell.

"So I'm jealous," I say. "So what? I can't turn into a beautiful horse, and I've never dated anyone before, and I saw you looking at her—*screaming* at her. It's upsetting."

They're lining us up, and it's time to focus, but my horse is laughing. "Quicksilver," I hiss. "Pay attention."

He practically saunters into his chute, totally unconcerned.

The other horses, even the palomino mare, are jostling around, eyes rolling, hooves pawing, nostrils flared.

Thankfully, when the bell rings and the chutes open, my very calm, very steady stallion still bursts out like a rocket. We break early—which I didn't really mean to let him do, but we're clearly going off script.

It finally hits me. If there's another shifter here, Leonid came.

As we round the first bend, we're running alongside three other horses. A black, a bay, and the stupid golden mare. Quicksilver's moving smoothly, totally unconcerned. It's almost like he's out for a morning jog alongside a friend. The mare keeps looking sideways at us, but whenever she does, her jockey crops her. That makes Quicksilver pin his ears.

"Let's give them some space," I hiss.

My big guy listens, and as we swing wide, covering

more ground to keep up with the leaders, the mare does the same thing. Her jockey's hauling on her face to move her back inside, but she doesn't care, throwing her head up to avoid the bit. Her visible eye keeps rolling our way.

I hate it.

I urge him forward, kissing and whipping my hands back and forth. Quicksilver listens perfectly, putting on a burst of speed that is still a little thrilling, even weeks into riding together. Most horses couldn't keep it up for a full furlong, but he does, widening the space between us and the others. One horse length.

I glance back again.

Two.

"Alright boy. That's good. Let's settle in."

He slows just a hair, swinging around at the halfway mark, handily ahead of the others. We maintain our lead for another round, not really pulling ahead, but maintaining.

As we go into the last round, the mare makes her move.

I hear it before I see her, the churning sounds of hooves striking dirt that's just a little too hard. Then I see a flash of gold, and she's beside us, racing top speed.

So much for pacing against the others. She's about to set records. I remind myself that I don't need to win. I repeat it over and over in my mind. Only, I don't really seem to be listening to myself. I crouch lower, urging Quicksilver to give it everything he has.

He listens.

His muscles strain.

His hooves clatter.

My heart hammers.

And we pull ahead, inch by inch, and then in the

last straightaway, I ask for everything, and it feels like we're truly *flying*. We pull ahead of her, finally. A full length. And then a bit more.

Until a wretchedly familiar *zing* runs through my entire body. It bows my back out. The reins slide through my numb fingers, my muscles unable to contract. I very nearly fall.

Quicksilver slows in response, and that blonde witch flies past us.

I scramble back upright and grab the reins, but we take second place. I want to murder that mare—it had to be her. She must have electrical powers, and I'm ready to hop off and find out how she's here and why.

Only, Mirdza, Kristiana, Aleksandr, and Grigoriy all close ranks around me almost immediately. They're all shaking their heads.

"She zapped me," I hiss. "That's illegal."

"Racing on a shifter probably is too," Mirdza hisses right back.

"But—"

"Just wait," Mirdza says.

I stand there like an idiot while the jockey and some random rich guy take all the acclaim and *my* prize money, and I crumple up my claim ticket and drop it on the ground.

I can't bring myself to clap, but at least I don't stab her. I finally slide off Quicksilver's back, my hands clenched around the reins so tightly, I worry that I might snap them.

"Who is she?" I ask, the second we've gotten a few dozen yards away from the milling crowds. "You must know."

"I'm pretty sure that's Boris's sister," Aleksandr says.

Boris, who kept me in that concrete room. Boris

who had electric powers. Of course it's his stupid sister. "Katerina." I remember Alexei's story. "She was in love with Leonid or something."

Mirdza frowns. "How could anyone love—"

"Later," Aleksandr says. "Right now, we need to try and get to Katerina."

We do try. But between waiting for the race celebrations to end, pushing our way past reporters, and handling our own horse appropriately, by the time we reach the parking lot, they're already gone.

"Do we know whether she's voluntarily helping Leonid, or sent here as some kind of threat?" I ask.

Aleks isn't even listening, though. "I think she was a distraction." He holds up his hand and waves us over. Even Alexei, in his horse form, comes over to see what's going on. "Pizdets!"

I'm a little confused. "But we need to load Quicksilver—"

Aleks stares intently at his phone, turning up the volume. "Watch."

The video's small, and there are five humans and a horse crouched around it trying to watch it, but the second we realize what's happening, we're all riveted.

"Russia has been in a political freefall since the fourth impeachment of a President in the time since communism crumbled. But no one saw this coming," one commentator says in English.

"I think you can say that again," the woman sitting next to him, also British, says. "On the heels of the revelation that there's an actual member of the Romanov royal family alive now—one of the children must have survived that savage massacre—we have confirmed evidence that there's also a member of the famous Riurik Dynasty, long thought to have ended in the early sixteen hundreds with Vasily the Fourth. Now there's a referendum that's being put to the Russian people that will determine what the government will look like going forward."

"How likely do our analysts think it is that Russians might vote to revert to a *monarchy?*" the man asks. "I mean, that really feels like a giant step back, doesn't it?"

"Well, seeing as it's in the hands of the people," the woman says, "I can't imagine it's very likely. What person would vote for something that would take away their future ability to vote?" She chuckles. "It's nonsensical, surely. Probably a publicity stunt."

"But you're applying our culture and beliefs to them," the man says. "This is a people who have long been ruled by might, and our research shows that more than anything else, they long for a return to the strength that used to mark Russia and Russian culture in the international world."

"A strong president," the woman says, "seems to be the obvious solution to that dilemma."

"What I want to know," the man says, "is who exactly becomes their next ruler if they *do* vote for this monarch? Is it the Romanov heir, or is it the Riurik Dynasty one?"

"I suppose we'll just have to wait and watch, and I hope everyone else will tune in with us as this all unfolds," the woman says. "But we do have some exciting news. The man who has been tested and proven to be a Riurikid heir is named Leonid Ivanovich, and he's released a public video. Apparently the people supporting him are the ones who gathered the required votes to get the referendum slated."

My hand's trembling on Quicksilver's reins. My jealousy over a palomino mare seems ridiculous. This is it. Leonid's move. He's trying to take over the entire

Russian government. It's insane. When his face appears on the screen, I realize that I'd forgotten how visually appealing he is. The people watching are going to love him. And unlike the day we met, this Leonid wants people to like him.

He's smiling.

He's approachable.

"Hello, and welcome," a man wearing a ridiculous toupee says.

"I'm delighted to be here," Leonid says in Russian. Then he turns toward the camera and says, "Thank you for having me," in English. "I'm so happy to be here," in Latvian. "It's an honor to be able to address everyone," he says in Italian.

"How many languages do you speak?" the commentator asks.

"Eleven," he says, switching back to Russian. "You see, when you're heir to a dynasty, communication's everything. That's the real difference between having a ruler who was prepared from birth and someone who has to grasp for that power all the way up. I won't have lobbies coming after me. I won't need to cater to mobsters or criminals." He smiles again. "The only people I answer to are the Russian people. They're also the only people I care to serve. It's my sole purpose. That's what makes a monarchy so much more pure than an elected president, whose interests can be bought and sold, changing like the tides along with his personal interest."

"I hear there's another heir who has surfaced, strangely at the same time, a hundred years after Russians cast their monarchy away. Some might call the idea of reinstating the monarchy madness—why would they give up their freedom?"

"Let's look at what that freedom has brought

them," Leonid says. "Burned churches. Starving people. Riots. Wars. Insurrections. Mobs and mafia. Arms dealers. Drug lords. The Russian people have paid in blood, tears, and misery for more than a century now. It's time to restore order and strength, and the prosperity that goes with those."

"You're making some big promises," the man says. "You're confident you can fulfill them?"

"Utterly and completely," Leonid says. "And I know we don't have much more time, but I did want to quickly address the questions you had about the Romanov heir." He shakes his head. "The Romanovs were always usurpers. They never had a right to hold Russia's throne, and they're the reason things fell apart like they did. Instead of looking back a hundred years, you should really be casting your recollection back further, back to sixteen hundred and ten, when the last legitimate ruler of Russia died. The throne has been empty since then, as far as I'm concerned. But I'm here now, and I'm ready to bring back the long-lost era of Russian dominance."

That sends a chill down my spine.

Quicksilver, Grigoriy, and Aleksandr look ready to do murder.

"I'm guessing this means our plan didn't work." I pat Quicksilver's shoulder.

"I think this time, Leonid won on all fronts," Aleksandr says. "But the best generals know how to regroup."

It's the first time in my life I've hoped that someone I knew was a decent general, because I think that maniac is coming for us next.

❦ 25 ❦

It's been almost a week since I decided to date someone.

In all that time, he's spent two hours as a human. I've fed him hay. I've scratched underneath his mane. I've ridden him and raced with him.

I haven't held his hand.

We haven't gone to dinner or a movie.

There has been absolutely no kissing, not since that very first day.

Basically, dating kind of sucks so far, and as soon as we get him home, and he can finally shift into his human form, the first thing he does is take a shower. I do the same thing, dumping my clothing in the wash and then showering faster than I ever have.

Then I race over to the big house where he's staying, and I jog up the stairs. The door to his room opens, and he walks out, his hair still wet. I've been so hungry for his face that seeing it lifts my spirits tremendously.

Sure, it's been a weird day.

Leonid has gotten the upper hand. Again. But I'm ready to grab Alexei and—

"Phone call for you." Aleksandr's striding down the hallway.

Alexei bites his lip, looks at me longingly for one moment, and then turns and scowls. "Tell them I'll call them back."

"It's the leader of United Russia—the single largest political party in the country, and the current party in power," Aleksandr says. "You want to take this call."

Alexei brushes one hand down the side of my face and sighs. "Fine." He holds out his hand.

"Remember our story," Aleksandr says.

We can't just tell the world that he's *the* Alexei Romanov and that he woke up from a curse last month. No one would believe it for one, and then they'd all assume he was insane. He'd never be chosen to rule so much as his own life, much less a country. Although, Russia *is* notoriously tolerant of maniacs, like Putin releasing serial killers to fight on the front lines. It's been a little like Cuba in that way.

I turn around to head downstairs, but Alexei grabs my arm and shakes his head, tugging me back into his room alongside him. While he sits down on his bed, I hover by the door, unsure he really needs a distraction.

Alexei points at the edge of the bed, and then he presses that finger to his lips to remind me to be quiet. As if I needed that reminder. I perch on the edge of the bed right as he puts the phone on speaker.

"I'll be brief—I'm sure you're quite busy right now. I imagine we have one major thing in common."

"What's that?" Alexei asks.

"We both despise Leonid Ivanovich."

Alexei chuckles. "I think his vision for Russia's not a good one. We agree on that."

"I'd like to propose a deal," the man says. "Right now, the referendum is basically a contest between the current regime—"

"Your regime."

"And this new, handsome young man."

"Leonid."

"Exactly," the man says. "But I hear you're young and handsome."

I nod.

"I'm young," Alexei says. "I'm not bad looking."

"And you appear to be well spoken."

"I only know six languages," Alexei says. "But I'm entirely fluent in each."

"Only six." He chuckles. "I think I can work with that." The man snorts. "Listen, I'd like to give the Russian people a choice between two young, likable men."

"You want me to be the face of your regime, because after the former president's disastrous mishandling of things, it'll be a landslide in Leonid's favor without me."

The man on the other end of the phone sighs. "That's about right."

At least he's honest.

"What do you think our chances are of winning?"

"We aren't sure yet," the man says. "But if you're as charismatic as we hope you are, we think it's about fifty-fifty."

Fifty-fifty that the people of Russia vote to reinstate a monarchy?

"Assuming that I agree to help you," he says.

"Yes," the man says. "With your help, we have a chance. Without it, that maniac's going to take over everything."

Alexei looks at me, lifting both eyebrows.

I want to stay here. Let Russia burn.

Whether Leonid rules them or whether some other nut does, the impact on my life will be minimal. I know that's selfish. I know that's greedy. Neither Mirdza nor Kristiana would agree with me, but that's how I feel.

But I also know Alexei, and I know he can't live with that. He's always said that Russia can stay as she is. . .as long as the people are well cared for. I also can't help thinking about what Baba Yaga said. She said she's supposed to serve all her people, not just a few. Leonid only cares about himself. He's definitely clinically insane.

Alexei will care for everyone, at any cost.

It pains me, but I nod.

No matter how much I may hate it, that's one of the reasons I admire him. He's a much better person than I am. He even took the time to see what I thought, and I'm nothing to him right now. I'm not his wife, his fiancée, or even his official girlfriend, really. I'm some girl who agreed to date him, but so far still hasn't actually gone on a single date.

"It seems like you're not sure yet," the man says. "Come back to Russia. Meet with me. Let me convince you that we share the same vision."

"I'm not worried about a shared vision," Alexei says. "Let me be clear. If I win, I want to do what's best for the Russians every step of the way. Not what's best for you. Not what's going to line your pockets. I want peace and prosperity and freedom. Those are my priority. Do you still think we have something to discuss?"

"Oh, bravo," the man says. "You're even better than I was led to believe. I can't wait to meet you."

"But do you understand what I'm saying?" Alexei doesn't let go.

"I do," the man says. "Absolutely."

"Our position with the Russian people must be that while I am of noble blood, I plan to earn my position as their leader. I'm not afraid of working hard for it. I'm not afraid of proving that I'm the best leader out there. In that way, they can maintain their freedom, and I will serve them as long as they feel I'm doing it adequately."

"All you have to do is say that, with a reasonable smile on your face, and I think we can beat him."

"This isn't just about winning," Alexei says. "I really do believe what I'm saying. I like the idea that I'll have to do a good job and that I'll be accountable."

"Leaders have to do things that the people won't like sometimes," the man says. "But we'll make sure we do them at the beginning of a new term, not at the end. Also, we recently abolished the term limits for the office of the President, so you could conceivably keep the position for your entire lifetime and pass it on to your own son."

"Or daughter," Alexei says.

"Right, of course. Wow." He sighs. "You really are perfect."

"When did you want to meet?"

"How soon can you get back to Russia?" he asks.

"I'll let you know." Alexei hangs up, drops the phone on the nightstand, and crosses the room toward me. "I know this is weird." His eyes are so intense. So dark blue. So deep that I could fall into them.

"How long do you think you'll be gone?" I ask.

"The referendum vote is soon," he says. "It'll all be over within a matter of weeks."

"The information age," I say. "Our world's quick and small now."

"It's an adjustment for sure," he says. "But it's also pretty amazing."

That's true enough, and for a century-old man, he's handling it all quite well. "Before you go, I'm going to show you something amazing." I whip out my phone. "See this?"

"The call button?" He looks unimpressed. "I'm not that backward."

"But this one," I point, "is called FaceTime. You can press this, and it brings up a video image of me. You'll be able to see me any time you want to chat."

He reaches out and grabs my hip with his right hand and drags me closer.

I squeal and nearly drop the phone. "Hey, I was showing you how to use—"

He presses the finger on his free, left hand to my lips. "Shh."

"Believe me. Even if it's only a few weeks, you'll want to know how to use FaceTime." Or maybe it's just me who longs to see his face whenever I can't.

He shakes his head, dragging me even closer, until our hips are pressed together and my body presses against his all the way up to my chest. My heart's racing so fast that my pulse's pounding in my ears. I know what's coming next. I lift my chin, looking into his eyes.

"I won't need to use that video thing," he says. "Because you're going to come with me to Russia. Right?" And finally, his head lowers over mine until his lips are just a tiny distance away. "Adriana."

My name's a caress.

Hearing him say it—a shiver runs through my entire body.

"Say you'll come."

"You're going out there to run for President," I say.

"As a Romanov heir, you're going to ask all the people of Russia to vote for you." I can't even explain why it's so crazy for him to take me with him. "I'm the daughter of a single mother who was married to her own brother-in-law. I can't possibly—"

"I don't care about any of that. No one else will either, trust me."

"I was a criminal, Alexei. Before you had that man arrested, he was ordering me around because I borrowed money from his brother. Money I couldn't repay until you gave me all that cash." I don't want to say any more, but I have to. "Money I tried to repay by throwing races."

I feel sick now, and I shove myself away from this man—this prince. I don't deserve him, and now he knows it, too. I can't meet his eyes, but I need to hear him say it or I'll keep hoping.

"How do you feel now? Knowing that I took that money you gave me and paid it to a mobster?"

"I feel like I should have had him arrested much sooner," he says. "But I don't blame *you* for any of it."

"I like nice things," I say. "I pick fights sometimes. And when I have to choose between saving myself and saving other people?" I shrug. "I pick myself, Alexei. I'm not a do-gooder like you or like Mirdza or even like Kristiana."

"Come with me." He leans toward me again, his eyes still fixated on my mouth. "Stop throwing out excuses."

I slap his chest, a little distracted by the muscles underneath my hands. But through sheer force of will, I focus. "You're not *listening* to me," I say. "I can't come with you, because if I do, there's no way you'll win." There. I said it.

"I told you that I want to help Russians," he says. "I

told you that I want to rule there, if that's what it takes, and although you find that personally distasteful, you understand and support my decision."

I nod.

"Now support me in mine. I want you to come with me, and I want to date you, just like you said we would. No excuses. No wiggling out of it." He pulls me close again, and this time, I collapse against him, dropping my head against his chest. "Any wiggling you want to do can be done right here, on top of me."

That makes me giggle. "Alexei, be serious."

"I am," he says. "In fact, I've never been more serious."

"I should stay here," I say. "You know it, too."

"So when you think about your future, are you here by yourself?" He peers down at me with curiosity.

I think about tomorrow. About next week. About next month. About next *year*. And in every single hope and dream I have, he's there.

Alexei's always there.

"I want you to come back when all this is done," I say. "I want you in my future."

He sighs. "I'm not the kind of person who would do that. I am who I am, and I want you with me now. I'm not going to lie to the Russian people about who I am or who's in my life, and I won't ever be ashamed of you, either. I think you did the best you could at the time, just like you're doing now. Just like I am." he says.

"I should have done better."

"My father should have done better. I should have done better, too. We've all made mistakes, but I won't compound mine by lying about them. Even if you don't want to be in Russia, even if that's not what you had in mind, if you see yourself with *me*, then you should come. Don't wait for next week or next month. Come with me now."

"What would that even look like?" I ask. "You're meeting with important people, and you're having these important dinners, and my Russian sucks. I never say the right thing. I'm a politician's worst nightmare."

He shrugs, and then he presses a kiss to my forehead. "Then you're in luck, because I'm not a politician. I was born to be a czar."

"Be serious."

"I am," he says. "If the Russians vote for me—and they're lying to me, by the way. The odds must be below fifty percent, or they wouldn't be calling me. But if they do vote for me, I'll choose to serve. I can't walk away from my country or from my people. But if they choose me, they'll have to accept you. They'll understand that your Russian isn't perfect, that your past isn't spotless, and that your future isn't certain. And most importantly, they'll see that your heart is big and brave. They'll see that you make me happy, and they'll be happy for us."

"That's a nice sentiment," I say. "But the world doesn't work like that. People are catty and jealous. They don't want what's best for others. And when push comes to shove, they pick themselves and their own interests every time."

"That may be the truth of the world," Alexei says. "But people only improve when you believe they can, so I'm going to keep seeing the world I wish existed, and then I'm going to work toward it every single day. It's the only way I know to move ahead."

That's the first truly beautiful thing I've ever heard from anyone about government. I can't tell him no— not when he's that bright and shiny. His ideas may be founded upon the complete delusion that people are good and noble deep down, but I hope he's right.

"Alright," I say. "I'll go."

He beams.

"Under one condition."

His brow furrows. "What's that?"

"You're going to be busy. You're going to be inundated by people who want to talk to you, who want to ask for favors, and who want to promise you things. You can do those meetings as you see fit, but your spare time all comes to me." I smile. "And I get one night a week for a date. A proper date, with a meal, an activity, and at least one kiss."

His mouth meets mine then, with a fervor I never realized was possible. He never officially agrees, but I'm taking his kiss as consent.

❦ 26 ❦

I'm not sure how I got to Russia the last time I went, since I was unconscious, but I feel like I might have been rolled up in a rug or something. This time is a little different.

Aleksandr knows how to travel in style. Our private jet—seats for twelve, but only the six of us on it—is met by the man from the phone. It turns out his name is Igor Baranov, and he lives larger even than Aleks. The man travels with an entourage that would staff a circus. The deep wrinkles in his face nevertheless don't give the impression that he spends a lot of time smiling. Quite the opposite.

Someone's dabbing his face as we deplane, as if he's going on TV.

"Alexei." His voice is deeper and more compelling in person. "You said you're not bad looking." He shakes his head and chuckles. "I wish I was as 'not bad looking' as you." His chuckle is low and deep.

"He's modest," I say. Or at least, I'm pretty sure I used the right word for modest.

Judging by the look he gives me, I might have said

something else. "And who's this?" His smile definitely turns forced in that moment.

"This is my girlfriend," Alexei says. "Adriana Strelkova."

"And where are you from?" Mr. Baranov keeps blinking, his brittle smile frozen in place.

"I'm from Latvia," I say.

"How lovely." He's one of those people who says one thing while clearly meaning the exact opposite.

"I'm worried we may have a problem right from the start," Alexei says. "You haven't *said* anything rude, but you're treating my girlfriend as if she's not welcome here. If she feels unwelcome, then so do I. We'll both leave together."

"I was merely surprised," Mr. Baranov says. "But of course, having a lovely girl on your arm will only help your image."

"It's fine," I whisper. "Really." It's not like Alexei can really force every single person we meet to like me. It's the exact reason I'm a terrible match for him. A Latvian with a shady past? Not good arm candy for the possible future president of Russia.

"It's not fine," Alexei says. "I can't control how other people treat you, but I can certainly ensure that the people who are working with and for me treat you well."

It's just that what they think I deserve and what Alexei thinks are unlikely to align.

"You said we'd have accommodations in St. Petersburg," Aleksandr says. "Novgorod is too far?"

Mr. Baranov waves his hand and a half dozen people rush forward, eagerly taking our bags from the airline crew. "The best hotel, of course. We'll get you settled right away, but depending on how tired Mr.

Romanov is, we'd love to get started on at least some of the preparation work today."

And here's where we find out how well the story Aleksandr crafted is going to hold up. Even though I may find him a little overbearing and irritating, most of his obsessive traits might actually help Alexei today. We're claiming he's Anastasia's great grandson—which the DNA mostly bears out—but thanks to a lot of Disney movies and conman schemes, no one trusts anything to do with Anastasia.

The rest of the day is very, very boring, but thanks to the ironclad evidence of his DNA, no one seems to question his lineage. I suppose some parts of modern-day technology are pretty cool. Aleksandr won't leave his side at first, but after several hours, it becomes clear that the people here don't need to be sold on Alexei's identity. Or the man himself.

They already adore him.

They're prepared to tattoo his name on their butts.

At that point, even Aleksandr realizes that there's not a lot for him to do. Eventually he decides to leave Alexei in their care and find a place to eat and rest. You can only eat so much of a cheese and fruit platter, no matter how nice, before it starts to look nasty. They all decide to head for the hotel around dinner time.

I decide to go with them.

It's not like I'm really getting anything out of the long, boring meetings and strategy planning. Since I'm secretly hoping none of this pans out, I feel like my very presence might be bad juju.

"I'm surprised you came to Russia, to be honest," Mirdza says. "You hate meetings, and you hate being stuck inside buildings, and you can't stand politics of any kind."

That makes me laugh, because it's so true. And also,

it's so very *my* life. I finally like someone, and it's a person who, by the very nature of being who he is, requires me to do all the things that I hate. Talk about ill-fated. Romeo and Juliet had it easy, for heaven's sake. Who doesn't have a little family drama?

At least they weren't interested in a stallion shifter who had been sleeping for a hundred years. Thankfully, the hotel is *amazing*. It looks like a palace—then I work out the words on the sign. It's the Four Seasons Lion Palace Hotel.

"Was this a property that Alexei's family owned?" I whisper as we approach the enormous front entry of the massive yellow palace, replete with tall white columns, and two huge white lions guarding the doors.

"Hardly," Aleksandr says. "It's been bought now, by some American computer guru named William Gates, but it was built by the Kurakin family. While we slept, they built palaces." He looks absolutely disgusted.

"At least it's nice," I mutter.

"I'm excited to stay here too," Mirdza says.

"And they may have been awake, but they don't own it now," Grigoriy says.

When we walk through the door, a man in a tuxedo walks briskly our way. I'm busy looking at the stunning frescoes, but he recognizes Aleksandr. "Your rooms are ready, sir. The Palace and Noble suites are arranged for you and Mister Khilkov, and the Lobanov Royal Suite is reserved for His Majesty, Alexei Romanov." His mouth is twitching like he's desperate to smile.

"It's not like he asked you to call him that," I say. "If you think it's funny, just call him Alexei."

The man's eyes widen, and he swivels and drops into a bow. "I'm so sorry, madam. I didn't find any part of this humorous." He straightens. "It will be the singular pleasure of my life to serve the rightful heir to the Romanov throne."

Oh. Weird. "Okay."

"You'll be staying in the Lobanov Royal Suite with His Majesty?"

Staying in the *same room*? I can't help spluttering a bit. "Certainly not. We haven't even had our first date yet."

The man's brows draw together sharply. "I have just the three suites reserved." He coughs. "I'll—let me get back to you."

"It's fine," Mirdza says.

"Excuse me?" Is she my sister or some kind of pimp?

"The rooms are suites," Mirdza hisses. "There are lots of places to sleep—it's like having a little apartment in each one. Calm down."

"Oh." The guys would probably insist on having us at least close to where they're sleeping for safety anyway. "Then, yes, that's fine."

"You will not require separate accommodations?" The man's quite intense for a hotel employee.

"No," I say. "It's fine."

"Right this way, then." Several porters materialize to take our bags.

"I can carry mine." I clutch the handle, bringing it closer to my body. I'm a little uncomfortable with all the people trying to pry my things away. It's not like my stuff is super nice, but I have no idea how I'd go about replacing things while I'm in St. Petersburg.

"It's my job," the porter next to me says in Latvian.

"You speak Latvian?" I'm surprised.

"We all speak at least four languages." He smiles. "It's a requirement to work at the Four Seasons St. Petersburg."

For the porters? Really?

I have no idea why, but knowing my porter speaks several languages makes me think he's less likely to steal my things. I doubt anyone with education and culture really wants a pair of heels that have been reglued on the left heel twice or a makeup bag full of half-used stuff from the convenience store. I finally surrender it with just one longing glance.

With our stuff magically being taken to where it goes, we're free to eat immediately.

"Reservations have been made for you at all four of our finest onsite restaurants," the man in the tux says. I notice that his badge says he's the concierge. "If you would like to make a selection, I can show you the way. If none of them suit, we can certainly find you a table anywhere else you'd like, and transportation to it."

"How can you do that?" I ask.

"All fine restaurants reserve a few tables for VIPs," he explains.

VIPs.

Very important persons. Until today, the only time that would have been used to describe me would have been if it meant very irritating person. Or maybe very impatient person. Actually, the most likely descriptor would have been very improper person.

And now I'm dating the lost Romanov heir. The VIP of VIPs.

What a joke.

Two hours later, after one of the best meals of my life, I'm standing in the poshest room I've ever seen. The chandelier—that's right, a chandelier—is made of Waterford crystal. My room attendant told me that little tidbit. He'll be waiting outside all night in case one of us needs something. The pillows are all embroidered with the finest golden thread, made of white, ecru, and gold linen and silk. The curtains, the duvets, and the carpet are all perfectly coordinated and luxe.

In lieu of a mini-fridge, there's a full-size fridge with dozens of drink and snack options that are all included in the room rate. I don't even want to know what the nightly cost is. Our attendant also told me he would be happy to bring us anything else we wanted to eat, day or night. When Alice went through the looking glass into Wonderland, she could not have been as lost as I am right now.

In that exact moment, as I stand bewildered, Alexei walks in.

He looks the same, but also slightly different as he bids Mr. Baranov a good night. His hair has clearly been cut—expertly. His suit's different now too—more expensive, if that can be imagined. And his shoes are brand new, which makes no sense because his other shoes were only a few weeks old. His tie's a soothing shade of blue that just matches his eyes.

If anything, he looks even more out of reach than he did before.

"You're still awake." He smiles.

"I wasn't sure how many more people might be rotating through here," I say.

"I'm sorry." He looks genuinely concerned.

"Looks like the meetings were a success?" I wring my hands, feeling like a frivolous house wife from 1952. No kids. No laundry to fold. No food to make. All I need is a string of pearls and a sweater set.

What am I doing here?

Why did I think he and I might work? That there might be an us.

"Mr. Baranov runs United Russia, but the other party leaders unanimously ratified me as their candidate tonight. It's going to be announced tomorrow—

they want me for a press conference first thing in the morning."

"How cool," I say lamely. I'm as bad at faking it as Mr. Baranov, it turns out. At least it's not part of my job.

That makes me think that maybe he wasn't really trying to fake it. Perhaps he wanted me and Alexei to know that I'm not really in line with what he needs. Better to know now, before it's done any damage.

"I should go home," I say. "I'm not sure why I came here."

Alexei's face falls, but I've never been one to suffer in silence.

"It's the first day," he says. "Of course it's overwhelming."

I shake my head. "It's not that. The hotel's amazing, and the food was to die for, but. . ."

"But?" He walks toward me.

I step back, bumping into the sofa and shifting sideways to crab walk my way around it. "None of this is me."

"It's not me, either," he lies.

Which makes me laugh. Even his effortless white lies are flawless. "It *is* you, though. The pomp and circumstance. The royal treatment—it's what you've always known. It's where you belong. But I'm. . .even if I didn't feel uncomfortable about it all, I don't want it."

"Neither do I," Alexei says. "But something Mr. Baranov said this morning kept me going. He told me that without my help, Leonid Ivanovich would win in a landslide, and with one single election, the Russian people would surrender the freedom they spent thousands of years winning."

"The power of a demagogue," I say.

"I might be able to stop it," he says. "I may not. I

may lose. But at least the Romanov name stands a chance with people who are tired of being overlooked, ignored, and neglected. They deserve to have a better government than what they've had, and I have to at least try to give it to them." He sits on the sofa and holds out his hands, reaching for me.

I can't help thinking that his pose right now, sitting down, entreating me to join him while I loiter a foot away, just out of reach, parallels our current position. He wants me here with him, or he says he does, but I know it's not right. For the very reason he just articulated.

"If you're the only thing standing between all those people and the loss of their freedom, I really do need to leave, because I think I'm going to tip the scales the wrong direction."

But Alexei doesn't drop it. He doesn't sit back and sigh in resignation like I expect. He hops up, grabs me, and pulls me back down onto his lap. With our height difference, I'm finally at eye level with him, my hands braced against his firm chest. He doesn't say anything else. He doesn't argue with me.

He just kisses me.

And all the arguments and guilt and the feelings that I don't belong evaporate like spit on parched, cracking soil. My hands slide up his hard chest to his neck, and I pull away for a moment, just to breathe in his scent. I shouldn't be surprised, but he smells like leather and a cool stream and a spring rain all at the same time. I could smell it all day long and never tire of it. My hands wrap around the back of his neck, and I pull him down even closer to me.

"You can't leave," he murmurs against my mouth. "I'm sorry it's boring and you hate it and I know we'll have to figure some things out, but I need you here with me. The Russian people need me, but I need you even more."

"Okay," I whisper back. Now that he's touching me, now that he's *here*, I remember why I came. I remember why I'm doing things I've never done, things I vowed never to do. Something inside of him calls to me. Something about him soothes me. Something about sitting in his lap, with his arms around my body, makes me feel safe in a way I never have before.

Which is ironic, because I'm probably in more danger now.

But for the first time in my life, it feels like I'm not alone.

He may be everything I never deserved, everything that my past decisions will complicate, but walking away from him feels harder than giving up breathing. It feels like turning down a chocolate lava cake and a tall glass of cold, frothy milk: impossible.

As he kisses me, I start to want *more*. Things I never thought I wanted. My stomach flutters. My heart races. My hands tremble. I unbutton the top of his shirt, but he catches my hand at the wrist.

"Adriana." His voice is ragged, and he drags in a breath. "You can't."

It's like he's dangling a truffle in front of me and telling me no. Or offering me the tooled, leather bridle I want and then tossing it away. "Why not?"

The corner of his mouth turns up. "Soon," he says. "But not yet. Our hearts and our heads need to sync first."

He's right. If we do more than we should tonight, tomorrow morning will be awkward.

"I don't want you to leave, Adriana." His voice is smaller than ever before, like he's about to share a secret. "My whole family's gone, Ana. I can't bring them back, and I need you."

Ana.

He made up a nickname for me. Mirdza calls me A sometimes, but not consistently, and it never really caught on. No one else has ever used a nickname just for me. It sends a tiny thrill racing through me, and I want to kiss him again.

I don't want to stop.

But then the rest of what he said sets in. *My whole family's gone.* He's telling me that even though he *looks* invulnerable, bulletproof, and larger than life, he's fragile.

He's scared.

And what frightens him is that I might leave. He's also scared that I might die.

"Are you at all excited?" I ask. "Do you think you'll love ruling?"

His laughter sounds so pained that I can't help dropping my hands and wrapping them around his waist.

I press my head against his chest. "No?"

"I hate it," he says. "But I was raised from birth to believe that it's a ruler's obligation to provide the best life for the people they rule. My dad was destroyed by evil people, and I know they're still out there. I can't just walk away from his legacy, no matter how it's been tainted and twisted by the victor."

"I've been thinking about something," I say.

"What?"

"Leonid came to your dad, you said."

He murmurs assent. "Hm."

"He wanted to regain the throne, presumably?"

"I think so."

"And then he managed to curse all of you—Boris

and Mikhail joined him to do it. But then, why did he wait? Why did he let the Bolsheviks or whoever take over? What happened?" I sit up enough to see his face.

Alexei blinks. "Why haven't we been focused on that?" He scratches his chin, and I love the sound of his fingers rasping against his golden stubble. "The mare we saw—things have moved so fast since then— she's Boris's sister. She and Leonid had something going on, but they had a falling out. I can't imagine she'd run against us, but she must have done that for him."

"What if she was cursed too?" I ask. "Each of you woke up when the one you—when someone who was fated to come into your life was in danger. That's what Kris and Mirdza think."

"I did wake up just in time to save you." His smug smile is kind of hot.

"You did," I say.

"So was she cursed? Or has she been with them all along?"

I shrug. "Maybe she's been with Leonid all along." Why do I secretly hope she's a villain. "It did seem like she was there as a distraction for us. Kind of a little dig —I see you, and I don't care about you, but I can still ruin you."

Alexei's brow furrows. "She didn't seem too excited to be ridden."

"Maybe she didn't like the jockey, but she agreed to the rest."

"We just don't know enough," Alexei says. "It's frustrating."

But he's talking to me, and I'm doing my best to help, and I didn't realize how much I needed that. For the first time all day, I feel like there's a reason for me to be here. "We'll figure it out." My smile's stupidly shy.

He slides his finger under my chin and lifts it until I'm looking right at him. "With you here, I actually believe that. You're not someone who gives up, not even after a fight is over."

It feels like he means it. "Speaking of fights, where exactly are you planning on sleeping?"

He laughs. "Anywhere you tell me to go."

"I know you don't want us to get ahead of ourselves, but would it be terrible if you slept next to me?" I bite my lip.

He kisses me lightly. "Not terrible at all. . .as long as you don't wiggle around and keep me from sleeping."

"I sleep like the dead." I cross my heart. "Barely even move."

Alexei, it turns out, does not. The man tosses and turns like a little kid, but every time he wakes me up, I stare at his beautiful face for a moment and think about how lucky I am that fate threw him at me. My knight in shining horseflesh—sent as an actual white horse to save me.

I never really did my three good deeds, but I'm wondering if God will count this. I'm sticking around even though I don't want to, just to try and help him be the leader the people need. If that's not altruistic, I don't know what is.

The next morning, things seem a little brighter. When I stand up and stretch, I realize that Alexei's already gone.

But he left a note on the fridge.

A*t the press conference. Turn on the tv.*
I miss you already.
A.

.   .   .

I t's short. It's to the point. And it makes me swoon.
The note's not all he left. There're also several
different breakfast options under little stainless steel
covers. Oatmeal, eggs, bacon, toast, and pancakes.
There's even a tiny omelette.

I turn on the television and start picking a little
here and there from all the plates of food. Within five
minutes, the news story starts.

"The United Russia party has been reeling since the
referendum no one expected to take hold was
approved, and since then, officials have speculated
wildly about what candidate they may present for the
Presidency, assuming they don't lose entirely to the
reinstatement of the monarchy." Commentators always
manage to sound exactly the same. It's crazy, how all
these different people in lots of different languages all
manage to sound identical.

"Today we're welcoming Mr. Igor Baranov, the
leader of the United Russia party. He has some pretty
exciting news for us."

Igor looks exactly as he did in person, but also
different. His hair is fuller, his wrinkles are less
pronounced, and he's glowing. How do they do that?
I'd really like to know. "Thank you for having me
today," he says. "As you may know, our party itself is the
combination of two powerful, conservative parties who
have joined in the hope of better serving Russia and its
people. It's been quite a long and bloody road for us to
get here, to a place where our people have the right
and the ability to vote for what they deem to be the
best option."

"Yes, yes, we know that you strongly prefer that we
keep the status quo instead of reinstating a single ruler.
Hardly a surprise."

Lots of people behind stage laugh.

Mr. Baranov himself smiles. "Of course we prefer to maintain the freedoms the Russian people were long denied. But it may surprise you to hear that we're not alone in this desire. Leonid Ivanovich took us all by surprise when he announced that he's the heir of the legendary Riurik line, but I think that almost as shocking was the existence of the more recently royal Romanov bloodline. They ruled Russia, nobly and well, for more than three hundred years. They were already moving us toward noted new freedoms when the Bolsheviks murdered their family."

"I expected you to dislike Alexei Romanov as much as you dislike Leonid Ivanovich, to be honest," the commentator says.

"Of course you did," Mr. Baranov says. "But in fact, I'm pleased to announce that in spite of his heritage, in spite of the brutal and violent way in which his family was removed from the throne, he's actually a supporter of United Russia, and we of him."

The commentator looks surprised, but the sounds from the studio audience are wild. Shouts. Cheers. Yelling. Clapping. The reactions are all over the place, but they're all passionate in their feelings.

"You may be even more shocked to hear that we see eye to eye on so many things that he's agreed to be our party's candidate for President, should the referendum for the monarchy fail to pass."

The absolute chaos that breaks out shocks everyone, myself included. I think it's probably indicative of what everyone in the country is feeling, however. No one would expect one of the displaced heirs to stand up for the usurping government, forgoing their supposed rights of noble blood to be dictated to by the whims of the populous.

The commentator touches his ear and nods. "Well, Mr. Baranov, you've shocked us all with that, but it appears you came very prepared. I understand that he's actually here today, this Alexei Romanov, the lost heir of the last tsardom of Russia."

"He did come, and he'd actually like to say a few words, if you'd welcome him on your show."

No matter how many people were booing, shouting, jeering, and hissing, the second Alexei, dressed in a sweater that perfectly frames his broad shoulders and well-defined chest, saunters into view of the camera, no one does anything but cheer. It's almost deafening, really.

I can't blame them, either.

It's strange, but for some reason his beauty seems even more untouchable when I see him on film. His skin is flawless. His jaw is strong and perfectly square. His eyes sparkle, their deep blue color almost accented by the lighting they chose. I'm sure we have Mr. Baranov's team to thank for that one. And when he looks right at the camera and smiles?

He was made for this.

Although he was born in a time before selfies and videography as we now know it, his natural smile and easy-going confidence radiate when he takes his seat.

Leonid was commanding. He looked fearful and impressive.

Alexei is *dreamy*.

"Welcome, Your Majesty," the commentator says.

"Please, call me Alex," he says.

Again, the audience goes insane.

"You really are a surprise, in more ways than one," the man says. "Especially since your namesake, your great grandmother's brother, if I have that correct, was said to be sickly, weak, and in fact he had a severe blood condition, did he not?"

I expect Alexei to cringe, but he just shakes his head and smiles. "You know, I didn't know him myself, so I can't say whether any of that was true or just slander made up by the people who murdered him."

Even the commentator laughs.

He has them laughing about a murder, one that hurt him badly.

"But I am delighted to be here today," Alexei says. "I am so pleased to have this chance to introduce myself to the Russian people, and to share with them my reason for stepping forward."

"Please do," the commentator says.

"You see, the Russian government has actually been quite gracious since I did my DNA test and came forward. They've returned some of my family's property and holdings, and I could easily have stayed out of the public view. Or I could be campaigning for the government to return to a tsardom. Certainly I'd have a compelling claim to bring against Leonid Ivanovich, whose family has not ruled in more than 400 years. But when I gave this some serious thought, even before United Russia reached out, I knew that what was best for the Russian people was to maintain the freedoms they suffered for so many years without."

More cheers.

"My most important role in this pivotal moment in history may be convincing those of you who are tempted by the promises of greatness to bet on yourselves. You see, I happen to think the greatest Russia, the strongest Russia, and the most successful Russia will require the help and the voice of each and every Russian citizen to be achieved."

The commentator asks him several more questions,

and Alexei does better and better with each. At the end, the commentator asks him whether he's nervous about the unreliability of his position as President. "You know that you'll have to be re-elected every six years in order to retain the office."

Alexei smiles. "That's the best part of all of this. I may be a Romanov, but that's not a guarantee that I'll do an excellent job. And if I'm not serving them the way I should, the people have every right to kick me to the curb. Actually, I'll vote to do that myself, if I can't get the job done properly."

In that moment, even I want to vote for him.

By the time he gets back to the hotel, I'm almost positive that he's going to beat Leonid. Charm, intelligence, sophistication, he has it all. The Russians would have to be complete imbeciles not to trust their future to Alexei Golden Boy Romanov, as they're calling him on the webchats I've seen.

Over the next three days, his ratings skyrocket, and there's no fear that Leonid and his proposed monarchy will win. The meetings are less and less intense, and we have our first date scheduled, finally.

I'm swiping on some mascara, listening to the hum of the Russian news in the background—I think my Russian has improved a lot with all the news I've been watching—when I hear something very concerning.

My own name.

I drop the mascara, smearing black all down my cheek. I turn slowly.

"Recent news reports have been confirmed. What we once believed to merely be nasty rumors have been confirmed as true."

A large photo fills the screen.

"Latvian criminal Adriana Strelkova, who has been connected with a prominent Lithuanian crime family for years, is Alexei Romanov's girlfriend. For those of you still holding out hope that this hotly contested rumor isn't true, we have a clip."

It's Alexei. He's wearing a chunky sweater, because the weather's already starting to turn here. Someone calls his name, and he turns back toward them, smiling beautifully.

"Is it true that you have a girlfriend?"

His smile broadens. "It is."

"And can you confirm whether she's from Latvia?"

"She is," Alexei says. "Her name is Adriana Strelkova, and I'm lucky she's willing to put up with all this." He gestures around, and then he turns back. "And for the record, she's not just my girlfriend. I love her very much."

My heart soars when I hear him say those words for the first time, but it's still very, very bad news. Because just as I predicted, the Russians aren't keen on their shining golden boy dating someone like me.

The front page of the newspaper the next day calls me the Latvian criminal whore. I can't even really argue with them, not about the criminal part, anyway. But worst of all, any argument I make won't help, because Alexei's not on trial.

He's up for election.

All that matters is their perception of me, and it's not good.

Not good at all.

Apparently security in Russia is not very good, because Mirdza just shoots through the door to my hotel room, even though to my knowledge, she should not have been given a key.

"You can't leave."

I'm nearly done packing my bags. "Why not?"

"That's what you always do," she says. "You run away."

I turn toward her slowly. "When have I *ever* run away?"

"All the time."

I shake my head. "I think not. I bash the bullies in the head with a rock. I spit in Nojus's face. I scream and rail whenever someone wrongs me. But no matter what I do, the only thing that can fix this mess is for me to leave." My eyes are welling up with tears, and I feel like I might be sick, but what I'm saying is absolutely true.

"That's a bunch of crap."

"Excuse me?" I throw the shirt I was folding down and step toward her. "We've been trying and trying to figure out how to beat Leonid, with his magic and his minions, and we've come up short. But Alexei might defeat him fair and square using the law. He might do it, because the people freaking love him. They should. He's amazing. It's no wonder people think I'm not good enough for him." I shake my finger at my twin. "I'm not. Not even close."

"You're being an idiot right now," Mirdza says. "So I'll humor you and name a few times that you've run. First, you told me you ran that night, when you heard Mārtinš come after me."

I flinch. That's a low blow.

"And again when you thought Nojus was going to kill you and I called pretending you were Kris, you ran straight at Leonid. Running away. When you first realized you liked Alexei, you sprinted away from Russia so fast, you left little flaming tracks behind you."

I have to admit, she came up with a few times. "Fine, but in this instance, I'm not running. It's a strategic retreat."

"How did you feel about it when Kristiana and I lied to you, strategically, to try and force you to be around Alexei more?"

I hated it.

"How do you think Alexei will feel when he comes back—he's on his way to the hotel now, frantic, by the way, because you won't answer the phone—and finds you gone?"

"Mirdza, if he's on his way, I need to go. Stop stalling me."

"What if Leonid orchestrated the whole thing, and he's waiting outside for you to be stupid? Then he can catch you and use you as leverage against Alexei."

I hadn't even thought of that. I was too panicked about what I'd done to Alexei to consider that it might have been an intentional attack. "Do you think Leonid planned it?"

"He kept you captive. He would have looked into everything about you, and the reporters know a *lot* about your connection to Nojus and his brother." Mirdza shrugs. "I have no idea where else they'd have found the evidence. All the people you worked with are in jail or dead now." She snorts. "Speaking of, Grigoriy's pretty upset. Someone in prison knifed that horrible brother who was threatening you. He wanted to end that one himself."

"I'm glad it's not weighing on his mind," I say. "But I'm going to sleep better knowing he's gone. Tell him there's always Mārtiņš."

Mirdza frowns. "My leg's healed. I've let it go."

I can't keep my lip from curling. "That makes one of us."

"Put your stuff away so Alexei doesn't know you were going to leave him." Mirdza's voice is soft, like she knows how hard it would be on Alexei if he did see that I was going to run.

"But—"

"He has shown you every way he knows how that he's committed to you, even declaring he loves you on air. He had to know what they'd find when they dug around, and he had to know a Latvian girlfriend—or any girlfriend—wouldn't be popular." She shrugs. "He's a big boy. Trust his judgment."

"I don't want to cost him the election." I can't live with that. "Leonid needs to lose."

"I agree," Mirdza says. "That's why I think you should do a press conference yourself."

I'm still laughing when Alexei walks through the door. His eyes take in Mirdza, my bag, and the tears running down my face as I laugh.

"What's going on?"

"Mirdza thinks I should do a press conference." I wipe my cheeks. "Can you imagine?"

"Igor wants you to do one, too. Would you?"

Is he kidding? "I barely speak any Russian."

"You've gotten better," Mirdza says. Which basically means that even she admits I suck.

"Plus, I'm a disaster on camera, and I'm terrible about answering questions on the spot."

"But you're honest, and you're kind," Alexei says. "The people will see that."

"You're their golden boy," I say. "You just said you loved me, so every woman in Russia is already predisposed to hate me."

"She's right about that," Mirdza says. "But if you went on stage and, I don't know, fell on your own face, they might pity him."

I'm going to slap her.

"Anyone who really gets to see you will love you," Alexei says.

"Oh, no," Mirdza says. "Remember how I said to trust his judgment? I take it all back."

Alexei shakes his head. "True political success comes from people being able to feel your authenticity."

"Says the spectacularly beautiful orator who speaks six languages and was raised with statecraft from the bassinet," Mirdza says.

I had no idea my sister was this feisty. Grigoriy's good for her.

Two hours later, Igor Baranov's people are dusting crap on my face that makes me sneeze, and I've been squeezed into a stupid, itchy suit with the most irritating tiny buttons I've ever seen. I've been practicing my smile for twenty minutes, but it only seems to be getting worse.

"Maybe don't smile," the woman Igor sent to prepare me says. "You seem serious and distinguished when you don't smile."

Oh, geez. Even she's lying to me now.

Ten minutes later, I'm tripping over my own feet—these heels are ridiculous—and they're showing me a stack of enormous cards that the person near the camera will be holding up. They're basically the written responses that Igor prepared frantically. They make me sound like that horrible American woman—Monica something or other.

Shoot me now.

Sixty seconds after that, the man by the camera is using his fingers to count down: three, two, and one. A big red light blinks and words on the top corner of the screen in front of me now say *On Air* in English. I wonder why they don't have it in Russian. Maybe the equipment's made in America.

I have the same commentator Alexei had, the friendly, chuckle guy who made him look so easygoing and approachable. Maybe that'll help.

"Today we have the woman who took our entire country by surprise, the Latvian criminal herself, Miss Adriana Strekkova."

At least he left off the whore part. "It's actually Stre*l*kova."

"Excuse me?" The commentator looks down at his papers. He squints. "Ah, yes. Sure."

"Anyway, it's nice to be here." Only, it doesn't sound like I think it's nice. My voice came out squeaky at first, and then flat. It sounds like I'm mocking him.

The commentator's scowling at me, possibly for correcting him on my name. Or it could have been my sarcastic-sounding tone. Either way, we're not off to a great start.

I decide to try smiling. How bad can it really be?

"Is everything alright?" he asks.

My smile falters a bit. "What?"

"You look as if you may be in pain. Are you feeling alright?"

I laugh. "Of course, Pavel," I say. "How about you? Are *you* alright?"

"Actually, I was diagnosed last week with prostate cancer."

"Oh no," I say. "That's terrible."

"Well, hopefully not," he says. "I have a procedure set up next week."

This entire interview is a trainwreck. I seriously consider standing up and walking off the tracks. "Well, if I was the kind of person who prayed, I'd be sure to pray for you."

"You don't believe in God?" Pavel asks.

I shrug. "Honestly? I don't know. I was in a bit of a bind last month—your usual criminal stuff—and I prayed when I was really scared. I wound up being fine, so maybe God saved me."

Pavel stares at me blankly.

Maybe I shouldn't be mocking God on television.

"Look, I know that no one here likes me," I say. "And I know that it's very bad for Alexei that he does." I shrug. "I'm not sure what else to say right now. The women watching will hate me for dating the most handsome, the most intelligent, the most respectful and eligible man in Russia. The men watching will hate me because, no matter what I say, they've already decided what kind of person they think I am. I'm not sure why I agreed to come talk to you, to be honest. My Russian isn't very good. My Latvian isn't welcomed.

I knew that coming here would be miserable and that it would go badly, and hey. What do you know? It is."

I stand up and start to walk away, but then I remember Mirdza. She said I always run away. Am I doing it again right now? Did I really even try?

Alexei deserves my best efforts. Then if people don't soften, that's on them. I turn back to face the camera again, and this time, I try to be as honest and sincere as I can.

"I'm very good at a few things, things no one cares about in politics. One of them is racing horses. One of them is defending myself. And the last one?" I look right at the camera and pause. Then I say, "Telling the truth, and you all know that's the worst thing anyone can do in politics, right? So if you want to hate me, go right ahead. Throw paint or eggs or something at me. Despise me in your homes. Slander me in your newspapers and on the streets. At the supermarket. I don't care. But what you *shouldn't* do is blame Alexei Romanov for liking me, because the things he doesn't hate about me are the same things that give him a reason to take this terrible job and try to serve you. He sees the good in flawed people. I'm guessing that describes most of you almost as well as it describes me. And none of us are good enough for him, but he cares about us anyway. That's the reason you should vote for him right there. He'll look the world in the eye and tell them all that he loves you, even when you're not perfect."

I turn on my heel, and I walk toward the edge of the stage, leaving Pavel to splutter and stammer until someone shows up with some cue cards for him to read. I'm nearly to the stairs when Alexei walks on stage across the studio. He's smiling.

"Isn't she brilliant?"

Of course everyone cheers for him.

"Much like all of you, things have not always been easy for Adriana. She's had to fight for what she wants, and she had to fight to protect herself in a world that never gave her what she deserved. She's had terrible men who stood in her way. She's had to deal with bigotry and sexism. She's had to overcome struggles, and she's had to forgive the people who wronged her. But in spite of all of that, she's a little spitfire, and she always helps the people who need it. I've seen that, and now you've seen enough to believe the truth in what I'm saying."

He walks toward me, and he holds up one hand, ducks his head a little, and waves for me to come back. I groan, but I listen. Walking back out there feels like being forced to chat with someone I just bawled out.

It's uncomfortable.

"This is a little unconventional, but I hope you'll forgive me. The news media outlets haven't been very kind to my girlfriend since they found out we were dating. Not just media outlets, either. Some of you on chats, on webpages, and on message boards have called her names, and they've even demanded that I should dump her." He shakes his head. "I will give my all to Russia as its president, but one thing I'll never do is let anyone dictate what's right and wrong in my personal life. I do love Adriana Strelkova, with every part of my being."

He drops to one knee and turns to face me.

"I want to marry you." He looks over his shoulder, a boyish grin tugging at his lips. "That's my answer to all of you asking me to dump her." He leans forward, and emphatically says, "In case I wasn't clear, it's a very firm *no*."

"Alexei," I say.

"I'm sorry," Alexei says. "I couldn't hear her. Did anyone else?" He looks around. "Did that sound like a yes? Or was it a no?"

"Alexei Romanov," I say. "Stand up right now."

"Not until you've said you'll marry me." He pulls a black box out of his pocket and holds it up. "Your sister told me you would want the largest, most ostentatious diamond I could possibly find so that *everyone* who ever treated you like crap would gnash their teeth in jealousy and rage when they saw it."

How embarrassing. My cheeks heat up furiously.

"This is what I came up with." He whips the lid off, and I'm suddenly staring at the largest, sparkliest diamond I've ever seen.

"Alexei," I say.

He stands up. "They say the third time's the charm, and guys, she's now said my name three times, but she's never said no. I'm taking that as a *yes*." He slides the ring on my finger—it fits—and then wraps one arm around my shoulder. "I hope that all of you will celebrate with us as we plan our wedding. It'll be in your hands whether Adriana marries the President of Russia. . .or just another guy." He leans closer to the camera one more time. "I think we'll be just as happy either way."

He's waving when the camera cuts off.

I cannot believe my eyes when they start showing me the responses online. They continue to roll in, even while we're all at dinner.

"You have got to be kidding," I say. "People love me, in spite of me. Alexei's just that charming."

"I think you might not be giving yourself enough credit," Kristiana says. "I was watching you up there too, and I wanted to be as cool as you. I think you may have made some real fans tonight in your own right."

"I thought you looked awesome too," Mirdza says. "But then, I always do."

When I go to bed that night, I can't help staring at my new ring.

"I was worried you were going to say no," Alexei says.

"Yeah, right."

"I was." His eyes soften. "Do you like the ring?"

"I hate that Mirdza knew just what I would want. I hate it even worse that you said it on live television." I can't help my smile. "But I do love it."

Alexei's smiling as he slides under the covers.

I'm glad that I didn't run away. It turns out, standing and fighting for what you want might be scary, but some things are worth it, and I'm pretty sure that Alexei Romanov is one of them.

✢ 28 ✣

When Uncle Mārtinš came to visit, two years or more after Dad died, Mom was delighted. She thought that, *finally*, after neglecting us for so long, his family might lend a hand. Or you know, give us some money, which would be more helpful.

But then Mārtinš never left.

His arrival turned out to be the very worst of luck.

The only wedding we ever had was the kind they do at the city records office. He marched her downtown and made her fill out all the forms so that he could say he owned her, basically. It didn't really leave me with the best impression of marriage.

Or weddings.

Yet, when Alexei proposed on national television—in Russia, yes, but it must've made it to Latvia too, because every single person I've ever met and some that I haven't are all texting me—I thought I'd be filled with fear. Instead, I felt *proud*. Proud that someone like him would ask me. Proud that, in spite of the damage I was causing to his reputation and popularity, he still wanted me by his side. Proud that in spite of my refusal to date, I was still proposed to by the most eligible bachelor, maybe in the world.

But I also felt safe in saying yes.

I'm not afraid, even now, that he'll change his mind. I'm not afraid that the whims of humanity or his people will sway him. In many ways, I barely know him. But in others, no one knows him better than I do. I've seen him in more than one form. I've experienced the wonder of his magic. I know the truth about his past. I know his dreams for the future and what he envisions my part to be.

And I know his greatest fear: losing his loved ones again.

I thought, with all that we have going on, that Kristiana and Aleksandr would either postpone their wedding, or that we'd be forced to miss it. A month ago, I wouldn't have cared much. I might not have even gone, had I not met Alexei.

Back then, I didn't realize quite how much of my decision-making was affected by my jealousy. I mean, I knew I was jealous of Kris. Her mom was worlds better than mine, for one, but her life in general was incomparable. Her family. Her home. Her money. And her fiancé. Most of all, though, she's always felt loved. She's always had a support system, even if her dad is a bit of a mess.

Whereas, I have always felt utterly alone.

It wasn't really fair for me to feel that way. I always had Mirdza, and Kristiana too, if I'm being honest. They've never wavered in their care for me. Even my mom, in her own way, has always loved me. There's value in that I never quite acknowledged.

Alexei insists that we go back to Latvia for their wedding and that they shouldn't postpone under any circumstance. Watching Kristiana and Aleksandr prepare the last-minute details is one part inspirational and two parts stressful. For some reason, when Alexei proposed, I didn't really think about the stress and decisions involved in having the *wedding* itself.

Bridesmaids and flowers, a venue and vows, a dress and a priest.

It's a lot.

Most girls talk about their dress, and their perfect spot, and their colors, and their favorite flowers. It's not anything I ever dreamed about, simply because I never wanted to be shackled to a man.

"—hold that?"

I realize that Kris is talking to me. "Right." I take the flowers. I blink. "Where do you want me to put them?" I should be paying more attention and not distracted by my own stress.

"They're for you," she says. "Are you alright?" She looks about one centimeter away from snapping her fingers in front of my face.

"I'm fine."

"Thinking about your wedding?" Her mouth curls into a smirk.

"Kind of," I say. "Except, do you really think we have to do one? Like, a big one? That people come to?"

Kris drops her own bouquet on the ground, lilies scattering all over the floor.

"Oh, no." I lean over and start gathering them up. "I bet we can tuck these back in."

"Who cares about the flowers?" Kristiana says. "Of *course* you have to have a wedding."

"You don't care about the flowers?" I ask.

She frowns.

"Maybe you get it then. I'm like *that*, except about all of it." I wave my hands around to encompass everything. We're standing in a pretty small dressing room on the side of the small chapel she chose, so there's not really a lot to gesture at, but I think she gets my point.

Mirdza walks through the side door, closing it quietly. "The coordinator says four minutes." Her mouth drops open. "Oh, no. The bouquet."

"I'm fixing it." I set mine on an end table and start poking the runaway lilies into gaps in the enormous bubble-shaped ball of flowers.

"Not like that." Mirdza slaps my hand away. "You're making it look like a helmet."

"Isn't that how bouquets are meant to look?"

Mirdza clucks at me, just like Mom always did. "Just stand over there and try not to ruin yours too."

"Hey, I didn't ruin that one," I say. "I didn't even touch it until she dropped it."

"Because Adriana says she doesn't want a wedding." Kris's mauve lips are pursed, and her perfectly plucked and outlined eyebrow is arched in frustration.

Mirdza crushes the flower she's holding.

"What's with all the melodrama?" I shake my head.

"If you're going to get married," Mirdza says, "you should do it right. You should throw the biggest party anyone has ever seen." She glances back at Kris. "But not bigger or nicer than this, of course."

Kris rolls her eyes.

"The last thing you want to do is what Mom did," Mirdza says.

"Mom got married," I say. "To a real loser. That's the example of hers I want to avoid. Neither of us would ever marry someone like *him*, so the kind of celebration we have is a little irrelevant, isn't it?"

Mirdza frowns. "I guess."

"We're not done talking about this," Kris says, "but maybe let's finish with the bouquet."

"Right."

We're shoving the very last lily into a gap in the bottom—for all her self-righteous indignation, my twin ended up doing the same thing I was—when the door pops open and the coordinator waves at us. "Come, come. Mirdza first, then you."

I was a little surprised when Kristiana invited me to be a bridesmaid, but I realized that she can't very well leave me out when I grew up alongside her just like Mirdza. Plus, my fiancé's best friends with her groom. Alexei must have said a dozen times that he wouldn't stand next to anyone other than me. It should have annoyed me. But. . .

When I heard him say that, it made me smile.

I've definitely changed. I hope it's for the better.

With Alexei in attendance, the paparazzi are understandably pretty bad, but Igor says it's fine. Attending a lovely wedding with respectable Russian nobility who are marrying wealthy Latvian girls can only improve both Alexei's and my images, apparently.

Or so Igor thinks.

The polls have been a little strange for the past week, which is hardly surprising. The voting happens tomorrow, and we'll be stuck spending all day on television and standing on stages making speeches. It's not the election for President, of course. That will still lie ahead of us, but if the referendum passes, there won't be an election. In most ways, the vote for the referendum is actually more important. With the way their political parties work, as I understand it, no one else would really have a chance if the grab at the monarchy fails.

When Alexei threw in with Russia United, he sort of gave up his right to challenge Leonid's right to rule.

He had to pick whether to support the current government or vie for his place in the new one.

The aisle we have to walk is stupidly long. I have no idea how Kris and Aleks can possibly know the number of people filling all these seats. Aleksandr has been in an extended coma for a century, for heaven's sake. We're almost there when I trip on a little kid's discarded shoe and nearly fall on my face.

Alexei catches me, his hands bracing my elbow and back. "You alright?"

"I am now." A month ago, that might have annoyed me, having to thank a man, but now I'm not even surprised that he lunged forward and caught me. I'm grateful for his attention and care.

I shuffle over and hop into line at the end, cameras flashing right and left. Clearly, in spite of Aleksandr's people being posted on every corner, a few reporters squeezed through. Either that, or some of the people in attendance are being paid a lot for their candid photos. Mirdza steps into place next to Grigoriy as gracefully as ever, the opposite of me in almost every way now that her leg has been repaired.

Mom's on the front row, already bawling. She told me this morning that all her wildest dreams are coming true. While I'm happy for Kris, Mirdza, and myself, I couldn't help being a little annoyed that her dreams for her daughters still revolve around them marrying the right guys.

Oh, well. Baby steps.

I'm a little surprised to see that their chosen pastor is a woman. Her hair's short, and her suit is sharp. "Welcome to all of you who are here to celebrate the marriage of Kristiana Liepa and Aleksander Volkonsky."

Kris holds out her hand, and Aleks takes it.

"I'm so pleased to be here today, officiating the wedding of such a beautiful couple. When Kristiana asked me to marry them, I told her I'd need to meet with them a few times first. It's been hard for them to make time, especially with all the things going on in Russia, but they've made time for it. It has been really special for me to talk to them about the things they have in common. Their love for horses. Their passion for racing. Their affinity for the earth and collecting minerals and rocks." She shakes her head. "They're a match made in heaven."

I can't help it—I glance sideways at Mirdza and smirk.

She's looking at me, too. No one in the audience has any idea about Aleks and his horse form or his earth powers. Kristiana had no interest in gardening, in rocks, or in gems. As far as I know, Aleks never rides horses. But I suppose none of that matters. It's what the world sees.

She drones on a little bit about the sanctity of the marriage covenant, and how they each promise one another to protect and preserve their connection and their bond. I'm a little distracted, because Alexei's writing something on the inside of my palm.

The first time, I don't quite catch it.

But the second time, I do.

I. L. O. V. E. Y. O. U.

He's said it on national television—twice—but I've never said it back. Between the election stuff and the travel and the meetings, we haven't had very much time alone, and what we've had has been a little. . .preoccupied. When we're together, I mostly want to be touching him and kissing him. Or I pass out and fall asleep. There's not much in between.

I decide that it's time.

Most couples would have a normal date, and they'd sit down and stare into each other's eyes, and then the girl would tell him she loves him too. She loves that he's always there. She loves that in spite of always being supportive, he gives her space. She loves that he hasn't wavered, but that he lied about wanting her so she wouldn't worry.

That might feel wrong to some people, but it was right for me.

It's strange to me how one person's love story might be someone else's disaster. Alexei came into my life as a *horse*, and he was a literal answer to the first prayer I ever made. He has stayed with me, biting anyone who means me harm—or wants to ask me out—and watching my back ever since.

So I squeeze his hand, and then in my really lousy Russian, I spell out I love you, one symbol at a time. He's much quicker than I was, because he releases my hand, turns my face toward his, and kisses me right on the mouth.

In the middle of Kristiana and Aleksandr's wedding.

The officiator's just now telling them to share their vows, and I don't think anyone even notices. That's a relief.

But Alexei's still beaming when I sneak a glance.

"When I started thinking about what I wanted to promise," Kristiana says, "I wasn't really sure. My mom died, as all of you surely know, and so I know better than most people that there aren't any guarantees. No matter what I promise today, I could die in an hour. In a year. Or when I'm eighty-five. Some things in life—a lot of things, really—aren't up to us."

Kristiana looks up at her soon-to-be-husband and smiles. "But one thing is entirely within my control, and that's what I spend my time focusing on. In the past, it was horses, horses, and more horses. From this day forward, though, I promise it will be horses, horses, Aleksandr Volkonsky, and more horses, for as long as we both shall live." She smiles then, and I'm standing close enough to hear her whisper, but only just. "Good thing you're the most beautiful horse I've ever seen."

Aleks is laughing when he starts sharing his vows. "My lovely wife will always keep me on my toes, and I love that about her. She races for her job, and it's been a joy of mine to run alongside her. But her other job, the one I've been taking her away from more often than not lately, is healing creatures who can't even say what's wrong."

He looks away from Kris and out at the audience. "Most of you know her well enough to know why that's perfect for her. Kristiana loves to champion the little guy. She loves stepping in and helping horses' lives to improve. She's like that in every single way. That was the first thing I noticed about her, and it's what made me fall so hard and so fast in love. She is always healing, always caring, and always watching, and she will do anything it takes to protect the people she loves. Thank you all for joining us today, so I can pledge to each and every one of you that I promise to take care of her in any way I can for the rest of my life."

John's sitting on the front row.

Aleksandr meets his eye. "John here, the Liepa family's long-time horse trainer, wasn't very keen on me at first. In fact, I think he kind of hated me. But over time, I think he's come to accept that I make Kris happy."

"Given how you met, you can't ever complain about

any horse she buys." John folds his arms. "Or any vagabond-looking trainer she hires."

"I suppose you're right," Aleksandr says. "From this day forward, *carte blanche* on horse purchases." He clears his throat. "I think two trainers is more than enough, though. Don't you?" He eyes John.

Unsurprisingly, this makes the whole room cheer. And after the pastor pronounces them man and wife, Kristiana's dad walks in, leading two horses. One of them I barely know—a sweet but very leggy chestnut mare. But the other one—it's Five Times Fast. The horse Kris was riding when she met Aleksandr.

"I thought that we could do the norm and just get in cars and drive to the reception," Aleks says. "Since you're wearing that." He points at her huge, fluffy skirt. "Or we could race there." The glint in his eye is all the evidence anyone needs to see that they're perfect for one another.

When he swings up on his leggy mare, I realize that he must be a decent rider. I suppose it makes sense. He came from a time when riding a horse was still an oft-used mode of transportation. I figured he might have just shifted into his horse form whenever he needed to go somewhere, but I suppose he couldn't exactly traipse around naked once he arrived back then either.

As they take off for the reception on horseback—a solid two and a half miles away—I walk hand-in-hand to the car with my fiancé.

"Do you want to chase them?" Alexei asks.

Part of me wants to say yes, but we're the hosts. We can't exactly run into a corner, have him shift into a horse and go racing across the countryside. Surely one of the guests would notice. Right?

But not fifteen seconds later, my jaw drops as Mirdza whoops and flies down the side of the road on top of her massive bay with the face stripe. She's riding freaking Charlemagne, so by golly. . .

"Yes." I point at the side room where Kristiana changed. It must be where Grigoriy just shifted. The side wall's blocked by a huge copse of trees. "Only, hurry. I know a shortcut, and I really want to beat them."

Quicksilver's definitely the fastest of the three, but we take so long to get his clothes off, folded up, and tucked into a bag that we're hopelessly behind when we finally start. The wind whipping through my hair knocks all the pins out, the dust from the road coats my Robin's egg blue dress in uneven patches, and I accidentally drop the bag, upending Alexei's clothes in a mud puddle.

Still, it's worth it.

By the time we rejoin the reception, everyone's already dancing and eating and smiling, and Kris and Aleks, and Mirdza and Grigoriy look just as disheveled as we do.

I take a moment to marvel at the fact that the three of us, all horse-obsessed idiots, managed to find the perfect men. Solid, steady, kind, and always willing to take us for a wild ride through the surrounding countryside.

Mirdza picks a few pieces of grass out of my hair, and then she smiles. "I'm not sure I could be happier than I am in this moment."

Grigoriy flings her into the air and spins her around, dropping her back down without having to use extreme care. Some days, I still forget her leg was healed until I see her do something she hasn't done in a decade. It's been a strange month, but a wonderful one in many ways. My sister's in love, and she's been healed.

I'm in love, and in a lot of ways, it feels like I've been healed even more than she was.

The next day, I hang on to as much of that calm and peace as I can while we fly into Russia at an ungodly hour. I cling to it while we're dressed up by a whole host of people. I'm still grasping it while we smile and wave and make stupid canned speeches.

And then as we sit and wait as the votes are counted, I try too.

But it's awfully hard to hold on to my joy when, in spite of our best efforts, in spite of Alexei's brilliance and generosity and in spite of my attempts to repair the damage I did by being who I am, the referendum passes.

We lose.

And more frightening, Leonid wins, fair and square. The Russian people voted to give up their freedom because they liked his vision for a stronger future. They're dumb, but we're the real morons for believing in them.

❧ 29 ❧

After Dad died, Mirdza and I lived in a rotation of homes that changed monthly. Only after meeting Kristiana's family did we find a home. And when Mom met Mārtiņš, that changed again. I stayed with Mom as much as I could manage it, in an attempt to keep her safe.

Or you know, saf*er*.

When Mom married him, she thought her money problems were over. Wrong. They were just getting started. People like him don't know how to do things that are hard. They've given up on everything difficult for the entirety of their lives. I did learn how to pack up quickly and head out when danger threatens.

Only, no one in my new group of friends wants to do that.

"In ten days, Russia transitions to a tsardom again," I say. "We need to be gone by then."

"We just got our homes back," Aleks says. "You haven't even been to see any of the palaces Russia agreed to give back to Alexei. Some of them are pretty nice."

"One was a church, one was a boarding school, and one was a hotel," I say. "Who cares? We can build a new house. We can't grow new heads."

"Have you forgotten?" Grigoriy asks. "We're powerful. Leonid's afraid of us."

I'm not at all sure that's true now that he has a massive standing army of innocent-ish soldiers at his command. "Even if he is, will you use your powers to kill his armies? Thousands and thousands of soldiers?"

I remember Alexei telling me what he could do to humans—thousands of them. I'm not the only one who thinks that through, because all three men frown.

"I'm telling you. We need to leave."

Aleks is staring at his phone.

"What now?" Grigoriy asks.

Aleksandr turns on the television, and it shows riots in Russia. Men who are angry at the elimination of their freedom are now destroying things. Shops with the double-headed eagle of the Russian Tsardom stickers in the windows. People with the United Russia bear symbol on their cars are having their windshields smashed in.

Tensions are running high all around.

We're still arguing over what to do when Aleksandr's butler knocks and pokes his head in the room. "A message has come for you by personal courier." He steps all the way into the room, holding a silver tray. There's a card resting on top of it. Nothing delivered like that is going to be good, no matter what kind of tray it's sitting on.

Alexei takes it, lifting the heavy cream envelope slowly. He slides his finger under the flap, waiting for Aleksandr's butler to leave.

Then he pulls the card out and reads it out loud.

"It's addressed to Alexei Romanov, *pretender* to the throne of Russia." Alexei grimaces.

His Majesty, Leonid Ivanovich, hereby requests your presence at a dinner at his personal residence in Moscow. Transportation will be provided.

The details follow, but he wants us to come to his house.

"And at the bottom, he's hand written something." Alexei lifts the card so we can all see.

Please do bring your delightful fiancée. My belated congratulations on your upcoming marriage. Tell her I'll be sure to prepare the finest charcuterie plate.

Charcuterie? I think back on the plastic boxes of crackers and cheese that Boris threw into my cell every day. I might try to wring his neck if I see him again.

"No way," I say. "We cannot go."

"I think we should," Aleksandr says. "We were hoping he'd come to the race."

I shake my head. "But he didn't. The one time we wanted him, he didn't show, and now that he wants us there?" I shudder. "Bad idea."

"I think we all go," Aleksandr continues.

"The invitation's only for Alexei," I say. "Well, and me too, I guess, but it's not like I can do much to help."

"He may not be angry anymore," Grigoriy says. "I mean, I'm still upset, but maybe he's not. He did win."

"I'd think that you, above all others, would want to go," Mirdza says, her voice characteristically soft. It irritatingly grabs my attention, like she knew it would.

"What does that mean?"

"The palomino mare who won that race—she's probably being held captive by Leonid." Mirdza folds her arms. "We could use this chance to check on her."

"It's more likely that she's helping them," I mutter. "She did her best to win that race."

"Even if she is, she may not know everything that's going on," Mirdza says. "There's more than one way to be trapped." No one knows that better that Mirdza and I. Our own mother was held captive without bars or locks for years.

"You think they'll just let all six of us waltz in to look around?" I frown.

"Nope," Mirdza says. "But I think people like Leonid rarely even notice the servants."

Now Aleksandr's frowning too. "What are you even suggesting?"

"Just a little misdirection. It's been used the world over for lots of things, from illusionists to spies."

Neither of which my sister is. "This is crazy."

"Hear me out," Mirdza says. "When they go for dinner, I can go too as the maid or the helper. Whatever."

"They've seen you," I say. "It won't work."

"I could dye my hair," she says.

"I like it how it is," Grigoriy says.

"I can always dye it back—a little perspective." Mirdza rolls her eyes. "They won't know I've been healed, either."

"I think they can guess," Grigoriy says. "The guys knew what Alexei's family could do."

Mirdza huffs. "They may have seen me, but I doubt they paid much attention to me. They held Adriana. They wanted Kris. No one cares about me. And if I can cause a distraction or sneak out and let you guys in—"

"No way," Grigoriy says.

"This may be our last chance to stop him from ruling all of Russia," Mirdza says. "Or at the very least, we can try to find out what measures we need to take. Maybe meeting with Alexei is a publicity stunt, and if so, it could help prevent rioting. But if he's planning something else, we could finally turn the tables on him." Mirdza shrugs. "I think we should try to do something before it's too late."

Too late.

All of Russia's children are mine—not just Riurik's.

Baba Yaga's words come back to me. She made the mistake of caring only about her own child for a time. She gave certain humans a power they never should have had. And in the process, she forgot to care for the others.

She gave the noble families—Aleks, Grigoriy, and Alexei's families—five smaller powers to try and fix her mistake. She wanted them to care for the people of Russia. Now someone who may not have that interest in his mind at all is about to take control. I think that's why she came to talk to me.

It hits me then—it all comes from the same main. "Baba Yaga was talking about Leonid. He can use more than one power, because he really is from Riurik's line."

"Right," Alexei says. "We figured that part out."

"But we haven't understood *why* Boris and Mikhail would listen to him." I say the next part slowly, as I work it out in my brain. "What if, when he uses their powers, they can't? Or they only can with *his* permission?"

"Then he really could be holding Katerina hostage," Alexei says.

I can't say I love that she's his first thought.

"And Boris and Mikhail as well," I say. "If he's the higher valve that she didn't know was still there. . ." I gasp. "He might be able to control you three as well."

Aleksandr's shaking his head. "He'd have come after us already if that was how it worked. There must be more to it than that."

"Why didn't she tell us what she meant?" Kristiana looks heartily annoyed. "Why be so cryptic?"

"She's not sure whether Leonid's going to do good or bad, maybe," I say. "Or, if he is descended from her child, she might be too invested to do what it takes."

"I hate her," Kristiana says. "If she gave him this power, she could just take it away."

"He'd still be about to take over Russia," I say. "So maybe it doesn't matter."

"He used those powers to get where he is," Kris says. "I'm sure of it."

She might be right, but the three men we care about have all used theirs as well. "If he could take Boris and Mikhail's powers, he can take Aleks, Grigoriy, and Alexei's as well."

"But only they can stop him," Mirdza says, "from doing exactly what they did to you to anyone else they'd like."

The words sound dragged out of me, but they do come. "We should go."

Alexei looks shocked. "I thought you wanted to live our lives, now that we've been freed."

I nod.

"Then why—"

"Because as selfish as she wants people to think she is, no one is as ferocious a defender of what's right as my sister is," Mirdza says.

Does she really believe that?

Tears well up in my eyes. I want it to be true. I want to be brave. I want to be good. And in that moment, I think about what I promised to do. I could be dead right now. I could have been killed by Leonid, the very man we're talking about going back to meet. It's possible that it was luck, but it's also possible that God helped me escape. . . For what purpose?

In that moment, something inside of me swells, and I know this is the right path. We're supposed to confront Leonid. If not us, then who? Who else would stand a chance against someone who can burn or electrocute anyone who attacks? Thinking about the zaps I've endured doesn't normally inspire, but instead of frightening me in this moment, the fact that I endured them galvanizes me.

Together, we sit down and make a plan.

A plan to find out what Leonid really wants. A plan to defend all the people of Russia from this person who thinks he's entitled to anything he can take. We can't just let him take things that aren't his and deprive others of what they need. We might be able to flee Russia and live in comfort and wealth in Latvia, but how many other Russians can do the same?

That night, when I lie down in my room, my brain won't stop spinning. I think about the time when I was locked up. I think about my first interaction with Leonid. I think about the things Baba Yaga said, and the things Alexei said.

Over and over and over.

I review our plan—which seems pretty thin, to be honest. Mirdza goes as my maid? Who needs a lady's maid in this day and age? They all think Leonid won't think a thing about it. She's then supposed to use some drug Grigoriy supplied to knock out the guards, and then she lets the men in through the side of the property. Thankfully, Aleksandr has some people who are good at hacking. Apparently they're plentiful in Russia, but at least we know the layout of the house and grounds.

Once they're inside, they'll search for Boris and Mikhail, and of course, Katerina. Grigoriy's quite good at searching, thanks to his wind power, and Aleks is decent at sussing out hidden basements and the like. They'll pump anyone they find for answers, and then the three of them will unite and face off against Leonid, threatening to destroy him, basically.

It's hard to know what more to do, since we don't understand how he stole the power from the other two or what he plans to do now that he's won the election and Russia's about to fundamentally change. Which means we don't really have much of a plan at all.

I hate it.

Which is why I'm still tossing and turning and not even close to sleeping. There's a very soft tap on my door.

I hop to my feet and throw on a robe.

It's a habit now, after staying in fancy hotels and houses for a while. But when I answer the door, it's Alexei. A tiny thrill runs through me.

"Were you sleeping?" He looks nervous. My big, tall, handsome czar looks nervous.

I shake my head.

"It took longer than I thought, but I have something for you." He's wearing navy blue silk pajamas. His eyes have never looked more sapphire. "I was worried

—the whole idea of taking you with me tomorrow, even though you have no powers—"

I grab his arm and yank him into the blue room.

He stumbles forward, bracing himself with one hand on the dresser, but his powerful chest and other arm still slam into me, pressing his hard angles against my soft ones. His eyes widen.

"Tomorrow's going to be a long day. A dangerous day." His voice is soft and low. "And I don't want you going in there without any kind of protection."

I swallow. "And?"

He opens his free hand, and I can't help looking. "What's that?"

"Dad wouldn't let me share this spell, at least, not while he was alive, but I think he'd understand my reasoning." Alexei reaches for my face, but his hands stop a little short. "Can I take a hair?"

That is not what I was expecting. "Um, sure?"

He yanks one out, a long one, and then carefully winds it around a deep red ruby. He waves his hand over them, and the hair disappears. "This necklace is a charm, now. I've spelled it with my water power, which will counter any attacks directly at your person from any fire, and Aleksandr spelled it with earth, which negates any electrical attacks."

Water counteracts fire, and earth grounds electricity. Interesting. "Okay. How do I use it?"

He shakes his head. "You shouldn't have to. It's keyed to you, so if your safety is threatened, it will activate."

Handy. "Well, thanks."

He sets it on the top of my dresser, and this time, when he reaches for me, his hand doesn't yank any hair out. It strokes the back of my head and pulls me closer. He kisses me then, and I lean closer, finally distracted from thoughts of tomorrow. My mouth opens against his, wanting more. When he crushes me even harder against him, I can't help a small moan.

He freezes, and his voice against my ear is rough. "I needed to be closer to you. I missed sleeping next to you."

"Yes."

"But we can't do anything stupid."

"Why would anything we do be stupid?" The corner of my lip turns up. "We're adults."

His chuckle's low and cocky. "That's true. But we have no idea what may happen tomorrow, and most important of all is that you feel *safe*. Wanted. Treasured."

"I do feel all of those things."

He's practically purring when he says, "Good. But not good enough. Not yet." When he lowers his head, slowly, his mouth barely brushes against mine. "I thought I might try something."

He kisses me again, but this time, I feel something brushing against my body *all over*. Everything. Every cell. Every single separate part of my body shivers in delight.

"What was that?" I ask.

It happens again, this time with a little more pressure. "It's a caress," he whispers against my ear. "Water's an amazing thing, isn't it? Depending on its movement, depending on its volume, the pressure can change. And there's water just about *everywhere*."

Alexei may have the power to dam up a river, the power to tear someone apart one cell at a time, and the power to redirect even rainstorms to bring water to drought areas. But he can also use water expertly in ways I never imagined, and boy does he.

"I love you," I whisper, late into the night. "I didn't think I would ever be able to say that to a man."

Alexei brushes his hand across mine. "Why not?"

"Because it means that I trust you." I snuggle closer to him, my head resting on his chest. "After my dad died and my stepdad was a miserable wretch, I didn't think I could ever trust a man. To love someone, you must first believe he'll keep you safe." I prop myself up on one arm. "I believe that you will."

"My love for you worries me a little." Alexei looks up at me. "All my life, I've known that I had to put Russia first. Everything else must follow my duty to Russia. Tomorrow, we're going to face the scariest foe I've ever imagined, and I need to be as strong as I can to defend my people."

"I'm worried about it, too."

He traces one finger across the top of my lips, and he shakes his head. "I'm not worried about Leonid or those idiots Mikhail and Boris."

I frown. "Then what?"

"I'm worried," he says, "because for the first time in my life, I care more about you than I do about anything else, including Russia. If I have to choose, I don't think I'll make my father very proud." His voice drops to the merest whisper. "If I have to choose tomorrow, I'll choose you."

❧ 30 ☙

Once, when I was in secondary school, I was supposed to get an academic award. I never had the best grades, but my English teacher chose me as the top student. After the awards ceremony, there was a banquet.

I didn't want to admit it, but I was pretty excited.

Mirdza went every year, almost, but I had never been invited before. Only when it was time to go did I realize that I had nothing to wear. The flier they sent home said I was supposed to wear 'business dress,' whatever that means. My mom came out of her room wearing her one dress—it was black. Short. And low cut.

It made me uncomfortable.

I didn't want to take my mom when she looked like that, but I looked even worse. All I had were pants and shirts, and none of them looked very good either. They were all worn and threadbare.

"I don't want to go," I told my mom.

She insisted I had to. "It's the only time you've ever

earned this, and it'll probably be the last." She pointed at the door. "Now, march."

When we reached the school, I felt even more out of place, because every other girl was wearing a dress. None of the boys' pants had worn spots or a hole in the knee, either. None of them were wearing the same beat-up sneakers they always wore to school. I survived that dinner, but I didn't enjoy it.

In spite of the gorgeous red dress Alexei ordered for me, in spite of the lovely red pumps, and in spite of the stunning red stone hanging around my neck, I have the same feeling as I had that night when we exit the car Leonid sent for us. My heart hammers in my chest as I walk up the steps to the ridiculous mansion he's occupying in the last few days before he starts ruling Russia.

I feel out of place, poor, and useless. My fingers keep reaching for my necklace, as if it's going to somehow save me from the anxiety I'm feeling.

"Try not to draw attention to it," Alexei whispers. "The last thing we want is for Leonid to notice what you're wearing."

He's right. He's always right.

Alexei takes my hand then. "It's going to be fine."

But he has no idea whether that's true. We could be walking into a firing squad. I could be leading Mirdza to her death.

"If they attack us, I'm ready." He squeezes my hand.

"How can you always read my mind?"

His half-grin looks utterly calm. "You're as expressive as a toddler. I hope you never played poker."

"I blew my money on horse races," I say. "Cards weren't really my thing."

"Thank goodness. You'd have owed twice as much." He lifts his hand to knock.

And the door opens before he can.

A sour-faced butler—why are they always sour-faced? Why can't they be comedians?—gestures for us to walk inside. "Come."

Mirdza keeps her head down as she scampers in behind us.

"Where can my maid wait?" I take off my jacket—thankfully it's cool enough to wear one now—and hand it to her.

"You didn't need to bring a maid," the butler says.

"I never trust my valuables to be left alone in a room." I shrug. "After I lost a really nice wallet and another time, a purse, I just can't risk it."

The butler arches an eyebrow at first, but then he nods. "Over there. She'll find a lounge with a settee."

Why can't rich people just say couch? Really, it's ridiculous. And if it's actually a couch with just one side, then they're especially dumb. Those don't look comfortable or nice. It's like rich people are the dumbest of all—they pay more for a useless sofa with fewer materials that go into it because it has a fancy French name.

"This way." The butler starts walking and never looks back to see whether we're following.

But when he turns down a huge hallway, we're still right behind him. And when he opens large double wooden doors, Leonid's behind them, standing almost at attention. When he sees us, his face lights up.

"You actually came. I didn't think you would."

"How could we refuse such a gracious invitation?" Alexei looks around the room, clearly looking for a camera.

It's in the corner.

"With our nation rocked by discord, of course we agreed to this dinner. We should both do everything we can to quell any revolution or unrest. It really hurts everyone." Alexei smiles. "The people have spoken, and if their decision was to restore the monarchy, so be it."

"Are you upset?" Leonid cocks his head. "Do you think you should be ruling Russia instead of me?"

"As the Romanov heir, you mean?" Alexei asks.

Leonid shrugs and then nods in one smooth movement. "Even so."

"I have a strong claim," Alexei says. "But my family was in the process of trying to allow the Russian people more freedoms. I never thought all the power should be returned to me or my family. And I won't try to foment discord now."

"You're such a *good* person," Leonid says. "Exactly what Russia doesn't need, of course, but a good person nonetheless." He turns to face the camera. "But as you can see, we aren't fighting, and as the gracious loser here said, neither should you. We're all united now, in a way we never would've been with all those elections and a dozen different groups arguing." His smile's a little too beatific. "I think if you watch our dinner tonight, you'll see that the riots, the unrest, the property damage—it's all a waste of energy. You should be looking ahead, at our glorious shared future."

The rest of the dinner is more of the same. I can't figure out why Leonid's still posturing, but maybe he's worried that something might happen between now and the official transition. Maybe he should be—he's not commanding the army yet.

As he promised, there's a large charcuterie board in the center of the table. He keeps offering it to me, and every time, I grit my teeth and remind myself why we're here. We're putting on a show to calm down the fury among Russians, and we're buying Mirdza time so that she can get us some backup to actually do something to this lunatic.

I'm hoping, since we haven't heard otherwise, that she managed to get the guys inside without being caught. For now, we have a performance to continue. After we've eaten—as little as possible for me—Leonid sets his utensils down. "Well. If we're done with dinner. . ."

But I worry they haven't had enough time. What if Mirdza got delayed or detained?

"I still haven't tried the cheese and crackers," I say. "You should tell me which ones you like."

Leonid's lip twitches. "You're more interesting than I expected." He turns toward the camera. "But I think our time today has come to an end. I'm afraid the network could only spare an hour. Why don't you wave goodbye to the audience before we go off air?" His mouth curls up into a genuine smile. "I'm glad to see that you look especially pretty tonight. It's fitting. After all, you are the reason your boyfriend—or is it fiancé?—lost the election."

"Excuse me?" Even knowing he's been trying to bait us all night, it still ticks me off.

"Surely Alexei showed you the polls." Leonid looks genuinely puzzled. "Even after your little press conference, he never could make up the lost ground. No one liked his Latvian lover, even if she did prove to be less of a prostitute than people were saying."

Alexei has been calm and collected the entire meal, but he stands up, his chair shooting back behind him. "You'll watch your mouth."

Leonid gestures again and someone shuts off the camera, the little red light blinking out. A flick of his wrist, and the servant bows and backs out of the room. "That was brilliant. With all your chivalrous generosity and forced cheer, I was worried the people might stop rioting and fighting altogether, but that last bit should get them all worked into a frenzy again."

"You want them rioting?" Alexei frowns.

"Why did you really invite us here?" I ask. "Was it just to gloat?"

"Actually." Leonid stands too, looking utterly nonchalant. "I think I've been pretty patient for the last hour, waiting and waiting for you to assemble your team of friends." He tosses his head and the doors open.

Boris and Mikhail walk through, followed fairly closely by Mirdza, Grigoriy, and Aleksandr.

"You knew they were here?" I'm so confused. "But—"

"Would you all have come, if I invited you?" Leonid looks utterly calm.

Aleksandr and Grigoriy are looking from one to another, clearly confused.

"I only wish the darling, elusive Kristiana could have joined us. You see, she presents a fairly large problem."

"Why?" Aleksandr asks. "What do you want with her?"

Leonid shakes his head. "Never mind all that. Let's celebrate what we've been able to accomplish today." He shoves the cheese and cracker plate closer to me. "I mean, a mere few weeks ago, you would barely eat anything I brought you, and now you're tossing down crackers and cheese in my home like we're old friends."

I clench my hands into fists. "What do you want?"

Leonid holds up his hands. "I have fire power galore, thanks to Mikhail." He holds out one hand and a flame bursts into life above it. "Fire's pretty useful, to be sure. It can destroy most anything, if I push it hot enough. People are scared by it. It's very satisfying." He closes his hand into a fist and the fire blinks out.

"How do you have that power, precisely?" Alexei asks.

Leonid laughs, but it's a hard sound. Ugly. "I'm sure you want to know."

"Baba Yaga already told me," I say. "She said she gave it to your ancestors. The power you have is connected to the power each of them has." I gesture.

"She came to talk to you, did she?" Leonid's nostrils flare. "The witch isn't very consistent. Not consistent at all." He shakes his head and holds out his other hand. "I also have the power of electricity, which has completely transformed our world in the last hundred years, wouldn't you say?" He extends his hand. Crackles of lightning dance around his fingers, and then he flicks his index finger and an arc shoots across the room, frying the video camera.

Wasteful.

Everything about Leonid is wasteful.

"Although I have these powers, Boris and Mikhail still have them as well." He glances at them and inclines his head.

Boris waves his hand, and sparks fly into the air. The lights flicker.

Mikhail smiles as he shoots a fireball at the tapestry on the wall.

Leonid scowls, balling one hand into a fist and extinguishing the fireball before it strikes the woven scene depicting some kind of war. "But what I do *not* have that I always wanted is the power to create life. To nourish. To sustain." He smiles. "So be a real friend and share, will you, Alexei?" He holds out both hands, palms up.

"You need my consent," Alexei says, realization

dawning. "For some reason, you can't take a power without the one using it allowing you to." He can't help his smile. "Which I will never do."

"Don't be so sure. Everyone has a price," Leonid says. "I could make you my Chancellor. You'd be a trusted advisor. I could even give you the Winter Palace back."

"Not a chance," Alexei says.

"How about you?" Leonid turns toward Aleksandr. "What would you like in exchange for your earth powers?"

"You disgust me," Aleks says.

"Why?" Leonid rolls his eyes. "Because I'm willing to negotiate?"

"You capture women," Aleksandr says. "You curse people to sleep for a hundred years on a greedy whim. You care nothing for the Russian people."

"Enough." Leonid begins to pace. "You think I really care what you think?" He shakes his head. "The real reason I've been asking you idiots questions is that I was waiting to secure my leverage."

"Your what?" Grigoriy asks. "I fail to see how you might have any leverage at all."

Leonid glances at his watch. "While the three of you are in here. . ." He tsks. "Your helpless wife is. . ." He turns and smiles. "Smart watches are easy to fry when your body is a conduit for electricity, but once you learn to keep that arm free of it, they are just the greatest thing, aren't they? The little text messages you can get on them aren't magic, but it really seems like it. Just instantaneous." He clucks. "Using similar technological advancements, my very mortal supporters were able to catch your very mortal wife."

Aleksandr's face drains of all color. "She's not here."

"Yes, yes, you told her to stay at your home. It was cute."

"But—"

"If you think I can't spy on you in your house because of those wards, you're dumber than I thought. Your plan wasn't *so bad*, but you never really understood what I wanted. I'm not the kind of person to attack head on. If I was, I'd have done that ages ago. No, I like to wait until people are ready. I feign attacks a time or two, and then I wait until they think they're safe and then—"

"My home's warded," Aleksandr says, color returning. "You couldn't have broken inside."

"But if she was stupid enough to follow her friends or desperate to have her chance to help, I could catch her when she walked out on her own." Leonid pulls an iPad off a side table and spins it around. "Like this."

Kristiana's face—clear, crisp, her eyes wide—fills the screen. "I'm sorry," she whispers.

Aleksandr looks utterly wrecked, but I don't feel much better than he does.

"She's what you've wanted all along," I say.

"Not quite," Leonid says. "But you're not entirely wrong."

Grigoriy appears to have heard enough. He attacks, wind whipping through the room, yanking things off the walls, pulling heavy objects from the tables. Silverware, steak knives, they all head for the three men, and suddenly, he's not the only one in motion.

"Behind me," Alexei calls.

Mirdza and I both race behind him, huddling down low under the table.

"Do you think they really have Kris?" Mirdza whispers.

"I think she was angry about being excluded when

their powers can't even harm her," I say. "I'm not surprised she followed us."

"Where would she be held?" Mirdza asks. "Maybe while they're distracted, we can get her loose."

I do have a charm. I notice Mirdza's also wearing a necklace with a similar stone. I bet she has one, too.

"It's three on three," I say. "But I brought a knife." I pull it out of my thigh sheath. "And I'd love to save the day."

While the men are fighting—which is pretty terrible to watch. Fire. Electricity. Water. Mounds of dirt that are coming from—oh. Right. Potted plants. And wind churning it all up, while Grigoriy flies through the air, shooting projectiles all around—we sneak for the door.

No one stops us.

At least, not until we get outside where there's a human guard. "You're not allowed to leave."

I'm brandishing my dagger when he looks over my shoulder, his eyes widening. I suppose watching six men flinging fire, lightning, earth, wind, and water at one another would be a little off-putting. I'm not really very surprised when he turns and runs.

It is a nice surprise, though.

And in an even bigger twist, Kristiana's being held in the next room over. Her guards aren't as easy to dispatch, though. The two men waiting with her come after Mirdza and me, and they're armed. They each pull out a gun, and they aim them at our heads. "We're not to harm the target," the bigger man says in Russian. "But no one said we can't shoot anyone else."

"How nice to know you can't harm me." Kristiana's hands are bound, but she picks up a large vase and she clocks the closest man on the side of the head with it.

It doesn't knock him out, but it does make him royally angry.

They both turn toward her, and she smiles. "Sorry about that, but you can't harm me. Remember?" She waves.

I slash the one closest to me across the back of his legs as hard as I can. Mirdza, in the most shocking move of all, snatches the gun out of the hands of the man Kris bashed.

And then she shoots him.

31

Since we were kids, Mirdza has hated violence. She hates all conflict, really, but maybe I shouldn't have been surprised. She did stand up for Mom that night, even if she took a beating for it. Tonight, she knows the stakes. Also, those men had guns trained on us first. Maybe that's it. But then she turns and shoots the second man, before he can do a thing about it. With both guards on the floor, taken down by Mirdza, Kris holds out her hands.

I cut them loose.

Both of us look at Mirdza.

"What?" She shrugs. "Grigory and I have been talking about this a lot. Violence is usually wrong, but sometimes, the only solution to violence is violence." She sounds confident, but I can see her hands shaking, and she swallows twice. And then a third time. She'll be shaken up later, but thanks to her, we may all have a *later*.

Nothing about today has gone according to plan, but the guys need to know that none of us are in danger. I pull out my phone and text all three of them. Hopefully one of them sees their smart watch.

WE HAVE KRIS. WE'RE LEAVING.

Now one of them needs to see that and signal the others. Then they can break away, and we'll be fine. We can head back to Latvia with the knowledge that Leonid can't possibly get worse or become any stronger without the three of them allowing it. I mean, he's the Czar of Russia now, but at least he can't gain more magic.

They'll have to come up with another plan to fight back on another day.

We're in the entry hall on the way out when a dozen or more men show up, all of them holding guns. "We may not be able to shoot her." The man near the front gestures at Kristiana. "But I'm guessing you'd rather we not shoot the two of you."

Well, that sucks.

We were about to win the night for the guys, but instead, we're ushered back toward the dining room, all of us with our hands tied, and all of us gagged, like mobile lambs headed for the slaughter. So much for impressing the men.

When we reach the dining room, it's *gone*. There aren't holes in the walls—it's more like, there are only a few chunks left of what used to be the walls. The table has burned to the ground. The paintings are gone. The chandelier's in pieces on the floor.

It looks like a war zone—literally.

But when they see us, all six of them freeze.

Leonid points, and the men shoving us along all press guns to our temples. "I know they have charms to keep them safe from the three of us," he says. "But I'm guessing those charms don't protect them from a bullet through the skull." He smiles. "I *love* modern-day guns. No gunpowder bags to deal with. No messiness at all, really. They're so easy to acquire and even easier to use. They barely even kick."

"What do you want?" Alexei asks.

"You know what I want," Leonid says. "Simply speak the words. Offer me your powers."

"No," I mumble. "Don't do it."

Our gags disappear, thanks to Grigoriy's wind power. And then, faster than I have time to think about it, the men pressed against us are whipped away as well. Their guns shift and spin, the bullets dropping out.

"Nice trick," Leonid says. "But you'll notice before you dispatched my men, they eliminated their charms."

I drop my head, shocked to see that my necklace is gone. I can't help swearing. Leonid really is the worst.

He's also been circling the room and now he's closer to us than anyone else. "You see, those necklaces, they almost *hummed* to anyone trained to listen. And while I don't yet have access to earth and water powers, I can sense them. You could say that I *yearn* for them."

"Just as you whisked the men away, just as you disarmed them, I'm now going to burn them alive, and you won't be able to stop me." Leonid reaches out his arm, and the floor around us heats.

Alexei raises his arm to block him with water, but they're both channeling their energy, both of them holding their hands extended.

"While you're distracted with that," Leonid says.

Boris scowls, but he holds up his hands, lightning already sparking. And then he directs those bolts at us.

Aleksandr barely blocks them in time, the dirt from

the potted plants churning furiously in strange patterns in front of us, pulling the electricity downward and keeping us safe.

"But you see, I have the advantage." Leonid smiles. "Because I have two streams of each power, with only one of you to block it." Electricity crackles across his left hand, and he grins.

"What do you want?" Grigoriy asks.

"All Alexei has to do is say the magic words," Leonid says. "Swear to share your power with me, and I'll free you all."

"Just like that?" Grigoriy asks. "Why would you do that?"

"As you can see, I don't mind sharing." He shrugs.

"But this is a bargain," I say. "Clearly the words used matter."

Leonid frowns, because I must be right.

I stare at Alexei. "Remember what you said last night? You said that you knew you'd pick me, but you can't. You have an entire nation to serve. I love you, and our time was a gift." I press the dagger against my own throat.

"Oh, for heaven's sake." Leonid flings his hand sideways and the dagger heats up, burning the palm of my hand.

I drop it reflexively, swearing as I do.

"I could never pick the nation," Alexei says. "Not anymore."

"You two are nauseating," Leonid says. "Truly. I'm sure you must know."

"You'll agree to release them all and allow us to leave Russia safely, and you'll allow us to retain or sell all our property freely." Alexei looks like he's about to agree.

"You can't," I say. "Don't do it."

"And you will swear never to harm Adriana, no matter what happens, not in any way."

"Or you," I say. "He has to swear not to harm you either."

"You'll never harm me or Adriana," Alexei says.

Leonid smiles. "Done."

"And in return, I promise to allow you to use the water power given to the Romanov line."

Leonid closes his eyes. The fire. The electricity. It all disappears. It just blinks out. And then he opens his eyes and *smiles*. "You should all leave now," he says. "Before I start thinking of ways to circumvent that stupid promise."

Grigoriy's spluttering.

"I'll give you three minutes," Leonid says. "Out of the generosity of my heart."

"If you think we're just going to walk out," Grigoriy says, "you've lost your mind."

"Suit yourself." Leonid lifts a hand and flings a fireball at Grigoriy.

Alexei will stop it, clearly.

Only, he doesn't. It barrels into Grigoriy, setting him on fire and knocking him backward into what's left of the wall behind him. Aleksandr immediately sends a flurry of dirt to extinguish the fire, but Grigoriy's wounds look really, really bad.

Both Alexei and Aleksandr rush to his side.

"What's going on?" I ask.

"Oh, *that*," Leonid says, beaming. "Did I forget to mention that I only share my power when I *feel* like it?" Now he's positively gloating. "And I'm not sure I'll *ever* feel like sharing the water power." He pauses. "Oh, and, two minutes left."

Alexei looks gutted. Grigoriy's unconscious and still

smoking. Aleks and Alexei lift him up and carry him toward the door. No one stops them, so the three of us rush to follow.

"Kristiana," Leonid says. "I have to allow you to leave Russia safely, but there are any number of ways you can leave that are safe, but not really very satisfying. While you're thinking on that, I'd love to offer you a follow-up bargain."

"What's that?"

"I'll heal your friend there. He should be exhausted enough that he won't have the energy to lash out again —and I'll let you all export your property out of Russia over the next month or two without interfering in any way. But in return, I want you to answer a very important question for me."

"What?" Kristiana lifts one eyebrow.

"Unfortunately, to be eligible for this deal, you must promise to answer before knowing the question." Leonid looks utterly pleased with himself.

"Screw him," I say.

"Do it," Mirdza begs.

I wonder what I'd say if Alexei smelled like the local barbecue joint.

"Fine," Kristiana says. "Now heal him."

"Don't forget your promise," Leonid says. "I can always throw a few more fireballs around before I allow you all to leave if you renege."

"I won't forget," Kristiana says.

We all watch as Leonid heals Grigoriy.

"Sheesh, that was clumsy," Leonid says. "But it worked. I healed him perfectly." He inhales slowly. "Water is everything I hoped it would be."

"Fabulous," I say.

"Now it's your turn." Leonid turns to Kris. "Other

than your father, what family do you have? My searches yielded nothing. Are you an only child?"

Kris grits her teeth.

But she's not going to be able to lie. Not after swearing that she would answer his question. "I have an older brother."

"Why isn't he on any of the paperwork?"

"After our mother died, he left. He had my grandparents adopt him. He wanted nothing to do with us, or with Latvia. With any of it."

Leonid looks happier than I thought possible. "That's why you're a null." He nods. "Now tell me his name and where he lives."

A null?

"Ah, ah, ah," Kristiana says. "You said one question, and I already answered it."

She practically sprints out, which is wise. Alexei and Aleksandr are still stuck helping Grigoriy walk—Leonid kept his promise and healed the burns, but it was draining for Grigoriy I'm sure. And I wouldn't put it past Leonid to lash out again.

But ultimately, with his resources and the knowledge that she has a brother, he'll find Gustav. It's only a matter of time. We can all guess what he plans to do when he finds him.

We follow Kristiana and the guys as quickly as we can. Thankfully, the SUV we planned is waiting for us. But when I hop inside, there's someone I didn't expect. Someone I've never seen before.

A redhead.

She's gorgeous. Her bright green eyes flash. "I thought you were never coming," she says in flawless Russian.

"Who are you?" I ask.

"I was late getting the guys," Mirdza says, "because I found her—Katerina."

"Let's go," Katerina says. "When Leo realizes I'm gone, he'll be really angry."

Just when I thought things can't get any worse, they somehow do.

32

True to his word, Leonid doesn't interfere when we drive back to Aleksandr's home, or when Aleksandr, Grigoriy, and Alexei begin liquidating some of their interests in Russia and shifting money to Latvia. I'm actually shocked at how well he keeps his word. I expected him to show up, dramatically, and attack us.

Even though things are going as well as they possibly could, Alexei's being really, really strange. We've been staying at Aleksandr's while they try and sort details and make a plan, and it's been getting worse and worse.

He's avoiding me all the time, so I can't even pin him down about it. I finally catch him as he's ducking out the back door.

"Whoa there," I say. "Where you going?"

Alexei freezes, but he doesn't turn.

"Are you just never talking to me again?"

He sighs, his shoulders slumping a little. "I thought that might be best."

I practically lunge toward him. "Are you kidding

right now?" I grab his shoulder and spin him around. "What are you doing?"

"The Romanovs were obsessed with two things," Alexei says. "Gemstones and horses. Did you know that?"

I can't help frowning. "I'm always happy to hear about your family, but can we go back to why you're avoiding me first?"

"My dad came home with seven horses once—Arabians he had bought from the finest breeder in Asia."

What's he talking about? He's not even meeting my eye.

"He brought us all out to watch them move. I fell in love with a beautiful, deep, blood bay."

"Alexei."

His eyes snap toward mine. "Just listen."

At least he's talking.

"He let me choose first. It wasn't fair, probably, but I was the only son, and I didn't question it. I chose the blood bay mare, and I never looked back." He's looking away again, eyes on the horizon. "But before I ever rode her, she got white line and foundered." He finally turns back toward me. "I never rode that horse. They worked with her for years, but she was never sound to ride."

"I'm sorry." And I am. Founder's the literal worst.

"I was sorry I chose her in the first place," Alexei says. "I should have chosen one of the greys, the chestnut, or the browns. It was my own fault. I'd made the choice, but I didn't realize she was going to have so many problems. I had to watch as my siblings rode their Arabians, delighted, knowing I'd never ride mine."

"But surely you had other horses."

"What if she was my only horse? What if I chose a horse that looked perfect, only to have her never be rideable?" His eyes are flashing now. "That's what you've done. You said yes to marrying me, but now, after you've chosen, I've gone lame."

Oh, geez. "Alexei."

He shakes his head and tries to walk away.

"I honestly thought you were smarter than that." I snort.

That makes him stop.

"Do you really think I agreed to marry you because you were going to be the next Russian President?" I step closer. "Or maybe you thought I agreed because you could make water do things with your hands. Or perhaps, you believe I said I love you because you thought I needed a massive grey horse to ride."

"I can still shift." He turns around.

"Oh, well then." I can't help my smirk. "The one thing I was going to miss the most, you still have. That's promising."

"You said yes, but things have changed dramatically," Alexei says. "Big things. And unlike me, you can get a do-over." He meets my eyes, and his are shattered. "You can change your mind. I won't even blame you."

I grab his hand and look at our fingers interlocked. His hand's huge. Strong. Masculine. Mine's small and feminine. Paler skinned. Weaker in every way.

"I love you because you're kind," I say. "I love you because you're chivalrous. Because you're brilliant. Because you're considerate. And most of all, because you're the most beautiful man I've ever met." I can't help smiling when his head whips upward, our eyes finally meeting.

"You—" He splutters.

"I hated the idea of being married to someone who

was stuck in the world of politics. Or tied to someone who was ruling other people. I hated the idea of living in Russia. And to be honest, the magic was cool, but I don't need it."

"I don't have a family home anymore," he says.

"I've never had one, remember? Welcome to real life!" I tug him closer, and he actually moves toward me. "None of us ever really have a place. We're stuck carving a place out for ourselves, and Alexei?"

He looks up, his eyes hopeful.

"You're the only person in the world I want next to me when I'm slicing and dicing. When I look at you, I don't see a lame horse. I see a vibrantly strong, brave, and noble grey stallion."

He doesn't look like he believes me, but he doesn't turn away either.

"I hate Leonid, because I think he's a greedy, manipulative, genuinely bad person. But I don't care that you don't have your water powers. And who cares that we're poor now? I've always been poor."

"Oh, we're not poor," he says.

"What?" I blink.

"The Russian government, under the control of United Russia, ceded loads of land to me as reparations for the war crimes committed against my family. They thought I'd be able to use them once I took office, admittedly, but they did it legally. I also now own several palaces, which I suppose Leonid may retake. And there are countless works of priceless art that were sent my way. It's nothing to the three hundred billion we once had, but Aleksandr says that even without the palaces and items that can't really leave Russia, I should have well over twelve billion euros."

I drop his hand.

"Of course, to liquidate, I'd have to sell some things

I'd rather not sell, like various paintings that were restored from the museums and storage vaults the government held. Even so, I should have nearly two billion that's usable, or so Aleks says."

Two. Billion. Euros.

"Yes, you sure are a lame horse," I say. "How could any girl want anything to do with you?"

"Adriana."

I shake my head. "You're even dumber than I thought."

"I want to be able to protect you," Alexei says. "My ability to do that was directly related to—"

I step into the space right in front of him and rest my head against his chest. "No one can really protect anyone else. We never have any idea what's coming. Health. Weather. Villains. The future's a big old question mark in the best of times. Healthy horses routinely go lame. Wells run dry. Powers get stolen." I look up at him, a smile tugging at the corners of my mouth. "But one thing you never have to worry about losing is my love. I'm so stubborn that you were the first man I ever loved, and you'll be the last, Alexei Romanov. So stop trying to run away. That's *my* thing."

He traces his finger along the top of my nose, and then he runs it across the skin under my eye, down the side of my jaw, and stops, his finger resting over the base of my neck. "You weren't easy to break," he says. "But the best horses are worth the investment, and I plan to love you my entire life, Adriana Strelkova. However long that may be."

"Oh, good," I say. "Then let's stop sulking, get out of Russia as soon as possible, and start planning our wedding."

He kisses me then, and although there's no stroking of phantom caresses or magical zaps of any kind, it's still the best kiss of my life. I have a feeling that's a measurement that's going to just keep changing, the longer I spend with him.

I pull away and say, "How about we go—"

But that's when I hear it.

We both freeze, listening. Alexei whispers. "Do you—"

"Shh," I say. Then I point.

Right around the corner, on the flowering path leading to the barn, Mirdza and Grigoriy are walking, hand in hand.

"It's precisely because I love you so much that I want to marry you," Grigoriy says. "And this time, I really think you'll like the ring."

Mirdza drops his hand and puts her hands on her hips. "Grigoriy Khilkov, I already told you. If you propose to me one more time, I'm going to dump you."

"But your best friend's married," he says, "and even your idiotic sister—"

Mirdza pokes him in the chest with her finger. "Don't call her that."

"You do all the time." He scowls. "Why can't I?"

"I can call her idiotic because she's my twin, but you don't get to insult her. It's not like she's your sister-in-law."

"Yet," he roars. "And about that, if you would just agree to marry me." He drops to one knee, and he holds up a box. "At least *look* at this one."

"I can't believe we're breaking up," Mirdza says. "I warned you, and I warned you, and you insist on making things difficult with another stupid proposal."

Although this is quite entertaining, it feels like an intervention might be in order.

"Mirdza?" I say.

Both of their heads whip toward me. "Adriana?"

"And me, too." Alexei's grin is a little smug, but I can't fault him for that. "What was that you were telling me this morning?" He coughs. "About how I needed to *man up*, I believe were your words?"

Grigoriy's hands curl into fists at his sides. "What I said was true."

"And yet, the manliest man I know. . .just got dumped while on one knee? Or did I misread some part of that?"

Alexei's about to get us stabbed. I drop one hand on his wrist. "Hardly helpful," I hiss. "Alright, Mirdza. How about you and I chat while these two think about how many years they've been friends."

Mirdza's scowling when I drag her over near the blooming bushes on the side of the mansion. "What on earth are you doing?"

"He's just proposing because both of his friends have," she says. "And I don't think there's any reason for us to be in a rush."

"Let's review," I say. "There's a maniac who's trying to take over the world and making good progress, there's your recent miracle healing, there's the ongoing threat of attack from who knows where, and oh, yeah. Your mom's getting older, and tomorrow's never guaranteed."

"Yes, but none of that is a reason to be hasty about—"

"No." I shake my head, and then I glare. "You told me I was running away."

"You were."

"And you're just as bad!" I soften a little. "I know it's scary."

"Mārtiņš held it together until they were married," Mirdza says. "What if Grigoriy changes?"

"Did Aleksandr?"

Mirdza frowns.

"Do you think Alexei will? He was just telling me how I should just let him go, now that he's a weakling disappointment—no throne, no water powers. He thinks I should dump him." I can't help laughing. "As if the only reason I loved him is that he could make it rain."

Mirdza's laughing now, too. "It is nice having money for the first time ever."

"He's still loaded," I say. "Probably richer than Grigoriy." I shouldn't gloat.

"I doubt that," Mirdza says. "Or at least, not for long. We're making money hand over fist on the—"

"We?" I smile, because I've got her now.

"You know what I mean."

"I do. You already consider him yours. You already trust him. Now throw the poor man a bone and just agree to *marry* him."

"You think I should? I actually wondered whether you'd back out."

"I won't," I say. "And. . ." I get ready to run. "I bet I get married before you do, and with a nicer wedding ceremony." As I jog away, I see her face—jaw dropped, eyes wide, competitive nature clearly activated.

Once I reach the boys, I slow a little, grab Alexei's arm, and start to jog toward the side entrance of the house.

"What's going on?" Alexei asks.

"There aren't many decent venues in Latvia," I say. "And I mean to book ours before Mirdza can."

Alexei's laughing as we head back inside, and he's not avoiding me anymore. Turns out, my lame horse just needed a little tap on the butt with the crop, and now he's on the bit again.

I can't believe I was worried about saving that

palomino mare. I haven't even seen her since we came back. All she does is hide in her room. I'm not sure why she even wanted to get away if that's all she was going to do.

"How'd you like to go for a ride?" Alexei says. "It's a glorious day."

"Oh, sure," I say. "Let me go change my pants."

"I didn't mean that kind of ride." His eyes are as devilish as his tone, and I've never loved him more.

"Now you're speaking my language."

But as we get closer to our rooms, I hear Mirdza coming from the other direction. "No, I don't think we could get flowers together that fast. But the next available option, maybe."

I freeze and turn toward Alexei.

"We're about to spend the next four hours on the phone, aren't we?"

Boy, does he know me.

"This is going to be the nicest wedding Daugavpils has ever seen. And I'm going to invite every single person I hate and they're going to be *so* jealous."

"Don't you want to invite your friends?" Alexei looks confused.

"You really don't know women." I pat his arm. "That's okay. I love you anyway."

❧ 33 ❧

KATERINA

I think everyone does something stupid when they're young. They might spend all their money on something they don't even like. Or perhaps they kiss the wrong guy. Maybe they make a stupid promise or trust the wrong friend.

For me, my dumb thing was falling for the wrong guy.

It wasn't long before I saw where I went wrong. He was clearly less in love with me than he was with the power my family held. That, and he was a sociopath. But as a result of that stupid fling, I lost the only man I ever really *did* care about.

Alexei Romanov.

I've been patiently waiting for months since I woke up, for Alexei to save me. We were friends. I know he was cursed, too. And above all else, he's always been a shining white knight.

He's handsome. Powerful. Rich. Noble. Gorgeous. And he's always been the light and bright hero who does the right thing in every circumstance. But while I was locked up in Leonid's stupid house, Alexei fell for someone else.

Watching him watch her on the way back from Leonid's mansion was possibly the hardest hour of my life.

So now that I'm finally free, I'm still hiding in my room. The world has changed so much that it's not even a place I recognize. Leonid's controlling all of Russia. He took Alexei's magic, and he has a plan to do more. I don't know what it is, but he'll never be satisfied with just one piece of something.

No, he wants it all.

His is the kind of hunger that consumes.

Everything.

It will never be sated. He will never stop pursuing for what he wants, because nothing is ever enough for him. He's got to be especially ticked that I escaped.

He still doggedly insists that he loves me.

It's a farce—he doesn't know how to love—but more concerning is that he knows that I know the truth. I was there, you see, when he convinced Baba Yaga to restore his powers. I know exactly what deal he struck, and exactly what he needs to regain control of all the magic his lineage should have provided.

None of them really understand what kinds of things he can do if he gains all five powers. None of them grasp what the Riurikid line possesses. It's been too long since anyone had it all.

I wish I knew these people well enough to trust them, but so far, I can't tell what their goal is, either. One thing I heard them talking about has given me purpose. Kristiana, Aleksandr's irritatingly cute wife, is apparently a null. The powers don't work on her—which means she's Riurikid as well.

It makes sense.

The first thing she did was restore to me the ability to shift and access my powers on command. And as she said it would, her generous words of forgiveness restored my abilities in a way Leonid refused to do.

Which confirms my suspicions she's Riurikid, and that she poses an ongoing threat to Leonid.

They think he's going to let them escape, but he will never truly free them. Her older brother, the primary heir in their Riurikid line, is a bigger threat. And that means Leonid will attack him first. I have no idea what kind of person this Gustav is, but he can't be worse than Leonid, which means I need to find him and warn him.

It's really his only chance.

Because Leonid's number one priority will be killing him immediately, before he can compete for the same power. I can tell that the people who saved me don't trust me, and I'm not sure I really have time to win them over. Which means I'm going to be stuck sneaking around to find out information about Gustav.

I'll have a decision to make once I do.

I can trade that information to Leonid and buy my way back into his good graces. Or I could gamble on Gustav and warn him about what's coming. I might even be able to give him a chance to win in the fight that looms before us all.

I chose wrong last time.

So whatever I decide, it really needs to be the right choice. I can't afford to lose twice in a row. The stakes are too high for me this time around.

I've hidden long enough. I open my door, and I'm in luck. The very person walking past my room is Kristiana. "I'm sorry for being so antisocial," I say, hoping she speaks Russian.

"Oh, it's fine," she says.

"Would you want to chat with me? Maybe over lunch?"

Kris frowns. "Of course," she says. "But it may have to wait. I'm about to get on a plane."

"A plane?"

"I'm headed to America," she says. "I can't get my brother to answer his phone, and I'm getting worried."

Whatever it takes, I'm going to be on that plane, too.

***I hope you guys enjoyed this book as much as I enjoyed writing it! AND I KNOW you don't want to wait for book four, which is planned to be the last book in the series... but don't worry! It's set for May 1, 2024, but I anticipate writing it sooner than that! I promise! <3

If you're excited about My Wild Horse King, go preorder it! That helps me know people want it and I move it up even more. THANK YOU so much for your love and support! It means the world to me.

And while you're waiting, go try my dragon shifter series, starting with Ensnared. It's out NOW! The second book in that series (Entwined) should be out in January 2024!

Here's the blurb for Ensnared:

**A love story that sets the world on fire. . .
Literally.**

Elizabeth spent her life preparing for the worst. As one of the fiercest MMA fighters in the USA, nothing scared her.

Until the dragons came.

To save her younger siblings, Liz makes a deal with the dragon prince sent to destroy them all. She also makes secret plans to take him down. But the more she learns and the deeper she gets, the more confusing things become.

. . .

The dragon prince isn't who she thought he was, and Liz begins to wonder what happens when an avenging angel falls for the devil himself.

If you like fantasy romance like the Fourth Wing, then this totally unique new series will probably knock your scaly socks off.

Grab Ensnared now!

ACKNOWLEDGMENTS

First and foremost: to my fans, THANK YOU. When you tell friends, when you gush on social media, when you leave reviews, it changes my day, my week, and sometimes my year. Thank you for your support, your excitement, and your love for my stories.

To my editor Carrie, you are amazing. You make this happen for me on a terrible and rude and ridiculous timetable... ALWAYS. THANK YOU.

To my kids: you are patient. You are supportive. Thanks for being my very smallest and also my very biggest fans.

To my husband, known as Mr. Bridget in my facebook reader group, THANK YOU for your ongoing patience, excitement, and support.

To my dogs, I don't appreciate your little paws on my keyboard (for which I often call you TYPO), but I do appreciate your licks and snuggles. They keep me typing happily.

ABOUT THE AUTHOR

I have animals coming out of my ears. Seven horses. Three dogs, three cats, thirty-ish chickens. I'm always doctoring or playing with an animal... and I wouldn't want it any other way. But Leo (my palomino) is still my very favorite.

When I'm not with animals, or even if I am, I'm likely to have at least one of my five kids in tow, two of which I'm currently homeschooling.

My hubby is the reason all this glorious madness is possible. He's the best parts of all the amazing men I write (although he's bald and his six pack sometimes goes into hiding because of cookies.)

I also love to bake, like to cook, and feel amazing when I find time to kickbox, lift weights, or rollerblade. Oh yeah, and I'm a lawyer, but I try to forget about that whenever I can.

I adore my husband, and I love my God.

The rest is just details.

(But one detail you might want to know! I have an active reader group on FB called the Bridget Baker Binge Readers, and I have a newsletter you can sign up for at www.BridgetEBakerWrites.com! I'd love to have you sign up for either thing!)

ALSO BY BRIDGET E. BAKER

The Dragon Captured Series:

Ensnared

Entwined

Embroiled

Embattled

The Russian Witch's Curse:

My Queendom for a Horse

My Dark Horse Prince

My High Horse Czar

My Wild Horse King

The Magical Misfits Series:

Mates: Minerva (1)

Mates: Xander (2)

The Birthright Series:

Displaced (1)

unForgiven (2)

Disillusioned (3)

misUnderstood (4)

Disavowed (5)

unRepentant (6)

Destroyed (7)

The Birthright Series Collection, Books 1-3

The Anchored Series:

Anchored (1)

Adrift (2)

Awoken (3)

Capsized (4)

The Sins of Our Ancestors Series:

Marked (1)

Suppressed (2)

Redeemed (3)

Renounced (4)

Reclaimed (5) a novella!

A stand alone YA romantic suspense:

Already Gone

I also write women's fiction and contemporary romance under B. E. Baker.

The Scarsdale Fosters Series:

Seed Money

Nouveau Riche

The Finding Home Series:

Finding Grace (1)

Finding Faith (2)

Finding Cupid (3)

Finding Spring (4)

Finding Liberty (5)

Finding Holly (6)

Finding Home (7)

Finding Balance (8)

Finding Peace (9)

The Finding Home Series Boxset Books 1-3

The Finding Home Series Boxset Books 4-6

The Birch Creek Ranch Series:

The Bequest

The Vow

The Ranch

The Retreat

The Reboot

The Surprise

The Setback

The Lookback

Children's Picture Book

Yuck! What's for Dinner?

www.ingramcontent.com/pod-product-compliance
Lightning Source LLC
Chambersburg PA
CBHW031002190726
48285CB00004BB/1426